THE VENGEANCE OF MOTHERS

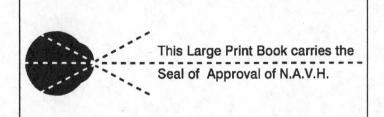
This Large Print Book carries the
Seal of Approval of N.A.V.H.

THE VENGEANCE OF MOTHERS

THE JOURNALS OF MARGARET KELLY & MOLLY MCGILL

JIM FERGUS

THORNDIKE PRESS

A part of Gale, a Cengage Company

GALE
A Cengage Company

Farmington Hills, Mich • San Francisco • New York • Waterville, Maine
Meriden, Conn • Mason, Ohio • Chicago

Copyright © 2017 by Jim Fergus.
Thorndike Press, a part of Gale, a Cengage Company.

ALL RIGHTS RESERVED
This is a work of fiction. All of the characters, organizations, and events portrayed in this novel are products of the author's imagination or are used fictiously.
Thorndike Press® Large Print Core.
The text of this Large Print edition is unabridged.
Other aspects of the book may vary from the original edition.
Set in 16 pt. Plantin.

LIBRARY OF CONGRESS CIP DATA ON FILE.
CATALOGUING IN PUBLICATION FOR THIS BOOK
IS AVAILABLE FROM THE LIBRARY OF CONGRESS.

ISBN-13: 978-1-4328-4360-1 (hardcover)
ISBN-10: 1-4328-4360-5 (hardcover)

Published in 2017 by arrangement with Macmillan Publishing Group, LLC/St. Martin's Press

Printed in Mexico
1 2 3 4 5 6 7 21 20 19 18 17

To my dear friends Moira &
Jon D. Williams III,
with love

ACKNOWLEDGMENTS

Writing and publishing a novel is a long, complicated, collaborative affair, and the author is indebted to a great number of people along the way.

I'd like to thank first my agent, Albert Zuckerman of Writers House, who has been a steadfast supporter of my work for twenty years now, as well as a wise editorial counselor and a dear friend.

After a long hiatus, I am delighted to be reunited with St. Martin's Press. I owe the publication of my first novel, *One Thousand White Women,* and its continued success to my terrific editor, now Executive VP Jennifer Enderlin. I am deeply grateful to her and to President and Publisher Sally Richardson, for welcoming me back to the house so warmly and generously.

It has been my great pleasure to have worked closely on the publication of *The Vengeance of Mothers* with an outstanding team at St. Martin's. My gratitude to Assistant Editor Caitlin Dareff, always prompt and gracious while serving as my liaison to the process. Thanks, too, to Production Editor Elizabeth Catalano and Production Manager Cheryl Mamaril, who are in charge of the many talented people working in the background, invariably making books better products for both author and reader. Among these are some of the anonymous unsung heroes of the business, in this case the copy editor, Amy Schneider, and the proofreader, Kenneth Diamond, who assiduously identified the typos, repetitions, anachronisms, grammatical and spelling errors, etc., making my work, finally, smoother and more literate than the original manuscript may have indicated. Virtually all authors rely on such critical service. (Having said that, I must take full responsibility if I failed to implement a few of their suggestions in the final draft.)

On other fronts of the publication grounds, my gratitude to Senior Designer Donna Noetzel and Associate Art Director Kerri Resnick for their sensitive work in making this novel both handsome and easy on the reader's eye.

It has been an equal pleasure for me to prepare the book for launch in the marketplace with Senior Publicist Katie Bassel; Vice President of Publicity Dori Weintraub; Marketing Director Nancy Sheppard; Assistant Marketing Manager Jordan Hanley; and Vice President of Marketing, Communications Brant Janeway. I lump you all together here in the interest of brevity, but I thank you each personally for your good cheer and hard work, and for making the process so painless. I can say frankly that in my long career as a journalist and novelist, I have never worked with a more talented, capable, pleasant, and professional team from top to bottom than that at St. Martin's Press.

Last, but certainly not least, a much overdue thanks to my old friend, Larry Yoder, who, when *One Thousand White Women* first came out twenty years ago, was the western sales rep for St. Martin's Press. These fine people, too, are frequently unheralded heroes, working tirelessly in the field for low pay, driving thousands of miles a year in all weather to sell our books. I have nothing but respect and admiration for you all, not to mention gratitude. I credit much of the success of *One Thousand White Women* to Yoder (as everyone calls him), a legend in his profession. He embraced this first novel by an unknown, middle-aged author, and he passionately hand-sold it to booksellers across the western states. In large measure, due to his efforts on my behalf, the book won the 1998 fiction of the year award from the Mountains & Plains Independent Booksellers Association, after which it began to take on a life of its own, eventually breaking free of the stigma of "regional fiction" to find a national audience.

Their prophet, Motsé'eóve (Sweet Medicine), told the Cheyenne of the coming of a person to them; this person was apparently the white man. Sweet Medicine told the Cheyenne:

"A person is going to come to you [pl.]. He will be all sewed up [enclosed in clothes], nowhere will he not be sewed up, this person who is going to come to you. He is going to destroy for you everything that you used to depend on, he is going to destroy everything. . . . And this one who is going to come to you will take over all the land throughout the world."

— excerpted from the story "Sweet Medicine" by Mrs. Albert Hoffman in *Cheyenne Texts: An Introduction to Cheyenne Literature*, edited by Wayne Leman, 1980

In those days the country was an extra two thousand miles wider, and an additional thousand miles deep. There were many undiscovered valleys to walk in where Indian tribes lived undisturbed though some tribes chose to found new nations in the heretofore unknown areas between the black boundary cracks between states . . .

All dogs and people in free concourse

Became medium sized and brown.
    — from the poem *The Old Days*
        by Jim Harrison

It is the mothers, not the warriors, who create a people and guide their destiny.
    — Luther Standing Bear,
        Oglala Lakota Chief
(December 1868 — February 20, 1939)

FROM THE FINAL ENTRY TO
THE JOURNALS OF MAY DODD

1 March 1876

Yes, truly it is finished now, it is over, the soldiers have come with the breaking light of dawn, like the vengeful hand of God, to strike us down. I am shot, I fear that I am dying, the village destroyed and burning, the people driven naked into the hills to crouch like animals among the rocks. I have lost track of most of the others, some still alive, some dead, I have taken refuge in a shallow cave with Feather on Head, Quiet One, and Martha. Here we huddle together with our babies as the village burns below, a huge funeral pyre upon which the soldiers pile our belongings, everything we own and all that we have — hides, furs and blankets, meat and food supplies, saddles and ammunition — and upon these piles they place the bodies of our dead, and with burning torches set all aflame, they ignite our lodges which burst into flames like trees in a forest fire, the ammunition and kegs of gunpowder inside popping and exploding like fireworks . . . all that we have. Gone.

I am shot, I fear that I am dying, the breath rattles in my chest, blood bubbles from my mouth and nose . . . as long as I have the strength, I shall continue to record these events . . .

From the Codicil to
The Journals of May Dodd

by Abbot Anthony of the Prairie
Saint Anthony of the Desert
Abbey Powder River, Montana
November 15, 1926

*The night after the Mackenzie massacre,
the mercury dipped well below zero.
Everything in the Cheyenne village had
been destroyed by the invading cavalry,
dozens of the People slaughtered in the
dawn attack — men and women, young
and old, our white women and their babies
among them — cut down indiscriminately
by blood-crazed soldiers wielding sword,
rifle, or pistol. Those who managed to
survive fled into the hills, many gravely
wounded, many half-dressed, with nothing
to protect them or their infants from the
elements. Although wounded seven times
himself, that night the great Sweet Medicine Chief Little Wolf led the bedraggled
remnants of his band across the moun-*

15

tains toward the village of the Lakota warrior Crazy Horse. I followed and did what little I could to aid and comfort these poor souls.

It was a ten-day journey of unimaginable hardship and suffering. Eleven Cheyenne babies froze to death in their mothers' arms the first night, three more the following night, including all the remaining white children . . .

The Irish sisters, Margaret and Susan Kelly, lost both their sets of twins in the course of that brutal march. The anguish of their grief was a terrible thing to behold. They cursed me, and they cursed the Lord in his heaven for taking their baby girls.

They were a sprightly pair, Meggie and Susie. Besides Martha Atwood, they are the only white women of whom I am aware to have survived the ordeal of Mackenzie's attack and its terrible aftermath. After the death of their infants, they went quite mad. They joined various bands of marauding Cheyenne and Sioux and fought like demons in the final days of the Plains Indian wars. They are reported to have ridden with Crazy Horse when Custer and his soldiers were killed that following summer at the Little Bighorn, and to have taken themselves grisly trophies of war there. I

16

made many inquiries on behalf of the Kelly twins over the years and heard many rumors, but I was never able to learn what finally became of those girls. God bless them both . . .

Martha Atwood Tangle Hair, the sole white woman to officially survive the Mackenzie attack, returned to Chicago with her son, whose Christian name was Dodd, in honor of her dear, deceased friend May Dodd. I never saw Martha again, but for many years after we kept up a correspondence. She eventually remarried and had several more children. Except to say in her very first letter to me that she had delivered May's final message to Captain John Bourke, Martha never mentioned the affair again — neither the Brides for Indians program, nor the devastating massacre that so definitively brought it to an end. Nor did I ever learn what arrangement she had made with the U.S. government to purchase her silence on these matters. It is not a monk's business to ask such questions. And silent on the subject Martha remained.

■ ■ ■ ■

PROLOGUE

■ ■ ■ ■

by JW Dodd, III
Editor in Chief, Chitown Magazine
Chicago, Illinois
May 14, 2015

My name is Jon William Dodd, III. Most people call me JW, to distinguish me from my father, the late J. Will Dodd, known familiarly as Will. I am currently the editor in chief of the Chicago city magazine *Chitown,* family owned and operated, for which publication my father served in this same position for thirty-four years until his recent passing.

Some readers will remember my father as the man who discovered and published *One Thousand White Women: The Journals of May Dodd* in serial form in this magazine almost twenty years ago now. At the time, the journals caused quite a controversy in the academic community and were roundly denounced as fakes by outraged history professors in various universities around the country, who argued in letters to the editor that the exchange between the Cheyenne and the whites upon which they are based

— that is, the trade of one thousand white women for one thousand horses — never took place, nor did there exist any historical evidence to support that claim. Although my father wrote the introduction to the series, he never directly responded to these attacks. To him, the search for and publication of the journals was a labor of love, undertaken out of a sense of familial responsibility — to learn the truth about the life and death of his great-grandmother, May Dodd; to expose the wrongs done to her by her parents; and to restore her good name in the family history. Dad never gave a damn whether the academics believed in their authenticity.

For those readers unfamiliar with her story, in the year 1875, May Dodd, age twenty-three, was abducted from her home in Chicago in the middle of the night, torn from her two young children, and committed by her parents to the Lake Forest Lunatic Asylum — all for the crime of having fallen in love with a man below her station in life. The official Dodd family history reports that she died in the asylum of undisclosed causes roughly a year later, in February 1876. However, there was an alternate, and considerably more romantic version of May's short life: a secret family legend passed down in hushed whispers through the generations that she did not die in the asylum at all. Rather she had escaped and "gone out West to live with Indians," a phrase that over the years had morphed into a widely used family euphemism for mental illness.

Dad's research into this legend eventually led him to the Tongue River Indian Reservation in southeastern Montana. There in the fall of 1996, over a century and a quarter after they were written, May Dodd's Cheyenne great-great-granddaughter, May Swallow Wild Plums, presented him with those extraordinary journals.

As a young teenager, I was fortunate enough to accompany my father on many of his travels around the Great Plains as he reconstructed May's own journeys. I had already planned on entering the family business and to pursue a career in journalism myself, and largely due to Dad's obsession with the subject, I had become fascinated by the native American experience — its tragic history, difficult present, and uncertain future.

Because of his familial connection to May Dodd, and his own essential decency, my father came to be received as a trusted friend on the reservation — which was not an easy accomplishment for a white man. During our numerous visits there, we camped out for weeks at a time in our Airstream trailer and became friendly with a number of tribal members. We were even invited to participate in certain sweat lodge and Sun Dance ceremonies. Although I made friends among some of the Cheyenne kids on the res, many of them maintained, quite understandably, an ingrained distrust and resentment of white people. I even got into a few fights over it.

As so often happens in this business, the publication of May Dodd's journals was both the end of one story and the beginning of another. Abbot Anthony, known as Brother Anthony by May and her friends, was a young Benedictine monk who lived with the white women among the Cheyenne and who participated in many of the events recounted in her journals, including, of course, the fatal attack by U.S. Army cavalry troops under the command of Colonel Ranald Mackenzie on a frigid winter morning in 1876. In his codicil, written exactly a half century after that event, the abbot mentions the uncertain fates of three white women who survived that terrible ordeal — the Irish twin sisters, Meggie and Susie Kelly, and Martha Atwood, who had been employed at the Lake Forest Lunatic Asylum and who helped May escape from that ghastly institution. Although by today's standards, such a military strike against civilians would certainly be prosecuted by the International Criminal Court as a war crime, as genocide, at the time it was unofficial, though widely accepted U.S. War Department policy, designed to exterminate the native population in order to make the Great Plains safe for the white invaders — a sadly familiar tale in the settlement of America.

Six months ago, only a few weeks before he was scheduled to retire, my father suffered a massive stroke, and three days later he died in Chicago's Passavant Hospital. In preparation for his retirement, Dad had long been grooming me to take over the editorial reins of the magazine in order to lead it into the digital age — a largely incomprehensible and vaguely intimidating world to his generation of "print-era dinosaurs," as he often referred to himself. I had already worked at *Chitown* for a number of years, starting out as a stock boy and gopher during vacations when I was still in grade school, and later on through high school, college and afterward, as a copy editor, then assistant editor, staff writer, and finally department editor.

25

One afternoon only ten days after my father's death, the receptionist sent me a text message informing me that there was a young woman at the front desk asking to see me.

Name? I responded in kind.

Won't give her name. She's dressed weird

What kind of weird?

Like an Indian

India, or native American?

NA

What does she want?

Says she knows you, wants to give you something. She's carrying a pair of old leather saddlebags. I mean, like, really old

And did she ride in on a horse?

Hahaha . . . you want me to call security, Chief?

I told you to stop calling me that, Chloe. No, I'll come out.

My father's sudden death was still so recent that I was not yet comfortable sitting in his chair. In addition to my own grieving process, I had the sense of being an impostor, pretending to be editor in chief. As I passed by the other offices on my way to the front desk, I remembered coming here with Dad when I was just a boy. How different he must have found the place by the end of his career: no longer the staccato clack of typewriter keys, the jangling ring of vintage corded telephones, the cacophony of passionate journalistic conversations; no longer a haze of cigarette smoke hanging in the air like a perpetual indoor smog, or the acrid smell of burnt coffee left too long on the hot plate. Now the office was oddly quiet and sterilely clean, our young editorial staff sequestered in their glass cubicles, agile fingers drifting effortlessly over the silent keys of their various devices, the only muffled sounds the tiny electronic bells and beeps, clicks and clanks, the little *whooshes* as messages tumbled into their respective in-boxes.

At the front desk, I was suddenly taken out of my nostalgic reverie, indeed out of the digital age altogether, by the sight of the young woman standing before me.

Noting my surprise, the receptionist, Chloe, smiled smugly. "Told you so, Chief," she said softly.

"Good afternoon," I said to the woman, who did not look familiar to me. I held out my hand. "I'm JW Dodd. You wanted to see me?"

She looked at my hand but did not take it. "In private," she answered.

"May I ask what this visit is in reference to?"

"I have something for you."

I glanced at the saddlebags that she carried slung over her shoulder, which were indeed old — the leather cracked and faded, with faint stenciled lettering I was unable to make out on the flap of the pouch. "Give me a hint."

"In private," she repeated. "I read the journals your father published. I met him some years ago on the res. I met you, too, but you probably don't remember. We were just kids."

"Very well, follow me."

As I escorted the woman through the office, one by one the heads of my editors popped up out of their cubicles, as if there was finally something more interesting to look at than their screens.

Having spent so much time with my father in both tribal and natural history museums around the country, I had become rather a student of native American artifacts and attire. It struck me that the woman's beaded buckskin shirt and skirt, sewn together with rawhide stitching, seemed almost eerily authentic. She wore leather leggings and moccasins and moved with a fluid, athletic gait, her step so light and soundless on the office carpet that she seemed almost to float upon it. She was a tall, lanky girl, quite lovely, dark-skinned, but with light brown hair and arrestingly blue eyes — somewhat unusual for a native American. She had strong features and an aquiline nose with slightly flared nostrils, which, along with the way she held her head high, gave her a certain proud, even defiant demeanor. She wore braids, with colored beads and small bones that looked like they had belonged to birds tied into them. Most astonishing, around her waist she wore what I couldn't help but identify as an old-time scalp belt, adorned with what looked to be real human scalps, examples of which I had also seen in various museum collections. Attached to it, as well, was a period scalping knife with an elaborately carved bone handle in a finely beaded sheath. I hesitate to say this, but in the vernacular of May Dodd's day, the young woman had a certain savage look about her.

I closed my office door behind us. Indicating her belt, I asked: "Is that what I think it is?"

She nodded. "Don't worry, I'm not going to add your scalp to it."

"Good to know. Please, sit down." I gestured to the chair in front of my desk and took my seat on the other side. "Just out of curiosity, how did you get past

29

security downstairs? They're very strict about not allowing any kind of weapon into the building."

She deftly swung the saddlebags from her shoulder to the desktop, where they landed with a heavy slapping sound. "I am a shape-shifter," she answered. "I take the form of other beings — birds, animals, other humans. To them I appeared as any other employee on the Chicago Mercantile Exchange. I walked right by with a group of professional women returning from their lunch hour. No one stopped me, no one saw my knife, for to their eyes it did not exist."

I looked at her very carefully now to see if she would reveal the smallest smile at this little charade. But she remained perfectly deadpan. "I see," I said, finally. "And how do you manage this shape-shifting business?"

"Ah, but that is an ancient trade secret we do not share, least of all with a white man."

"Fair enough. What is it you wanted to give me?"

"I said I had something for you," she said, "but not to give, only to lend. I had intended it for your father. I am sorry I did not have occasion to see him again before he went to Seano, the Happy Place, but at the same time I am glad to know he has moved on there."

"And how did you learn about his death?" I asked.

"You must know that your father was well liked by many people on the reservation. Word travels fast there."

"You say we've met before. But you're right, I'm afraid I don't remember you."

"We were just kids. We didn't know each other well. But one day you invited me to go the movies at the res community center."

I laughed then, suddenly remembering. "How could I forget? I had just turned thirteen years old, and you were the first girl I ever asked out on a date. I was walking from Dad's trailer where we parked on the res to pick you up at your house, and a group of Cheyenne boys waylaid me and beat the crap out of me. You're Molly Standing Bear . . . all grown-up."

She smiled and nodded. "That's right. When you asked me to the movies, you overstepped the boundaries for non–tribal members."

"That was made quite clear to me," I said. "But after they beat me up, I went to your house anyway, and your mother told me you weren't home. I never saw you again after that. It was a long time before I got up the courage to ask another girl out."

"My parents did not allow me to see you." Now Molly Standing Bear touched the saddlebags lightly with long slender fingers, as if in a kind of blessing. "I must go now. Everything you need to know is contained here."

"Need to know about what?" I asked. "I should tell you that the magazine does not accept unsolicited manuscripts. Which doesn't prevent people from sending them to us . . . though usually they arrive as e-mail attachments, not inside antique saddlebags."

"This is not for the magazine," she said. "This is just for you. Your father was one of the few white men we trusted. I'm hoping that you, as his son, can also be trusted."

"Trusted with what?"

"Take good care of these," she said, again lightly placing her hand on the saddlebags. "I'll be back for them. If you lose them, I *will* take your scalp."

"You're kidding about that, right?" I asked.

She touched the handle of the knife at her waist and looked in my eyes without answering, which seemed like a kind of answer to me.

"Yeah, OK, one last question then."

"I remember your father, too, asked a lot questions," she said. "We forgave him for that because we respected him, even though in our culture it is considered impolite."

"It's our job," I said. "I'm just curious to know: what's up with your outfit? I mean, this is downtown Chicago. You are clearly an intelligent, well-educated woman, but you're dressed like you just walked out of a museum display case featuring nineteenth-century Plains Indian attire."

"That's just the look I was going for," she said.

"I'm surprised the police haven't stopped you."

"Is it illegal here to be a native American?"

"No, but the Chicago police force doesn't see many traditionally dressed Cheyenne women on the streets. Not to mention the fact that you're wearing what appears to be an authentic scalp belt and knife. I would think they might just stop you out of curiosity."

"I told you, I blend in. I become whatever, whomever I need to be in the eyes of the beholder. They do not see me for who I really am."

"And who are you, really?"

She stood to leave, smiled, and held her open hands out to her sides. "I am who you see me as."

In that moment, I saw Molly Standing Bear as a young girl again on the reservation, and myself as a thirteen-year-old boy with a mad crush on her. "You know," I said, feeling a flush of gooseflesh, "you know, Molly, I really liked you when we were kids. I remember you had kind of an edge, an attitude. The res boys were all intimidated by you, because you were smarter than they were, and you didn't put up with their bullshit."

"They're still intimidated by me, I'm still smarter, and I still don't put up with their bullshit." She said this not in any boasting kind of way, but simply as a statement of fact.

I laughed. "Yeah, I can see that. Any chance we could have that movie date while you're in town? Or maybe even dinner, now that we're grown-ups?"

"None."

I laughed again. "OK, then. I'll walk you back out to the lobby."

"I know the way."

"Sorry, company policy. All visitors must be escorted from the premises . . . especially those who are armed."

But she was already at the door, and without turning she slipped out of my office, silent and graceful as a spirit being.

I stood from my desk and followed her. But when I opened the door and stepped into the hallway, she was gone. The only person walking ahead of me toward the lobby was a woman in a tailored gray business suit and heels, carrying a briefcase. "Madam, excuse me," I called after her. "Did you just pass a young Indian woman in the hall?"

Without breaking her brisk stride, the woman looked over her shoulder and smiled politely. "No sir, I'm afraid not, I haven't seen a soul."

I stood there for a few moments in the hallway regarding the departing figure of the woman, the hairs on the back of my neck rising with a tingling sensation.

"Did the native American girl just come out through here?" I asked Chloe when I reached the front desk.

"No, I thought she was still with you," she answered. "But some other lady came out who I don't remember coming in. She must have slipped by when I went to the ladies' room. You want me to call security, Chief? That Indian girl really creeps me out. Like, what was that weird hairy thing she was wearing around her waist?"

"You don't want to know, Chloe."

I heard the ding of the elevator in the hallway outside the office, and I came out just as the doors were beginning to slide shut. The woman in the gray suit stood in the back of the elevator. Her hair was pinned up neatly and she wore makeup; she looked like a professional — an attorney, a doctor, perhaps a university professor — but there was no doubt in my mind: it was Molly Standing Bear. She smiled wryly as the doors closed on her.

I hurried past the front desk toward my office. "Chief," Chloe called after me, "you sure you don't want me to call security?"

I stopped and turned to her. "Hey, Chloe, haven't I asked you to stop calling me Chief?"

"But you know I always called your dad that," she said. "I think he liked it. Kind of a retro thing."

"I'm not my dad, Chloe, and I'm not into retro. So please, just call me JW like you used to, like everyone else does. And while you're at it, shut up about security."

"Grumpy, grumpy, grumpy," she muttered, shaking her head. "OK, JW, I got it. So what happened to Pocahontas, anyway? Where'd she go?"

"I'm not sure."

"I told you she was weird."

Back in my father's chair, I dragged the saddlebags toward me across the desk. On close inspection I was just able to make out the faded stenciling on the flap of the pouch. It read *Miller 7th U.S. Cavalry.* I remembered the one fact that every Plains Indian buff knows: the Seventh Cavalry was under the command of General George Armstrong Custer at the Battle of the Little Bighorn. I was almost afraid to open the saddlebags. But of course, I did.

From the first pouch, I slid six antique ledger books with faded cloth covers. Stocked in trading posts throughout the West during the late 1800s and early 1900s, these were one of the few sources of paper readily available to native American tribes, whose pictorial artists highly valued them for use as drawing pads. On a trip to New York with my father, I had seen one of the most famous ledger art books on display at the Museum of Natural History. The drawings in it had been executed by a young Cheyenne artist named Little Fingernail, who when traveling or in battle wore the ledger strapped to his back, as did May Dodd. With an eerie similarity to her journals, there is a bullet hole passing through both covers and all pages of that book. Fired by a soldier as Little Fingernail fled an

Army attack, the bullet killed the young artist, just as it had May. Both of them shot in the back.

In the second pouch, I found seven more such ledgers, all numbered. Flipping through the pages of the first book, I saw that it contained neither old accounting records — which, of course was the original purpose of these ledgers — nor native American drawings. Instead, the lined and columned pages were filled with a woman's handwriting in different colored pencils, the only medium available to the Indian artists of the day. On the inside of the cover was written:

This book belongs to
Margaret & Susan Kelly.
Private property. Keep out!

I picked up one of the ledgers from the second pouch, opened it at random, and saw that it was written in a different hand, though also that of a woman. Assuming that Molly Standing Bear had arranged them in some order, I put this one back, picked up the first again, and began to read. I stayed in my office all the rest of that workday and all the night. I took no calls, responded to no text messages or e-mails, and did not stop reading until I turned the last page of the final ledger book.

The following journals have been rearranged in alternate but roughly chronological order. As they were written by two different authors, covering some of the same events, there is some inevitable overlapping of dates. Except for very minimal and occasional corrections of spelling and punctuation, they are largely unedited. In some cases, quotation marks, italics, paragraph breaks, and obviously missing words have been added, simply for the sake of clarity and continuity. Although it is always difficult for those of us trained in this business not to "clean things up" as my father used to say of the editing process, I have kept in check as much as possible my more anal-retentive editorial impulses, thus leaving intact the voice and style, as well as the literary shortcomings of the respective narrators. Because, of course, this is their story, not mine.

■ ■ ■ ■

Ledger Book I
In the Camp of
Crazy Horse

■ ■ ■ ■

We curse the U.S. government, we curse the Army, we curse the savagery of mankind, white and Indian alike. We curse God in his heaven. Do not underestimate the power of a mother's vengeance.

(from the journals of Margaret Kelly)

9 March 1876

My name is Meggie Kelly and I take up this pencil with my twin sister, Susie. We got nothing left, less than nothing. The village of our People has been destroyed, all our possessions burned, our friends butchered by the soldiers, our baby daughters gone, frozen to death on a godforsaken march across these rocky mountains. Empty of feeling, half-dead ourselves, all that remains of us intact are hearts turned to stone. We curse the U.S. government, we curse the Army, we curse the savagery of mankind, white and Indian alike. We curse God in his heaven. Do not underestimate the power of a mother's vengeance.

We have reached the winter camp of Crazy Horse on the Powder River. We been here six days now. The Lakota family who took us in has given us a stack of ledger books and a rawhide pouch full of colored drawing pencils. These belonged to one of their tribal artists who was killed in battle. Because me and Susie don't speak Lakota, only Cheyenne and sign talk, they wished us to make drawings of the attack on our village so they could see for themselves how it went. These are a real visual people, and we got no other way to communicate with them. We did the best we could, but me and Susie are not real good drawers.

The thing is we can write a little better, at least I can, though we ain't fancy educated girls, like our old friend May Dodd. Aye, we may have all been from Chicago, but me and Susie grew up on the streets, orphans who lived by our wits . . . and our bodies in times of need . . . because we was a handsome pair of lassies back then and the fellas was always sniffin' around after us. When we was split up and sent to different foster homes, one of my families gave me a little more teaching than did Susie's, who just made her a servant like in many foster homes, didn't care if she knew how to read or write, long as she could do their housework and laundry. So when she has somethin' to say here, she is just going to tell me and I will write it down best I can, and together we are going to keep up this journal in honor of our friend May. For

Brother Anthony tells us that she, too, is dead, along with all the others, except Martha. But just now we have no tears left to shed . . . we expect that will come later.

The night before the Army attack, a number of us white women slept in Brother Anthony's tipi. Earlier that evening we had watched our Cheyenne husbands dancing proudly over their trophies of war — a bag of twelve severed baby hands taken in a raid that day against their enemy, the Shoshone. They had ridden with a band of other rash young men out to prove themselves for the first time in battle. None of the experienced warriors such as Little Wolf, Hawk, or Tangle Hair had participated, but it is the tradition of the tribe that all must attend the victory dance. As they pranced, these boys chanted the tale of their triumph, they sang that in taking these babies' hands they had captured the power of the Shoshone nation . . . aye, the grand power of a baby's hand . . .

After the horror of what we saw the lads had done, we white women fled from the celebration, and we could not bear to go back to our own lodges, could not bear to look upon our husbands ever again. We slept that night in Brother Anthony's lodge, and we tried to make sense of something that made no sense at all. What were those boys thinking? How could they have done such a thing? And maybe, after all, what happened in the morning was God's just punishment . . . though still we curse him for putting us and our children on earth and then abandoning us.

Even though we were flyin' white flags of surrender, the soldiers attacked the village at dawn. We woke to bugles blowing, galloping horse hooves pounding frozen earth, the sharp metal-on-metal sound of swords unsheathed, gunfire, and the battle whoops of the invaders. Course, those of us with babies had but one thought — to run, to save our children. Me and Susie gathered our twin girls in their baby boards and strapped them to our breasts. Brother Anthony went immediately through the tent flap and with no fear for his own safety raised his arms to the heavens and begged the soldiers to stop this madness. But the killing had already begun, and the soldiers did not heed Anthony's pleas.

As our own men took up their arms, the women, children, and elders ran from the tipis, confused and terrified . . . they were knocked down and trampled by the soldiers' horses, shot by rifle and pistol, slashed by swords, there were screams and cries everywhere, chaos and death . . . everywhere chaos and death.

We ran for our lives with the others. We saw some of our own fall to the soldiers and we tried to help 'em best we could. But finally we had to make the terrible choice to leave 'em where they fell, so we might save our own babies. The attack went on for several hours, as the men of the village fought bravely to defend us. But they were no match for the Army. We who managed to reach the hills sought any shelter we could. It was so cold . . . so bloody cold . . .

After the cavalry secured the village, they went about their business of destroying it and finishing off the wounded. Crouched shivering in the rocks, trying to keep our babies warm, we heard the terrible sounds of the killing. Some bravely sang their death songs until they were silenced. We heard the keening of mothers mourning their dead children, before they, too, were slaughtered. We heard screams from some of our women, and we knew what was happening to them . . . before they, too, fell quiet.

With the wounded finally dispatched, the soldiers began to stack all our goods in huge piles and light them afire, lighting, as well, the tipis, leaving nothing for us to salvage, nothing for us to return to. The cold flames rose, offering us no warmth, the smoke bearing its sickening odor of burning human flesh . . .

It was dusk by the time the cavalrymen remounted and rode off. Brother Anthony joined us in the hills, came to us weeping . . . *"the horror, the horror,"* he cried. "I tried to protect God's children, I tried to save them from the soldiers' madness. But there were too many, too many . . ."

"Where is May?" I asked. "Is May alive?"

Anthony could only shake his head, so broken up was he by grief.

"Is anyone alive?"

Again he shook his head. "All dead," he managed to say, "all dead except for Martha and her baby. Captain Bourke has taken charge of them . . . he was riding with the soldiers, but not as their commander . . . he, too, tried to stop the carnage, but their bloodlust was not to be denied . . . The captain swore to me . . . he swore to me on his life and in the name of God that he would see that Martha and the child were returned safely to Chicago."

Aye, Martha was May's best friend, and besides me and Meggie, she and her baby were the only other survivors of our entire group. It offers us great solace to imagine them back safe in their home . . . a place that seems to us so far away.

That night under the cold full moon, Little Wolf led us across the mountains toward the village of Crazy Horse. We ain't got words to tell of the sufferin' we endured on that journey, the children and the wounded who died, includin' our own Daisy Lovelace and her baby that first night, and on the second night me and Susie's twin girls. We were told to leave their bodies in a tree, for there was no timber available to build a burial scaffold in the manner of the Cheyenne, and the ground was frozen so they could not be interred as was our own custom. But we could not bear the thought of the carrion peckin' at their wee bodies, and so we carried them in their baby boards the rest of the way to Crazy Horse's camp . . . we feel still, and will forever, the weight of the tiny frozen corpses heavy on our breasts.

And so you see we got nothin' left but our hearts of stone.

The Lakota, too, are being pursued by the Army, and they have little to share with us. Captain Bourke told Brother Anthony that when the Army attacked our village, they thought it was the village of Crazy Horse, he was the one they were really after. All that death, all that pain and destruction and heartbreak . . . because the Indian scouts who were guiding the troops made a mistake. But you know what the soldiers say around the fort? We heard it ourselves when we were trading at Fort Laramie before winter came on. They say the only good Injun is a dead Injun. Who cares whether they be Cheyenne or Lakota? I guess the Army decided that white women who consort with savages also deserve to die . . . and their half-breed babies as well, even though our government sent us here in the first place.

Crazy Horse himself is a strange man. He hardly speaks, stays to himself, and does not socialize with the rest of the tribe. Even his own people think he's a peculiar fella. Although the Lakota are allies of the Cheyenne, our chief Little Wolf has never cared for their people, has never learned their language, and has avoided contact with them as much as possible. Among other things, he thinks their women are loose. He and Crazy Horse do not get on together, and keep out of each other's way; two great warriors from different tribes behavin' like a pair of fightin' cocks keepin' their distance. Men are hopeless creatures, me an'

50

Susie lay all the violence and troubles of the world at their feet.

Little Wolf is angry with Crazy Horse. He thinks he ain't been generous with us since we got here. It's true that the Lakota don't have much to give, but to the Cheyenne stinginess toward those who need help is the worst insult. Then again, Crazy Horse got his own people to look after. Game is scarce, the buffalo herds shot out and scattered all the hell across the plains. The white settlers want to raise cattle on this land, and so they slaughter the wild beasts to make room for their cows . . . in the same way they slaughter the wild Indians to make room for themselves.

Many of the people talk now of surrender. We got nothing. We kill and butcher our horses to eat. Others wish to fight on. Me an' Susie will never surrender to those who murdered our babies. Never. We have taken a holy vow to fight the whites to the end, to kill and scalp as many bluecoats as we can. Brother Anthony came to our tipi today and has tried to talk to us, has tried to bring us back into "the arms of God who loves and keeps us," says he.

"Is that so, Brother?" asks Susie. "An' if he loves and keeps us so well, then why did he kill our wee infants? What did they ever do to deserve that? We curse God for his cruelty, his savagery . . . the fooking hypocrite who blames the very people for our behavior he himself created in his own image. What kind of arsehole is he anyway, Brother? Aye, we curse him and we damn him in the name of all mothers." It is true that though we be identical twins, me and Susie still each got our own ways, and if anything she may be the harder girl between us.

"It is not God who is cruel and savage," the monk answers. "Those are the actions of men who have fallen from the path of our Lord, or who, perhaps, have never known it."

"So what good is he then, Brother, if he hasn't even the power to protect babies?"

"It is your grief that steals your faith, my children, your grief that speaks for you now. Not your hearts."

"Our hearts are stone, Anthony," says I, "and as stone they speak."

"And with those hearts of stone," says Susie, "we will bash in the soldiers' brains, and with our knives, sharpened on those same stones, not only will we take their scalps, but also cut off their bollocks."

"Right ya are, sister," says I, "and those bollocks we will string together with rawhide and wear proud around our necks as trophies of war."

"Aye, Brother Anthony," says Susie, "our husbands cut off the hands of Shoshone babies. The fools believed that in so doin' they were capturing the power of the tribe . . . imagine that . . . But it is men's bollocks that cause all the war, all the death and destruction in the world. That is where we will take our revenge."

"Aye, Brother," says I, "and as the legend of the mad Kelly twins grows across the plains, the soldiers will so fear runnin' into us they will refuse the orders of their officers, they will mutiny and begin to desert, they will leave this country once and for all until all have fled."

"The traders and the sodbusters and the cattlemen and the gold diggers, too," Susie continues, "as they learn of our savage exploits, will be driven from the plains by sheer terror at the sound of our names. And then the People will live in peace and the buffalo and the game will return, and all will be as before."

Anthony can only shake his head sadly. "Yes, my children, all will be as before," says he. "Except that your infants will still be gone, and all your anger, all your hatred, all your schemes of bloody revenge will not bring them back."

"Maybe not, Brother," says I. "Maybe not . . . but do not underestimate the wrath of a mother's vengeance. It is only that which keeps us alive, don't ya see? We will stay here and fight to the end, because what else is there to do, where else do we have to go? And if we survive we will bear more babies for the savages, and we will make for them a better world ruled by mothers, not by the bollocks of men."

15 March 1876

These past few days bring a false spring thaw, the snow melting on the surrounding hillsides. The wet rocks shine and steam in the morning sun, the plains that stretch beyond the river bottom even showing a few patches of pale green grass. Brother Anthony has come again to our tipi to tell us that it is fixed now — Little Wolf is fed up with the stinginess of the Lakota, and he's leaving with most of the rest of our band to turn themselves in to the Red Cloud Agency at the Army's Camp Robinson in Nebraska Territory. Aye, that is where the already surrendered Lakota, Cheyenne, and Arapaho are now living, and where all those hostiles who have not yet turned themselves in have been ordered by General Crook to report . . . once they do, forbidden to leave again.

Only a handful of the other Cheyenne who have family here among the Lakota will stay, and those like me and Susie who would rather die than give up. We don't blame Little Wolf, he's the bravest man we've ever known, the finest leader and the toughest warrior. But his first responsibility as the Sweet Medicine Chief is to protect the people from harm, to feed and clothe them best he can and it is for this reason that he has decided to surrender.

"You girls must go in with Little Wolf," Anthony says to us again.

"Have we not made it clear to you, Brother," says Susie, "that the Kelly sisters will never surrender?"

"Please, listen to me, my children," says he. "You are white women. It is not a matter of surrender, for you are not at war with the Army or the United States government."

"Not at war with the Army or government, you say, Brother?" asks I. "That would be grand news to us, wouldn't it now, sister? But were it true, then who was it attacked us, who was it responsible for the death of our babies and all our friends?"

"This is now simply a matter of your own survival," says the Brother, "of seeking food, shelter, and safe passage back to your homes."

"But we have no homes to return to," says Susie. "Have you forgotten, Brother, that we are felons? We will be returned to prison if we go back to Chicago."

"No, Captain Bourke will see to it that this does not happen. As he has promised to do for Martha, he will see that you are cared for."

"Aye, just as he saw to it that our peaceful winter village flyin' white flags of surrender was not attacked by the cavalry with which he himself was ridin', ain't that so, Brother Anthony?"

"The captain did not know it was Little Wolf's village. They were misinformed by the scouts. He is filled with remorse and guilt over what happened, and will be for the rest of his life."

"As well he should be," says Susie.

"You girls are incorrigible," Anthony says sadly. "Although I rather expected this answer from you. If you insist on staying, then please at least grant me one request."

"And what would that be, Brother?" says I.

"There is a group of white women here."

"White women?" Susie and me answer together as so often happens among twins.

"And where in bejaysus did they come from? What are they doin' here?"

"It appears that they were intended to be another installment of the Brides for Indians program," says Anthony. "The wheels of government bureaucracy turn slowly, and as you well know communications out here are difficult. Evidently these women had already been sent to join the Cheyenne before word that the program was terminated had reached the proper authorities."

"But how did they end up with the Lakota?"

"As I understand it, their warriors built a fire on the tracks to stop the train, and when it came to a halt, they attacked — overpowering the escort of soldiers, stealing the Army horses, guns, ammunition, and other kit meant to resupply the troops at Fort Laramie . . . and abducting the women. They are now being kept isolated in a guarded tipi on the edge of the village. I was allowed to meet with them, and, understandably, they are deeply distraught. I powwowed with Crazy Horse and the other Lakota leaders and did my best to convince them to let the women come with us to the agency. I explained that releasing them into my custody would be considered by the Army as an act of good faith on their part.

But the chiefs flatly refused my request."

"What do you want from us then, Brother?" asks Susie.

"I want you to help them, to look after them," says he. "Anticipating that you would refuse to come in with us to the agency, I did at least manage to convince the chiefs to let you see the white women. My hope is that with your own experience among the Indians, you will be able to counsel these girls and see them through this ordeal."

"Aw, holy Jaysus, Brother," says I, "me and Susie ain't no damn babysitters. We got more important business to attend to than lookin' after a bunch of crybaby white girls."

"And what important business would that be, ladies?" Anthony asks. "I am simply asking you in the name of the Lord, in the name of Christian charity, to help a group of deeply distressed, captive women of your own race. You remember what it was like when you first came out here a year ago. You must yourselves have been terrified, although knowing you two as I do, I suspect you hid that fear behind your Irish bravado. At the same time, you had the support of each other and of your friends. You had a peaceful transfer into the hands of the Cheyenne, you were not violently abducted from a train and held hostage. A number of their party were also killed in the attack, which has further traumatized them. I beg you, do what you can to help these girls, counsel them, offer them succor and support, try to transfer to them some of your own fortitude. For all you have both suffered, for all you have endured, you are strong women, you are survivors. Give them some hope that they, too, can find a way through this predicament."

"We don't know much about hope, Brother," says Susie.

"But I believe you do. And so does almighty God in his heaven."

16 March 1876

And so me and Susie go to see these white women. The Lakota are keepin' 'em in a communal tipi used by the Indians for official functions like war councils and pow-wows, a tipi so grand you can stand up inside it. It seems that the women of the tribe are a wee bit unhappy about the arrival of the white lassies and wish to have them isolated from the general population, particularly from their men. As all the tribes do with female captives, the Lakota squaws probably plan to make slaves of 'em. But you can be sure we're not going to tell the lassies that part just yet. Nor do we intend to tell 'em straight out what happened to our group. We figure they must be scared enough as it is with what they already been through, and that'll only scare 'em more.

As the Cheyenne do themselves when they go visiting, we thought we should bring some kind of gift for the white girls. Cheer 'em up a wee bit. But we got nothing ourselves besides the clothes on our back, so all we could think to give 'em was some of our stock of ledger books and colored pencils. We figured maybe that would at least give 'em something to do, other than to sit around all day long worrying about what was going to happen to 'em.

The young Lakota boy guarding the entrance opens the tipi flap for us and we duck inside. A fire burns in the center and the women are seated in a circle around it, wrapped in trade blankets or buffalo capes worn over their dresses. At first they seem a little confused to see us, frightened even. It is true that maybe me and Susie have a scary look about us after these last hard days of want and suffering and grief — identical twins with our red hair wild and tangled around our faces, bright green eyes and deathly pale complexions, bone skinny from hunger, dressed in ragged animal hides and ratty trade blankets given us by our Lakota family. Sometimes we catch sight of each other, and we share one of those twin mirror moments, realizing how much we have changed, how far we have come in this past year, so far that there is no turning back to the world we once knew.

A quick head count tells us that they are but seven in number. Although most of 'em look to be about our own age, they seem like mere girls to us, as if we ourselves have aged a full decade in our one year on the plains. They, too, are a wee worse for the wear, what we can see of their white-women clothes stained, frayed, and torn here and there. Still we can tell they're makin' an effort to keep themselves as tidy as possible in captivity, which is an important sign that they haven't given up hope — their faces are clean, their hair in place. Though thin, they clearly ain't starving, and it appears to us that the Lakota are treating them kindly and with respect, which is the way of these people.

"Alright, lassies," says I straightaway to calm 'em, "you've nothing to fear from us. I be Meggie Kelly, and this be me sister, Susie. We might not be lookin' our best, that's the God's truth, but we are white women ourselves as you can plainly see.

Make a wee bit of room for us so we can sit down with you by the fire."

Several of 'em scoot over to make space, and Susie and me get settled cross-legged. Pale late-afternoon light filters through the hide walls of the tipi, giving everything a kind of golden hue. "We came here a year ago," Susie begins, "under the same program as you. We were with the first group of women sent out to marry among the Cheyenne. And so we did. And now, as you may also have guessed from the look of us, we have gone over to the other side. We are white Cheyenne. We come here to help you. We know you been through a terrible ordeal. We know you're tired and scared. We been there, too, believe me. But the first thing you must learn is that whinin' and behavin' like sissies will gain you nothing from these people but scorn and abuse. They do not respect weakness, nor do we. Now which of you be the leader among you?"

"What do you mean by the leader?" ventures a timid girl seated beside me in a wee Liverpudlian voice. "We are all of us just prisoners."

"Aye, but in every group like this," says I, "there is usually one who takes charge . . . at least until such time as everyone else gets their feet under them, so to speak. Let us put it this way, then, who is the one you look to first in a tough spot? Ours was a lass by the name of May Dodd. She didn't ask for the job, just kinda fell into it. So whoever that be among you, go ahead and introduce yourself."

Me and Susie could tell right away by the number of girls who all looked over at one particular girl on the other side of the circle that she was the top dog alright. She seemed reluctant and a wee embarrassed to claim the title, but finally she stood up. She was a handsome lass, maybe a few years older than some of the others, tall, big-boned, a blue-eyed fair-haired lass who looked like she knew how to take care of herself.

"I don't know why," she said, "but for now I guess that might be me."

"Alright, that's a fine start," says Susie. "And what would your name be then, lassie?"

"Molly. Molly McGill."

"Aye, a good Scottish name. Where do you come from, Molly McGill?"

"It's true that my family was of Scottish origin," she says. "We had a farm in northern New York, up near the Canadian border not far from Champlain. However, I was living in New York City."

"What kind of work did you do in New

York City?"

"I was a schoolteacher and a charity worker. I worked mostly with children without homes."

"That had to be hard work."

"Hard enough. With all the immigrants arriving, there are so many of them."

"Susie and me been there, too . . ." says I. "We grew up in an orphan asylum in the Chicago tenements, farmed out to different foster families who mostly took us right back soon as they could because we were a pack a' trouble, we Kelly twins. We could not bear to be separated and when we were we tried to run away first chance we got. Finally they said we were unadoptable and locked us up in one a' the orphan asylums reserved for repeat runaways. But we ran away from there, too. We spent a lot of time livin' on the streets. So you see, we know a bit about such matters and we know you must be a tough lass to work that kinda job."

Molly McGill shrugs. "Not always tough enough."

"Ain't that always the way, though?"

"And you must be smart to be a teacher," says Susie. "Meggie and me admire those that know something more than the mean things we learned growing up. The only useful talent we came away with was how to take care of ourselves. You look like a girl who knows how to do that, too."

"I do what I have to do."

"Good, then you got the job."

"And what does that job entail?" she asks.

"Stayin' alive, and keepin' your friends that way, too," says I. "That's the first responsibility. You'll soon find out, if you haven't already, it's full-time work in this country among these folks."

Molly looks us hard in the eyes for a long moment. We get the sense that this is a girl who has known some considerable trials in her life. "That we have already learned," she says, finally. "And how did your friend May Dodd do in the performance of this duty?"

"She did just fine for a long time," says I. "And then in two shakes of a lamb's tail not so fine. She didn't make it . . . through no fault of her own."

"I'm awfully sorry to hear that," says Molly McGill. "What happened to her?"

"All a' that in good time, missy," says I. "Right now, it's we who want to get to know about you. First off, there being only seven of you, we're curious . . . How many did you start out with?"

"We were a total of nineteen when we boarded in Chicago," says Molly. "By the time we reached Omaha, four women had had second thoughts and jumped train at various stops along the way. We lost two more in Omaha for the same reason . . . and six of our party were killed when the Lakota attacked the train . . . God rest their souls." Some of the girls started to get teary again at this fresh memory, and maybe at the reminder of their fast-dwindling number.

"We're real sorry about that," says Susie. "If your group was anything like ours, we know you made friends fast on the trip out. We know how it is to lose friends."

"Why don't you begin for us, Molly," says I to get off the subject quick as possible. "How is it that you came to sign up for the program?"

"To gain parole from Sing Sing prison," she answers.

"Did you now?" says I. "And what were ya in for, if we may ask?"

"Murder."

"Who'd ya kill, then?" asks Susie.

"A man who deserved it. But I cannot speak further of that."

"Aye, that's fine, lass," says I. "We are none of us required to say any more than we choose, and all have a right to guard our

66

secrets. That's how it was among our group."

"Meggie and me has been in stir ourselves," says Susie. "I imagine being cooped up in this tipi might remind you a bit of that."

"As a matter of fact, as I have been telling the girls, this place is preferable to Sing Sing. The prisoners there aren't allowed to speak. Ever. Not a word. Absolute silence is the rule. And if we were caught at it, we were whipped, beaten . . . or worse. I was not what you would call a model prisoner. I was considered an agitator, and I spent a good deal of time in solitary confinement. When the recruiter for the brides program came, the warden was delighted to be rid of me. And I was ready to go anywhere. *Anywhere.* For me, compared to that place, this is a stroll in Central Park on a Sunday afternoon. Even the food is better."

"Brilliant," says I, "excellent start, we've got a murderer among us. Have we a lunatic or two?"

Now another woman in the circle raises her hand. She stands, brushes herself off, clears her throat. A manly-lookin' bird, tough and built like a spool of wire, she has short cropped hair, wears jodhpurs and fancy English riding boots. "I hope I do not disappoint you ladies," she says in a hoity-toity British accent, "when I tell you that I am neither a criminal, nor am I insane. If I may present myself: I am Lady Ann Hall of Sunderland." Susie and me exchange a glance then, because this is a name we have heard before. "And the young lady here beside me," continues the Englishwoman, indicating the girl who sat at her feet, "is my maidservant, Hannah Alford from Liverpool. Raise your hand, Hannah." The tiny slip of a girl, timid as a mouse, raises her hand.

"You won't have much use for a servant here, m'lady," says Susie. "Like May Dodd said at the beginnin' of our own journey, you'll soon find out that you are all equal here, regardless of where you come from, who your family was, what you did in your past lives, how much money you got, how much education, your accent or the color of your skin. Because you see, you'll learn real quick if you haven't already that none of that matters in this country."

"Quite the contrary," says Lady Ann Hall. "I believe that even in the wilderness, it is essential to observe civilized social hierarchy and conventions. I consider myself no less a lady here than back in Great Britain."

"That's all very well, m'lady," says I. "But

out here it's the Indians who decide the hierarchy and conventions, and, believe it or not, they really don't give a rat's arse about British titles. In fact, you'll be lucky not to be workin' as a maidservant yourself in the household of a Lakota squaw."

"Not bloody likely," says Lady Hall. "You see, in addition to my title, I served for three years as the president of the London National Society for Women's Suffrage. I lead women, I do not follow, nor, I can assure you, do I do housework."

"Well, then, do tell us how you joined the program, Lady Hall."

"I have come here in search of my companion," says she, "the ornithologist and artist Helen Elizabeth Flight. I received one short letter from her posted from Fort Laramie almost a full year ago. She told me of her enrollment in the Brides for Indians program, and a little about the group with whom she had been dispatched, of which I must assume you ladies were also members. After that, I had no further word from her. I attempted to make inquiries of the authorities in America via representatives of my own government, but to no avail. It seemed, finally, that the only hope I had of finding her was to come out here as a volunteer myself. You ladies must have known Helen.

Can you give me news of her?"

Susie and me look at each other again, our memory well refreshed as to where we had heard Lady Hall's name. "Indeed we can, m'lady," says I. "Helen Flight is a dear, dear friend of ours. We shall tell you later, in private, all we know of her."

"Ah, splendid news," says Lady Ann Hall, "then I am on her trail, after all. A stroke of good fortune to have come across you ladies. Thank you."

We do not wish to disabuse the English-woman of this notion just yet, and neither me nor Susie says anything further about Helen. But a shadow crosses our hearts at the prospect of havin' to tell her the truth of what happened to our dear brave friend who fought the soldiers to the end.

"Alright, then," says Susie. "Now, we brought you girls a wee gift, a stack of these ledger books and some colored pencils. As the leader, we're givin' 'em to you, Molly, to distribute as you please."

"For what reason do we need ledger books?" she asks. "Are the Lakota going to put us to work keeping their accounts?"

Susie and me laugh. It is already clear to us that this Molly McGill is a direct girl, not afraid to speak her mind. "See, we don't have much to offer," says I, "but we came into a nice stash of these when we got here. All the tribes have artists among them, who trade hides for the books at the white trading posts, and use 'em to draw pictures on. Helen Flight calls their work 'primitive' because you see they paint everything real flat, without 'perspective,' she says. But we all liked it anyhow, even Helen, and she taught them a few of her own tricks. Now if you don't want to draw on 'em, you can do like me and Susie, and our friend May did, and use 'em to keep a diary. Either way, we thought it'd give you girls somethin' to do besides worry yourselves sick all day long."

"I kept a diary myself on the train," says Molly. "But like all our other possessions, it is lost now. Needless to say, our abductors did not allow us to bring along our bags. We are grateful to have this paper and pencils. Of course, we will share them."

Now Susie points to a pretty young girl sitting cross-legged in the first row, her head downcast. "And you there, darlin'?" she says. "Speak up, tell us your name and how you came to be here. Don't be shy."

She looks up, smiles real friendly. "But I am not shy," she says, speaking with a French accent. "My name is Lulu LaRue. That is my stage name, and that is what I call myself, for I am an actress. I sing and I dance." One or two of the other girls snicker at this.

"Aye, in the theater then, are you? And where are you from, Lulu LaRue?"

"I come from Marseille, France," she says, "and from there I go to Los Angeles, California."

"And what brought you to the program?"

"I go to Los Angeles with other women from France to work in a laundry," she says. "It is very hard work and the hours are long and we are hardly given a day of rest. When one of those days arrive, I look for work in the theater. But you see, my English is not so strong and no one has interest in a little French girl with funny accent. One day I answer advertisement to try out for a theater group from St. Louis, Missouri. The man who auditions me is very handsome, charming, very kind with me. His name is Earl Walton. He ask me if I know how to dance. *Mais oui,* I say, of course, I dance, I am very good dancer. And so for him I do a French dance called the cancan. He say he like me, he like the way I dance, and he want to give me a job in his theater. He ask my address and say he will be in contact. The very next day, he come to our rooming house. He say that he must leave Los Angeles *immédiatement,* and go back to St. Louis, that if I want the job in his theater, I must go with him now. He does not give me time to think . . . it sounds so exciting, and I am glad to leave the laundry. And so that same afternoon, I go with him. It is a very long trip to St. Louis, very hard. This man Earl is all I have in the world . . . I begin to fall in love with him . . . at least I think I am in love. He say he love me, too, and that after we arrive we will marry together."

"I think we're beginnin' to get the picture, Lulu," says Susie. "So tell us about this theater in St. Louis."

"Well, you see . . . it is not really a theater at all," says Lulu. "Earl is the proprietor of a private gentlemen's club. There the girls dance and sometimes put on shows to entertain the gentlemen . . . and, of course, they must do other . . . certain other service."

"Aye, say no more, Lulu," says Susie, holding up her hand. "Meggie and me has taken similar employment in times of need. And so you signed up for the brides program in order to escape this Earl fella, is that how it happened?"

"*Oui* . . . you see, it become clear that the only reason he hire me is so I learn the others to dance the cancan. He is not going to marry me, he does not love me . . . I think he not even like me . . . the other girls say he make the same promise to them. We are prisoners at the club. We are not allowed to leave there, not even to go shopping, unless one of his men is with us. When I finally escape, I know that I must go as far away from St. Louis as possible, or Earl find me and bring me back."

"In that case, lassie," says I, "lookin' on the bright side, you have come to the right place. Earl won't be findin' you here in Crazy Horse's camp, that is for certain."

"Yes, well I always try to look on the bright side," says Lulu LaRue. "I was even thinking life as the wife of a Cheyenne Indian will make bigger my palette . . . no, wait, how do you say? . . . make bigger my *range* as an actress."

"Quite possible, Lulu," says Susie, "for one never knows when learnin' to fook Indian style will come in handy onstage." At this some of the other girls giggle nervously, both shocked and amused at our language.

"There, you see, ladies," says I, "one thing our group learned in our time out here is that a little laughter goes a long way toward lightening the dark times. We know you don't feel like it most of the time, but it's the only way to keep your spirits up, the only way to survive. We were all the time makin' fun and teasin' each other. You'll find that the Indians themselves have a sly sense of humor if you can engage them on that level. The truth is, Lulu, I'll wager your acting skills *will* serve you well here."

"Do you have any idea what the Lakota plan to do with us?" asks Molly. "Are they going to keep us prisoner indefinitely?"

"That's what we're gonna try to find out," says I.

"Will they give us to the Cheyenne?" asks another girl, who seems to have a Scandinavian look and accent about her. "It is to them we are to be married. To help keep the peace on the Great Plains, to teach the savages the civilized ways of the white man."

"Aye, aye," says I, "we know all about the civilized ways of the white man. Brother Anthony didn't tell you lasses much, did he? He wanted to leave that to us. We are sorry to inform you of it, but you are not going to be the brides of Cheyenne warriors. The program has been ended and most of the Cheyenne are surrendering. Nor is the Army or your government going to come to your rescue as you must be hopin'. To them, you see, the Brides for Indians program never existed, and they wish now to bury all evidence of it."

"And what exactly do you mean by 'bury'?" asks Lady Ann Hall. "Where are the rest of the women in your group now?"

"We'll get to that in good time, m'lady," says Susie. "Right now, we just want you to understand that you're on your own out here. You have only yourselves and each other to count on. No one is comin' to save you, and that is something you'd best get used to right off."

"For whatever wee consolation it may bring you," says I, "you also have us . . . for now anyhow. First thing we're going to do is try to powwow with the Lakota chiefs and see if we can't figure out a way to get you out of here."

Susie and me were hopin' maybe we could slip out of the girls' tipi quick like without having a private conversation with Lady Hall about Helen just yet. However, she asks to step outside with us, and when we do, she comes right to the point. "My dearest companion Helen is dead, is she not?"

Susie and me look long at each other, neither wishing to be the one to say, as if tellin' of it is like a second death for Helen . . . and for us. "Yes, m'lady, she is," I answer at last. "How did you know?"

"It was quite obvious from the looks on

76

your faces when first I spoke of her," says the Englishwoman. "However, I pretended not to notice for I was afraid I might fall apart in front of the others. I do not grieve publicly."

"You are a strong woman, Lady Hall," says Susie. "As was Helen. We loved her . . . all of us did. We are very sorry for you."

"Please tell me how she died. Tell me everything you know, and do not try to shield me from the truth."

"She died like a grand heroine, m'lady," says I. "The reason we have not told your group what happened to us yet is because it will only scare 'em worse than they already are. So please keep this to yourself for now. Several weeks ago the Army attacked our village at dawn. Helen stepped out of her tipi with her scattergun to defend against the invaders, while the women and children tried to escape. We were fleeing past her tipi with our babies. Helen had her corncob pipe in the corner of her mouth and she was firing at the charging soldiers. She blasted two of them right out of their saddles. As she paused to reload, she saw us running. 'A right and a left double, girls!' she called out to us. 'Lord Ripon would be envious! Run! Save the children! I've got you covered!'

"That was the last we would ever see of our dear friend Helen. After the attack was over, Brother Anthony, who stayed bravely in the village himself, came upon her body. She had been slashed across the neck by a saber, and a bullet had pierced her forehead. A soldier lay dead beside her, one side of his skull caved in. The stock of Helen's scattergun lay broken. Anthony thinks she must have been reloading as the soldier charged her. As he swung his saber, she swung the stock of her gun, hittin' him a blow to the head that unseated him from his horse. Another soldier must have finished her off with a bullet."

Lady Hall nods. "Yes, doesn't that sound just like my Helen? She was a tenacious girl. She would not have gone easily." We see the tears beginning to cloud the Englishwoman's eyes, but she keeps talking as if to avoid breaking down completely. "Helen, as you probably know, was a wonderful shot. She is the only woman who has ever been allowed to carry a gun at the grand driven shoot at Holkam Hall, Lord Leicester's estate in Norfolk, or at any other estate shoot for that matter. She outshot all of the men that day, including Lord Ripon, who is widely considered the finest wing shot in all of England. Indeed, after her magnificent performance, Helen was never again invited to participate in an estate shoot. Evidently the men could not tolerate being outshot by a woman, and wished to ensure that it did not happen again."

"She was a bleedin' fine artist, too," says Susie. "The Cheyenne warriors felt she possessed big medicine. Before they went off on raids, they had her paint animal and bird images on their bodies, and on their horses, too. They believe these protect them in battle. Last summer and fall, they returned victorious from every raid, and the warriors credited Helen's artistic skills for their success. She became quite famous among the tribe."

"Thank you for telling me this," says Lady Hall. "It means a great deal to me. I should like to know if any of her work on the birds of the western prairies survived?"

"Not that we know of," says I. "After the attack, the soldiers burned everything in the village. It is not likely that Helen's sketchbooks were spared from the flames."

19 March 1876
Well, goddamned if she doesn't ride right into the village this afternoon, astride a big gray mule, head held high like she owns the place, like a conquerin' hero come home.

Aye, our old friend Dirty Gertie, aka Jimmy the muleskinner. She must somehow have slipped past the Lakota sentries, which, believe us, is no easy thing to do, unless you be Indian yourself. For her to show up like that, alone and without warning, is not the normal way of things here, and it causes no small confusion in the village. The people come out of their tipis to watch silent and with a sense of wonder as she rides by. No one molests her, nor do the children run out to count coup on her as they like to do. As if taking their cue from the behavior of the adults, they stand real close together, hugging the legs of their parents or older brothers and sisters, quiet and watching round-eyed as Gertie makes her way through the village, now and then touching the grimy brim of her hat in friendly greeting to those she passes on either side.

Aye, they know who she is, pretty much everyone on the plains, Indian and white alike, knows Dirty Gertie. But like us, they heard she was dead, killed by the half-breed Jules Seminole and his band of Crow scouts. Such news travels fast out here, for Gertie was well-liked by the Cheyenne and the Lakota, having herself lived among these tribes. She's been in this country for years, got captured off a wagon train as a girl, married young the first time to a French trapper, who traded her for her weight in hides to the Southern Cheyenne, with whom she lived for a number of years, married a Cheyenne fella. Since then Gertie has moved easily between the Indian and white worlds; she's scouted and driven mule trains for the Army, served as an informer to the Indians, been shot, knifed, and left for dead by both sides. You name it, Gertie has seen and done it all, and no one, Indian or white alike, seems to hold it against her. She's just that kind of person who gets a pass from both sides, maybe because they know she does the right thing. So everyone took it real hard when they heard that the murderous scoundrel Seminole, who was hated as much as Gertie was loved, had done her in. Now as she rides through Crazy Horse's camp, the people wonder if they're seein' a ghost, because everyone believes she's dead.

But me and Susie know she ain't a ghost and I cannot say how happy we are to see her. Unlike the Lakota who just watch her silent as she passes, as soon as we part the tipi flap to see who is clip-cloppin' by and we recognize Gertie — dressed in her regular old fringed buckskins she hardly ever changes out of, her braided hair startin' to go gray, her face as leathery brown, beat-up, and wrinkled as an old boot — we come out at a dead run to her. With a whoop I swing up on the mule's withers facing her, and Susie jumps on his back behind her, and we both give her big hugs, kind of a twin sandwich. "Goddammit all, Gertie, they said you were dead!"

"I ain't dead yet, but if you two Irish scamps don't stop squeezin' the damn wind outta me, I will be soon."

"We heard Jules Seminole killed you."

"Son of a bitch give it a real good try," she says. "Invite me in for a cup a' coffee, girls, and I'll tell you the whole story."

And so Gertie pickets her mule outside our tipi, and we send the horse boy to bring a pile of dried grass for him to chew on. We boil up some coffee in the tipi and when we all get settled, Susie asks: "What are you doing here, Gertie? You didn't seem surprised to see us. Did you know we were here?"

"I was at Camp Robinson when Little Wolf brought his people in to surrender," she says. "Brother Anthony told me you gals had stayed out with Crazy Horse."

"But how did you ever find us?"

"Aw hell, girls, I know this Powder River country blindfolded, you oughta know that by now. It weren't hard at all for ole Dirty

Gertie to find ya."

"Then you know what happened to us down on the Tongue . . ." says I.

Gertie gazes into the fire, tears rising into the corners of her bright green eyes, peerin' out beneath hooded lids and sparklin' wet now in the flickerin' flames. We never seen Gertie cry before. We didn't even know the tough old bird was capable of it. "Yeah . . . I know all about that," she says in a low voice. "Broke my friggin' heart when I heard. And it was all my damn fault, too. After that last visit I made to your village, I was on my way back to the fort to deliver May's message to Cap'n Bourke. She wanted to tell him where you was located, and that Little Wolf had decided to come into the agency as soon as the weather cleared and it was safe to travel with the newborns. But Seminole had it in for you folks, and he didn't want that message delivered. So he and his Crow scouts were layin' for me on the trail, shot me the hell fulla arrows, until I looked like one a' them damn voodoo dolls they poke needles into. Left me out there for dead. If it hadn't been for a coupla Arapaho braves who come upon me and took me back to their village, the coyotes and the buzzards woulda been shittin' me out for a week. As it was, I was

83

laid up a good long time, touch-and-go. If I'd a' made it back, you'd a' never been attacked. It was that goddamned Jules Seminole who guided the cavalry to you, who told Colonel Mackenzie it was Crazy Horse's camp, not Little Wolf's. It was all on account a' that half-breed bastard all this has come to pass."

"Where is Seminole now?"

"They tell me he's livin' with the Crow," Gertie says. "Right after the attack against you folks, General Crook called off the winter campaign on account a' the cold weather. Too many soldiers was gettin' frostbit, losin' fingers and toes. That's why they haven't found this village yet. But if spring comes on early, like it's maybe fixin' to do, the Army'll be on the move again real soon, and the Injun scouts will be back hangin' around the fort lookin' for work . . . When the bastard shows his face, I'll be ready for him, that I can promise ya."

"But why would the Army use Seminole to scout for 'em again," asks Susie, "if they know now that he led them to the wrong village?"

"Hell, girl, you oughta know by now that the Army don't give a damn they wiped out Little Wolf's village 'stead of Crazy Horse's. It's still just one less band of renegades for 'em to deal with, either way. Sure, they lost some white women in the bargain, but the newspapers don't even knew about you gals anyhow, so no one is the wiser. As to the babies they killed . . ." Gertie pauses here and tears up again. *"Damn, I'm gettin' soft in my old age, ain't I,"* she whispers as if to herself.

"Brother Anthony told me what happened to your little girls," says Gertie after she collects herself. "I'm real sorry for you. I think you know I was with the Southern Cheyenne at Sand Creek in sixty-four when Chivington's troops attacked our village. Our head chief, Black Kettle, wanted peace, he was flying an American flag from his tipi that day to show his loyalty. But Chivington ordered the attack anyhow. An' before he did, he told his soldiers, *'Kill and scalp them all, big and little, nits make lice.'* See, that's how highly they think of the Injuns, that they ain't even human beings, they're insects . . . nits and lice . . ."

Gertie stops here and gazes long into the fire. "The soldiers killed my two babies by my Cheyenne husband that day," she whispers finally. "I never told that part to May, I never told her I had kids, didn't want to scare her, her being a new mother and all. I took three bullets in the attack and the

85

soldiers musta thought I was dead. But I wasn't and when I come to, I was lyin' under a pile a' bodies. Maybe on account a' the fact I was at the bottom, they hadn't bothered to take my scalp. But I was hurt real bad and I didn't even have the strength to crawl out from under. The soldiers were still sacking the village, rapin' our girls, killin' the wounded. Then I saw my little boy, Hóma'ke I called him . . . Little Beaver . . . five years old he was . . . he was cryin' and wanderin' around a ways off. He was lookin' for me, see? He was scared and lookin' for his mama . . . Two soldiers standin' not too far from me, spotted him, and they pulled their pistols. They were laughin', an' bettin' each other and they started takin' turns shootin' at him . . . I could see their bullets hittin' the ground all around him, I tried to holler, I tried to scream, but no sound came out, and my little boy just kept walkin', cryin' . . . lookin' for his mama . . . and then I saw my little girl, Little Skunk we called her, Xaóhkéso . . . she was runnin' toward him . . . she was seven an' she always took care of her little brother . . . I tried to scream, I tried to holler, but no sound came outta my mouth an' I couldn't crawl out from under the bodies. Just before Little Skunk got to him, one a' the bullets

86

struck her in the back and she went down . . . and the soldier who shot her hollered to the other, *'You owe me a nickel, you sumbitch'* . . . and that's the last thing I remember . . . *'You owe me a nickel, you sumbitch.'*

"I don't know how long I was out, but when I woke up the soldiers were gone, and the village was quiet. It took me some time but I finally managed to drag myself out from under the bodies and I crawled on my belly through the burnt ruins of the village until I found my babies . . . both of 'em dead . . . scalped . . . yeah . . . nits make lice . . . an' you know what else? That Colonel Chivington was a preacher . . . that's right, the Denver newspapers called him the Fightin' Parson, a man of God. I tell you all this now, girls, so you understand that I know firsthand a little something about what you been through . . . it breaks my friggin' heart . . . I am so sorry for you . . ."

And then we all had a good long cry. The three of us, me and Susie and Gertie, held on to each other and we bawled like babies. It was the first time me and Susie had been able to cry for our daughters, and for our friends lost.

Brother Anthony had told Gertie about the new group of white women here. Aye, that's another reason she came to us, she says, figuring we could maybe use a little help with the situation. She was sure right about that, because when me and Susie tried to set up a powwow with Crazy Horse and the other chiefs we were told that they do not council with women. We shoulda known that because it's the same with the Cheyenne, too. Even though women have considerable power in the tribe . . . in fact, they can be said to run the show from the background, they are still not allowed to participate in council. For that matter it's the same with the U.S. government, ain't it? We aren't even allowed to vote. And why do you suppose it is that these very different societies have this in common? I'll tell you why, it's because the old men who make the decisions for everyone else don't have the same amount of man juice runnin' through their veins anymore, only the fadin' memory of it, so they use the young men to stand in for their own shriveled bollocks and limp weenies. But mothers don't want to send their babies off to war, and the old men know that if they allow women a voice in council, they will only get in the way of all their war plans. It's as simple as that.

But for some reason me and Susie couldn't figure out until she explained it to us later, the Lakota chiefs were willing to council with Gertie. We were allowed to attend, and bring Molly along, but were not allowed to speak. Gertie knows the Lakota language, too, so we didn't even need a translator. We love our Gertie and don't hold it against her in anyway, but she can be rough as a bear's arse, and often smells like one, and it's true that despite her soft side, she's got a manly way about her — walks like a man, cusses like a man, dresses like a man . . . about the only thing she doesn't do is piss like a man, which is how she got found out by May, when we all still thought she was Jimmy the muleskinner.

Now when it's Gertie's turn to speak, one of the chiefs, who she tells us is named Rides Buffalo, passes her the pipe. She takes a long pull on it, which makes me and Susie a wee bit envious, because we enjoy a smoke now and again ourselves. Then Gertie starts talkin' and she goes on at some length, but of course, we understand nothing of what she says. We can see that the chiefs listen to her very respectful as she speaks. She finishes with what seems like a fancy flourish of language, and passes the pipe with some pomp and fanfare to the chief on the other side of her. Like the Cheyenne, these men do love to talk, and each goes on at some length when it's their turn, all except for Crazy Horse, that is, who says only a few words, but seems to listen thoughtfully to everyone else.

It's useful havin' Molly there with us. She's real alert and pays attention and it's clear that she makes a good impression on the chiefs. She's a fine thing, a grand lassie with a real presence about her. She appears not to be at all intimidated by these men, who can be a wee bit scary, truth be told, and they in turn seem to admire both her appearance and the bold, direct manner she has.

After the powwow finally concludes, we want Gertie to give us a full account of how things went with the chiefs before we inform the other girls. So the four of us go down and sit on the banks of the creek, which is still mostly covered with ice, except for the water holes kept open.

"No decision has been reached yet by the chiefs," Gertie begins. "It's always like that with these folks, they like to mull things over for a good long while. I gave 'em a lot to think about, told 'em something I haven't even told you gals yet. About ten days after

Little Wolf surrendered his band at the Red Cloud Agency, they left again. The chief could not tolerate life there, with no game to hunt and nothing to do all day long, eatin' outta tin cans what little food rations was given to 'em by the government. So they made a run for it. You Kelly girls know as well as I that no one can sneak off as quiet as a band of Indians when they set their mind to it, you and me have seen 'em do it, ain't we? They don't move like white people, who make a lotta noise even when they're trying not to, they move like the wind, like a light breeze in the air, with only the faintest rustling no more noticeable or unnatural than that made by the movement of spirits. By the time the Army figured out what had happened, they were well on their way."

"Where did they go, Gertie?" I ask.

She shrugs. "Who knows? I expect Little Wolf took 'em north, lookin' for open country and some buffalo herds, maybe trying to hook up with another band or two of Cheyenne who ain't surrendered yet."

"And why did Crazy Horse and the chiefs need to know that?" Susie asks.

Now this is what surprised me and Susie, and when Gertie said it we realized that she really has gone over to the other side: "I told Crazy Horse the Army was plannin' another major military campaign against the Lakota and all the other scattered bands that hadn't observed General Crook's order to surrender. I told 'em more soldiers were headed out here from the East, more horses, more guns and supplies. I said that the Cheyenne and the Lakota had long been strong allies, and that Little Wolf and Crazy Horse were the two greatest warriors and leaders of their people. I said the only hope they had against the Army was to put aside whatever differences were between 'em, join forces and fight together. Then I asked that the Lakota give up a dozen of the horses they stole off the train, and let the white women go. And I finished up by sayin' 'Now I have spoken true what is in my heart. I have told you what I know about the movements of the Army, and I have told you what I believe is good for your people and good for these women. I thank you for hearing me.' See, the chiefs like it when you speak to 'em real respectful and formal like that. I give 'em valuable inside information and I ask for the horses in return without really having to say it's tit for tat, 'cause everyone already understands how these things work."

Now me and Susie thought it was one thing for Gertie to be offered the pipe, and make a case for releasing the women in her custody, and something else altogether for her to be givin' war counsel to the Lakota chiefs. What we learned in our time among the Cheyenne was that the best way for us to address the men with any kind of advice was real indirect, what May called "by allusion," which was too fancy a word for me and Susie, but means kind of a way of hinting that allows 'em to think maybe they came up with the idea themselves. We found it was never a good idea to come right out and tell them what they should do because men almost always take offense to that.

"But how is it, Gertie," I ask, "that as a woman you can speak so frank that way to the chiefs? Even though we couldn't understand 'em, we could see that they were listening real close to everything you said."

"Aw hell," she answers, "don't you gals know? . . . both the Cheyenne and the Lakota consider me to be a *he'emnane'e* — half-man, half-woman. See, everyone knows I was married to a Cheyenne fella and had babies by him. And they also know I ran a mule train for years as a boy named Jimmy. They believe the *he'emnane'e* have big medicine, that we got all the qualities, wisdom, and power of both sexes . . . which . . . what the hell, might even be true.

That's why they pass me the pipe, which gives me the right to speak my mind in council. And because I can speak as a man, I got some real influence. Course, even though I don't have all the necessary body parts to qualify me as a real *he'emnane'e,* I never tried to set 'em straight on that notion, because it's real useful to be treated as both man and woman if you get what I mean. On the one hand, they gotta behave toward me with a certain kinda manners they reserve for women, on the other I have the full voice of a man. Comes in mighty handy sometimes."

"Aye, such as right now, Gertie/Jimmy the muleskinner," says I. And we laugh.

■ ■ ■ ■

Ledger Book II
Captured

■ ■ ■ ■

The first Lakota to board the train approached me, took me by the arm, and pulled me from my seat. He drew a knife from the scabbard at his waist, raised it, placing the flat of the blade beneath my chin. He looked at me with no apparent malice . . . even, is it possible? a certain tenderness . . .

(from the journals of Molly McGill)

18 March 1876

What an extraordinary luxury to have this paper and pencils with which to write. When all has been taken from you, when you have nothing left but the clothes on your back, it is remarkable how much such a gift means. It is like giving a drink of water to a woman dying of thirst. As it was in prison, one of the worst things about this incarceration is the boredom of it. We have virtually the entire day to do nothing. And so I have distributed paper and pencil to anyone among us who has asked. Some draw, some write letters that they hope Gertie might be able to post for them, some simply doodle (which I find a waste of valuable paper). We all thank the Kelly sisters for this gift. About them I will write more later . . .

I was keeping my own diary on the train trip west. Of course, all that came to an abrupt halt upon our abduction, and my diary is forever lost. And so I will tell first of this terrible event . . .

It had been thus far a mostly uneventful trip across the plains. We had more or less exchanged our personal histories, or, at least, as much as we each wished to reveal of them. With few exceptions, most of the women felt they were escaping a fate worse than that to which they were headed, and some needed to tell their stories by way of reassurance. This seemed particularly true now that we were drawing closer to our destination, and the reality of the bargain they had struck began to reveal itself in this vast plains landscape wilder and more desolate than any of us had ever before seen or imagined.

It was early morning and I was looking out the window of the train, seated next to a woman named Carolyn Metcalf, a pleasant, quiet, demure lady, who had thus far on the trip kept very much to herself. By appearance and demeanor, she seemed rather an unlikely candidate for the brides program. By way of making conversation, I asked her idly where she came from.

"I am from Garden City, Kansas," she answered. "My husband . . . no, I should say my *former* husband, is the pastor in our Baptist church."

"I'm sorry, I did not mean to pry," I said. "That's quite alright," she said. "You are not prying. And in case you're wondering what I am doing here, I signed up for the program in order to gain release from the state insane asylum. However, I can assure you that I am of no danger to you."

I laughed. "Yes, well, I signed up to get out of prison. But I'm no danger to you, either."

"You see, I had begun to question certain tenets of our religion," she continued, as if having finally told someone of her incarceration, and not having been censured for it, she was now free to fully unburden herself. "This, I naively believed, was a right of all American citizens, even women. Early one morning before I had even risen from my bed, the church bishop, escorted by two members of the Bible class at which I had voiced some of my reservations, and in the company of our local sheriff, appeared at our house. I barely had time to cover myself in a dressing gown. Their visit, of course, had been arranged by my husband. Now in the presence of these gentlemen, the good pastor explained to me that there is a law in the State of Kansas that a husband has the right to commit his wife to the insane asylum without any proof, that he had filed the necessary forms, and all was quite legal. It appears that the diagnosis of insanity was based simply on the fact that I had questioned our faith.

"In this manner was I kidnapped from my house, forbidden even to say good-bye to my three children. I was sent to the asylum, where I have spent the past two years. When the doctors there asked my husband's consent for me to participate in the brides program, he quite readily gave it. You see, the good pastor had taken up with the organist in our church, presumably a more devout soul than I, and he wished to marry her. Thus he arranged our divorce, as he had arranged all else, and was delighted to send me out west to marry an Indian, rid of me once and for all . . . The organist now raises my children . . . and here I am. On a train into the wilderness . . ."

At this moment in Carolyn's story, we came to a long curve in the tracks with low hills on either side, last year's yellow grass poking out in places where the wind had blown clear the snow. Just as the engineer sounded the horn and slowed the train, I spotted a plume of smoke rising ahead of us.

As a precaution, several of our escort of a dozen soldiers were dispatched to climb atop the train as lookouts. We heard their footsteps overhead as they passed from car to car. Now the engineer blew the horn again, at the same time sharply engaging the brakes, the wheels making a heavy metallic squeal. We were thrust forward in our seats and then abruptly backward as we came to a halt in front of a large bonfire burning on the tracks.

In that very instant the shooting began, in concert with the terrifying unearthly cries of our attackers, like the ululations of a pack of coyotes under a full moon. A soldier fell heavily on the top of our car, rolled off, and tumbled past my window to the ground below. Some of the women began to scream.

"Get down!" a soldier hollered at us. Carolyn and I dropped from our seats, crouching as low as we were able on the floor. Several women, already hysterical, were crawling down the aisle as if they might somehow escape. The soldiers began returning fire from the windows, others climbing over those women in the aisle to take up positions between the cars. But the bullets seemed to come from both sides of the train, and at all angles, shattering the windows and spraying us with shards of glass. In a matter of moments, six of our own women were shot, four of them immediately dead, the other two mortally wounded, the soldiers, too, falling one after the next, the cries of the dying and wounded, the screams of the terrified . . . blood spraying . . .

And then suddenly it was over as quickly as it had begun. The soldiers fired no more, and the attackers, too, quit their assault, an eerie silence falling over the train, broken only by the moans of the wounded and the weeping and whimpering of those still alive, lying or crouched on the floor. I looked up from my prone position to see the first Indians entering our car, three of them, all brandishing rifles. "Stay down," I whispered to Carolyn. I am not sure exactly why, but I stood, brushed the front of my dress and took my seat again — not because I am an especially courageous woman, rather simply one for whom there is little in life left to fear, least of all my own death. However, I did not wish to die cowering on the floor of a train.

The first Lakota to board the train approached me, took me by the arm, and pulled me from my seat. He drew a knife from the scabbard at his waist, raised it, placing the flat of the blade beneath my chin. He looked at me with no apparent malice . . . even, is it possible? a certain tenderness . . . Nor when he spoke to me in his incomprehensible tongue was there anger in his tone, rather I thought I sensed a kind of reluctance. Although I knew he was about to slit my throat, I felt no fear, only a strange detachment, the heightened sense of observation one sometimes experiences in dreams, as if I were standing outside myself, watching, noting every detail with perfect objectivity. He smelled of gunpowder and sagebrush, winter prairie grass, horse sweat, and a deeper odor, a kind of animal man scent. He was fairer than the other two Lakota who followed him down the aisle, stepping as they did so over the dead and dying. His light brown hair was braided, his eyes hazel, his skin the chestnut color of burnished saddle leather, taut and unlined across a proud nose and broad cheekbones, the latter adorned with slashes of red paint. I felt some sadness in his gaze, even a kind of affinity, as if we had come instantly to some unspoken understanding. "Go ahead, kill me," I said softly in encouragement, my voice, too, coming from a great dreamlike distance. "I am not afraid. I have nothing left to live for. Go ahead, I welcome the solace of death. Go ahead, please, release me." But he did not slit my throat, he lowered his knife, and spoke sharply over his shoulder to the others. Only later, in the manner in which we assess a fading dream upon waking, did it occur to me that, of course, the man certainly couldn't have understood me. Now he took me by the arm and led me down the aisle, and through the door at the back of the car, and there between the cars he lifted me from the platform and swung me to the ground with a gentle grace that suggested I had not yet awakened. Pointing with his rifle, and speaking to me again in Lakota, he indicated that I was to sit down. One by one the other surviving women, including my seatmate, Carolyn Metcalf, were similarly escorted from the train. We sat on the frozen ground waiting to see what was to become of us next. Some wept and blubbered, others seemed in a state of shock.

The rolling hills on either side of the tracks were sculpted by the wind, the virgin snow without imprint of man or animal, until several dozen more mounted Indians suddenly materialized, riding soundlessly toward us from all directions, the snow kicked up by their horses' hooves swirling like clouds of vapor, covering their tracks behind them so that they seemed a kind of mirage. Now as they converged upon us they began uttering their strange yipping ululations of victory.

In this way did they ride in, a different race of man than any we had ever before seen, dressed in moccasins and buckskin leggings and wrapped in trade blankets or buffalo hides against the chill winter air; they wore braids and ornately painted faces, and rode with such natural harmony that they and horse seemed one being together, a kind of centaur. All carried rifles and it became clear from their sheer number why our dozen poor soldiers — raw young recruits, some of them recent immigrants, who like most of us had never before been west of the Mississippi — were so quickly overwhelmed.

We had each only been allowed by the authorities to bring with us one small carpetbag of possessions, and these the Indians now threw from the train, some of them bursting open upon impact. Those Lakota who had dismounted began emptying out their contents. If a bag contained shiny objects such as coins or jewelry, these they might pick up, as well as certain articles of clothing, winter coats or woolen sweaters. Otherwise they seemed to have only a cursory interest in our meager belongings. When one of them opened my bag and turned it upside down to empty, my diary fell to the ground with everything else. Instinctively, I made a lunge for it . . . it seemed important to me in that moment to recover this one object, this one small connection to my past life, the last record that remained of my little girl. But one of them kicked it out of my grasp. They clearly wished to leave us with nothing. And so they have.

There were only two passenger cars on the train, one for us and one for the soldiers, followed by three cattle cars full of horses that had been shipped from the stockyards in Omaha to resupply the cavalry at Fort Laramie. The Indians on the train now opened the doors of the stock cars, slid the loading ramps to the ground, and began leading the horses off single file. Coming from the close, warm quarters of the train into the cold afternoon air, the horses nickered, snorted, and threw their heads, steam rising off their bodies and streaming like smoke from their nostrils.

How cold we were sitting in the snow on the frozen ground, and we huddled together seeking warmth and physical contact. We did not speak. I think we all had the same sense of having entered some primal new world in which we owned no language.

Now those Lakota who were still afoot

made us stand and began leading us each to one of the mounted warriors, who offered us an arm and with the help of the man on the ground swung us onto the back of the horse behind the rider. This we submitted to as docilely as children, reminding me of the submissive frame of mind one assumes in prison, the utter helplessness of captivity, the futility of resistance. The man who held his arm out to me, and behind whom I was seated, was he who had led me off the train.

When we all were thus seated, the riders wheeled their horses with the precision of a flock of rising birds, and broke into a gallop across the rolling plains, the warriors issuing again their ungodly warbling cries, half-man, half-beast. We put our arms around the waists of our abductors and hung on for dear life . . . a strange intimacy of necessity . . . I did not turn my head to look back at our train, the carnage around it, the tracks running ahead into the distance without us, our last link to the world we once knew.

We traveled thus all night, beneath more stars than I had ever seen before, and a thin sliver of new moon, alternately walking, trotting, galloping. Another group of Lakota drove the herd of horses, but these we soon left behind. I drifted off to sleep several times to the rolling cadence of the horse's gait, waking abruptly with my head resting against the man's back, my arms still around him, feeling the warmth of his body and smelling again his scent of wildness, taking even I must confess some simple human comfort in it. The odd thought occurred to me that it had been a long time since I had held on to a man, and I wondered if it was equally strange for him to have a woman he did not know clutching him thus.

We arrived finally in the Lakota village just as the sun was cresting the horizon, flooding the rolling plains with the hard white light of winter. The people began coming out of their tipis to watch our passage, the women taking up a high-pitched trilling to welcome their warriors home. Small brown children ran out to lightly touch our feet and legs, squealing and giggling with delight, then running back to their tipis, sometimes turning and running back to touch us a second time. Their simple pleasure in this game made our entrance into this strange new world seem less threatening, for it is hard to be afraid of children. In direct contrast, their mothers watched us as we passed with varying expressions of suspicion, distrust, dislike, even hatred, one arm crossed holding their blankets over their opposite shoulder, as if closing themselves off from us. We would later talk about this among ourselves, all agreeing that we hoped it was not the women of the tribe who would decide our fate.

We are now being held in a single large tipi, where we have at least been given blankets and buffalo hides to warm us at night. We have a fire pit in the center and a stack of sticks and dried buffalo droppings to burn outside the opening, replenished when necessary by the young Lakota boy who guards us. Some of the others have spoken of trying to escape, to which I ask the simple questions: "Escape to what? Where would we go? In what direction? We do not even know where we are."

Some days ago a young white man came to see us. He introduced himself as Brother Anthony, a Benedictine monk. We were so happy to see him, and thought for a brief moment that perhaps he had come to rescue us. However, he quickly disabused us of this hope, telling us that he had no such authority. Still, he was a kind, gentle man; he asked us to pray with him and offered us some small solace.

The next day he sent the two Irish twin

sisters, Meggie and Susie Kelly, to see us. Wild, strange creatures who call themselves "white Cheyenne," which seems an accurate description, for they appear to exist in some state of limbo between savage and civilized, neither quite Indian nor altogether white . . . and at the same time . . . I hardly know how to put this . . . somehow part human, part mythological beings, like twin elves from another land. They are small, pitifully thin girls, dressed in tattered animal hides over which they wear ragged trade blankets, their pale severe faces framed by a mass of tangled red hair, their demeanor that of certain hardened souls such as I knew in prison, girls full of equal measures of rage and a deep underlying heartbreak. The sisters put up a brave façade, a kind of bravado, and although they would not reveal the details of what has befallen them, it is clear that they have suffered greatly. They, too, have been very kind to us, giving us hope and sound advice, and even a rare laugh or two, their visit making our group feel less helpless and alone.

As it was for me in prison, we are learning to appreciate whatever small "luxuries" we are offered — our hides and blankets for example, fire, a daily trip to the creek, where we break the ice, splash ice-cold water on ourselves, and fill a vessel fashioned from the stomach of a buffalo in which we carry water back to the tipi. The boy who guards us, Yellow Bird, he is called, or so the twins tell us, brings our food every day, sometimes cooked, sometimes raw. This includes dead rabbits and beavers, and various parts of deer, elk, and buffalo, as well as wild root vegetables, dried wild fruits, and strips of dried meat. We boil the roots and fruits in a tin trade pan given us, to soften them and make a kind of stew. As I grew up on a farm in upstate New York, I learned the ways of self-sufficiency — animal husbandry, gardening, putting up fruit and vegetables for the long winters. Like virtually all farm people there, my father was also a hunter, and as a result I know a bit about such matters and am able to butcher as well as cook the dead animals, which is a great relief to some of our more squeamish girls, who would probably starve to death were they required to perform such tasks themselves. At the same time, I must confess that I am unable to identify certain items that come our way. I believe that one day we were presented with the carcass of a small dog, but I made up a story for the others, telling them it was a plains animal that lived in underground burrows and was entirely

111

unrelated to canines. As there is never much food, and we are always hungry, we eat what we are given on blind faith, and whether it tastes good or not. One day recently the Kellys even managed to bring us a small leather pouch full of coffee beans, which evidently the Indians obtain at the trading posts in trade for buffalo hides. We ground the beans with a rock on a flat stone and boiled the coffee in our pan over the fire. It seemed quite the greatest luxury we had ever known. As I learned in prison, it is astonishing how quickly human beings can learn to adapt to severe changes in circumstances, and to deprivation.

We are being kept isolated from the tribe. We even perform our bodily functions in a different place than the Lakota women, although occasionally we catch a glimpse of some of them walking to another part of the river some distance away from ours, where presumably they bathe and gather their own water. We are trying to make some sense of all this, to find any small reasons to think that we might one day be free. Thus far about all we have to hang on to is that we are still alive, and have not yet been violated by our abductors, both of which things we must take as hopeful signs.

Despite the Kelly sisters' admonition that "no one is coming to save you," as they warned us on their first visit, it appears that there may be a savior in our midst, after all. This would be in the person of an extraordinary woman known as "Dirty Gertie" . . . or, alternately, "Jimmy the muleskinner," who rode in several days ago on a big gray mule, stunning the Lakota with her brazen, unannounced entrance, having evidently slipped past the sentries who are constantly posted around the perimeter of the village to protect against intruders. I liked her right away, a rough, tough-looking character who speaks her mind and who, to hear the Kellys tell it, has achieved some legendary status across the plains, with both Indians and whites alike. Indeed, she had not been seen for several months and was reported to have been killed by a band of Indian scouts who work as guides for the Army. Many of the Lakota seemed to believe that the reason she was able to evade detection by the sentries was because she was a spirit being, a ghost. Gertie and the sisters tell us that the Indians make no real distinction between the natural and the supernatural worlds, and believe that both humans and the other animals are capable of moving freely between them . . . an interesting concept to be sure . . .

With Gertie's invaluable help we were able to arrange a "powwow" with several Lakota chiefs and prominent warriors. I was allowed to attend with Gertie and the Kellys, for I have been selected by default as the nominal leader of our group, some of whom seem to have mistaken my relative sangfroid for strength of character, when in fact it is simply indifference to my personal fate. Among the native attendees was the one called Crazy Horse, who barely spoke, but appeared to listen thoughtfully to all the proceedings. He does not at all seem to fit the image of fearsome warrior and great leader of his people which the twins tell us is his reputation on the plains.

I came away from the powwow with the first genuine hope I have felt since the attack that we might actually be set free. Gertie speaks fluent Cheyenne and Lakota, and she addressed the Lakota leaders eloquently and formally, asking that they give us horses and safe passage from the village, after which, of course, we are entirely on our own. They seemed to listen respectfully to her words and are now considering her request.

After the powwow, Gertie came back to

our tipi to meet the other girls and give them a report. Of course, all were greatly heartened by the news that we might possibly be freed.

"Let's say the Lakota agree to cut loose a' some horses and let you gals go," Gertie said. "How many of you know how to ride?"

Only three of us, myself included, raised our hands. The second was a strong, Sapphic Englishwoman by the name of Lady Ann Hall, who, indeed, I was rather surprised had not been elected leader of our troupe. Lady Hall commands sufficient natural authority that everyone calls her thusly by her title and family name, rather than her given name, as the rest of us do each other. I admire the woman, for she came all this way to locate her lover who joined the brides program with Meggie and Susie's group last year.

The third to volunteer her equestrian experience was our Mexican girl, Maria Galvez, the former mistress of an infamous gentleman bandit from Mexico City. I use the term "mistress" with reservation, for evidently when she was a young girl the bandit purchased her . . . or stole her from her impoverished family in a village in the Sierra Madre mountains of Sonora. She is a small but sturdily built girl, who clearly has

Indian blood herself for she is dark-skinned and shares certain common facial features with the Lakota . . . a kind of Asian or Mongolian appearance.

Now our Norwegian girl from Minnesota, Astrid Norstegard, raised her hand uncertainly. "My people were fishermen," she said, "and had little use for horses, for we lived in a world of water. However, like all of us, I rode holding on behind my captor when we were first brought here. Does that count?"

"No, missy, that don't count," Gertie answered. "That's like saying you know how to drive the train, because you once rode in one. The reason I ask is that these folks have a real eye for horseflesh, and they're the finest damn riders you ever seen. One thing for sure is that they ain't gonna give you the pick of the string. They'll keep the best mounts for themselves, and let you have what's left over. You're liable to end up with some real wild-ass mustangs."

"Then we'll just have to take whatever they give us," I said, "and consider ourselves lucky."

"Well now, that is another matter I'd like to talk to you gals about," said Gertie. "As you know by now, the brides program has come to an end. It is way too late for you to help civilize the Cheyenne." She looked now at the Kellys. "Didn't work out so good for the first group that came here, did it now, girls?" The sisters did not answer, but in their gaze was all the pain they had experienced and not yet described to us.

"And since then, things has only got worse," Gertie continued. "The Indian bands still at large, mostly Lakota, Cheyenne, and Arapaho, are scattered and on the run. Meggie and Susie here are gonna try to find their Cheyenne people and fight on with 'em, and for that I respect 'em, I truly do. But the thing is, you new gals are greenhorns, and believe me, you do not want to get caught in the middle of the shit storm that is headed this way. General Crook is resupplying and come spring the troops will be on the move again. He has orders from General Sheridan to clear the region of hostiles from the Black Hills south to the Platte River and north and west to the Yellowstone. That means attack and destroy every Cheyenne, Lakota, and Arapaho village they come across, because every band still out there are now considered hostiles. The Army will show no mercy. If they haven't already, Meggie and Susie can tell you all about that, can't you, girls?"

The Kellys cast their eyes to the ground

and nodded in unison.

"OK, so if the Lakota do let you go and do give you the horses," Gertie continues, "the sisters are gonna ride out north and west with some of the other Cheyenne to try to hook up with Little Wolf's band again. And you all are gonna ride south with me back to Fort Fetterman. You ain't even supposed to be here in the first place, so the Army'll take you down to Medicine Bow station, put you on a train, and send you right back where you come from."

I noticed Meggie and Susie sharing a look at this point. Clearly, this is just what they had been hoping for — that Gertie was going to take us off their hands. "That's the God's truth, lassies," says Susie. "Like Gertie says, you got here too late and there ain't a damn thing you can do for the Cheyenne. They don't need any more wives or babies just now, they need warriors, horses, guns, and ammunition. And you all need to go back home."

"Home?" I said. "My home is a life sentence in a windowless prison cell in solitary at Sing Sing, where I am not allowed to speak . . . even to myself. I won't go back there. I prefer to take my chances on the unknown."

"And my home is a bed in the Kansas

118

state insane asylum," said my friend Carolyn Metcalf, "to which I am frequently tied and abused by sadistic attendants and doctors. I would rather die out here than return to that."

"My home is a bedroom in a bordello," said our French gamine, Lulu LaRue, "where fat old men sweat on top of me, and the proprietor beats me for not being sufficiently *enthousiaste* with the clients."

"I lived in Mexico City with a bandito named Chucho el Roto," said Maria Galvez. "And when he believed that I betrayed him, he put an order out to have me killed. Until I crossed the border, I lived in a different room under a different name in a different hostel or posada every night. And often I slept on the street or on the ground. That's what I have to go home to. That and a death sentence."

"Well, my goodness," said Lady Ann Hall. "I, on the other hand, as you all know by now, have a magnificent estate in Sunderland . . . a quite satisfactory home in which to live, I must confess. However, it does feel rather lonely there without my dearest companion, Helen Elizabeth Flight. If the others are considering staying here, I would join them in the adventure. Having come all this way, I believe I owe that to my Helen."

"My home is with m'lady, wherever she requires my services," said the Liverpudlian girl, Hannah Alford, in her tiny voice.

"Listen now," said Susie Kelly, "if you lassies are thinkin' you might be comin' with me and Meggie, then think again. Aye, we offered to look after you, but that was before Gertie showed up. Now you got a way out of this country. We are sorry for you, truly we are. Believe me, we understand about not having a home to go back to, we been there, too. But we got our own troubles and we ain't responsible for yours."

"Aye, and neither are we babysitters," added Meggie. "So let us be clear: you ain't invited to come along with us. Period. We are goin' to be traveling with other Cheyenne here who also want to rejoin their people, and who know where to look for Little Wolf. The last thing in the world they're gonna tolerate is being burdened by a bunch of greenhorn white women, half a' whom don't even know how to ride a damn horse."

"Then those of us who choose to stay," I said, "will do so on our own. We'll follow you and not get in your way. We'll take care of ourselves."

"Aw, c'mon now, Molly," said Susie, "You know you'd last about a half day before you

120

come cryin' to us. And if you fell behind, which you're sure to do, we'd have to leave you. There are all kinds of hostile bands wandering the countryside, not to mention some real unsavory white men you do not want to run into, either."

"Aye, that is the God's truth," said Meggie. "And how do you plan to feed yourselves while you're traveling? Besides horses, if they be that generous, the Lakota will not give you much when you leave here. Who'll do your hunting for you?"

"I will," I said.

"As will I," said Lady Hall.

"You gals are dreamin' if you think the Lakota are also going to give you valuable guns and ammunition," said Susie. "I suppose you're both handy with a bow and arrow? Aye, it's true, maybe they'll part with one or two a' them."

"Ladies, please," Gertie interjected, "let's talk about this when and if the time comes. We don't even know yet if they're gonna turn you loose, let alone give you horses."

"They're going to let us go *and* give us horses, Gertie," I said. "I know it. I watched them as you spoke. Of course, I didn't understand what you said, but I could see you had them eating out of your hand."

Despite my intransigence on the subject, I

fully understood that the Kelly sisters wish to send us off with Gertie. They clearly have their own troubles, having already witnessed enough horrors, and still facing sufficient trials without having to look after us . . . *greenhorns,* as they put it. At the same time, despite their insistence, I sensed some reluctance in their resolve to send us back with Gertie. Whatever they have been through in the past year, I suspect that in us they see some mirror of themselves and their friends when they first came out here. We are the innocents they once were, escaping dark pasts into uncertain futures, and in denying us that chance, they would be turning their backs on their own experience, denying themselves and their friends.

And so I decided to try another tack. "Tell me," I said to the twins, "which among the Cheyenne going with you will make the final decision about whether or not we are allowed to come?"

"Why do you want to know?" Susie asked.

"Because I want to talk to him."

"Going over our heads, are you now, Molly?"

"If I need to. Didn't you tell me that I was the leader of our group? Didn't you say I was responsible for keeping us alive?"

"That don't mean you're *our* leader,

Molly," said Meggie. "That don't give you the right to make decisions over us."

"I don't want to be your leader, or make decisions over you. I want to talk to *your* leader and let him decide *our* fate."

The sisters exchanged a glance. "His name is Aénohe," said Meggie, grudgingly. "That means Hawk in English. He was at the powwow. He'll be leading us back to find Little Wolf."

"Which one is he?"

"The fair one. He's mixed blood."

"That's perfect."

"What's so perfect about it?"

"Because I know him."

"Whoa, easy now, lassie," said Susie. "What do you mean you *know* him?"

"I mean, he's the one who took me off the train. I can't explain it . . . he was going to kill me but at the last instant we came to some kind of understanding . . . I felt him change his mind. And I rode holding on to him for six hours. I know that much about him."

Meggie and Susie shared another twin look that suggested some surprised acknowledgment of what I said. "It's true that the only reason the rest of you weren't killed and scalped," said Meggie, "was because Hawk was the leader of the raiding party and he stopped the other warriors from doin' the dirty deed. We heard this from another Cheyenne fella who was there with him. They weren't supposed to bring any survivors back, just the horses, and any rifles and ammunition they could collect. They don't need any more mouths to feed here. But Hawk wouldn't let 'em kill you, don't ask us why . . . but you're right, Molly, you can all thank him for still being alive."

"Can you tell me anything about him?" I asked.

Now between them, and with some additions from Gertie, they told us about the man called Hawk.

His mother was a white girl kidnapped by the Cheyenne when she was ten years old, taken during an attack on her family's wagon train, which was headed west to the gold fields of California in the early 1850s. This was not uncommon in the day, one of the great hazards of travel through Indian country. When she was fourteen, the girl married a young Cheyenne warrior named Lone Bull, whose father was Oglala Lakota, Crazy Horse's people. She had three children by Lone Bull, two daughters and a son, Hawk. Because she had blond hair, the girl became known among the Cheyenne as Heóvá'é'ke — Yellow Hair Woman.

When Hawk was eight, he was gathering wood along the river bottom with his mother, who was now around twenty-two years old. A company of U.S. Army soldiers came upon them. Recognizing her as a white woman, the soldiers managed to catch her before she could run away. They questioned her, and she admitted that she had been taken as a child, but said she did not remember the name of her white family, although, in fact, she did. However, after twelve years among the Indians, with a Cheyenne husband and children, Yellow Hair Woman had become fully integrated into the tribe, and she had no interest in returning to the white world.

As it happens, the girl's parents had survived the attack on the wagon train when she was abducted, and had never given up looking for their daughter, whose Christian name was Samantha. The attack and her abduction had convinced them to turn back from their original destination of California and settle in Grand Island, Nebraska, where her father became the minister in the Methodist church. For those twelve years her parents had continued to post flyers in the trading posts and at the forts around the region asking for information about their daughter. Among the soldiers who caught the girl were several who had seen these fly-ers. And so they took her and her son, Hawk, with them back to Camp Robinson, in northwestern Nebraska. Her parents were contacted and they traveled there. In a sense, in this way she was kidnapped back to her first family.

Of course, as delighted as her mother and father were to be reunited with their long-lost daughter, Samantha was not the same little girl who had left them. She had lost much of her English and refused to even acknowledge her white name. Her parents recognized that to bring her out of what they considered savagery and back into the civilized world would be no easy task. Toward this end, and because they also knew that it would be unacceptable for the Methodist minister and his wife to return to Grand Island with an unbaptized, illegiti-mate, half-breed grandson in tow, her parents decided to ship young Hawk away to a special school for Indian children in Minnesota, run by Jesuits who were tasked with civilizing and educating the young savages. This her parents arranged with the fort commander, who sent four soldiers one morning to the family's quarters to take the boy. Against this separation, both Hawk and his mother fought the soldiers like wild animals, scratching, biting, shrieking, but finally they were subdued and the boy dragged away.

Hawk spent four years at the Indian school, which was virtually a prison. There he learned English but little else besides a hatred of whites and the white world. He gained a reputation among the priests as an incorrigible troublemaker. At age twelve he escaped with two other Indian boys, one a Dakota, the other Ojibwe. They traveled for three days together and then went their separate ways to find their own people. Of the three, Hawk was the farthest away from his home country — over a thousand miles. But somehow he made his way, walking the entire distance. One day he appeared in Little Wolf's village, where he was reunited with his mother, who had run away from her parents before they even reached Grand Island. Because she had no idea where her son had been sent, Yellow Hair Woman returned to Little Wolf's people, and for those four years, she waited for Hawk, hoping that somehow he might find his way back to her. And so he had.

"Hawk will be the ranking warrior when we leave here," said Susie when they had finished their little biography. "He is the one you would want to talk to, Molly."

127

"Thank you for that," I said.

"That don't mean he's going to let you girls come with us," she said. "And me and Meggie still ain't in favor of it."

"Understood," I said. "But can you arrange a meeting between us? You say that Hawk learned English in the Indian school, so we should be able to communicate."

"We have never heard Hawk speak a single word of English," said Meggie. "We were told he tried to forget everything about his time there, including the language. Despite his mother having been one, he hates the whites. Even more now since the soldiers attacked our camp. That's why Susie and me are surprised he didn't kill you lassies."

Meggie and Susie looked at each other again in silent twin communication. They both nodded.

"Aye, that's it, then," said Susie, "we been trying to protect you girls from the full truth, but maybe this is the best time to tell you what happened to our own group of white women. It would not be fair to you if we didn't. And maybe this'll discourage you once and for all from wishin' to come with us.

"You see, a company of U.S. Army cavalry attacked our village at dawn on a bitter cold morning in February. Out of a baker's dozen of us white brides who had still stuck with the program, only me and Susie, and one other lass lived to tell about it . . . all the rest of our friends died . . . and the infants of those who had 'em were killed, too. Meggie and me lost our own twin babies to the cold the next night, trying to make our way here . . . we were married to twin Cheyenne boys, and both of us gave birth to twins . . . four babies froze to death, one after the next . . . That's all you need to know about us so don't ask any more questions . . . and that's why we're goin' to fight the Army. In the end we expect that we, too, will die. But see, we don't give a rat's ass, 'cause we already lost everything we had to live for and we got nothin' left to lose. Aye, that's what you have to look forward to if you stay with us. You'll be gettin' mixed up in somethin' way over your heads. You lassies are not that far down the road yet. Before you go any further, maybe returning to your 'homes,' wherever and whatever they be, ain't really such a bad choice for you, after all. And Molly, just so you know, Hawk's wife, son, and mother were also killed in the attack. Like us, he's got a heart full of vengeance."

Now we fully understood what we had suspected all along but had not yet heard voiced. Of course, we had seen glimpses of the Kelly sisters' barely concealed anguish, but I believe that because our own situation was so precarious, and we so fragile, we had not really wanted to hear the full story, had not wanted to know that the brides program had ended in the butchery and death of nearly all their friends, as well as their infants. Attacked by the very government that had been charged with protecting them, no wonder they wanted us to turn back. We all sat now in silence, as if in a kind of memorial . . . to Meggie and Susie's fallen comrades, and to our own, and most of all to their babies, to all the infants and children who have perished senselessly . . . my own daughter included. What kind of God, what kind of world, what kind of human beings allow such horrors to take place on earth?

28 March 1876

It has been decided. Today we learned that the Lakota leaders have agreed to give us the horses, and all that is still in question is with whom we are to ride — with Gertie back to Fort Fetterman, or with the Kelly girls and the Cheyenne to wherever they lead us . . . assuming that they even agree to accept us. Although the Kellys' words

130

were sobering to our girls, appearing not to offer a single good option, that same night around the fire circle in the tipi, we spoke again privately and at length among ourselves. We remembered Meggie and Susie's advice the very first time they came to see us, that we had only ourselves and each other upon whom to rely. And so it was decided that above all we must stick together. It was agreed that after seeing so many of our own group killed in the attack on the train, and then having been held hostage these past weeks, the notion that all had been for naught, and what we faced now was simply a return to the grim fates we left behind, seemed out of the question. Susie was wrong about one thing: we had already come too far down the road and there was no turning back for us.

To their credit, Meggie and Susie arranged for me to meet with the man called Hawk, and they said that if I was able to convince him to let us ride with them, they would not stand in our way. As I had suspected all along, I sensed their relief that the decision had been taken out of their hands.

Rather than going to Hawk's lodge as a humble, beseeching captive white woman, or have him come to our own tipi, where he would see us all as such, I wanted to meet him alone and on more equal footing. I proposed that the meeting take place outside the village, and that I would arrive there on horseback. As the representative of our group, I wanted him to know that we were not so helpless, after all, that I could at least ride. I asked the Kellys to let me choose my own mount among the horses given us, and I asked that Gertie accompany me to the meeting place. "However, I wish to speak privately to Hawk, Gertie," I explained, "and unless I need you, I want you to hang back when we get there."

"You're takin' a real chance, honey, that you'll even be able to communicate with Hawk," she said. "You heard what the girls said, they never heard him speak a single word of English in the year they've known him. And neither have I, and I've known him since he was a boy."

"I'm a teacher, Gertie," I said. "If Hawk spent four years between age eight and twelve at an English school run by Jesuits, believe me, he speaks English, whether he chooses to or not. Children that age absorb language like sponges, and he has not forgotten it. Of that I am certain. I spoke to him when we were captured, and I believe now in looking back that he understood me."

A meeting place was set in a copse of cottonwoods on the river at a short distance from the village. From among those horses offered us, I chose a chestnut mare to ride, a compact little filly with a white blaze on her forehead, who seemed to possess a certain calm maturity that attracted me. Many horsemen don't care for mares because they can be difficult and cause trouble among the geldings and stallions, but I've always gotten on well with them. I've named her Spring, because it is the season of renewal, of new beginnings.

Gertie on her big gray mule, and I on the smaller chestnut, rode away from the village together, some of the people coming out of their tipis to watch us. I don't pretend to be an accomplished equestrian, but when I was growing up on the farm when they were working in the fields, my parents set me on the backs of Percheron draft horses before I could even walk. Early babysitters, these were huge gentle giants, with hooves the size of frying pans, and later I used to ride one to school, as did many farm kids. I hadn't been on horseback since I left the farm those years ago, but right away it felt natural and after our long confinement gave me a wonderful sense of freedom. However, I experienced again a pang of homesickness and regret for ever having left there, a terrible mistake that changed my life irrevocably, can never be righted, and will haunt me to the grave.

Gertie must have seen it in my face now as we rode. "Honey, I know sumpin' real bad has happened to you," she said. "I don't know exactly what it is, but I see the rough form of it, and if ever you need to talk about that, ole Gertie here is a pretty damned good listener. I've had some rough times myself, lost a coupla chillun along the way, so I know damn well what that's like."

I turned and looked at her then in some surprise. "Are you just taking a stab in the dark, Gertie," I asked, "about what might have happened to me?"

"Sure, honey, you can say I'm taking a stab in the dark if you like," she said. "But I have hunches about people, Molly. I see things . . . not always real clear, but I see things."

I nodded. "OK, I will keep that in mind."

As we approached the meeting place, Gertie reined up and pointed. "That's Hawk there in the trees." He sat motionless on a paint horse beneath the cottonwoods, bare of leaves still, his back to us, looking off across the river.

"Good, I wanted him to arrive before we did," I said. "I'm going to ride in alone, Gertie. You don't need to wait for me. I know the way back."

"I like your style, honey," she said. "You remind me of myself some years ago. Good luck to you."

I pressed my heels lightly to the mare's flanks and was pleased to see that she responded by quickening her step into a trot, and when I nudged her again she broke into an easy lope. I had been given only a kind of native rawhide hackamore, little more than a glorified halter with reins really, but I was accustomed to that from the farm, and I had already ridden the mare briefly and knew that she had been trained to neck rein. In this way we rode into the meeting place, where I slowed her to a walk. Hawk had turned at my approach, so that as I came alongside him the horses were head to butt and the two of us faced each other.

The unseasonably warm weather continued, and in the river bottom the whorled flattened yellow grass of last fall was studded by a few optimistic shoots of pale green just breaking through, while tight buds were still waiting to swell on the cottonwood trees.

We sat our horses and looked in each other's eyes for a long moment.

"My name is Molly," I said finally. "Molly McGill. Thank you for agreeing to meet me."

He did not respond, or give any indication that he recognized me.

"I'm sorry I don't speak Cheyenne or Lakota," I said, "but I think you know what I'm saying. We met before, as you may remember, on the train. I rode with you. And I was at the powwow."

Again Hawk simply watched me, his expression giving nothing away.

"You can answer me in Cheyenne, if you like," I said. "Of course, I won't understand you, but I intend to learn your language. I've always had a facility for languages. I speak French, because my family lived close to the Canadian border and we had French neighbors. And I speak some Norwegian, as well, because we had neighbors on the other side of us from Norway . . . they raised dairy cows . . . ah, yes, I imagine you're finding all this quite fascinating, aren't you?" I don't know whether or not it was just my imagination, but in that moment I thought that something like a tiny smile might have flickered across Hawk's mouth . . . no, no, just as quickly, I realized that this was

136

simply wishful thinking on my part; his expression remained utterly neutral, revealing nothing.

"I think you know why I am here," I continued. "The twins must have told you. It is to ask you to take my friends and me with you when you leave here. We wish to join Little Wolf's band, and take up life there among your people. We were sent here by our government, volunteers in the Brides for Indians program, but we are no longer affiliated with that . . . no, forgive me, that is a poor choice of words on my part . . . that you would surely not understand. I mean to say, we no longer work for the government. You see, the brides program is defunct . . . that is to say, it has been terminated . . . ended . . . yes, the program has ended. Now we are strictly on our own, completely independent, you see . . . oh, dear, I am sorry, I'm babbling, aren't I? . . ."

"I know what 'affiliated' means," the man named Hawk said.

"*What? You do? You speak?* I knew you spoke English. You understood me on the train, didn't you? I knew it. I sensed it . . . but . . . but . . . how do you know what 'affiliated' means?"

Hawk held his hands out to me, the backs of them badly scarred. "I went to an Indian school run by Jesuit priests. I had a good teacher. I refused to speak the white man's tongue, I would only speak my people's language. Every day he beat my hands with a stick until they bled. And he said, 'Don't you understand, you little savage, that you are no longer *affiliated* with the Cheyenne tribe? You live in the white world now. You will never see your people again. You will become a Christian, and you will speak our language.' "

Despite the scarring, Hawk had finely formed hands, with strong, tapered brown fingers, which I now reached over and took in mine, a gesture of intimacy that seemed somehow natural between us, without artifice, as if we had known each other for a long time and shared some complicity. "I am sorry for you," I said. "I have known teachers like that myself, men and women who enter the profession expressly as a pretext to be cruel to children. I don't blame you for not wanting to speak English."

But then he did and we talked. Hawk had no objection to having our group join those returning to the Cheyenne. Indeed, he said that the Lakota had agreed to give us the horses for no other reason than that they wished to be rid of us now. How popular our little group is! The government abandons us, the Lakota want nothing more to do with us, Meggie and Susie Kelly want to send us "home" . . . wherever that be. However, Hawk seems to feel that Little Wolf, who lost so many of his band in the attack the sisters described to us, will accept us, having already had experience with white women among his people, including his own wife, May Dodd.

"But why did you bring us here?" I asked Hawk. "Wouldn't it have been easier just to kill us on the train?"

"I didn't kill you because you weren't afraid of me," he said. "You said it was a good day to die. It is the Cheyenne way to sometimes spare enemies who display bravery" — he paused and looked away as if embarrassed — "and also because you have hair the same color as did my mother."

"I am pleased to remind you of your mother, if that is what saved us," I said, "but I am not your enemy, nor am I brave. As the twins say of themselves, I simply have nothing left to lose. That is much less heroic than courage. It is only the longing for nothingness."

Hawk looked at me again and nodded. "Yes, I understand that," he said.

The warm weather continues, nearly all the
snow already off the plains, a faint blush of
green grass sprouting on south-facing hills.
The early spring and the news of our release
has offered a small surge of spirit, a bit of
hopefulness. Our horses have been corralled
near our tipi, and we have been conducting
riding lessons for those girls who are inexpe-
rienced. Indeed, as Gertie suggested, the
Lakota clearly did not give us the pick of
the string, and some of the mounts are skit-
tish and unpredictable. Lady Hall is by far
the most accomplished rider among us, and
has been working with the horses in addition to instructing the beginners. "Let me
observe, first of all, ladies," she said, "that
as our friend Miss Gertie warned, these are
hardly hunter/jumper thoroughbreds we
have here. Indeed, if one were to arrive for
the hunt seated upon one of these nags at
any of the estates at which my noble class
pursues that distinguished sport, one would
be roundly ridiculed and summarily forbidden from participating. However, in our
rather diminished circumstances, as Miss
Molly here has suggested, we are required
to ride the horses we have been given, not
the horses we wish we had been given. And
crow bait though the majority be, grateful

for them we are. When I have finished my training course, the lot of them should be biddable enough for all of you to manage, and I shall keep the wildest of the wild as my own. I have never shrunk from an equestrian challenge. Indeed, as a girl I refused to ride sidesaddle, I donned men's breeches, and rode unladylike, scandalizing the British nobility with my spread legs.

"Now, ladies, regarding your personal relationships with your mounts," Lady Hall continued, "let me just say that each will size you up in the same manner in which you do them. If they find you timid or wanting in authority, they will sense it immediately and take advantage of you. This is a very poor precedent to set. Thus from the beginning, a firm hand is essential. As incompetent as you may feel on the back of your horse, establish your mastery over the beast, even if you have to pretend it. They will respect you for that, and respond accordingly."

This was sound advice from Lady Hall. Nevertheless, the equestrian efforts of some of our girls were not without a certain comedic value, and fortunately, but for minor bumps and bruises, no one so far has suffered any serious injury. Oddly, our Norwegian girl, Astrid, who hails from a family of fishermen, took rather naturally to horseback. She said the rolling motion of the horse's gait was not unlike that of a boat bobbing on water, which comparison seems to possess a certain logic. Our irrepressibly optimistic gamine, Lulu, on the other hand, appeared to have no natural aptitude whatsoever for riding, although the horse chosen for her was one of the most gentle of the bunch. She somehow managed to slide off its back at a walk, and when helped back on, she slipped off the other side, which gave all of us a jolly chuckle at her expense. She's a sweet girl and allowed us our moment of merriment with her usual perfect good nature.

Despite her lady's expertise on the subject, our Liverpudlian girl, Hannah, was one of the most recalcitrant of equestrians, refusing even to mount her horse. "I shall walk alongside my lady's horse," she announced in an uncharacteristically firm voice, and no amount of commanding, cajoling, or threatening from Lady Hall seemed able to move her from her position.

"Very well, Hannah," said Lady Hall finally in exasperation. "But you will hold the rest of us up if you insist upon walking, and we will eventually be forced to leave you behind." She swept her arm across the vast open country that lay beyond the village. "Of course, you will be all alone out there, and as you become weaker and weaker, the wolves will begin following you, the entire pack yipping and howling at the prospect of their coming meal. Soon they will be further emboldened and begin nipping at your heels, while high in the air above you, the buzzards will now be circling, biding their time, waiting to pick clean your bones when the wolves have finished feasting on your entrails. No, it will not be a pleasant end for you, my dear Hannah, of that I can certainly assure you."

Poor Hannah's lower lip began to tremble as the tears flooded her eyes. Quite matter-of-factly, Lady Hall strode to the side of the horse she had chosen for the girl, and whose halter I held. "Enough of your nonsense," she said. "Come here right now, young lady." As Hannah timidly obeyed her, Lady Hall bent over, lowered her arms, and interlocked her fingers to make a little stirrup of her hands. "Put your dainty little foot right there," she said, "take hold of the horse's mane with your left hand, put your other hand on its withers, and I shall give you a leg up. Go ahead, girl, do not hesitate, I will not make this offer a second time. You are already holding us up, the wolves are gathering behind you . . . *quickly* now." Hannah did as she was told, and Lady Hall boosted her onto the horse's back, and with a small cry the girl grasped it around the neck, as if even at a dead standstill, she needed to hang on for her life. She wept openly now, whether out of relief or fear, it was hard to say.

"Splendid!" said Lady Hall. "Well done, Hannah! You see, this horse is going to be your best friend. And never forget, he is the only thing that stands between you and the wolves."

And now, something else that seems to bode well has occurred. This afternoon a contingent of five Lakota women, escorted by Gertie and the Kelly girls, came to our tipi. The women bore bundles of native attire, deerskin shifts, moccasins and leggings, additional buffalo robes and trade blankets. They did not look us directly in the eye, which we have noticed is the manner of the natives, but seemed to focus their gaze somewhere in the middle of our foreheads, or just off to the side, and one by one, they began to relieve of us our own clothing. Only Lady Hall did not submit to this, for she already wore practical attire — riding boots and jodhpurs, a flannel blouse with a moleskin vest and a waxed cotton coat, while the rest of us were dressed like "ladies," in attire and footwear that all quickly recognized did not in the least lend itself to travel through this country on horseback. For my part, I wore the dress in which I had arrived at Sing Sing, and which had been given back to me upon my release. Like the rest of our girls, I had tried to wash certain items in the creek when we were allowed, but this was problematic at best. All these weeks here we had worn the same set of clothing, and so we did not object when the Lakota women ceremoniously undressed us, bundled our filthy attire, washed us from a pouch of water scented with sagebrush, and redressed us in native costume. Indeed, it felt quite liberating to give ourselves over to their gentle ministrations. And our comfortable new clothing of soft animal hides and fur gave us the sense of having left behind at last this limbo state in which we have lived these past weeks, and of being reborn into the new world.

The Kelly girls tell us that we ride out tomorrow morning. I write these words at night by the fire's faint light of embers. All are suitably apprehensive about our departure, and I think will sleep fitfully. None of us can know, of course, what is to come in these next days and weeks, or even if we will survive this journey. All we know for certain is that something is coming to an end, and something new is beginning . . .

11 April 1876

Having been six days on the trail thus far, we "greenhorns" are all still in the full agony of saddle soreness. Even Lady Hall and I are suffering though we rode more than the others before departure. The muscles used for riding seem exercised in no other activity, and this discomfort is inevitable. Nor should we complain, for at least we have the use of excellent new cavalry saddles that were in the freight cars of our train for delivery to Fort Laramie, and which were Hawk's to keep as the spoils of war.

I must write of the country through which we are traveling, as if by describing it, I might somehow be able to contain its sheer immensity. I think most of us are rather stunned and intimidated by the huge scale. It was one thing looking out the window of our train car, for that vehicle served as a kind of cocoon in which we felt encapsulated and protected . . . until, of course, that false sense of security came to a rapid halt of screeching wheels and gunfire.

We do not know our exact location, for

we simply follow the Cheyenne, who seem to be taking a circuitous route, headed generally west and north. The Kelly sisters tell us we are somewhere between the Powder River, upon which the village of Crazy Horse is situated, and the Tongue River, where they were formerly encamped with Little Wolf, and attacked in February. However, sometimes we turn to the south, then back to the north, then south again, which deviations, say the twins, are taken to avoid other travelers whom we might encounter, as well as with the hope of cutting Little Wolf's trail.

"What other travelers are we avoiding?" I asked as we were riding.

"All of 'em," said Susie, "other than our own people. Soldiers first off and the Indian guides and scouts who travel with 'em — mostly Crow, Shoshone, and Pawnee — all mortal enemies of the Cheyenne. Then there are the white prospectors, settlers, land speculators, miners, and ranchers, who are flooding into the region and who are also often guided by Indians of these same tribes friendly to the whites. Finally, you have the general riffraff that always follows such a boom — bandits, murderers, petty criminals — who prey on the weak and vulnerable like a pack of wolves trailing a herd of buffalo . . . Aye, it may seem empty to you lasses, Molly, but the country is being invaded, especially since the discovery of gold in the Black Hills last year. Gertie told us that the local newspapers are full of editorials recommending that the savages be exterminated once and for all. And the government tells settlers and travelers to be well-armed, and to shoot every Indian they come across. Bounties are offered for scalps. So you see, all of these are the people we avoid."

Thus we make our way through a complicated network of canyons, draws, and coulees. Through many of these run rivers, creeks, or springs in which to water the horses, and ourselves, and small stands of cottonwoods and willows, their buds just beginning to swell with a flush of green.

Then suddenly our horses climb a swale of land like the crest of a wave at sea and lying before us as far as the eye can see is an endless vista of plains and rolling hills, punctuated by dramatic rock formations that seem to erupt violently from the earth, running to mountains on the distant horizon, a landscape of unimaginable, even terrifying grandeur, so that some in our party draw a deep inhalation and exclaim in astonishment. Here, visible for miles around, we feel exposed, as if naked, both to the elements and to those whom we wish to avoid, indeed to any or anything that may come upon us. This is the biggest, the emptiest, the most forbidding country we have ever seen, and how tiny and helpless we feel in the midst of it. So that when finally Hawk leads us back down into the folds of land we feel a great sense of relief to be secreted thus again.

A word about the wind . . . it is a nearly constant presence in this country, and has a broad range of moods — everything from a warm gentle spring breeze like a soft caress, to a howling, angry maelstrom that stings our eyes and faces with grit. In between that there is a grumpy wind that comes in brief, whining gusts, and then subsides, like the complaints of a querulous old man; and an ominous wind, heavy and deep-toned that you hear first arising out of dark clouds on the distant horizon, and you know is headed your way with its cargo of rain, snow, or sleet, or sometimes a combination of all three. The wind also seems to own a palpable corporeal presence in the formation of the landscape itself; it molds the plains in its image like a painter's brush, gouges the rock outcroppings like a sculptor with hammer and chisel. When it blows hard, the only protection from it can sometimes be found in the deep gulches, or the small, narrow river valleys, where it sails overhead like a flock of birds winging by. But even there, you can't always hide from it; just when you think you have escaped, and are safe at last, it seeks you out like an insidious warrant server, curling over the crest of a hill and diving down to intrude upon your haven.

In this way our party travels, we, the white women, bringing up the rear, following our Cheyenne guides, and happy to be doing so, for how could we possibly negotiate this countryside alone? I will never admit it to them, but Meggie and Susie were right, we would have lasted about a half day out here alone.

■ ■ ■ ■

LEDGER BOOK III
THE LONG ROAD
HOME

■ ■ ■ ■

By now we're all real worried that Molly
ain't come back yet. But we can't afford to
be left behind, and we have to make the
hard decision to follow the Cheyenne and
have faith that Molly and the chaplain can
pick up our trail . . . Goddammit all, didn't
me and Susie tell you not to go off like
that?

(from the journals of Margaret Kelly)

5 April 1876

It is a fine morning, clear but chilly when we saddle up and head outta Crazy Horse's village. We are small in number, only twenty-two altogether — includin' me and Susie, the seven greenhorns, and thirteen Cheyenne — four men, four women, and five children of different ages. Of course, there's our leader Hawk (Aénohe), the warrior Red Fox (Ma'hóóhe), his wife Singing Woman (Némené'héhe) with their two boyos . . . maybe seven and nine years old or so . . . whose names at that age keep changing, so we can't ever keep track. Then there's the lad Little Buffalo (Hotóáso) 'and his wife, a wee young lass named Lance Woman (Xomóó'e), who got the name during the Mackenzie attack when, fleein' with her babies, she picked up the lance of a fallen warrior and speared a soldier right out of his saddle as he was bearin' down on 'em with his sword drawn. Their baby boyo is about a year old, their daughter about three. There's an old couple named Bear (Náh-kohe) and his wife Good Feathers (Påhávééná'e), tough old birds the two of 'em, who have taken in the little orphan girl, Mouse (Hóhkééhe), maybe six years old, whose parents were killed in the attack. Finally, there's the Arapaho lass, Pretty Nose (Ma'evo'óna'e), who is herself a warrior chief due to her accomplishments on the battlefield.

It is good to be small in number so we can move quiet through the country without attracting attention — not so good if we run into the wrong folks and have to fight with so few warriors, and so many women and children. The Cheyenne, with Hawk at their head, ride in front. Me and Susie ride just behind, on either side of Gertie on her big gray mule, but she'll split off shortly to head back south toward Fort Fetterman. The greenhorns ride behind us.

"You know, Gertie," says Susie. "It ain't too late for you to change your mind and come with us — fight the good fight."

"I told you gals," says she, "I can be of more service to you if I go back to the fort and keep my ear to the ground. If your people got any chance at all of winnin' this war . . . which, I gotta tell ya . . . *you ain't* . . . you're gonna need all the inside information you can get about what the Army is up to. I'm gonna do what I can for ya. You might be fightin' the good fight, but you gals have seen the soldiers in action, and I think you know in your hearts that you're also fightin' the losin' fight. They're better armed, better equipped, better mounted, and there are a hell of a lot more of 'em than there are of you, and more comin' all the time. More soldiers, more settlers, more miners. The whites are like a plague of locusts, and they're gonna chew up this countryside like nothin' you ever seen before. You know why they're killin' all them buffalo, don't you — shootin' 'em from trains, leavin' 'em to rot where they fall, soldiers told to kill every one they come across, whether they need it to eat or not? May told me you seen it from the trains yourselves when you first come out here last year. They ain't just doin' that for fun, though most of 'em are havin' a pretty damned good time at it. They're doin' it because it's part of War Department policy to finish off the tribes. Take away their commissary, their way of makin' a livin', their main source of food, and what do they got left? Nothin', that's what. Without the

buffalo, they can't feed and clothe themselves, or make their tipis, and they got no
hides to trade. Course, that's why most of
your people have already surrendered,
turned themselves in to the agency. Those
like Sitting Bull and Crazy Horse, who
refuse to come in, and Little Wolf who tried
it but couldn't tolerate it, still believe that
they can somehow keep livin' the way they
always have . . . well, the truth is, they don't
stand a chance against the plague of locusts.
I wish things was different, girls, truly I do,
but you know as well as I do that they ain't."

Aye, to be sure, me and Susie ain't stupid,
we do know in our hearts that Gertie is
right. We've come upon the killing fields
ourselves during our travels with the Cheyenne — the plains littered with the rotting
carcasses of buffalo, in some places just the
bones left, already bleached white by the
sun. Aye, we are a destructive people, we
whites . . .

"The thing is, Gertie," says Susie, "Sitting
Bull, Crazy Horse and Little Wolf, don't
really believe they can beat the whites. But
that's not why they won't surrender. Little
Wolf tried, and you saw how long that
lasted. No, they're fightin' on, because
they'd rather die than give up their way of
living. And if you believe everything is so

156

damn hopeless for 'em, why are you helping us? I'll tell you why, because win or lose, we're fightin' the good fight, and you know that."

"And you gals, then? You're willin' to die for a people who ain't even your own?" asks Gertie.

"Aye, we are, Gertie, for you know yourself that as soon as we had our babies with 'em, they became our people."

"Sure, I know . . . Alright then, but I got one last plan to propose to you. I been thinkin' real hard on it. I been thinkin' we could all — all you gals could go to the newspapers, and I'll go with you though it'd surely cost me my job. We could blow this brides program wide open, maybe that'd slow the Army and the government down if the public got wind of all this."

"Ah, Jaysus Christ, Gertie," says Susie, "imagine what a circus that'd turn into, will ya? Imagine what fun the press would have with a bunch of girl criminals, lunatics, and whores takin' up with savages. Why, we'd be a damn freak show, the laughingstock of the whole fooking country. The public wouldn't blame the government, they'd blame us. Look, we told ya, me and Meggie already got a plan, a real simple plan. We're gonna kill some soldiers, cut off their bollocks and dance over their scalps, and we don't give a good goddamn if we die while we're at it, which we expect we will . . . . it'll probably be a relief for us from the pain. Don'tcha see, Gertie, that's all we got left to do on this earth — to avenge our murdered babies."

We ride now in silence, all of us lost in our own thoughts. It feels fine to be out of the village and back into the open country. Because me and Susie were city girls when first we came out here, it used to kind of scare us, all this land lyin' so big and quiet in all directions. All we can hear is the faint whisper of a breeze in the air, and the singing of morning birds wakin' up, and the soft creak of saddle leather. That's a grand way to begin the day.

After another hour or so passes, Gertie reins up. "Well, this is where I leave you all," she says.

Now Molly breaks off from her group of greenhorns and canters up to us. "I wanted to say good-bye to you, Gertie. And to thank you for everything you've done for us."

"Don't you mention it, Molly McGill. You just take care of yourself and your gals, best you can."

"Sure, Gertie, I'll do that."

"As to you two Irish scamps, I got only one last thing to say to ya."

"Tell us, Gertie," Susie says.

"You know all those young soldiers you're plannin' to kill, cut off their nuts and dance over their scalps? . . . I just want you to remember that those boys got mamas, too."

Gertie swings her big jake mule south, and without turning to look back at us, raises her hand in the air and kicks him into a lope. We watch her until she disappears over a far rise.

12 April 1876

Now truth be told, me and Susie can't say we're all that charmed to be traveling with the greenhorns. We did our best to convince 'em to go with Gertie, but this girl Molly is a tough nut, and I have to say they picked themselves a good leader for she took the decision right out of our hands and into her own. Aye, and because we been in their shoes, we couldn't object too strongly to bringin' 'em along. We know better than most how it is to have no place to go home to, and in our hearts we didn't want to be responsible for sending 'em back where they came from. It's a funny thing how for me and Susie home now is with Little Wolf and with what remains of his band, and we're excited to be headin' that way . . . assuming we can find them.

Having only been on the trail now for a few days, we can report that so far the trip has been uneventful, which is just the way we want things. I'll say this for the greenhorns, there's only been a wee bit of whinin' from a few of 'em, mostly because they're real sore from ridin', which is to be expected these first days out. No telling how long we'll be on the trail, but by the time we get wherever we're going, they'll all be saddle-hardened veterans. As me and Susie and the others found out a long time ago, it's amazing how fast you learn this life when there ain't another one available to you.

One thing for sure is we're lucky to have Hawk leadin' our party, for he's a real competent lad, and no one knows this country better. He keeps a scout ridin' ahead, another behind, and one to either side of us, and if there is any sign of even the possibility of runnin' into anyone, he diverts our path so that we seem to be taking a kind of zigzag route. Because Hawk was the head of the war party that attacked the train, along with horses, he got to keep some of the Colt .45 pistols and Springfield carbine rifles taken off the dead soldiers, as well as other guns, ammunition, and saddles found crated on the train and meant to resupply the Army at Fort Laramie . . . so it's a comfort to know that at least we're well armed, and we got good tack.

Tonight as I make these poor scribbles, I watch Molly doin' the same on the other side of the fire ring. Hawk and the rest of the Cheyenne with him make a separate camp every night a little away from us, but we can see their figures seated cross-legged around their own fire, and that offers us some sense of security, too.

I showed Molly how to strap the ledger book to her back with rawhide thongs while we're traveling, the way our May did. She's a real different kind of girl than May, both in the way she looks and acts. But to see her ridin' with that book strapped on, or writing by the fire like she is now, me and Susie can't help but think of our own group traveling across the plains with the Cheyenne people in happier times. 'Tis a real bittersweet memory, and after all that's happened . . . seems already like another lifetime ago.

We ain't quite altogether figured out this Molly lass just yet, but we're workin' on it. Tough as she seems on the outside, we think maybe it's just a suit of armor she wears to hide something soft and wounded on the inside.

"So what are you writin' about then, Molly McGill?" I ask her across the fire.

"Nothing much, Meggie," she answers. "Just a few impressions of our travels so far. And you?"

"Aye, same here," says I, "like you say, impressions . . . I was wonderin' if maybe every now and again, we should trade notebooks to see how the other is thinkin' about things. Might help me and Susie's vocabulary and spelling, too, to see how an educated girl like you writes. How would you feel about that, Molly?"

"I would not be in favor of it, Meg," she answers. "Isn't that the whole purpose of a journal, so you can write things no one else is ever going to read? It frees you up to be completely honest. If you and I knew we were going to share each other's notebooks, we'd be cautious about what we wrote. And being cautious means you're not telling the whole truth."

"Aye, we admit you're right about that," says Susie. "But you know, me and Meggie are a nosy pair of foxes, no one ever said we wasn't. We was always trying to sneak a peek at May's journals, but she wouldn't let us, either, though sometimes she would read passages aloud to us. She had a real nice way a' puttin' things, our May did, but she never read us the juicy parts we knew were in there somewhere. We figure her journals got burned by the soldiers along with everything else . . . leaving no trace of us behind, like none of us ever even existed, and no one would ever know we had . . . . May always told us she was keeping those journals for her two children back in Chicago, a boy and a girl, who her father took from her when he committed her to the asylum. She said she wanted them to know the truth of what became of their mother . . . course now they'll never know, either . . . In light of that, would you do Meggie and me a favor, Molly?"

"What's that, Susie?"

"When we get killed, which is sure to happen, if you're able to, will you try to keep our notebooks safe? And we'll do the same for yours if it happens the other way."

"Yes, of course, I'll try," says Molly. "But why? You say May was writing to her children. But I don't care if my notebooks survive me, because I'm not writing to anyone but myself. Who are you girls writing to?"

"No one in particular," says Susie with an embarrassed shrug. "We don't have anyone to write to, either. We just . . . you know, we just want someone to know what it was like . . . what happened . . . what they did to us . . . . what became of our friends . . . and our babies . . ."

And then Susie says: "Aye, sister, but maybe we're really writin' to our babies, after all . . . and to our friends. Tellin' them a story they didn't get to live."

Molly, still scribblin' away as we talk, raises her head from her journal and looks at us across the fire, flames flickerin' in her blue eyes, a haunted look on her face that is all too familiar to us. She nods. "Yes, I think you're right, Susie," she says. "And maybe I'm keeping this journal for my daughter. She may be gone, but she's still all I have left . . ."

16 April 1876

Well, then just when we got finished saying that things have been quiet, we've had a wee bit of excitement of a strange nature. Travelin' north along what the Cheyenne call Crazy Woman Creek, we stop to water the horses and all of a sudden the head scout, Red Fox, lets out a whoop and kicks his horse into a run, splashin' into the river — Little Buffalo and Pretty Nose, who also serve as scouts, right behind him. And there a bit downriver on the other side we see what looks to be a lone soldier, squattin' on the bank, filling a canteen with water. He doesn't appear to have a horse, or a gun or anything else. Seein' three of our people comin' across the river toward him, he turns and starts runnin' quick as a cat chased by a pack a' dogs. Hawk has given everyone instructions not to fire guns as we travel unless it's a matter of life or death because the noise will alert others in the area to our presence. For the same reason, even the hunting parties when they go out to find game only take bow and arrow with 'em.

When he has nearly caught up to the soldier, with a neat sidearm motion Red Fox twirls a weapon in the air made from a length of rawhide with a stone tied at either end and slings it at the fella's lower legs, tripping him up. The soldier cries out as he hits the ground hard, Red Fox already off his horse and on top of him, knife drawn and about to slit his throat and take his scalp with two fast slashes of the blade like only a savage knows how to do. The two other scouts have caught up now, and from their horses they each touch the soldier with their coup sticks. Just then Hawk makes his screeching whistle that sounds exactly like the cry of a bird of prey, and what's more sounds like it's comin' from overhead rather than on the ground, so that people look up rather than at him. It's an odd talent we've witnessed before in our time among the Cheyenne, and that no one even questions because there are things that happen among these folks that just can't be explained, and there's no point in tryin'. But as if taking a signal from Hawk's cry, instead of killing the soldier, Red Fox hauls him to his feet, takes a rope off his saddle, throws a loop over the fella's head, pulls it tight across his chest, pinning his arms, remounts his horse and drags the soldier — stumblin' and fallin' down and gettin' up, sputterin' and gaggin' — back across the river. Hawk, who no matter what Molly says on the subject has never uttered a single word of English to me and Susie, now asks us in Cheyenne to question the soldier, find out where the rest of his company is, so we can be sure to make a wide berth of 'em. Then Hawk tells Red Fox he can kill and scalp the soldier after we get our information, and the two of 'em lead their horses down to the creek to water, and we are left to interrogate the soldier.

Now this is one scared laddie, I can tell you, breathin' hard and blubberin' like a baby, blowin' river water and snot out his nose, so skinny he looks like he's starvin' to death. "What's your name, cubby?" I ask him, and he seems real surprised, and relieved, that I speak English. "That's right, we're white girls even if we don't really look it. Pull yourself together. If you cry like a sissy, like you're doin' right now, they'll kill you real slow, make you suffer more. There ain't nothin' they hate more than a cry-baby."

This kinda gets his attention. "They're going to kill me?" he asks, sniffling.

"Well, what do you think, boyo? You wear the uniform of a soldier in the United States Army, or at least what's left of a uniform, ragged though it be, and these folks are Cheyenne, at war with your government. What the hell you think they're gonna do, hold a feast in your honor?"

"Why are you with them?" he asks.

"That's a long story you don't need to know," says Susie. "Where's the rest of your company? Tell us everything, maybe they'll go easy on you."

"I don't have a company, I'm all alone."

"What are you doin' out here, then?"

"Hiding."

"Well, you're not doin' a real good job a' that at the moment, are ya, sonny boy?" says I. "You look like you been out here for a

167

good long while. You a deserter?"

"Yes."

"How long ago?"

"I'm not sure," says he, "what month are we in, I've lost track."

"Mid-April."

"Well, then I guess I have been here since early March."

"Where's your horse and the rest of your kit?" Susie asks.

"I had to kill my horse to eat. The rest of my gear is in a cave where I have been camped not far from here. I do not have much, just standard Army issue."

"Where did you desert from?" I ask.

"I was with the Fourth Cavalry under the command of Colonel Ranald Mackenzie," says he. "We attacked the winter camp of the Lakota warrior Crazy Horse at dawn on the morning of March first."

Me and Susie exchange a look as our blood runs cold. *"Did ya . . . did ya now?"* says I. "And *did ya* manage to kill some savages yourself then, boyo?"

"No, no, I do not kill people. You see, I am a noncombatant. I am the company chaplain . . . or I should say, I was . . . It was my first campaign, I had only recently been conscripted. I am Mennonite, we do not bear arms against others, we do not kill,

we follow the way of Jesus Christ. I was sent to Camp Robinson because the Army was experiencing a shortage of chaplains on the plains. When our troops attacked the Indian village and I saw what was happening . . . I saw women and children being killed . . . shot in the back as they tried to escape . . . I . . . I panicked . . . I ran away . . . I abandoned the soldiers to whom I was supposed to provide spiritual guidance, and I abandoned the victims of their terrible wrath . . . I lost my courage . . . I abandoned my faith . . ."

"*Holy . . . mother . . . of Jaysus . . .*" whispers Susie under her breath. "I was just about to cut his throat, Meggie, and take his bollocks and scalp as our first trophies of war, and I know you were thinkin' the same . . . but somehow . . . ya know, cuttin' the bollocks off a damn chaplain don't seem like such a grand idea now, does it sister?"

"Hawk has already told Ma'hóóhe that the soldier belongs to him, sister," says I. "Which relieves us of the responsibility of killin' him."

Meanwhile the greenhorns have been sittin' their horses real quiet, near enough to hear all this, watching kind of wide-eyed, and now Molly and the Englishwoman, Lady Ann Hall, confer for a moment, dismount, and walk over to us.

"Our group is of the unanimous opinion," says Lady Hall, in her hoity-toity way of speakin', "that this young man's life should be spared."

"Well, now ain't that just *lovely,* Meggie?" says Susie. "The greenhorns have decided to save the poor lad. The only thing is, m'lady, no one cares what your unanimous opinion is, because you don't have any say in this matter. You may be a suffragette where you come from, but you ain't got the vote here, either. Hawk is in charge, he does what he wants with the lad. And we don't interfere. That's how it works with these folks, see?"

"You girls talk tough," says Molly, "but I don't think you want to see this boy killed, either." She looks at the chaplain now. "It appears to me that he's suffered enough just staying alive out here."

"He is kinda pitiful," says Susie. "What's your name, anyhow, sonny?"

"Christian."

"Well, that figures," says Susie. "What's your family name?"

"Goodman."

"*Christian Goodman?* Jaysus Christ, you make that up?"

"No, it's an old family name," says he, "a

not uncommon one among my faith."

"I'm going to speak to Hawk about this," says Molly. "I don't mind interfering. As you girls keep telling us, we're greenhorns and we don't know any better."

Me and Susie don't try to stop Molly. In fact, we're glad she volunteered, rather than us havin' to do it, because she's right, there ain't much honor in killin' such a pathetic little fella as this one. We give her one piece of advice and that is to tell Hawk that the boy is a holy man, that he's got big medicine. We know that makes a real impression on the Cheyenne. It was enough to keep them from killing Brother Anthony when he first came among us. "And you tell him the boy quit the Army because they were killing Cheyenne babies," says I, "that he's been livin' for weeks in a cave on a vision quest. You tell him he wants to help our people.

"Now ain't that the way it is, cubby?" I ask him.

"In fact, it is," says he. "I do not know what a vision quest is, but it is true that I have been praying to God since I came here to show me the way."

"That's close enough. Aye, you tell Hawk all that, Molly."

So Molly walks down to the river where Hawk is squattin' on his haunches as his horse takes a long drink. We watch as she sits down right beside him, practically touchin', like they're old pals. It's true this lassie's got a lot to learn about Cheyenne etiquette, for it is not a woman's place to behave so familiar like that with a man she hardly knows. Still, we gotta admit, the girl's got a pair of bollocks on her.

Also . . . and we would never say this to her face . . . but me and Susie think Molly is sweet on Hawk. We catch her lookin' over his way all the time, though he doesn't pay a bit of attention to her. Now, it ain't like we think she doesn't genuinely want to save the chaplain's scalp . . . but at the same time we're thinkin' maybe the way she was so quick volunteerin' to speak to Hawk was partly an excuse to get next to him.

Aye, he's a good-lookin' lad, Hawk, no denyin' it, with all the best qualities of both races, Cheyenne and white. He's got a real noble expression of countenance . . . in the same way Molly does, except on the manly side. He's a little taller than most of the others, his skin a real nice shade about like that of brand-new saddle leather, his hair a fine chestnut color. He walks light across the earth, movin' with the soft, easy gait of a man who would be flyin' if he had wings.

When the tribe holds their footraces for

fun, Hawk almost always wins when he wants to. About the only one who ever beat him was our Phemie once or twice — aye, could that lassie ever run! . . . God rest her soul — they was always neck and neck, cut from the same cloth, that negro lass and the Indian lad, both half-white, both of 'em with a kind of native grace, exceptional at all they did, whether it be ridin', runnin', huntin', or makin' war, and they had a good, friendly competition, too.

Me and Susie don't know how really to explain it, but we seen it in most members of the tribe, as well, no matter what their blood — Little Wolf, for example — these are men and women who fit so natural into this savage world, and live with a kind of deal they made with the other animals, eatin' and being eaten, killin' and being killed. What they can't tolerate is the way the white world tries to close 'em in, make slaves of 'em, lock 'em up on the reservation and throw away the key. I suppose it's the same way me and Meggie were born smart about the streets of the city where we came up . . . but different, too, of course . . .

Anyhow, Hawk is not old enough yet to be a chief, but he already has the bearing of one, has proved himself as a warrior, and commands respect from the others. Sure, it's easy to see why Molly might have a hankerin' for him, especially after spendin' all the time she did in prison. Course, we don't know what wound she carries herself, and maybe me and Susie are just writin' a story here, trying to soften our stony hearts by imaginin' romance between others, because those days are long gone for us . . .

We have to admit that what Molly says about us is true. Aye, it's funny . . . all this time, we been dreamin' of findin' the soldiers who attacked our village and takin' our revenge on 'em. And here the very first one we run into was actually there, but he's a damned skinny Mennonite chaplain named Christian Goodman . . . for Christ's sake . . . who got scared and ran away. Aye, we don't want to see him killed, either. I wish we could tell Brother Anthony about this. We know what he'd say, too, he'd say this was God's way of revealin' himself to us. Well, me and Susie ain't quite ready to believe that . . . For God had plenty of time to reveal himself by savin' our babies, but he surely came up short in that regard, didn't he?

To pass the time while we wait on Molly, we ask the lad how he managed to survive out here in the dead a' winter. He tells us the Mennonites are a simple people and live close to the earth, self-sufficient country folk, who make their way farmin', raisin' animals, and huntin'. He says the only tool he has is an Army-issue knife, a fork and a tin plate and cup, and that he carried a small bag of salt, some hardtack and bacon in his saddlebags, long since used up. He doesn't know exactly how many days he traveled after he deserted, eatin' just enough to get by, not even knowing where he was headed, and not caring. Finally, he came upon a cave hidden in a rocky bluff, where he was able to get in outta the weather and make a fire. By then his horse was already half-dead from hunger, because with the ground frozen and covered in snow, there was little forage. So he killed the animal, butchered him, and was able to keep much of the meat frozen so it lasted a good long while. He made snares with strips of rawhide, and managed to trap small rodents and rabbits, and others he hunted with stones. He says he was plannin' on stayin' out here until he died, or until God spoke to him, givin' him some sign about what he should do next to make penance for his sins — for being a coward, for losin' his faith, for not tryin' to stop the soldiers from their bloodlust.

"You see, I had never seen war before,"

says he. "We are a peaceful people, I had never experienced violence, or seen human beings behave in such a fashion. I had never seen a person killed by another, let alone a child. I did not flee because I was afraid for my own life, I fled because I could not bear to witness such sins against humanity, against Jesus Christ our Lord. And in so doing, I became complicit in those sins. I know I should have stayed and tried to stop them, to save both the children and the souls of those who killed them. And I did not . . . I did not."

"If it is any small consolation to you, sonny," says I, "you could not have stopped them."

"How do you know that? I could at least have tried."

"We know because me and Susie were there, we were livin' in that village your soldiers attacked. It wasn't the camp of Crazy Horse, that's just what the Army believed at the time. It was the winter village of the great Cheyenne chief Little Wolf. Our village."

"You . . . you were there?"

We nod.

"Yes, now I see how all this has come full circle," he says. "I see God's presence, I hear his voice. It is no coincidence that you came upon me, it is all part of God's plan, his gift to us. You saw how frightened I was when I was captured, for I had turned away from God's love. And now you see how calm I am. If the Cheyenne wish it, I am no longer afraid to die. Perhaps it is just punishment for my sins at the hands of those whom I have wronged. Although perhaps, they, too, will find the Lord's forgiveness in their hearts. Excuse me, for I must pray now and thank Jesus for his infinite mercy."

The chaplain sits down cross-legged on the ground, closes his eyes, and begins whispering his prayers in a voice so soft we can't make out the words.

Me, Susie, Lady Hall, and the rest of the girls lead our horses, including Molly's, down to the creek, some distance away from where Molly sits with Hawk. She stays with him for a good long while, until finally he stands and walks away from her. We're all dyin' to know how it went for her and when she joins us, Lady Hall asks her what decision Hawk has reached.

"He is considering the matter," she answers.

"But what did he say?" asks Carolyn Metcalf. "Did he not give you any indication, any discernable hint about how he was feeling?"

"He didn't say anything, he didn't speak, he just listened to me, and he didn't react to what I said. That is just his way."

"Molly, you really think he understood you?" Susie asks. "We know you mean well, but Meggie and me ain't so sure about this idea you got that Hawk understands English. Maybe that's why he didn't say anything. You claim he's considering the matter, but you don't know that."

"I've already told you, he understands me. He has spoken to me before. He speaks English as well as you do . . . maybe better. Do you think I'm imagining that?"

"Alright then, lass, don't get your knickers in a twist. We believe you."

It is late enough in the afternoon now that the Cheyenne begin settin' up their night bivouac. It's as good a place as any, with live water nearby and deadwood along the creek bottom to gather for the fire. And so we, too, set up our own camp. Hawk hasn't returned yet, but just as dusk comes on we hear again that shriekin' whistle overhead and we look up to see a red-tailed hawk soarin', followin' the tree line above the river bottom. That's how Hawk got his name, for among the Cheyenne it is believed that he is a shape-shifter and has the ability to turn himself into a hawk, they say he's been doin' it since he was a boy. Now me and Susie got tribal blood in our own veins from way back when in the history of the old country, and we can be real superstitious about such matters. Our people were savages, too, so we ain't sayin' it's true, but we ain't sayin' it's untrue, either. Aye, and it's somethin' to hear how much Hawk's whistle sounds like the real thing, so much so that no one can tell the difference between the two.

Now all this while, that damned skinny chaplain has been sittin' in the same spot, prayin' quietly to himself. We leave him alone, figurin' he'll come over to the fire when he smells the antelope meat we're cookin' for supper. But he doesn't and he's still in that same position when we're ready to get under our blankets for the night. It gets plenty cold out here this time of year after the sun goes down, so Molly takes a buffalo robe over and drapes it around Christian Goodman's shoulders. He doesn't open his eyes or speak to her, just keeps whisperin' his damn prayers like he's in some kinda trance. Me and Susie figure he'll either be dead in the morning at the hands of Red Fox, or he'll have run off back to his cave. We go to sleep hopin' he'll make it through the night.

And damned if the chaplain is not still there at dawn this morning. It is cold enough that you can see your breath, and a sheen of frost has settled sparklin' on the ground. We see that Hawk and his people are already breaking camp without even havin' made the mornin' fire.

Pretty Nose comes over to us now to say we're headin' out soon as possible, that the scouts have come upon a party of white men camped upriver. She says there are Crow and Shoshone warriors with them, probably guides for whatever business they are on. Hawk seems to have more important things on his mind than the chaplain, and since he's still alive and Red Fox has made no move toward takin' his scalp, we figure the lad is in the clear in that regard.

We wake the others and tell 'em what's goin' on, and then we start packin' up our own night camp. Me, Susie, and Molly go over to the chaplain.

"Time to wake up now, sonny boy," says I. "We're movin' out. You can go back to your cave now if you want."

The chaplain opens his eyes, blinks a few times like he's shakin' off his trance. "Go back to my cave? You mean they're not going to kill me?"

"You're still alive," says Susie, "in case you hadn't noticed. If they were goin' to kill you, your hair'd be hangin' off Red Fox's belt by now."

"I do not wish to return to my cave. May I not accompany you? Perhaps I can do God's work among these people. But first I must go back to retrieve my possessions."

"If you want to come with us, laddy, you got no time for that."

"I cannot leave without my Bible. It is not far. I can be there and back in only a few minutes."

"Hurry up then. But understand that we can't wait on you, we're movin' out with the Cheyenne. And if we're gone before you're back, you'll have to catch up. Just so you know, there's a band of white men camped in the vicinity. They got Crow and Shoshone scouts with 'em. These tribes are old enemies of the Cheyenne. We don't know who the white men are or what they're doin' here, but if their scouts cut our trail, there will be blood spilled, that much is sure."

"I'll take you on my horse to fetch your Bible," says Molly. "It will be faster."

"Don't do that, Molly," says Susie. "You need to stick with us. The chaplain is on his own."

But she's already headed to the rope corral where the horses are held overnight. She leads her mare out, slips the bridle over its nose, throws the saddle on its back, cinches it up, swings on, and rides back to us. "Can you mount behind me?" she asks the chaplain.

"Of course I can," says he. "I grew up among horses on our farm." And the skinny little fella climbs aboard.

"Jaysus Christ, lass," says Susie, "are ya really goin' to risk your fookin' life for a bleedin' Bible?"

But she is already headed to the river, the chaplain with his arms wrapped around her waist. I look over to the Cheyenne camp, which is nearly ready to head out, and I see Hawk watching Molly's horse splashin' across the river with the chaplain ridin' behind her. He looks worried, and a wee bit perplexed, for he must be wonderin' where in the hell she's headed.

It takes us another ten minutes or so to finish packin' up our own affairs and preparin' the horses. It seems like Hawk dawdles a tad in movin' out, but his first responsibility is to look after his own, and soon they get under way. By now we're all real worried that Molly ain't come back yet. But we can't afford to be left behind, and we have to make the hard decision to follow the Cheyenne and have faith that Molly and the chaplain can pick up our trail.

We travel fast for better than an hour, due west, keeping to the river bottoms. Hawk has gone out himself with the scouts, leaving Red Fox in charge of us. We figure we're headin' toward the foothills of the Bighorn mountains, hazy and just barely visible on the horizon, where we can get into the timber for cover. The country we're passing through is rich in game and we scare up a number of elk bedded down overnight along the river. They get up as we pass with gangly alertness, blowin' clouds of vapor from their nostrils, and bound off with a grand rustling of underbrush. When we are forced to leave the river bottoms to cross a section of plains, we see small herds of buffalo grazing. Yet none of this game do we hunt as we ordinarily would, for Red Fox seems in a hurry to put distance between us and the white men with their Crow and Shoshone escorts.

As the time passes and the distance between us increases, and still Molly and the chaplain do not appear, we cannot but imagine the worst. We do not speak of it, for we each know what everyone else is thinkin'. One after the other, we turn periodi-

cally in the saddle to look behind us, hopin'
that by some miracle Molly will appear. But
Hawk has clearly made the only choice he
can, and if one of our group must be
sacrificed for the survival of the rest, so be
it. It is the way of this wild country. She
took it upon herself to leave us, rash and
reckless girl that she is, goddamn her. If she
has fallen into the hands of the wrong men,
this pretty blond white girl will not be well
used. Aye, and she will have no one to
blame but herself . . . Goddammit all, didn't
me and Susie tell you not to go off like that?

Tonight we are bedded down in a rough
bivouac with no fires permitted. We don't
even put up our little Army tents, we just
cover ourselves with the canvases in a tight
group. We don't talk much. All of us are
double worried now, for when the other
scouts came in from their different directions at dusk to confer with Red Fox, Hawk
was not among them. Too dark now to write
more. We chew a little dried buffalo jerky
for our meager supper and now we try to
sleep . . .

Ledger Book IV
Red Painted Woman

I looked now at the Indian girl on the donkey. She wore a buffalo robe over a dirty deerskin shift, leggings, and moccasins, and her face was covered in red clay greasepaint, clearly mixed from the local soil, the same color as the striated earth of the bluffs above the river. On each of her cheeks were three parallel slashes of black paint, which gave her a fierce, warlike appearance. She seemed to be in a kind of trance, dazed, her eyes fixed and staring straight ahead . . .

(from the journals of Molly McGill)

This afternoon, when we stopped to water the horses, the scouts caught a young soldier who was filling his canteen from the river, and dragged him into our camp at the end of a rope. He was pitifully thin, terrified. When he had sufficiently composed himself, he told us he was a deserter, that his name was Christian Goodman, and that he had been the chaplain of the same cavalry company that attacked Little Wolf's village — indeed, he had been witness to the massacre. He said he panicked and ran away. We felt sorry for him. He seems so young, so sincere in his faith, genuinely contrite. He has somehow managed to survive out here for a number of weeks, living in a cave, eating his horse and whatever else he could scavenge and hunt, including rodents. From the look of him, he appears to be near starving to death.

Even Meggie and Susie, whose hearts are so hardened in vengeance against the soldiers, felt that the young man's life should be spared by the Cheyenne, and I took it upon myself to speak to Hawk on this matter. I walked down to the riverbank where he was watering his horse and sat beside him. It is the first contact I have yet had with him on this journey, and I felt oddly nervous in his presence.

"He is not really a soldier, you know," I said. "He is a chaplain, a holy man. He carries no weapon. He does not believe in taking the life of another human being. He deserted from the Army because the soldiers were killing your people, were killing children. He got scared and ran away. That's all. Please, we ask you not to kill him."

Hawk did not look at me as I spoke, nor did he answer, he simply gazed across the river. We sat there for a time . . . I don't know exactly why but I leaned my shoulder lightly against his . . . yes, of course, I do know why . . . I did so because I wanted to touch him. We held this contact for a while . . . until he stood, gathered his horse's reins, and walked away from me without looking back.

When I returned to our group, the chaplain was sitting cross-legged, his eyes closed, praying in a whisper. The Cheyenne had decided to make our night camp here, and he remained in this same position for the rest of the afternoon and into the evening. After the sun went down, I covered him with a buffalo robe. We ate our dinner and prepared to take to our tents. Still Christian Goodman sat praying. "He'll either be dead and scalped in the morning, or gone." said Meggie. "And there ain't a thing more we can do about it."

21 April 1876

After the passage of several days, I must finally make note of a harrowing experience that almost cost me my life. The Kelly girls accuse me of recklessness, of jeopardizing the safety of the entire group . . . and surely they are justified in doing so . . .

The morning after my last entry, we prepared to break camp early, for our scouts had discovered a party of white men with Crow guides, bitter enemies of the Cheyenne, camped upriver from us. The chaplain, Christian Goodman, was in fact still alive, whether due to my entreaty or simply because Hawk was distracted by this information, I have no way of knowing. The chaplain announced that he would like to join our party, but he insisted upon first returning to his cave to retrieve his Bible. In the interest of saving time, I offered to ride him across the river, much to the disapproval of Meggie and Susie, who wondered why I would risk my life for a Bible . . . a fair question, for with the death of my daughter, I have lost whatever small religious faith I once possessed . . . Not heeding their objections, I quickly fetched my mare, the grateful chaplain jumping on behind me, pressed my heels lightly to Spring's flanks, and across the river we splashed.

His cave was in the rocks partway up a bluff only a few minutes' ride from the creek bank. "Let me slip off right here," he said when we reached it. "It will take me only a moment to gather my Bible and saddlebags."

"Make haste," I said.

Not visible from my vantage point, the cave entrance was concealed by large boulders, into which the chaplain now climbed, agile as a monkey. I waited uneasily, with a sense of impending danger which I may only now be feeling as I tell of it in retrospect. He took longer than I expected.

Perhaps it was the murmur of the river and the slight morning breeze in my face that prevented me from first hearing their approach, but suddenly Spring raised her head in alarm and nickered softly. And when I turned, there they were riding up behind me — a man, if you can call him such, astride a hammer-headed paint pony, leading by a halter rope an Indian woman mounted on a donkey.

The man raised his arm as if in friendly greeting as he approached. "Ah, *bonjour ma belle fille*!" he said. "*Quel plaisir* to find a beautiful woman out for a ride on such a fine morning! This must be Jules's lucky day!" He wore a tattered U.S. Cavalry uniform, the jacket navy blue with yellow stripes on the sleeve, the pants a dirty pale blue with a matching yellow stripe on the outside of the leg, high brown leather riding boots, the seam split open above his calf, and a broad-brimmed Army hat worn sideways with the brim turned up, a tassel from the braided gold hatband hanging off one side. Beneath the hat, long ringlets of black hair spilled over his shoulders and down his back, leaving dark grease stains on his jacket. He was swarthy of complexion, whether by natural pigment or by filth it was difficult to say, and from his features he appeared to have Indian blood. As he rode up beside me, Spring snorted and side-stepped skittishly.

Side by side on our horses, I could smell the man. If evil has an odor, it would be his, a stench somewhere between that of rotting carrion and excrement. "Allow me to present myself, *mademoiselle,*" he said, taking off his hat and sweeping it across his upper body to his waist in a gesture meant to be gallant. "I am Sergeant First Class Jules Seminole, chief Indian scout of the Fifth U.S. Cavalry under the command of Général Georges Crook. But I see that you are traveling alone, *ma petite.* Be not afraid, for Jules is here to offer you his full protective services under the generous wing of the United States government." He smiled a malevolent grin, exposing a partial mouthful of rotted teeth.

Yes, this was a name I had heard before, from both the Kelly sisters and Gertie. I felt a cold tremor run up my spine. "I am not afraid," I answered, "and I am not your petite. Nor do I require your protective services, or those of your government, although I thank you for the offer."

"Ah, but of course you need Jules, *ma belle,*" he said. "You *juste* do not know it yet."

I looked now at the Indian girl on the donkey. She wore a buffalo robe over a dirty deerskin shift, leggings, and moccasins, and her face was covered in red clay greasepaint, clearly mixed from the local soil, the same color as the striated earth of the bluffs above the river. On each of her cheeks were three parallel slashes of black paint, which gave her a fierce, warlike appearance. She seemed to be in a kind of trance, dazed, her eyes fixed and staring straight ahead.

"Aren't you going to introduce me to your companion?" I asked the man.

"Ah, *oui, pardon mademoiselle,* how terribly *impoli* of Jules. Allow me to introduce you to my wife, Vóese'e, which in your language means Happy Woman. It is a name I have given her myself, for we are so very happy together." He turned and looked at the girl with a mock expression of tender devotion. "Is she not beautiful? We are very much in love."

"She doesn't look so happy to me," I said. "She looks like your prisoner."

"Mais non," Seminole said in a tone of feigned offense. ". . . Ah, *oui, oui,* perhaps you might say she is a prisoner of the heart. You see, she fell crazy in love with Jules when first she laid eyes upon him. Which I think you may understand yourself, *ma petite,* for this often happens when women meet Jules . . . they cannot resist his charms. Love at first sight . . . I think . . . do I not

detect? . . . yes, I think perhaps, you, too, are already just a little bit? . . ." He held his thumb and forefinger up to me, parted slightly in the gesture indicating "small," *juste un tout petit peu* in love with Jules, are you not, *ma chérie?*"

"Is she drugged? Is that why she stares like that? Does she speak?"

"She is terribly shy with strangers," he said. "She speaks only to Jules . . . ah, *oui,* at night she whispers tender endearments to Jules, *'please, please,'* she says, *'please don't do that, please don't hurt me anymore,'* and she weeps, the poor thing . . . she begs and she weeps . . . ah, *oui,* you see, she knows exactly how to excite Jules's darkest passions."

Out of the corner of my eye, I saw the chaplain peer over a boulder on the bluff above us, and in the same moment, Seminole, too, must have caught the flash of motion for he quickly slipped off his horse and took Spring's halter roughly in hand. She whinnied, threw her head, and sidestepped, but he held her firm. "Dismount," he said. "Now." Before I had a chance, he grasped my arm and dragged me off her back. He was very strong and he pulled me close so that our faces were inches apart. I felt I was going to vomit from the foulness of his odor, his breath like a cesspool. "I believed you were all alone, *ma petite.* You have lied to Jules . . . Jules is so disappointed . . . Jules does not like his women to lie to him."

"*You* said I was alone," I answered. "I never said so."

"But you did not correct me, *ma petite.* You see, that is the same thing as a lie." Seminole drew his Army revolver with one hand and pulled me tight against him with the other. He pressed the barrel against my temple. "Whoever is up there," he called, "show yourself now or this lovely girl dies." He kissed me hard on the lips, the bile rising in my throat. I gagged, I could feel his manhood pressing against my leg. "Jules likes dead girls," he whispered. "Sometimes they continue to twitch a little after death, but they do not struggle so much as the living."

Now the chaplain called from the bluff: "Please, don't harm her! I'm coming down!" He scrambled over the rocks, his saddlebags, to which were strapped a rolled Army blanket, slung over his shoulder. Seminole released me. Unable to prevent myself from it, I bent over at the waist and vomited.

"*Mais, mais,* is it really you?" Seminole said as the chaplain reached us. "*Good*

195

Chaplain Goodman? Truly is this Jules's most lucky day ever? Another beautiful woman has fallen under his spell . . . *oui, ma belle,* fear not, your romantic dreams will soon come true. Jules shall take you as his second bride . . . we, the three of us together, shall share many nights of love ahead . . . and . . . and at the same time, I have captured a notorious deserter! Jules shall be so well rewarded by *mon général . . .* perhaps . . . dare he hope? Perhaps Jules shall even be awarded another stripe and a medal of honor for distinguished service. Yes, *Lieutenant* Jules Seminole, I shall become."

"Sergeant Seminole," said the chaplain, "please, in the name of God, let us pretend that this encounter between us never took place. We mean you no harm. Let us go our way in peace, I beg of you."

"Ah, but my dear Chaplain Goodman, you know perfectly well that Jules cannot do that. You are a coward who deserted your post in battle, and it is my duty to bring you to justice. I am sorry to tell you, but you will surely be court-martialed and executed by firing squad."

At that moment, we heard the startling shriek of a hawk directly overhead, and as Seminole looked up, I reflexively performed the one effective act I had learned to neutralize my late drunken husband when he began to beat me: I kicked Seminole between the legs with all my strength, a direct hit. He groaned loudly and went down, doubled up in agony and temporarily incapacitated. I snatched his pistol from the ground where he had dropped it, and to the chaplain I hollered, "Take his horse!" As he swung onto its back, I scooped up the lead rope of the Indian girl's donkey. Although the girl still stared straight ahead, seemingly oblivious to all that was happening around her, I could not leave her here with this wretch. I leapt onto Spring and kicked her into a run. Again there came the shriek of the hawk that seemed to issue from above and ahead of us now as we raced for the river, the donkey's little legs working as fast as they could to keep up with the horses. I glanced behind me to make certain that the girl had not fallen off in her stupor, but now she had wrapped her arms around the donkey's neck, holding on for life, wearing an entirely different expression on her painted face, one of utter intensity, as if she had suddenly awakened and was aware that she was escaping. We could hear Seminole cursing loudly, shouting at us to stop . . . I need not repeat in writing what filth he spoke.

Crossing the river, we quickly regained our night camp and found it abandoned; our party had moved out as the Kellys told us it would. How far ahead they might be and in what direction exactly, I did not know, or have time to consider, I simply rode at as fast a gallop as I was able to while holding on to the donkey's lead rope and still allowing it to keep up. The little beast ran remarkably swiftly, as if intent himself on escaping Seminole. The chaplain rode on my other side and slightly behind me.

We rode and we rode, seeking the path of least resistance, following game trails and the natural contours of the land, keeping as much as possible to the coulees, draws, and creek bottoms, trying to put us as much distance behind as possible from that creature. We rode . . . we rode . . . I do not know for how long, until finally it occurred to me that I was lost. I reined up, and so did the chaplain.

"Do you know where we are?"

He looked at the sun, still quite low in the morning sky. "Roughly."

"Yes, but do you know where we're going? Do you have any idea how we can find our party?"

"Back at the river, we might have picked up their trail."

"But we did not."

"We did not. We had no time to look for it. I simply followed you."

"So then we are lost."

"Perhaps a little . . ."

"You cannot be a little lost," I said. "Either you are or you aren't."

"My sense is," he said, "that if from here we strike roughly the same trajectory your group has been moving these past days, we should perhaps come upon them. You must know at least what direction you've been traveling?"

"Roughly west and slightly northward," I answered, "with many detours. Meggie and Susie told us we were heading toward the Tongue River." I pointed vaguely to the faint outline of the Bighorn mountains on the distant horizon. "That way."

"A good beginning," said the chaplain, "although there is a great deal of country between here and there."

"And what do you propose we do now?"

"I suggest we continue on, and we trust in God to lead us on the right path."

"I don't believe in God."

"Yes, but I do."

On we rode, mostly walking the horses

now, occasionally breaking into a brief trot, traveling west and north, not knowing where we were headed other than the general direction, or if we would ever find our people, not knowing if anyone was following us. We assumed that Seminole must have been with the party of white men our scouts had discovered camping upriver. We took some small comfort in knowing that, at least for a time, he was afoot, though we had no idea how far away from them he had been when he came upon us.

All day we rode like that, stopping only to water and rest the horses. We had no food or supplies and we did not stop to hunt. I came quickly to believe that we were going to perish out here, and it rather surprised me to recognize that I no longer wished to die.

The painted girl, as I came to think of her, had resumed her trancelike state. She sat steady on her donkey's back, but she did not speak or react to us when we tried to address her. Nor did we know if she even understood our language. I could only imagine what degradation and perversity she must have endured at that man's hands, and I understood that the only means for her to survive the ordeal must have been to retreat to some untouchable, unreachable place. I had seen women in prison, victims of violation and beatings, accomplish this sort of disappearance, becoming like phantoms . . . I had nearly done so myself . . .

On we rode, feeling so tiny, so helpless, so hopeless in the task of finding our people in the vast rolling sea of this big, empty country.

We stopped for the night beside a small creek. We had nothing to eat, but in his saddlebags the chaplain carried a length of fishing line and a hook. He cut a green willow branch and tied the line to the end of it, dug worms in the soft dark soil of the creek bank to use as bait, and with this makeshift rig quickly caught a half-dozen trout. I have to admit he is a resourceful fellow, this chaplain, with a great deal of energy. We allowed ourselves a small fire, and roasted the fish impaled on willow sticks. The chaplain also had a little bag of salt in his bag, which he removed as reverently as if it were a sacred object. "All this time," he said, "I have only used a tiny pinch now and again on special occasions so that it would last. I am so grateful now to share this with you."

"What kind of special occasions did you have alone in your cave?" I asked.

"Well . . . modest ones, to be sure . . . for

instance, if I happened to acquire a little fresh meat . . . something other, of course, than rodentia."

The painted girl ate her trout hungrily. She clearly still possessed an instinct for survival. We had only the one Army blanket for the three of us, and when the evening air grew cool, I draped it across her shoulders. Our sleeping arrangements seemed at first a bit complicated. On the one hand, we needed to share body warmth; on the other we had discovered over the course of the day that the girl had an understandable aversion to being touched, particularly by the chaplain. Thus we made a bed of dried grass, and he took his place on the outside, I in the middle, and the girl beside me. She tried at first not to have any contact with me, which only resulted in her lying outside the blanket. Yet she fell asleep quickly, and when she was breathing steadily, I took her gently in my arms, pulled her toward me, and covered her again. In the course of the night, I think she took some small comfort in lying against me, some solace in a woman's soft embrace that perhaps recalled the safety of infancy when she lay in her mother's arms . . . indeed, the embrace brought back painful maternal memories of my own. She was such a skinny little thing, I could feel her bones poking into me. I felt that I needed to protect this girl, whoever she was . . . as I had failed to protect my daughter.

As if from a dream, we were awakened abruptly at first light by the cry of a raptor overhead. I lay on my back and looked up to see the bird, wings set, circling high above. At that moment, we heard the hoof-beats and rustling brush of an approaching horse, and fearing the worst the chaplain and I scrambled to our feet. As we did so, the girl, too, sensing danger, sat up, and crabbed backward in a kind of panic. It was then that the Cheyenne warrior, Hawk himself, rode into our bivouac. The chaplain, not recognizing him, not knowing whether he was from a hostile or friendly tribe, said: "Welcome, friend! Welcome to our humble camp!"

"Do not be afraid, Christian," I said. "This man is with us . . . or I should say, we are with him. Or at least, we are supposed to be."

"But I am not afraid," said he. "I am always joyful to receive a visitor! It is a tradition of my faith. Please, sir, allow me to build a small fire to warm you, and catch a trout or two to cook for your breakfast. God provides us with his bounty. And . . . and I have salt!"

"You came back for us, Hawk," I said, gratefully.

He did not answer, or even look at me, as is his way. He dismounted and approached the girl, squatting down beside her. He looked closely at her, then spoke to her in Cheyenne. She did not respond, but her eyes focused upon him. He nodded, placed the fingers of his right hand lightly against her cheek, and spoke to her again. I had the distinct impression that they knew each other.

The chaplain scurried about, gathering sticks and rebuilding the fire, blowing gently on the few embers that still glowed beneath the ashes, finally coaxing a small flame to life, to which he held thin strips of dry willow bark until they flared. When he had a decent fire burning, he went down to the creek with his fishing pole and proceeded to quickly catch another mess of fat trout, which he cleaned with his knife.

We ate our trout, and as there was little to pack beside the chaplain's blanket, we were mounted and ready to move out just as the sun was cresting the hills to the east. Having ascertained that I no longer needed to lead the donkey, I had tied his halter rope around his neck, and he followed along in his cheerful trotting gait, ears alertly pricked forward.

After the previous day's sense of helplessness at being lost wanderers, I felt such peace in being again under Hawk's wing, as I believe did the chaplain, who, giving full credit to his God for the man's appearance, chattered on gaily to the three of us as we rode. After all that time alone in his cave, it seemed he had stored up an inexhaustible torrent of words, which he now released upon us. It did not seem to bother him in the least that I was the only one who responded, and even then, only occasionally.

It was late afternoon before we finally caught up with our band, who had already made their evening camp. All the girls were so relieved to see us, and we them, there was much hugging and shedding of tears . . . with the exception of the Kelly girls' welcome. "What the fook were ya doing back there, Molly?" Meggie asked angrily. "And who the hell is this ya bring with ya?"

"We were detained by your charming friend, Jules Seminole," I answered. "I have no idea who the girl is. He said she was his wife. I brought her with us when we escaped because it was clear that she was not with him of her own free will. As you can see for yourselves, she is terribly damaged."

"*Seminole? Holy Jaysus . . .*" the twins said in unison. "I'll wager, he's guiding the party of white men, ain't he?" said Susie.

"I don't know about that. He was alone with the girl when he came upon us."

"Aye, they'll be after us for sure now," said Meggie. "You'd a' done better to leave her with him."

"The chaplain took his horse," I said, "so at least he was on foot for a time."

"How in the hell did you get away from him, and with his wife and horse to boot?"

"There was a distraction of sorts . . . a hawk scream overhead . . . When Seminole glanced up, I kicked him hard in the . . . in the bollocks as you put it . . . and we managed to escape."

"You've brought danger down upon us all, Molly," said Susie. "Hawk left us to find you, and we could have lost him, too."

"But you did not," I pointed out.

"And now you've kidnapped Seminole's wife," said Meggie. "We know this man . . . there will be hell to pay, believe us. He will hunt us down to take back what is his."

"I did not kidnap her," I said. "I liberated her from that monster. Yes, perhaps it was foolish of me to go off like that. I'm sorry. But Seminole will have to catch us first, and

206

I believe Hawk will evade him, and protect us, as he has thus far."

"Just so you know," said Meggie, "me and Susie talked about it, and we decided that even if you made it back, which we were beginnin' to doubt . . . we decided Lady Hall should be the new leader of your group. We believe she is a wee bit steadier than you, a wee bit less rash."

"That is just fine with me, girls. I agree with you. I do not wish to be the leader any longer. You're quite right, I am not fit for the job."

"Rubbish!" said Lady Hall. "I won't hear of it. I say that Miss Molly has performed a rather brave and admirable service. She saved the chaplain from what could only have been an unpleasant end, and —"

"Yes, Seminole was going to turn me over to the Army," Christian interrupted her. "He said I would be court-martialed for desertion, and executed by firing squad. Molly saved my life."

". . . and she rescued this poor girl," continued Lady Hall, "from the clutches of that unsavory fellow. I say, to quote the great Shakespeare, that all's well that ends well."

Meggie now walked up to the painted girl, who still sat her donkey and had fallen again into her trancelike state. "Susie, come over here," she said, peering at the girl curiously. "Bring your canteen and a piece of cloth."

When Susie came to her, Meggie began wiping the red clay grease-paint from the girl's face. "Aye, look, it's just as I thought," she said, "she's not a savage at all, she's a white girl beneath all of this."

"Aye, and she stinks, too, don't she?" said Susie. "The mud must be mixed in bear fat. Nothing stinks worse than fooking bear fat."

Meggie poured more water on her rag and continued scrubbing the girl's face. Suddenly she stopped and stared hard at her. *"Holy . . . mother . . . of Jaysus,"* she whispered under her breath. "Do you see what I see, sister?"

"Aye, Meggie," Susie whispered back. *"I do . . . I do . . . I see . . ."*

"But it ain't possible, it cannot be," said Meggie. *"Is that you? Is it really you?"* The girl did not answer or react in any way, she just stared straight ahead, one side of her face half-cleaned. Meggie shook her violently, then dragged her off the donkey's back to her feet, and shook her again. *"Wake up, lass, wake up now, speak to us."* Still no reaction. Finally Meggie hollered: *"Goddammit all, is that you, Martha, is it really you?"* And she slapped the girl hard across the

208

face. *"Wake up, goddamn you!"* Now the girl seemed to struggle into consciousness, her eyes coming into focus. She looked back and forth between Meggie and Susie. *"Don't hurt me,"* she said in a tiny, wounded, pathetic voice, *"please, please don't hurt me anymore,"* and she began to weep.

"Oh Jaysus, Martha," whimpered Susie, the twins now weeping as well. *"Jaysus Christ."* Together they embraced the girl, the three of them bawling in each other's arms. *"No, no, Martha, please don't cry,"* said Meggie through her tears, *"we won't hurt you, no one will hurt you, dear Martha, we'll take care of you . . . you are home . . . aye, don't you see, you are home with us, you are safe now."*

25 April 1876
No time to make entries these past days . . . We have been traveling with greater haste since the encounter with Jules Seminole, departing at dawn without making fires, eating only strips of dried buffalo meat, and what roots and meager greens, mostly dandelion leaves, we are able to gather in the creek bottoms. Only after several days of this, when the scouts were unable to find any evidence that we are being followed, and no further sign of the party of white

209

men, has Hawk permitted small fires to be built again — but only long enough to cook and take some brief warmth before being quickly extinguished.

Due to my liberation of their friend, Martha, I have been profusely forgiven by Meggie and Susie for riding off that morning with the chaplain. The twins have even offered to restore me to my position as "leader" of our group, which I have declined. I told them that Lady Hall was far more reliable and competent than I in fulfilling such a role. Indeed, it is true that I am impulsive . . . stubborn . . . rash . . . reckless, all the words the Kellys have used to describe me. And indeed, my coming upon Martha was entirely an act of happenstance for which I can take no personal credit. Things could have turned out quite differently.

Meggie and Susie believe the party of white men are either prospectors, land speculators, cattlemen, or some combination thereof, and that with most of the tribes now subdued and moved onto the Indian agencies, they must have hired Seminole and his scouts to guide them through the countryside, to protect them from whatever hostile bands remain — most of them, like ours, in hiding or on the run.

After only these few days riding with us, Martha has by no means been miraculously "cured" of the terrible ordeal she has clearly suffered. The girl is so wounded and terrified that we all wonder if she will ever fully recover. As we ride, she still slips regularly into her dazed, nearly unconscious state, as if only there can she find some peace, some escape. And since she's been with us, she has experienced terrible nightmares, weeping, crying out in her sleep, and waking in a state of great agitation. We take turns sitting up with her, holding her, trying to offer her some sense of security, but she remains so far inconsolable and she does not speak to us.

The Kellys are still trying to sort out how Martha came to be in Seminole's captivity in the first place, and what became of her infant. Given the girl's extremely fragile condition, they dare not broach the subject with her, nor has she revealed a single clue. According to Gertie, after the Mackenzie attack Captain Bourke escorted Martha, who was considered to be the sole surviving white woman of the Brides for Indians program, and her infant — the son of the Cheyenne warrior Tangle Hair — back to Fort Laramie. Because the government wished to keep the brides program secret, especially from the press, Bourke quietly arranged safe passage for Martha and the boy back to Chicago. We all try to avoid the darkest, though most plausible explanation, that somehow Seminole captured them on their way there . . . in which case the child's fate can only be imagined . . . none of us can bear to consider the possibility.

In the morning, at least several of us go down to the creek with Martha and there she makes her paste of mud and bear fat, a greasy leather sack of which she carries in her leggings. This she slathers all over her face as if donning her mask for the day. In the evenings, the Kelly girls patiently wipe the greasepaint off again. Our Cheyenne women now call Martha Ma'etomoná'e, which the Kellys translate as Red Painted Woman. They tell us that her former Cheyenne name translated to Falls Down Woman, due to the fact that she was rather a clumsy girl with a habit of tripping. They say we will all be given Cheyenne names . . . and yesterday they told me with a twin smirk between them that I have one already.

"Oh, and what would that be?" I asked.

"Well, see, they know about your encounter with Seminole," Meggie said. "And now they call you Mé'koomat a'xevà. It's not a name that sounds real pretty in Cheyenne."

"How does it sound in English?"

The twins looked at each other again, and it was clear that they could barely contain their delight. "It ain't so pretty in English, either, Molly," said Susie.

"Go on?"

"Roughly translated . . . Woman Who Kicks Men in Testicles." The girls now dissolved in uncontrollable laughter, all the others joining them.

"We just hope you're not lookin' to find a husband among the Cheyenne," said Meggie when she was able to speak again. "Because with a name like that, 'tis not likely to be an easy task for you." And then Meggie and Susie danced a little Irish jig of mirth, laughing like crazy women.

"Lookin' on the bright side, lass," sputtered Susie, "at least ya can be assured that you won't be pestered by a lot of fellas asking you to step out with 'em!"

I could not help but join them in their laughter, of which there has not been enough of late.

26 April 1876

A word now about some other members of our party, to whom, with all that has happened these past days, I have given rather short shrift so far in these pages. The long days in the saddle have given us ample opportunity to visit with one another, either as a group or individually. At the same time, this immense country in the face of which we feel so tiny and inconsequential seems to encourage a certain intimacy among us that our close confinement, first on the train and then in Crazy Horse's village, did not permit, freeing some of the girls to unburden themselves frankly and without artifice. In this way, while the landscape can sometimes seem terrifying, it is also liberating.

And so I have had occasion to learn more about several of the women in our group. The Norwegian, Astrid Norstegard, has been heretofore perhaps the most taciturn among us, as well as the most stoic — quiet, never complaining, and revealing little about herself. I wonder if perhaps this is a characteristic of her people. At the same time, she is not what one might call an especially cheerful girl; it might even be said that she has a rather dour disposition.

This morning I found myself riding beside Astrid. The prairie wind had come up, as it frequently does, and black rain clouds were massing on the horizon. "You know," she said, "if I squint my eyes in a certain way, and feel the rhythm of the horse rocking beneath me, and the wind in my face, I can almost imagine myself on a fishing boat in the North Sea. Even those distant buttes and rock formations jutting from the earth bring to my mind the islands and peninsulas where my family has lived and worked as fishermen for generations."

"But you are such a long way from home," I said. "How did you come to be here, Astrid? You've never told us."

"I married a man named Nils Norstegard," she answered. "A very fine man, who dreamed of immigrating to America. We had heard much about the Great Lakes, particularly Lake Superior, for we had relatives who had gone to the city of Duluth and made their way as fishers on the North Shore. Life in Norway was very hard, and we were very poor, but we were young and full of the spirit of adventure. And so we left . . .

"It was a long and difficult passage but once we arrived and were settled we were happy doing what we knew how to do, what our families had always done. We built a simple hut on the lake, and Nils built a fine fishing boat, and I made and mended his nets. Lake Superior is rich in trout, whitefish, sturgeon, lake herring, and other fishes.

"One day, less than six months after our arrival, Nils's boat was found drifting a half

215

mile offshore . . . he was not in it . . . perhaps he fell overboard . . . However, he was a fine, experienced boatman and I believe that he was the victim of someone else who forced him overboard . . . His body was never recovered . . . I will never know what happened to him . . ." Astrid paused here, raising her head to gaze across the plains, composing herself with her usual stoicism, though the rawness of her loss was written clearly on her face.

"We had not yet had children," she continued, "which I suppose was a good thing. I found work in the fish house, and between that and mending nets for other fishermen, I earned just enough money to get by. I had many suitors — older men who had lost their wives and needed a woman in the house, and other single younger men who had come alone to the North Shore from the old country. But I was not yet ready to remarry, and I was afraid to marry another fisherman, for too many men in my family over the generations have died at sea . . . and now my own husband.

"I had suspicions about who may have been responsible for Nils's death — one man in particular who had made improper advances toward me while he was still alive, and who was the first to approach me with a romantic proposition after he disappeared, before even the suitable period of mourning was over. I was afraid of this man. I did not wish to stay there for he was always watching me, always coming by my hut, looking at me, making insinuating remarks. Nor did I wish to clean fish for the rest of my life. But I had nowhere else to go, and no means to get there. Then I saw the advertisement in the newspaper, asking for young, single women to go west . . . and I answered it . . . and here I am . . ."

"At least if you remarry here," I suggested, "one thing you will not have to worry about is losing your husband at sea."

She smiled. "Yes, Molly, I did consider that. I thought if I marry a Cheyenne man, he will probably not die by drowning. But look," she said, indicating the plains with a sweep of her hand, "this country is not so unlike the sea, and as we have already learned, other dangers lurk. One could certainly lose a husband out there."

27 April 1876

Let me say that greenhorns though we be, I believe our group is proving to be quite adaptable. Our actress/dancer/songstress Lulu LaRue has been particularly effective in ministering to poor Martha, holding her

217

gently in her arms and singing sweet French lullabies to make her sleep again. Others of us are learning the words to some of these ditties, and we frequently join in a kind of chorus.

This morning, as we were packing the horses for departure, one of the Cheyenne women, whose name we are told translates to Singing Woman, came over to our campsite, leading a young girl by the hand.

The woman conferred with Meggie and Susie for a moment, in Cheyenne, of course, and as she did so the child walked over to where I was saddling Spring. She was barefoot and wore a simple hide shift, a pretty little thing with a slight, willowy build, tawny skin, dark hair, and a round, open face, and she stood looking up at me with solemn brown eyes. Then she reached her hand out toward me in a kind of tentative, supplicating gesture. I knelt down beside her and cupped her cheek in my palm. "What is it, dear?" I asked.

"Her name is Hóhkééhe, Molly," Susie said. "That means Mouse. She's an orphan. Her parents were killed in the Mackenzie massacre."

"What does she want?"

"She has never seen a blond woman before. Singing Woman says she's been fascinated by you ever since we've been travelin'. She just wants to touch your hair."

"Aye, Mol," said Meggie, with a laugh, "she doesn't believe it's real. "She thinks it's made of straw."

I laughed. My hair has grown long these past months, and I often wear it loose, as I did today, rather than in braids. I took now a handful where it fell over my shoulder and held it out to the child. "Well, of course you can touch it," I said. I knew she didn't understand my words, but she would the gesture and my tone. She smiled shyly, and touched my hair very lightly with just the tips of her fingers, as if afraid it would burn her. Then, emboldened, she took the tress in her hand, rubbing it lightly between her thumb and fingers. As I watched her, I could feel the tears coming, for I realized that I had not touched nor had I been touched by a child since my daughter's death . . . and this little brown Mouse looked to be roughly the same age as was my Clara. In that moment, I had the haunted sensation of looking again into the eyes of my own daughter. I raised the girl's other hand to my lips and kissed it.

When finally she let go of my hair, I took the tress in hand, twisted it several times to tighten it, pulled my knife from the sheath at my waist, and cut off a length about six inches long. I stood then, and sliced a sliver of rawhide off the end of the strap that secured my bedroll to the saddle, and with this I tied the tress in a little bundle. Kneeling back down, I handed it to the girl. She smiled proudly and raised it to her nose to smell. Then she scampered back to Singing Woman.

"It's a fine thing for you to give her a lock," Susie said. "It will be much prized as a trophy when she shows it to the other wee ones. You've made yourself a friend for life, Molly."

"Please tell her that she must also give me a lock of hers," I said.

As we rode out this morning, Meggie and Susie explained that Singing Woman had come to see us on another mission, as well. The Cheyenne women have heard us singing softly these last few nights, and the music pleases them. They wish for us to teach them our songs, and they sent her as their emissary, for, as her name suggests, she is said to have a lovely voice. We all thought this an excellent idea, as given the constant chores involved in traveling — making and breaking camp each day, hunting, gathering, cooking, putting up our rough shelters for the night, and taking them down in the morning — we have had little time to visit each other's evening bivouacs, and therefore very little personal interaction.

And so today, after the first morning break to water the horses, we rode for a time with the Cheyenne women. We sang our songs, and tried to learn a bit of each other's language. Because they have had contact for at least two generations with French trappers and traders from Canada, a number of whom have married into the tribe over the years, many of them speak a kind of limited French patois, that is to say, a linguistically impure regional version of the language. This proves to be quite helpful in teaching them Lulu's songs, and we had a fine time, the universal language of music seeming to bring us closer together.

As requested, just as we were setting out, my new little friend, Mouse, brought me a lock of her hair. She, or perhaps one of the women, had tied my tress to one of her black braids, and I now tied hers into mine. Speaking Cheyenne, with a kind of pleading look on her face, she touched the horse's neck, then herself, then my leg in the stirrup, and I realized that she was asking if she could ride with me. And so I helped her up; she swung aboard light as a spirit being and straddled Spring's withers, and we rode out, her tiny, slender brown body warmed in the sun, leaning against me as she sang along in a high, sweet voice. I, in turn, held her lightly with one arm, both the orphan child and the bereaved mother taking solace in this simple maternal contact. How I have missed it . . . how it breaks my heart . . .

The Cheyenne women, in turn, are trying to teach us the rudiments of sign language, by which means the various plains tribes "talk" to each other, and which the Kellys tell us is how their group was first able to interact with the natives. It is a wonderfully effective form of communication, and a native practitioner is able to converse as quickly in hand gestures and facial expressions as in spoken language.

This entry I make as we sit around our evening fire. Encouraged by Lulu's efforts, our Mexican girl, Maria, has also begun to sing some of the folk songs she learned as a child growing up in a tiny village in the mountains of Sonora. Although none of the rest of us speak Spanish, we can imagine from the tempo and inflection of her voice that some of these are romantic love songs, and others about the hard, frequently tragic life in that rugged land.

She tells us tales of Apache raiders who

kidnap Mexican women and babies from the villages, and other dark legends of the Sierra Madre. She tells us that when she was only twelve years old, she was sold by her impoverished family to an infamous Mexico City bandito named Chucho el Roto. She says these songs were the only possession of her lost childhood that she was able to take with her, and that they helped sustain her through the many lonely days and nights to come, running finally into weeks, months, and years of what was essentially captivity.

Then even Astrid, so usually quiet and watchful, shares the music of her own land with us, haunting songs of the North Sea, in which one can hear the wind moaning, feel the waves cresting over the bows of the fishing boats, and in the distance see the craggy bays of her home country.

Finally, timid little Hannah Alford, spellbound by the songs of the others, gets up the courage to offer a few Liverpudlian tunes of her own, which, in her lively voice with its distinct accent, are as gay as can be. She says these are mostly drinking tunes her father brought home from the pub after having a pint or two with his friends at the end of their day's work in the rail yard.

In this way, while all try to assimilate into

this strange new world, they bring with them at the same time something of their past, of their former home, something familiar to remember, to hang on to in the face of these endless plains, covered by this vast, star-filled night sky, which if we lie on our backs and look up, gives us a sense of vertigo, as if we are tumbling headlong into it.

Only Carolyn Metcalf does not join us in song, for she says that the only music her husband, the pastor, permitted the family were church hymns, and after what he and the deacon have done to her, and knowing that the organist now lives in her home, she is a little soured on singing.

28 April 1876

We have all made one observation regarding Martha: she is terribly attached to her donkey. I suspect that the creature was her only friend through the ordeal of her captivity, and given the alacrity with which he ran away with us without a moment's hesitation, as if fleeing for his own life, we believe that Seminole probably mistreated him as well. Never have a donkey's little legs moved so rapidly! Although she does not speak to us, Martha made it clear that she wants the beast picketed by the entrance to her tent, and when she wakes in the night she sometimes goes outside to caress and hug it around the neck.

My parents kept donkeys as working animals on our farm, and I've always enjoyed them. Despite their well-earned reputation for stubbornness and unpredictability, and the fact that they can be quick to kick when the opportunity presents itself, and to bite, I find them to be quite intelligent creatures, more so even than horses. And I have to admit that Martha's donkey is a comely little fellow . . . as donkeys go . . . with a grayish-tan coat, dark brown mane, white muzzle and belly, and a series of pale spots on his hindquarters. He has a jaunty, one might even say slightly cocky disposition, and he steps out quite smartly when we travel. He does not tolerate any encroachment upon his person from the horses, at whom he nips when they come too close. Sometimes he simply raises his upper lip, baring his huge teeth in a kind of warning, an expression that makes us laugh and earns the full respect of the horses. We all take it as a good sign that Martha is so attached to the little fellow, for it seems to suggest that perhaps she will eventually be able to make a similar connection to people. She continues to slip in and out of her trance state. We try to engage her in conversation, ask her questions, and sometimes we just chatter on together, hoping that somehow she is absorbing our words, or at the very least, our kindly intentions.

Finally, this morning as we were riding, Lady Hall asked: "Martha, do tell us, please, have you given your splendid little donkey a name?"

And to our great surprise, and delight, for the very first time, Martha spoke: "Dapple."

"I say! Dapple!" said Lady Hall with gusto. "A grand name for the little fellow! I presume this is a literary allusion, for if memory serves me well, Dapple is the name of Sancho Panza's donkey in *Don Quixote.* Am I not correct about this, Martha?"

But for now this single word was all we would have from Martha. Still, it filled us with hope that she might yet return to us.

A final disturbing word about the donkey, Dapple . . . he has one annoying and potentially dangerous habit that is evidently ingrained in his species. Once or twice a day, and for no discernable reason, he raises his head and lets loose with a piercing bray that surely carries for miles across the plains. Lady Hall, who is quite knowledgeable about all matters equine, tells us that before they were domesticated and spread around the world as beasts of burden, the wild ass was originally indigenous to India. She said that unlike wild horses, donkeys do not travel in herds, but rather are solitary creatures, and that the males developed this loud bray in order to announce themselves across large distances to potential mates for breeding purposes.

This morning while we were traveling, one of the scouts rode in to tell Hawk that they had come upon a detachment of Army cavalry not far away. Hawk, in turn, rode back to impart this news to Meggie and Susie, telling them that in order to avoid the soldiers, we were swinging a wide berth that would take us some distance away from our intended route. Just then, Dapple let loose with one of his brays, and from some indeterminate distance and direction, another donkey, presumably a beast of burden traveling with the soldiers' pack train, answered him. Hawk spoke angrily to the Kellys, and they responded in kind, entering into an aggressive argument with him. The rest of us had no idea exactly what was being said, except that the subject was clearly Martha's donkey, toward whom Hawk kept gesturing.

Lady Hall and I rode up beside them. "I say, ladies, and gentleman, what seems to be the trouble here?"

"He wants to kill the donkey," said Meggie. "He says it will give us away. As always, the soldiers are travelin' with Indian scouts, who will discover us now in short order."

"Well, sir," said Lady Hall, "you see, that is quite out of the question. That would kill our dear Martha. Hasn't the poor girl suffered enough?"

"Aye, exactly what me and Meggie are tryin' to tell him," said Susie. "We say if he harms the donkey, he'll have us to deal with, and he'd best be prepared to slit our throats, too."

"Well done, ladies," said Lady Hall. "And sir, you will have me to get past, as well. Believe me, between us, we shall be formidable opponents. Have you perhaps heard of the three Furies of Greek mythology? . . . ah, no, I expect not . . ."

Ignoring Lady Hall, Hawk reined his horse to move past them, clearly intending to make good on his threat.

From my saddlebag, I pulled Seminole's Colt .45, cocked it, and pointed it at him. He brought his horse up short in front of mine. "Leave the donkey alone, Hawk," I said. "The girl has been through hell. That animal is all she has. We can't let you destroy her. If you are so worried about the scouts finding us, let us stop talking about this, and get moving again."

Hawk looked at me with a quizzical expression, as if trying to sort out whether or not I would actually shoot him over a donkey. Then he did something strange . . . he broke into a wide smile, shook his head with a certain incredulity . . . and he laughed — the first time I'd ever heard him laugh. He reined his horse in a tight circle, touched its flanks with his moccasined heels, and galloped back to the front of our loose assemblage.

"Jaysus Christ, girl," said Meggie, astonished. "Were you really going to shoot him?"

"Of course not," I answered. "And he knew perfectly well I wasn't. That's why he laughed."

"Well, then," said Susie, "ain't it pleasin' to know that Hawk has a sense of humor. Wouldn't a' been in the least bit amusin' if he had killed that donkey . . . not to mention me, Meggie, and Lady Hall."

We watched as Hawk conferred a moment with Red Fox, who peeled off to resume his scouting duties. Then he turned us to the southwest and we moved out at as fast a pace as we could travel. Meggie, Susie, Lady Hall, and I all broke into a light canter, and the rest of the girls, who have all by now achieved varying degrees of competence in the saddle, followed suit behind us.

We rode hard for several hours, alternately walking, trotting, cantering, and making only brief stops to water the horses. Red Fox and Singing Woman's two boys ran alongside their mother's horse at a brisk jogging pace, each of them taking turns riding behind her, for the horse they shared had come up lame yesterday. They do this without complaint. Truly, this is the hardiest race of people I have ever known, almost like another species altogether. It was all we could do to keep up with them.

It occurs to me how much of their life is spent running from and evading others, all with what seems to be the rather modest goal of living free. In these past days with them on the trail, we, too, have come to feel like fugitives, with the inescapable recognition that virtually everyone outside our little band — the white settlers, the miners, the soldiers, and the Indians who guide them — are all mortal enemies wishing to do us harm. For all our lack of skill at communicating with them, we have in this short time come to have a sense that we, too, are members of this tribe . . . a strange sensation . . . we against the world . . .

We stopped just after sunset to make our

night camp. It appears that Hawk has succeeded in evading the cavalry, as he has thus far evaded contact with all. Clearly, he knows this country intimately, how to hide in it and how most efficiently to travel through it. Still, he has given us a new worry.

"Don't be surprised if one morning we find Dabble lying in a pool of his own blood," Meggie warned as we were setting up camp. "Or more likely gone from here altogether — butchered and cooked by the Cheyenne. And we'll never know until it's too late that Hawk, or someone else he sent to do the job, has been here. These people move as stealthy as ghosts in the night. They can steal a whole herd of horses without hardly making a sound. We can't say we recommend you try it again, Molly, but you caught Hawk off guard this morning, and that ain't an easy thing to do with a lad like him. Where in the hell did you get the pistol, anyhow?"

"I took it from Seminole."

"Damn, lass," said Susie, shaking her head ominously, "you took his horse, his woman . . . *and his gun.* I just hope you never run into the bastard again. We don't need to tell you he's right crazy, that one, and if you do, he'll gut you like a deer and eat your organs raw. It's a damn shame you didn't kill him while you had the chance."

"All I had in mind at the time was getting away from him," I said. "I am not a killer . . ."

"Oh? But that ain't what *we* heard," said Meggie. "Why, we thought you were in prison for that very crime?"

"All we're tryin' to tell you, Molly," said Susie, "is that you may have sent Hawk off today, but he ain't goin' to risk his whole damned band just to spare a fooking donkey. You can't know this but the Cheyenne teach their children not to cry from the day they are born. This they do by pinchin' their noses shut whenever they start bawlin'. See, there are times when attacked by enemies that the women, children, and old people must hide themselves for protection in the tall grass or in the bushes outside the village. If a baby cries, its mother is required to smother the child in order to avoid giving away the others. Aye, imagine that? . . . having to kill one's own infant for crying? . . . it goes against every mother's instinct, don't it? So I think you can understand of what little consequence in comparison is the life of a donkey to these people."

"By the by, Molly," said Meggie. "While we're at it, me and Susie think you're sweet on Hawk. We seen you moonin' over him."

"What? That's nonsense."

"Don't be denyin' it, lass, we seen how you look at him. And maybe he's a little sweet on you, too . . . hard to say with Hawk, he's got such a good poker face. But even if he is, don't count on that to get you any kinda special treatment. In case you ain't noticed, around here everything is done for the benefit and protection of the tribe. Anyone who gets in the way a' that, whether it be a donkey or a person, can get dead real fast."

"Believe me, I've noticed. And I don't expect special treatment, nor is Hawk sweet on me. The only time he's even looked at me on this journey was when I pointed the gun at him. And even then he just laughed."

"Aye, there you go, lass, you just let it slip, didn't you?" said Susie. "You wish Hawk would pay a bit more attention to you, don'tcha now?" And the two of them look at each other and laugh in twin conspiracy.

I confess that I flushed in embarrassment then, and with no ready riposte I simply walked away. Damn those Kelly girls, anyhow, poking their noses in everyone's business. But now that they have opened the Pandora's box of my conflicting emotions, I may as well expose here in the privacy of this journal something I have tried thus far to ignore . . . and to hide . . . obviously unsuccessfully.

After Hawk found the chaplain and me on the trail, and led us back to the group, he did not address a single word to me, did not even look at me. I wondered at first if perhaps he was angry that I had gone off on my own, until it occurred to me that I have been acutely aware for some time that Hawk has not noticed me the entire time we've been traveling, nor has he spoken to me since our meeting by the river in Crazy Horse's village.

It is true what the twins say, and why I walked away from them blushing like a schoolgirl. I have come to realize, or at least finally here admit, that I wish for Hawk to notice me, at least to look at me now and again. I have myself been experiencing a certain unfamiliar longing of late, vague stirrings long dormant and buried . . . and this shames me deeply . . . Hawk has so recently lost his wife, his mother and his child, his wounds even fresher than my own. Why should I possibly expect him to pay heed to me? And how selfish such thoughts on my part are. In addition, they seem a betrayal of my own grief, my interminable mourning of my daughter. It was oddly easier for me when I was in prison, in a tiny dark cell in solitary, dead to the world, dead to all emotion, to all hope for a future, my only longing that for my own death.

Now somehow in the course of this strange adventure, at large in this big empty country, as I learn about the lives and struggles of the other women in my company, and of these people — hunted and herded onto Indian agencies like animals into a corral — I feel myself coming back to life. It was in the monstrous grip of Jules Seminole when I first became aware of this. I was afraid again, desperately afraid; I wanted to live. Could being afraid and wishing to live suggest some small faith in a future, or is it simply a basic animal instinct for survival that has returned to me? I am unable to answer this question.

All I know . . . and I am ashamed to write this even in the privacy of my journal . . . all I know is that I long to be held in the arms of this man Hawk . . . and I speak here not of carnal matters, although there is that, too . . . rather I speak of the simple notion of being loved and protected, which I have never known as an adult . . . Good Lord, I must now redouble my vigilance against the prying eyes of the Kellys. If ever they were to read these pages, I would die of embarrassment.

There . . . I have unburdened myself of such thoughts, and perhaps in having done so, I can now put them behind me.

1 May 1876
We have reached the Tongue River, but due to our many detours and delays, we are far to the south of what seemed to be our initial general direction. The Kellys now say that in addition to evasive tactics, the long and circuitous route of travel Hawk has led us on these past weeks has been undertaken in order to cover as much ground as possible in the hope of cutting Little Wolf's trail. In addition to being a superb tracker, because Hawk grew up in his band, he knows all the chief's traditional campsites and hunting grounds. Thus, as well as looking out for potential enemies, Hawk and his scouts are seeking signs of their own people. To all of us unfamiliar as we are with this vast land, there is an unimaginable amount of country to cover, and it seems virtually impossible that we should ever locate them. What then, we wonder? Are we fated to wander these plains indefinitely? Yet we remind ourselves that as a boy Hawk found his people's village after walking over a thousand miles from Minnesota. And so we keep our faith

in him . . . what else is there to do?

We have all been making an increasing effort to ride with the Cheyenne women during the day whenever possible, and in addition to my little Mouse, I have begun to form a particular friendship with the Arapaho girl, Pretty Nose, with whom I frequently ride when she is not on scouting duty. She speaks rather good English and French, for she tells me that her father was a French trader, who spoke both languages, and between the two we are able to communicate quite well. She herself married a Cheyenne boy, and they spent time living with both tribes. They happened to be camped for the winter with Little Wolf's band when the Mackenzie massacre occurred, and since then she's been riding with the Cheyenne. She is a lovely young woman with a broad face, high cheekbones, clear brown skin, almond eyes, and full lips, and, as her name suggests, a particularly finely shaped nose, as if chiseled by a master sculptor. Yet for all her natural beauty, somehow, together, her features create an oddly mournful expression . . . a kind of melancholy, a weariness, as if she bears some deep burden. She has not spoken of it, and so I finally asked Meggie and Susie about her. They say that when the soldiers attacked that morning, rather than running from the village with most of the other women and children, Pretty Nose took up arms, killing several of the enemy and valiantly providing cover for those fleeing, saving a number of lives in the process. So furiously and effectively did she fight, it is now believed by both tribes that she has special powers in the making of war. And thus she owns the exceptionally rare status as a woman war chief.

"And she had not fought before?" I asked Meggie and Susie.

"Never," they answered together.

"But how do you explain that? How did she even know what to do? Where did she get weapons?"

"Me and Susie did not witness her actions," said Meggie. "But after the battle was over, she made the trek over the mountains with Little Wolf and the rest of us survivors. The way we heard it told was that her three-year-old daughter and her husband were killed in the first charge of the troops. See, Gertie told us the Army has figured out that dawn is the best time to attack an Indian village, for the people are still asleep. The soldiers are instructed to shoot low into the tipis to kill them in their beds. That is what happened to Pretty

Nose's husband and daughter, dead before they even got up for the day . . .

"We heard she took her husband's tomahawk and ran outside, full of grief and rage. As one of the soldiers was riding by, she swung up behind him on his horse with a cry, they say, that would freeze your blood. She split his skull with the tomahawk, pushed him out of the saddle, reined up, slipped off the horse, collected the soldier's pistol where he had dropped it, slid his sword outta the sheath, and remounted. The soldier's rifle was still in the scabbard attached to the saddle. So now she was mounted and fully armed, and the rest of the morning they say she fought with the crazed power of a wife and mother's vengeance."

"Aye, Molly," said Susie, "that is the mournful expression you recognize in Pretty Nose's face . . . and the burden she bears . . ."

4 May 1876

We have had three days of rain and cold, and traveling has been miserable, our soggy evening encampments only slightly less so. However, we can hardly complain too much as we are fortunate to have enjoyed mild spring weather these past weeks. We woke this morning to clear skies again, but colder as always after the clouds lift during the night.

I write these brief words by the fire of our evening camp on the Tongue River, at the end of a very trying day. Now we know yet another reason Hawk has led us so far south. This afternoon we arrived at the scene of the Army's February attack upon Little Wolf's winter encampment. He had not forewarned Meggie and Susie of this return, and they were unaware of it until we actually approached the burnt-out village and the Cheyenne women took up a mournful primordial keening, heartbreaking ululations of implacable grief that seemed to speak directly to the ghosts of their dead loved ones, and brought shivers of compassion up our spines.

"Oh, sweet Jaysus, Meggie," said Susie, her voice breaking as they both recognized the place where so many of their friends had died, and from which they had fled in terror with their babies on that frigid winter dawn. "Look where we are, Meggie . . . look where he's brought us . . ."

"Aye, sister," said Meggie, in a low, equally tortured voice, "full circle, right back where it all began . . . and all came to an end." Now the twins themselves took up the keening, their wailings indistinguishable from those of the other women, truly their transformation to white Cheyenne complete.

To the great surprise of us all, Martha, atop her little donkey, also began to keen, clearly recognizing this place herself, tears flowing down her cheeks, her unfettered howls of grief joining the others, an unearthly spectacle such as none of us had ever before witnessed.

Good Lord, what have we done to these people?

■ ■ ■ ■

LEDGER BOOK V
THE GRAVEYARD

■ ■ ■ ■

Holy Mary, mother of Jesus . . . goddamn
you, Hawk . . . what have you done this
for . . . of all places, why have you brought
us back here?

(from the journals of Margaret Kelly)

Me and Susie still don't know quite what to make of this damn Molly girl. She's stubborn as a mule and has a mind of her own, that is for certain. Now our May was a strong woman, no denyin' it, a fine leader, but she was real thoughtful, she picked her battles careful, after a good deal of consideration. But this lass Molly . . . this one is fearless . . . and reckless, qualities that together can get you in awful trouble real fast in this country.

Aye, and that's damned near what happened after she went off with the chaplain that morning on Crazy Woman Creek. She didn't come back, we were all worried sick, and me and Susie were right furious. As it turns out, goddamned if she didn't run into that filthy arsehole, Jules Seminole, who caused all our troubles in the first place. All we can figure is that he musta been guidin' the party of whites the scouts discovered camped upriver from us. Molly and the chaplain were real lucky to get away. Still, Hawk had to go back and find 'em and he was gone for a whole day, too, so that we were thinkin' the worst, that they were all in trouble. So when they finally rode into camp, while there was a great sense of relief among us, me and Susie went off on Molly, gave her hell for puttin' the whole band at risk like that . . . Aye . . . course then we found out she brought our Martha back to us . . . and we had to forgive her real quick.

How Martha ended up with Seminole in the first place we haven't been able to sort out yet. All we can say is that she's not the same girl she was when last we saw her, which is to be expected when you've been taken by Jules Seminole. We don't know how long she was with him, or what he did to her, and that we can only imagine . . . which ain't a pretty thing to do. He broke her down in a terrible way, and we wonder if she'll ever get up again. She can't even talk to us.

It's true that had Molly not gone off with the chaplain that morning, Seminole would have eventually killed Martha for sure . . . it appears he damned near has killed her . . . killed her spirit at least. We've seen more than our fair share of wounded souls, me and Susie have, but we never seen a woman damaged worse than this lass is now. She's like a damn ghost of herself, and among all of the women in our group, Martha may well have been the one least equipped to handle such a thing. And here we thought she was the lucky one because both she and her child survived the attack and they were going home, back to Chicago where they could live a normal life . . . if such a thing still exists for any of us . . . hard for me and Susie to even remember what that would be like . . . a normal life.

But now her baby son is gone and we don't know what happened to him, and Martha can't tell us, either . . . can't tell us much of anything, other than the name of her damn donkey that almost got us in so much trouble . . . but that is another story. We try not to imagine the worst, but where Seminole is involved that ain't an easy thing to do. Because with him there ain't any limits to the worst.

A couple days ago Molly surprised us again by pullin' a gun on Hawk. Aye, that's what we mean by reckless, acting before she thinks things through, because doin' that to a lad like him can get you dead in two shakes of a lamb's tail. Hawk said he was goin' to slit the throat of Martha's donkey because its braying would give us away to the soldiers. Me and Susie and Lady Hall all stood up to Hawk, told him he'd have to get through us if he tried to do such a thing. Aye, this we done because we knew he would lose face in front of his people if he were to get into a wrestling match with three lassies. So we bluffed him on the matter, and we don't believe he was really goin' to kill the donkey, after all.

But before we could find out for sure, Molly pulls the damn gun on him. You see? What she doesn't understand is that had Hawk wanted to, he could have thrown his tomahawk dead between her eyes, cleavin' her face before she even had time to pull the trigger, which we don't believe she woulda done anyhow. She, too, was bluffing, and Hawk knew it. But he just laughed and rode off. It is a lucky thing the lad has a sense of humor . . . but she needs to watch herself, that girl, think a wee bit longer before she acts. Yet to be fair, takin' her side for a moment, we think she learned that way of behavin' while in prison, where we know from experience you sometimes have to act first just to protect yourself, and consider the consequences later.

We're pointed southwest now, moving

fast, tryin' to get out of the way of the Army. Me and Susie are wonderin' if we are ever goin' to find Little Wolf, and we're wonderin' if Hawk is havin' doubts about that, too. We're tired a' travelin' and startin' to feel vulnerable out here, with the countryside crawlin' with enemies all wishin' to do us harm. We'll say this for the greenhorns, they are keepin' right up with us, and we haven't heard much from them in the way of whinin' like the sissies we figured they'd be. For that we gotta give 'em some credit.

4 May 1876
This afternoon, we're ridin' on a high bluff above a canyon carved by the Tongue River . . . . Gradually the canyon opens up into a narrow valley, which in turn broadens to a wide meadow, green with spring, a real pretty spot lookin' down from up here. As they usually do, the little group of Cheyenne ride ahead of us, and for a reason me and Susie can't figure out yet, the women among 'em begin to keen, that high-pitched wail they make that doesn't sound like anything one ever heard in the white world. Me and Susie are used to the keening, but we can see that it sends shivers through the greenhorns, the same way it did our group at first. Our May, fancy, educated lassie that she

was, used to say it was a sound of the most "elemental human expression of grief, a cry that issues from some primordial time before the first people even had language."

We haven't yet recognized the country, but as we ride on, we see the burnt-out village down below in the river bottom . . . aye, and then we know it is our very own village that was wiped out by the Army those months ago . . . the very place where our babies were born, where our friends died . . . and their babies. Our blood runs suddenly as cold as it was on that winter morning, all the terror of that day droppin' down upon us like a black storm cloud. We take up the keening with the Cheyenne women, aye, that's what it's for, a way to let out the horror and grief that cannot be expressed in words, only by weepin' and wailin' our bloody hearts out. Martha, too, atop her little donkey, begins to keen. She has clearly recognized the place herself.

As we approach closer, we see the charred skeletons of burnt tipis spread out across the valley floor. Some are still standing upright, their lodge poles blackened by fire, others have collapsed into piles of charcoal. The spring grass sproutin' among them seems so out of place, for to us it will always be winter here, where nothin' livin' can ever again grow.

Aye, the Cheyenne believe that everything that has ever happened in a place lives on forever in the earth — from the first lusty cry of each baby born there, to the last death song of all those who have died — all the joys and sorrows of life and death, all the blood spilled upon the ground throughout the generations, the soil soaked with the long history of the People. As we drop down off the bluff and ride into the village, it is almost as if we can feel the attack rising again from the earth, can hear again the sounds of cavalry chargin', the gunfire and screams, can see the ghosts of half-dressed mothers fleein' from the empty shells of the tipis, carrying their infants in their arms, the children, old men, and women runnin' in terror and confusion, fallin' to the soldiers' bullets, cut down by their swords. We were there, me and Susie, and we see our own ghosts runnin' among the others, fleein' the wrath of the Army, our little girls in their baby boards strapped to our breasts . . . *Holy Mary, mother of Jesus . . . goddamn you, Hawk . . . what have you done this for . . . of all places, why have you brought us back here? . . . . what have you done this for?*

We make our way slowly through the dead

village, our keening dyin' down, our grief exhausted by this haunted place. A silence falls upon us, broken only by the crunch of our horses' hooves, releasin' the bitter odor of cold cinder and ash that still covers the ground.

It takes us better than thirty minutes to wind our way through the broad encampment. We were over three hundred tipis here, a number of different Cheyenne bands had come together for the winter, a village rich in food supplies, robes and hides, everything we needed to see us through the long season of cold and snow, all destroyed. Me and Susie try to get our bearings, searching for the remains of our own lodge, but it all looks so different now it is impossible to do, everything is gone . . .

Finally reaching the far end of the village, we see risin' against the late-afternoon sky a series of burial scaffolds built of cottonwood poles and willow branches. Into these Hawk now leads our party. The wind moans through the scaffolds, their rickety legs creak, the voices of the dead speakin' to us.

"What is this place?" whispers the French girl, Lulu, nervous, for they, too, can feel the presence of the unsettled souls of the dead.

"A Cheyenne graveyard," answers Susie.

"The savages don't bury their dead in the ground like we do, they place them on these platforms where their spirits can rise to the heavens. You see those bundles on top, wrapped in buffalo hides or trade blankets? Those are their remains. And look, you see that some have objects placed upon them? — a tomahawk, a bow and arrow, a water vessel, a pot for cooking, a beaded necklace. Somethin' for them to take with them to Seano. Ain't that right, Meggie?"

"Aye, sister," says I. "You see, ladies, people place these things on the platforms beside their dead friends and relatives, so they don't arrive empty-handed in Seano. That's what the Cheyenne call their heaven — Seano, the Happy Place, which their spirits reach by followin' the Milky Way, the hangin' road in the sky, they call it. There all the People who have ever died live again just as they did on earth, reunited with the souls of those who went there before them. In Seano they hunt and play, dance and hold ceremonies, cook and feast and make love, just like before. They even make war against their enemies. The warriors dress in their best beaded war shirts and head-dresses, and the medicine men paint them and their ponies with figures meant to bring them good fortune in battle. The only difference from war on earth is that because everyone in Seano is already dead, they cannot kill each other. So they just count coup, meaning being the first to touch the enemy with your hand or your coup stick, like a kind of game."

"But that seems a splendid idea," says little Hannah Alford. "Why don't men do that here on earth, before they are dead?"

"Aye, now that would be the question, wouldn't it?" says Susie. "For what's the good of gainin' wisdom such as that after one is already dead? Men are foolish creatures, ain't that the truth . . ."

"But who constructed these scaffolds?" asks Molly, "and put the remains and the items upon them? I thought all the survivors were driven from the village to Crazy Horse's camp?"

"Me and Susie are wonderin' that, too," says I. "The scaffolds are not that old, nor the bundles themselves. So we're thinkin' Little Wolf and his people must have come back here after they escaped from the Red Cloud Agency. You see, it ain't a good thing to leave the dead unprepared for the journey to Seano, or they may never find their way there. We're thinkin' maybe that's one reason Hawk brought us here. He must have known Little Wolf would come back, and he figured we might be able to pick up his trail. Or else it is simply because Hawk and most of the others travelin' with him have dead of their own, and he came to lay them to rest."

Now the Cheyenne spread out among the scaffolds, searching for some sign of their own family members, studying each platform as they pass.

"Tell me, girls," Lady Hall asks, "do you suppose it is possible that my dearest companion Helen Flight may be upon one of these?"

"Entirely possible, m'lady," says I.

"Then I must look for her," she says, ridin' away from us.

Me and Susie have no one left to look for, nor do we believe is it a good idea to disturb the dead. And so we stay with the greenhorns who sit their horses in a tight knot, real quiet they are, needin' the closeness to each other to protect them against the crushin' sorrow here. They have, finally, a tiny window into what we been through, and we can see it scares 'em.

From time to time as we wait, one after another of the Cheyenne identifies a scaffold bearin' a kinsman, and a high keening rises again on the wind to join the others. As we look over we see Lady Ann Hall slide limp off her horse's back and fall to her knees beneath a platform. She does not make a sound, but buries her face in her hands, her body shaking in silent sobs. It's clear she's found the final resting place of her dear companion, our dear friend, the artist Helen Elizabeth Flight. We all look away to allow the woman some privacy in her grief.

When Lady Hall finally rides back to us, she carries a rolled deer hide cradled in her arms. "Well, then, ladies," she announces; amazin' how calm she is, as if nothing at all out of the ordinary has happened, "it appears that I succeeded in finding my Helen, after all."

She unrolls the deer hide and inside lay the blackened side-by-side barrels of Helen's shotgun. "I saw this poking out of the bundle, which I can only assume contains her earthly remains . . . charred bones, I'm afraid, are all that is left of her. She was so proud of her scattergun, a bespoke piece . . . that is to say, custom fitted by Featherstone, Elder & Story, gunmakers of Newcastle upon Tyne. I know this, of course, for it was I who gave her the gift. Whoever built her scaffold must have found these barrels . . . and the bones . . . among the ruins and placed them there . . . so that . . . so that . . ." Here Lady Hall falters, her stoic façade beginning to crumble away, her voice breaking, tears flooding her eyes, until with another heroic effort, she manages to say . . . "so that Helen would have her gun with which to hunt when she went to Seano. She was a wonderful shot, you know . . . truly one of Great Britain's finest."

Here Lady Hall draws a deep breath, which she releases slowly, giving herself another moment to pull herself together: "And look what else I discovered upon the scaffold," says she. She spreads the deer hide open and holds it up for us to see. Painted upon it, in the natural earth pigments Helen used to mix her paints, is the image of a golden eagle. "Somehow this must have escaped the fires of that day," says Lady Hall. "I can only assume it is all that remains of Helen's body of work here . . . But isn't it magnificent? Had she lived and her work on the birds of America been published, I believe Helen Elizabeth Flight would have been recognized as an ornithological artist of the same stature as John James Audubon."

"M'lady, just so you know," says I, "it ain't a good thing to steal from the dead. Aye, the Cheyenne believe that it is very bad medicine to disturb the burial platforms.

You should put those things back, for they will only bring you trouble."

"Nonsense," she says, "I do not believe in such atavistic superstitions."

"Aye, but how will Helen be able to hunt in Seano, then, without her scattergun?" asks Susie.

"Alright then, I shall put the barrels back, but I am keeping the hide. Helen would have wanted me to have it. She was not superstitious, either."

"You would be surprised, m'lady," says I, "had you seen the care that Helen put into the figures she painted on the warriors and their horses before they went off to war. We think she came to believe in her art's power to protect them in battle."

Martha now dismounts from her little donkey and walks unsteady to us. She is real agitated. *"Where is Brother Anthony?"* she asks, and we are all astonished to hear her speak. *"Where is Captain Bourke? May has been shot."* She points at the rocks in the hills above the river. *"We must go to her. She is in a cave with her baby, Little Bird. She needs our help. We must go to her."* Now she turns her hands palms up and looks down as if seeing them for the first time. *"But where is little Tangle Hair?"* she asks of her empty hands. *"Where is my baby?"* She falls to her knees and begins to weep uncontrollably. *"Where is my little boy?"* she whimpers through her tears. *"Oh, no, I have lost my baby!"*

Me and Susie get down off our horses and kneel on either side of Martha, each of us puttin' an arm around her. "Don't cry, Martha," says I. "No, you haven't. You've not lost your son. We'll find him."

She looks me right in the eyes, the first time, I realize, she's done so since she came to us. *"No? Haven't I?"* she asks. *"Will we? Are you certain? Ah yes, perhaps I left him with May in the cave. Yes, that's right, May is looking after him . . . but . . . but May has been shot,"* Martha says, as if just now remembering again. She stands suddenly. *"May has been shot. Hurry, she needs us. She is very cold. Please, follow me, I will show you where she is. Hurry!"* And she begins to walk away from us toward the hills.

"Ah, Jaysus, Meggie," whispers Susie, "she's gone mad. What do we do now?"

"I don't know, sister . . ." says I. "I suppose we must go with her. What else is there to do? Perhaps if she finds the cave and sees that it's empty, she'll come to her senses."

"I don't know that she has any senses left," says Susie.

"Nor do I. But at least she's speakin'. That

we must take as a good sign."

So we follow Martha, Molly, too, dismounting to come along, the four of us afoot. In the confusion of the attack that morning, everyone in the village had scattered like a covey of prairie grouse jumped by a fox. Me and Susie had run a different direction into the hills with our babies than had May, and so we got no idea where the cave is located in which our friend passed her last hours on earth. We do know from Brother Anthony that afterward her body was taken by John Bourke for burial in the military cemetery at Camp Robinson. It is not what May would have chosen as her final resting place . . . surrounded by soldiers . . . we believe she'd have preferred to be on one of the scaffolds here . . . but there she lies . . . and we hope in peace.

We doubt after all Martha has been through, and given her deranged mental state, that she will be able to find the place again. But as we climb into the rocky hills, she seems so certain and determined in her direction.

"May has been shot," she keeps sayin', "she is very cold, she needs our help. Follow me, the cave is right this way."

We follow, climbin' a faint game trail that winds its way up the bluff. We squeeze between large boulders and pick our way careful across narrow ledges that fall away to the rocks below. And damned if after twenty minutes or so, Martha doesn't lead us right to the entrance of the cave. It woulda been easy to miss, too, just a shallow depression under a rock shelf, into which we have to crawl on our bellies.

"We're here, May," Martha calls out, "hang on, my dear friend, we're coming for you." It chills me and Susie to hear Martha speak this way, to realize that this is probably exactly what she said when she first led Brother Anthony to this place those months ago. It is like she is relivin' it all over again . . . and so maybe are we.

Once we crawl through the entrance, we find that it opens up into a shallow cave. A gap in the rocks above allows a faint light to enter, just enough for us to see as our eyes adjust. In the center of the cave is a fire pit; the gap in the ceiling musta worked like a natural chimney. In the pit are the remains of ash and blackened animal bones from travelers who have probably been takin' shelter here since the first people walked this land.

"Where are they?" cries Martha when she sees that the cave is empty. *"Where is May? Where is Little Bird?"* Suddenly, she holds

261

her arms out and turns her empty palms up again. *"But where is my baby boy? Oh, good God, I've lost my baby!"* And she begins to sob.

"Try to remember, Martha," says Susie. "You came back to this cave with Brother Anthony. You found May here, but she was already dead, remember? Quiet One, Feather on Head, and Pretty Walker took Little Bird with them. They joined Little Wolf and the rest of the band on the trek across the mountains to Crazy Horse's village. Meggie and me were with 'em, see? Our little girls died, you understand? . . . We couldn't keep 'em warm enough . . . they froze to death. But May's daughter, Little Bird, survived, because she had three mothers to keep her warm. We think she must still be with Little Wolf. We're going to find them soon. You'll see."

Molly has taken Martha in her arms and is tryin' to calm her. *"But where is my baby?"* Martha asks through her tears. *"I've lost my little boy."*

"We don't know, Martha," says I. "We don't know what happened to your boy. We been hopin' you might be able to tell us about that."

But now we watch as Martha in Molly's arms fades away from us again, we see the light go out of her eyes as they lose focus. It seems that the shock of this terrible day and her own confusion and dark imaginings are just too much for her to bear. "Martha?" says Susie. "Stay with us now, lass." But it is too late, she has gone again, seekin' escape in the place where nothin' can harm her.

Maybe just out of respect to May, we sit in silence for a while in the cold, dim cave. Molly still holds Martha in her arms . . . all of us imaginin' what those last hours here musta been like for May — wounded and freezing, knowing she was dying but fearing far more for her daughter's life than for her own. We know from Quiet One, Feather on Head, and Pretty Walker — Little Wolf's two other wives and his daughter — who were all here with her, that May insisted they leave to join Little Wolf and the others, and to take her baby, Little Bird, with them. She feared she would die here before Martha came back with Brother Anthony or Captain Bourke, or that Martha wouldn't make it back at all. She couldn't ask them to risk their own lives by waiting with her, nor could she risk dying with her baby in her arms after the others had left. So they did as she told them. How hard it must have been to give up her daughter and die here alone . . . Aye, she was a fine brave woman, our May . . . God rest her soul.

As we are leaving the cave, Molly spots a piece of paper in the shadows of the corner. She picks it up, looks at it, and hands it to me. Straightaway I recognize it as a page torn out of May's notebook, written in her hand. But it is too dark to read here, and so I fold it and put it inside the small beaded leather pouch I carry at my waist.

By the time we crawl out from under the ledge of the opening, the sun has set, and dusk is coming on. We make our way real careful back down outta the rocks, this time leadin' Martha, who follows passive with not another word spoken. By the time we reach the river bottom, the Cheyenne have set up their camp a bit away from the village and the burial scaffolds, for there'd be no rest for anyone from the unsettled spirits swirlin' in the air like dust devils, their silent keening bubblin' up from the troubled earth.

Our girls have set up their own night camp beside them, closer than usual for they, too, feel the presence of the spirits. They have picketed our horses and Martha's donkey with the other mounts. As we approach on foot, Dapple, apparently recognizin' Martha, raises his muzzle in the air, peels his lips back, and gives off one of his brays of welcome. She goes to him and throws her arms around his neck. We're glad to see that she's got somethin' to hold on to. Me and Susie and Molly lead Martha down to the river, where we wash up and remove her greasepaint like we do every evening. She's runnin' low on the bear fat and we're ho- pin' she'll run out soon. Maybe once she can't hide herself anymore, she'll have to face the truth . . . whatever that is . . . plus she'll smell a whole lot sweeter.

By the time we return from the river, the Cheyenne have a large fire burning, and Pretty Nose comes over to our camp to invite us to share a dinner of two antelope they killed this afternoon. Our own Lady Hall participated in the hunt, and she tells us how it went. The hunters, including m'lady, went out on foot each wearin' a cape made of a full antelope hide with the hair still on. Spottin' a herd in the distance, the hunters pulled the capes over their heads so that they were completely con- cealed and they got down on their hands and knees, and began crawlin' around like that. The antelope, being curious creatures, drew closer little by little, thinkin' maybe these figures were members of their own kind. When the herd had finally come into range, the hunters stood up and drew their bows. Lady Hall, a wiry lass, all muscle and sinew, has gotten right proficient herself with the bow and arrow, and she let one fly that hit the animal broadside right behind the foreleg, a perfect shot in what she calls the "sweet spot," the place where the heart and lung are located. The animal ran for twenty yards or so before droppin' stone dead.

When we arrive at the dinner, two antelope are roastin' above the fire and the Cheyenne are seated around it. Now is the time for the two men whose arrows together killed the other antelope to dance the hunt, accompanied by drumbeats. They begin hunched low, holding their capes pulled over their heads with both hands, dancin' like antelope themselves move, we got to admit. Suddenly together, they stand up straight, letting the hides slip away to the ground, and gesturing as if they are drawing their bowstrings and releasing the arrows, all the while still dancin'. When they have finished their pantomime, they dance over in front of Lady Hall, who is seated cross-legged with the rest of us. With hand gestures, they beckon her to stand.

"Oh, no, but I couldn't possibly," she protests. "You see, I have two left feet, I am not at all gifted in the art of dancing."

Course the hunters don't understand her words, but they sense her shyness. So they each just take hold of one of her arms and lift her to her feet. "Oh, dear!" Lady Hall cries. "Oh, my goodness!" One of them has picked up his antelope hide and now drapes it over m'lady's shoulders, prancing before her. "Well, alright then," she says, takin' hold of the hide and pullin' it over her head "if you insist. As my dear companion Helen Flight always said: 'When in Rome . . .'" And she begins to dance, tentative and clumsy at first. Aye, it is true what m'lady says, she has two left feet alright, and she doesn't dance at all like an antelope moves. The rest of us can't help but giggle at her efforts. She relaxes after a bit, prancing with . . . well, we ain't goin' to call it exactly grace . . . let's just say, she dances with plenty of energy, which makes us giggle all the more. Especially when she begins actin' out her hunt, hunched over, shrouded by the cape, then straightenin' and lettin' it drop dramatically behind her, drawin' her imaginary bow, and releasin' the arrow, pointin' straight with the index finger of her right hand as if showin' its path, and then raisin' her open left palm and striking it with the tip of her finger, to suggest the arrow makin' contact with her target. We are all in a fine state of hilarity now, we cannot stop giggling, even Lady Hall's maidservant, Hannah, who is watching her lady in wide-eyed amazement, gigglin' her little head off. The Cheyenne, too, are laughin' with us . . . not makin' fun of her, see, just enjoyin' the show.

Exhausted finally by her performance, Lady Hall collapses back into her seated position among us. "Oh, dear!" she says, breathing heavy. "I must say, the recounting of the hunt is more tiring than the hunt itself! But I did rather well, don't you think, ladies? That is . . . for one with two left feet. My Helen always said I was too straight-laced. I believe she would be proud of me."

" 'Deed she would!" says Susie, wipin' the tears of laughter from her face. "You did splendid, m'lady!"

"Mais oui, you must appear in my *revue cancan!"* says Lulu.

And later we find out that the Cheyenne have given Lady Hall the honorary name Vó'aa'e'hané', which means Kills Antelope Woman.

We have a fine dinner of the roasted animals, a grand end to what has been a hard day of heartbreak, tears, and bitter memories . . . but maybe a necessary return, after all, to this place to say a proper good-bye to our lost friends and loved ones, to lay their ghosts to rest, though we know they will never lie quiet, nor will we ever forget them . . . Still, we laughed again . . . here, of all places . . . they would be happy to know it, maybe they do know, maybe their spirits are even laughin' with us. Aye, that's what we like to think anyhow. For better or worse, for all its pain and trials, life goes on for the living . . .

8 May 1876
Hawk has kept us camped here by the winter village for four days now. It has been a welcome rest for both us and our weary horses. The scouts have been goin' out every day so he must know no one is followin' us, and that the Army would never bother comin' back to a place they already destroyed. There is good game in the valley and the men have had time to hunt and restock our dwindled supplies.

To be sure, those of us who were here during the attack can't help but remember this village as it was then, so rich and well-provisioned for the winter, our new babies warm and happy, swaddled in their buffalo furs, we just tryin' to live our lives in peace and calm . . . all this . . . all this laid to waste by the Army. Aye, what comin' back to this place has done for me and Susie is only to further harden our stony hearts . . . if that is possible.

For three days and nights, Hawk himself has sat cross-legged atop the burial scaffold of his wife, Amé'ha'e, Flying Woman in our language, and their five-year-old son Mónevàta, Youngbird, gone to Seano that cold morning in his mother's arms. Next to their scaffold is that of Hawk's mother, the white woman, Yellow Hair Woman, who joined her daughter-in-law and grandson on the journey up the hanging road.

Me and Susie and the other girls in our group knew Hawk's family real well. Yellow Hair Woman may have been as white in features as can be, but she was as Cheyenne as they come, and gray of hair by the time we came among 'em. We were real surprised to see a white woman there, and we hoped maybe she might help us to get settled. But she never spoke a word of English to any of us, nor did she ever act like we and her were even of the same race. She treated us just like any of the other Cheyenne women did, that is to say, like outsiders, which of course we were.

But the longer we were with 'em, the more the lasses softened toward us, especially

270

when we had the babies in our bellies and after their birth, because that is something that just naturally brings women together, no matter their race, the color of their skin, or the language they speak . . .

We believe Hawk has been makin' a vision quest these past three days and nights, sittin' upon the scaffold, and though his eyes are closed, we don't believe he has slept in all that time, for sleepin' people do not sit up straight like that. Somethin' else we can't help but remark upon is that circlin' high in the sky above him and the scaffolds are three hawks.

Now Lady Hall, who wrote the letterpress for Helen's bird drawings, is well versed in matters ornithological — and the only reason me and Susie even know that word is because Helen taught it to us. Lady Hall says that the largest of the three is actually the baby bird, the fledging they are called, while the other two are the mother and father teachin' it to fly. She says the reason the fledging is bigger than its parents is because it's been well fed by them without benefit yet of exercise, which burns off the baby fat once it gets flyin' with the grown-ups.

That is something we never would have thought about . . . and what exactly those hawks mean, we ain't sure, either. Much could be made of it, but the Cheyenne don't do that. They just accept things that can't be explained in earthly terms as part of the real world behind this one, and all are quite accustomed to the way Hawk, and others like him, have of movin' between the two. It makes life a whole lot easier not to question such mysteries, and me and Susie have begun to think that way, too. Even so, we can't help but wonder if Hawk is up there circlin' with his wife and son . . .

Hawk finishes his vision quest, and on the following morning we break camp and begin movin' out. Everyone is feelin' a little better for havin' had this rest, but at the same time we're happy to be travelin' again, leavin' this haunted place and hopin' that at last Hawk will find Little Wolf's new village.

All this while, Martha has not yet come back to us. She's not speakin' again, nor does she seem to be hearin' us, just as when she first arrived. Aye, and though she goes through the motions of livin' — eatin', slee- pin', shittin', and puttin' on her greasepaint in the morning, she does so like a sleep- walker.

After we been ridin' an hour or so this morning, Molly suddenly takes it upon herself, like she does everything, to break away from us and canter up to the head of the column, pullin' her horse up alongside Hawk's. Really the lass has no sense of etiquette, for women do not ride with the men. We can see that she's talkin' to him, course we have no idea what she's sayin'.

Every now and again, Hawk turns his head and looks at her as she chatters on, but we can't tell if he's answerin' her or not. Their conversation, if such it be, only lasts for about ten minutes, but she stays ridin' beside him for a good half hour or so, during which time the wee lass Hóhkééhe, who has taken a shine to Molly, climbs down off old woman Good Feathers's horse and runs up and leaps on Molly's.

Finally, Molly turns her horse away from Hawk, drops Mouse back with Good Feathers, with whom she speaks a word, and canters back to us.

"So what was that all about?" Susie asks her.

"None of your concern," she answers.

"As long as you lassies are in our care," says I, "everything is our concern."

"I'm not in your care," says she. "I told you, I take care of myself."

"Aye, we've noticed, Molly," says Susie. "Or at least, you try to. We just don't want you makin' trouble for us with Hawk or any

of the other Cheyenne. You know . . . talkin'
outta turn and such."

"I'm not making trouble for anyone, it is
a personal matter between us."

"Ah, a personal matter, Susie," says I.
"Ain't that sweet? The lovebirds were just
havin' a little . . . a little . . ." I turn in the
saddle and call back to Lulu LaRue, "Lulu,
what's that French word you taught us that
means when lovers are havin' a private
conversation between themselves?"

"Tête-à-tête!" she calls back.

"Aye, that's it! You and Hawk were havin'
a wee tête-à-tête together, weren't you,
girl?"

"I suppose you could say that," says she.
"If you must know, I asked him to marry
me."

With that Molly smiles, reins her horse
around, and rides back to rejoin her friends.

"She's pullin' our leg, right, Meggie?" says
Susie uncertainly.

"I don't know, sister . . . hard to say with
that lass, ain't it?"

11 May 1876
Three more days on the trail, and we're
movin' mostly north, tight against the
foothills of the Bighorn mountains, which
are still well covered in snow up high. It is

274

rich country, of broad grass meadows, beginnin' to green up already, crisscrossed by creeks, streams, and rivers, their water rising with spring runoff, but still clear, and not yet cresting the banks. Our chaplain, about whom me and Susie have not much written in these pages, is a canny angler and keeps both us and the Cheyenne well supplied with fresh trout. The Norwegian girl, Astrid, has taken to going out with him on these excursions, for she herself comes from a long line of fishermen. In addition, there is a fantastic richness of game in this country — between the foothills, meadows, and prairies that surround us there are mountain sheep, deer, elk, antelope, moose, bear, buffalo, grouse, turkeys, ducks, geese, just about every damn kinda wild animal you can imagine.

As to the good Chaplain Goodman, let us just say that he is a right cheerful, optimistic, and competent fella, and he has settled real comfortable into this nomadic life, seems even to delight in it. Me and Susie were raised in the Roman faith, that is to say, in and out of Chicago's St. Mary's orphanage, which was run by mostly stern, humorless, sometimes outright cruel nuns, they themselves overseen by an even harder and more dour priest . . . Father Halloran was his name . . . speakin' of a fella with no sense of humor. Aye, it was a place where religion was not so much taught as enforced. We inmates, many of us bastards born out of wedlock, and all treated as such even if we wasn't, were made devout not because we so loved God, but rather because we so feared him. We were indoctrinated into the faith through beatings and dark threats of burning for eternity in hell . . . the kinda things that get a child's attention.

Likewise, when we were farmed out to various Irish foster families, members themselves of the only Church, our religious training remained a joyless business. Even the painted glass windows in the churches we were dragged to, not to mention the bloody paintings that decorated the walls of Christ sufferin' on the cross, scared me and Susie shiteless. We have come to the opinion that the young should be kept away from such places, for they only serve to give you nightmares for the rest of your life. We much prefer the way the savages worship Mother Earth, the Great Spirit, the heavens, and the animals.

All of this to say that the young chaplain's simple good faith is appreciated in the same way as was Brother Anthony's when he came among us. To the lad's further credit, he does not try to convert us or the Cheyenne to his way of thinkin', as did, for instance, the pederast Reverend Hare, who was assigned to our group when first we came here, and whose missionary zeal was particularly tiresome. So that when he got run out of our village by angry parents for havin' been caught practicing a perversion unknown to the Cheyenne, we were all real relieved.

Aye, the chaplain keeps his religion to himself, practicing it by good example, rather than fire and brimstone and evangelical rantin'. Anyhow, me and Susie have long since given up on the notion that God will save our damned souls, and recent events in our lives seem to have well borne that out.

All three scouts, Red Fox, Pretty Nose, and Little Buffalo, ride in now from different directions to report to Hawk, and then all of them ride off together, their horses at a full gallop. Hawk adjusts our path of travel to follow them at a brisk pace, headin' us north and west into the foothills. We don't know exactly what yet, but something is clearly up, and we just hope it ain't that we're bein' trailed again.

We climb into the timber, mixed pine and aspen, the air much chillier up here, a good deal of snow still on the ground. We travel for another hour or so, coming to a low pass in the hills, which marks a kind of summit, from which we begin to drop down on the other side. We hear now in the hills around the whistles of Indian sentries so adept at mimicking the voices of birds that only those of us who have lived among them can tell the difference, and even then not always. Me and Susie's blood runs cold, for we fear we are ridin' directly into the ambush of an enemy tribe hidin' in the hills around, ready to open fire from all directions.

But then we hear Hawk call back in his hawk cry, and the whistles of our own scouts in response, and in the valley below we spot the village of maybe forty, fifty tipis spread out, smoke risin' from some of 'em, women seated in small groups in front doin' their various labors, children playin' in the sun, dogs barkin'. With the bird cries of the sentries and our reply, the women come to their feet and others appear through the openin's of the tipis and all take up the trilling, a beautiful lilting musical vibration that issues from deep in their breasts, risin' in their throats and rollin' off their flickerin' tongues, a sound as joyful as the keening is mournful. Me and Susie never could quite master that one. But we know then with a grand flood of relief, gooseflesh runnin' over our skin, that we are home at last.

The trilling continues as we ride into the village, the People, our people — men, women, and old folks — welcoming us, some smilin' broadly as we pass, others watchin' with the same expression of curiosity as spectators at a parade. The younger children as is their habit scamper out to count coup on the greenhorns, touchin' their feet or legs, squealin' and scamperin' back to their families. The lassies themselves appear a wee bit overwhelmed by this reception, but in a good way, they, too, smiling in wonder, for there is nothin' that feels threatenin' about it.

But one thing me and Susie hadn't quite considered is the fact that the chaplain is still wearin' his Army uniform . . . for lack of any other attire, tattered so much now that he looks like a damn scarecrow. And when the People start noticin' him ridin' among us, they assume he must be a captive. Captive soldiers are usually given over to the women and older children to do with as they like . . . which ain't a pretty sight to witness, we can tell you. Sometimes they kill 'em real slow with sticks and rocks, knives and tomahawks . . . piece by piece if you know what we mean.

We see a group of women gatherin' together, eyein' the chaplain with hate in their eyes and talkin' angry, and we know trouble is comin'. He's ridin' kinda in the center of the greenhorns and the Cheyenne women start movin' through our horses toward him. When they reach him, one of 'em, a stout lass you don't want to mess with named Méona'hané'e, Kills in the Morning Woman, grabs him by the front of his jacket and hauls him right off his horse and the whole pack of harridans set upon him, strikin' him with sticks. Christian covers his head with his hands, but he doesn't struggle or try to defend himself, nor does he cry out, he doesn't utter a sound. Now Molly dismounts and runs to him, and she grabs big Méona'hané'e by the scruff of the neck like you break up a dogfight and she hauls her off the chaplain. Then she does the goddamnedest thing, somethin' you don't ever see happen among the savages. She punches Kills in the Morning Woman right in the chops, lays her out flat on the ground. Now me and Susie used to like to bet on the fights in Irish town. We even stepped out with a pugilist or two in our day, and we ain't seen a straight right like that since Paddy McClintock knocked out Denny O'Connor in the fifth round, and we won five dollars on a five-cent bet.

Course, this gets everyone's attention and a low murmur arises from the people. The other harridans quit their assault upon the chaplain, scramble to their feet, and begin backin' away from the big blond white woman, the likes of whom they never quite dealt with before. Christian stands and dusts himself off.

"Chaplain," I call to him, "me and Susie kinda forgot to mention to you that it's not a grand idea to ride into an Indian village wearin' a U.S. Army uniform."

Christian goes over to Méona'hané'e, kneels down beside her, cradles the back of her neck in his hand and raises her head up a little. She comes to in a moment, but doesn't quite know where she is yet or what happened to her. She's not ever taken a punch before, that much is certain. He slides his arm under her and raises her to a sittin' position, her legs splayed out in front, steadies her for a moment, finally helps her to her feet, supports her with his arm around her, leads her over, and delivers her to the other harridans. He sits down on the ground then, and pulls his boots off, stands again and removes his Army jacket, his shirt, and his breeches, folds them up real neat, picks up the boots, and hands the whole bundle to Méona'hané'e, givin' her a little bow as he does so. Course, now he's standin' there in his dirty socks and long johns, and a ripple of approval and then of good-natured laughter begins to run through the People. Even Kills in the Morning Woman, tough old bird that she is, smiles kind of sheepish an' starts laughin' along with everyone else. Sometimes all it takes among these people to be accepted is a gesture such as Christian Goodman summoned, just because that's the kinda fella he is. Too soon to say how Molly's punch is goin' to be taken, but she was, after all, only defendin' her friend, whose life she saved once already, and after that she's gotta look after him forever, according to the way things work among the savages. When word gets around about her encounter with Jules Seminole, we expect she will have earned everyone's respect . . . if she hasn't already . . .

After this little bit of excitement, we ride on through the village, me and Susie wavin' to Cheyenne friends and acquaintances, who welcome us home. There are new faces among them, as well, other tribal members from different bands who have joined up with Little Wolf.

Still, happy as we are to be here, it is a bittersweet homecoming for us, on account a' all the faces that are missing. Aye, an' just as me and Susie are feelin' again that sharp sense of loss of our friends and our wee dear babies that comes upon us from time to time like a knife thrust to our guts, our eyes scannin' the people fall upon . . . *"ah, no, Susie, it ain't possible,"* I whisper.

"Pay no heed, sister," says she, "we're seein' a ghost this time for sure, you and I. Take our eyes off her a moment, an' she'll go away as all the other ghosts have."

Me and Susie know all too well the tricks of ghosts, and so we both look the other direction at the Standing Elk family, friends of ours, who stand in front of their lodge to greet us — mother, father, a small boy, and a smaller little girl. We smile and wave at them, and they do back. Finally, we cannot resist any longer, and we cut our eyes again toward the ghost and there she still is, smilin' wry at us. Aye, it ain't no ghost, after all, it is our dear old friend the black woman Euphemia Washington . . . Phemie, back from the dead!

Me and Susie leap from our horses and run to her and she takes us both in her long brown arms, we feelin' like children ourselves returned to the bosom of the mother we never knew.

"Ah, Phemie," says Susie, "our dear Phemie, you're alive, you've come back to us!"

"Everyone said you were dead, Phemie," says I, "that the soldiers killed you. Even Brother Anthony said so. What happened? How did you survive? Where have you been? How did you get here?"

"I will tell you everything later, girls," says she in her calm, musical way of speakin', which was always such a comfort to us, and is so wonderful to hear again. What joy! "But first, you must tell me, is that not Martha, wearing the greasepaint, riding the donkey?"

"Aye, Phemie," says Susie, " 'deed it is, how did you know so quick? That's another story for us to tell *you* later."

"But does she know that her child is here?" asks Phemie.

"What?" says we together. "But how is it possible? No, she doesn't know, nor did we. She knows nothin', Martha, she barely speaks. She was taken captive by Jules Seminole, we don't know how. That big blond girl who just punched Méona'hané'e rescued her, but not before Seminole destroyed Martha's mind. But who here has her son?"

"His father, Martha's husband Tangle Hair, and his second wife, Mo'ke a'e, Grass Woman," says Phemie, "they brought the boy here from Red Cloud Agency upon their escape with Little Wolf. It is said that the Army took him away from Martha before they put her on the train east, and returned the child to Tangle Hair. I do not know for what reason. By the way, who is that girl, and who are those other white women? Are they captives?"

"Not exactly. We'll tell ya all about it later, Phemie," says Susie. "After we get 'em settled. You and us got a lot to catch up on."

We take our leave of Phemie, gather our horses and remount, and ride to the far side of the encampment, where Hawk has led the greenhorns to set up their own camp. The rest of his party has been reunited with their family members, absorbed back into the village.

The news of Martha's baby boy surprises me and Susie almost as much as did finding Phemie, and we are eager to sort out how all this came to pass. So we gather Lady Hall and Molly for a powwow.

"By the way, Molly," says Susie, "where the hell didya learn to punch like that?"

"Defending myself when my drunken husband started to beat me."

"Fair enough," says I. We know better than to ask her any more questions, for Molly plays her cards real close to the chest.

We tell 'em about Martha's baby being here, and our fear that as fragile and confused as she is, the shock of seeing him again might be too much for her. We wonder if we shouldn't wait a wee bit, let her get settled in and stronger before we spring the news on her.

"On the contrary, ladies," says Lady Hall, "I believe that a good shock of a positive nature, which this will no doubt be, might be exactly what Martha needs to bring her out of her state of somnolence."

"I agree with Lady Hall," says Molly. "I don't think you should waste another minute before you take her to see her son. We were mothers, girls, the three of us, wouldn't we wish to be reunited with our children as quickly as possible, wouldn't we wish to know that they are safe . . . that they are alive? Can you imagine any greater joy than that?"

"Ah, Jaysus Christ, Molly," says Susie in a small, busted voice, "didya have to put it like that? No, we can imagine no greater joy on earth . . . or in heaven, for that matter."

So me and Susie make some inquiries as to the location of Tangle Hair's lodge, and we lead Martha there. She walks between us, docile and passive as ever, takin' no recognition of the people we pass, most of whom she knows from our year among them. Some address her like old friends, by her former Cheyenne name, Falls Down Woman, but she does not react, nor even look at them, and they quickly realize that she is not herself.

Susie scratches at the lodge opening, and the flap is parted by a young lass we know to be Mo'ke a'e, Grass Woman. She looks at me and Susie and nods in recognition, neither real friendly nor unfriendly either. Then she looks at Martha. It clearly takes her a moment to sort out, especially with Martha's greasepaint still disguising her features, but Grass Woman quickly makes the connection and ducks back into the tipi.

We can hear them talkin' softly inside, and after a minute or two passes, Tangle Hair himself comes through the opening. He's a tall fella as he straightens in the sunlight, well named for his mess of curly hair, a fearsome-looking character and a great warrior who strikes terror into the hearts of enemies. He looks at Martha, but she does not return his gaze. He speaks to her but she does not react. He peels the tent flap back and invites us in. We duck down and slip through the opening, and as she always does, Martha follows us, docile and obedient as a pet dog.

It is a large tipi, for Tangle Hair has counted many coups, killed many enemies, and owns a large string of horses taken in raids — a rich fella by savage standards, and a generous one, too, a quality most highly valued in tribal life. As modest as the village still appears compared to the riches of our old winter encampment, with a bit of time and with the benefit of this game-rich country Little Wolf's people have clearly begun to recover and replenish their supplies.

It takes a moment for our eyes to adjust to the dim light inside, filtering yellow through the hide-skin of the tipi, a small fire burning in the center. It smells like the inside of all savage tipis — of wood smoke and food cooking, of animal furs, hides and human beings, young, in-between, and old, all overlaid by a kind of herbal incense they burn to purify the air. It is not at all a bad smell once you get used to it, and me and Susie feel right at home.

We see the baby now, propped up in a cradle board leaning against a backrest so he can look around. In this way infants learn early on about the world around them, and the daily activities of the lodge — the sounds and motions, the comings and goings — keep them engaged. To see the child, so calm, happy and alert . . . so alive . . . me and Susie don't want to say we're envious . . . no, it's a lot deeper feelin' than that.

On either side of Martha, we kneel with her before the child, like visitors come to see the baby Jesus. We got no idea what to expect, but we're disappointed to see that Martha remains distant and unfocused, she doesn't even seem to see her son.

But now she looks around the inside of the tipi, like she's noticing her surroundings for the first time. Finally, she looks at the child. Something that may be a spark of recognition flashes in her eyes. She rubs the fingers of one hand down her cheek and then looks at it real curious. Now she runs both hands down the length of her face, and regards her open palms, smeared red with greasepaint, like she's never seen them before. All of a sudden she starts hollerin' and clawin' at her face, drawin' blood with her fingernails. Me and Susie each grab hold of one of her arms to try to keep her from doin' more harm to herself. We may not be real big girls, but we ain't weaklings, either, we're all muscle, bone, and sinew, but it's everything the two of us can do to restrain Martha in her rage, like she's possessed by the devil. Aye, just as we had feared, Lady Hall and Molly were wrong, seein' the child has set off some terrible force inside her. As we try to hang on to her arms, Martha, struggling fierce, weeps and hollers. *"Wipe it off!"* she cries. *"Wipe it off!"*

"We ain't lettin' go of you, Martha," says Susie, "until you stop fightin' us. And we can't clean your face until we let go. That's all up to you now, lass."

"Pull yourself together, Martha," says I, "calm down now. Is this any way to behave? Look how you're scarin' the lad." It's true, the child has started to cry. He has surely never before witnessed such strange and violent behavior.

This seems to get Martha's attention, and her struggles begin to subside. But me and Susie don't let go of her arms just yet. We're worried that in her madness she might hurt the child. Grass Woman also fears this, for she picks up the cradle board and moves it away from the crazy woman.

Speaking Cheyenne in a real small voice, Martha says to her: *"Please, please, don't take him away from me."* She begins to weep softly, and we feel all the strength of rage flow from her body until she goes nearly limp. Only then do me and Susie let go of her arms. *"Please don't take him away again,"* she says in English. Martha touches her face, but gentle this time, and looks at the red paint, mixed now with blood. *"Wipe it off, please wipe it all off,"* she begs us.

We ask Grass Woman for water and a cloth and she brings us a tin trade pan full from beside the fire and a strip of calico cloth that must be a remnant from fabric she got at the trading post. Martha sits quiet as we wipe the grease, mud, and blood from her face.

"Just out of curiosity, Martha," says Susie, as we are doing so, "why is it so important to you that we clean your face now? We been tryin' to get you to stop wearin' the damn paint since first you came to us. What's the big rush now?"

"I don't remember when I first came to you," she answers softly.

"So why is it so important, then?"

Martha looks puzzled, seems to struggle a moment to find an answer. "Well . . ." she begins slowly, ". . . well . . . I don't know exactly . . . I suppose . . . I suppose I just want my little boy to recognize his mama."

■ ■ ■ ■

LEDGER BOOK VI
ADAPT OR PERISH

■ ■ ■ ■

We have been informed that a feast and a dance is to be held in our honor, this in order to formally welcome us to the village, and so that the young men can have a look at us as prospective wives. "Let us think of it as a kind of savage debutante ball," said Lady Hall when we heard the news.

(from the journals of Molly McGill)

9 May 1876

I need not elaborate on the several days we
passed near the burnt-out Cheyenne village
mentioned in my last entry, other than to
say that it was a harrowing experience. All
in our group were deeply affected by this
haunted place, the charred remains of which
offer incontrovertible evidence of the massacre these people endured. We witnessed
firsthand the excruciating pain the return
caused the Kellys and the Cheyenne, who
had been there on that terrible morning. At
the same time, it gave us a chilling sense of
the dangers we ourselves face.

During our time there, I watched Hawk
sit on the burial scaffold of his wife and son,
next to that of his mother, for three days
and nights. I would awake several times during the night and leave the rough little tent
I share with Carolyn Metcalf to see if he
did not sleep at last. And each time I

looked, he was still sitting there under the stars in the same position, cross-legged, his back rigid.

On the fourth day, we took again to the trail. I'm not sure why . . . perhaps simply because our pace quickened, but I had a sense that we were nearing our destination, whatever that might be. Later that afternoon and much to the chagrin of the Kelly sisters, I decided that I must speak with Hawk, and I rode forward to the head of our procession, taking my place beside him.

"I only came to tell you that I am sorry about your family," I said. ". . . No, no, forgive me, that is not what I wish to say . . . how meaningless that sounds. I wish to say that because I bear one myself, I know that there are wounds we suffer . . . wounds so deep and permanent that no solace can ever be offered in words or expressions of sympathy, wounds that never heal, never scar over, but remain raw and open forever. I saw in your eyes when first we met on the train . . . well, if you can call that a meeting . . . I could see that we share this common bond. Now I understand a bit more about what happened to you, and someday perhaps I might be able to tell you a little of my own story . . . though it is not something I have spoken of to anyone else before. Until then,

I wish for you to know that when we find Little Wolf's village, and the time comes that we white women are to be given as brides to Cheyenne warriors . . . I wish for you to choose me. I wish to be your wife."

Hawk turned his head then and looked me directly in the eyes, the first time, it occurred to me, he had done so since that very first moment on the train. He did not respond to my proposal, but did I not perhaps detect a slight nod of his head as he regarded me . . . or is that simply wishful thinking on my part?

We rode on in silence for a time, side by side, our horses in step. I wondered at the absurdity of falling in love with a man who didn't even speak to me. And I wondered if it was even possible to fall in love with a man because I had held on to him as a captive on the back of his horse for hours . . . and I liked the feel of his body against mine . . . and I liked how he smelled. I wondered if this experience we were all having, in which everything familiar to us on earth has crumbled away under our feet, leaving us with a sense of falling into a chasm, has not caused me to grasp hold of this man in order to break the fall. Or perhaps I hold on simply because how else could I continue to live after having lost all that was dear to me?

Now I heard little Mouse call to me, and I turned to see her running up behind us, fleet and light-footed as a deer. Strangely enough, she calls me by the same name by which Hawk's mother was known, Heóva'éhe, Yellow Hair Woman, which I assume she has learned from the Cheyenne women. I put my left arm out and down, in the motion we have adopted for her to mount while I'm riding — she grabbed hold of it with both hands, at the same time springing off the ground like a quail launching into flight, and I swung her aboard, light as a bird. Hawk glances over and smiles at Mouse, and says something to her. She answers . . . I must learn their language, and teach her mine.

"When we marry," I said to him, "I would like this child to come live with us."

Hawk looks at me again with the same bemused expression with which he greeted my gun, just the hint of a smile at his mouth. We ride on in silence for another half hour or so, I indulging myself in an absurd fantasy of the three of us as a happy family on a leisurely horseback ride in the country.

Finally, I reined Spring around to drop Mouse back with Good Feathers and return to my group. "One day I hope you might speak to me again," I said to Hawk, then touched my heels to the horse's flanks until she broke into a lope.

I knew well that I was in for an interrogation by Meggie and Susie, and surely yet another lecture about savage etiquette. But I did not give a damn. I decided to tell them the truth. That would give those Irish scoundrels something to think about.

14 May 1876

At last . . . Hawk has led us to Little Wolf's village, in a lovely secluded valley on a tributary of the Tongue River in the foothills of the Bighorn mountains. After all the trials these beleaguered people have experienced, it was wonderful to witness the joyful homecoming our Cheyenne and the Kelly girls received as we rode into the camp. It brought back certain memories of our own strange arrival into Crazy Horse's village, riding behind our abductors, fully two months ago now . . . with the rather substantial difference that in this case, we are no longer captives . . . or perhaps, in a different manner, we are.

We rode in three days ago, having climbed all that morning from the edge of the foothills, gaining altitude into forests of mixed aspen and pine, the former not leafed out yet, traveling at times through snow midway up our horses' forelegs, all of us wrapped in buffalo hides or trade blankets against the chill mountain air. Through a high pass and down the other side, losing altitude quickly, the temperature warming in the sunlight. It was then that we heard in the hills around us the wild echoes of birds whistling, an eerie sound that seemed to issue from all directions, as if the birds were communicating with one another. We looked at Meggie and Susie, upon whom we so depend to interpret this world for us. They were clearly made anxious by the song of the birds. "Get ready, girls," Meggie warned, but for what she did not say, nor could we guess.

Then Hawk answered himself, in his distinctive raptor cry, and our horses pricked their ears forward alertly and quickened their pace with no prompting from us. We rode up a long grassy slope, just beginning to green up in the sunlight, the Cheyenne riding ahead of us already disappearing over the crest. When we reached the summit ourselves and began to descend on the other side, we saw the village in the valley down below. It appeared to be considerably smaller than Crazy Horse's winter encampment from whence we had come.

As if they had been expecting us, the people began to come out of their tipis, and those women who were seated, working in front of the lodges, stood. The women and girls took up the trilling they make that is also not possible to describe . . . a kind of melodic warbling, an orchestration in varying tones and notes, a beautiful, welcoming music that clearly also has its origins in the avian world, and that like birds singing in the spring makes one feel part of the earth, grateful to be alive.

Into this village we rode, the twins clearly delighted to rejoin their people, waving and greeting friends, which was heartening for us to witness, as we are so much outliers of this world, and it gave us small hopes of our own future.

Reminding us again of our status as curiosities, the impish young children, small, brown, and healthful, chattering and giggling like strange little elves, ran up to touch us, as they had upon our arrival in the Lakota village — counting coup, the twins tell us it is called, an act of courage that they can then recount proudly to their friends.

We had a moment of distress when a group of Cheyenne women, mistaking our chaplain Goodman for a captive soldier, dragged him from his horse and began to beat him with sticks. I managed to intervene on his behalf, and the matter was settled to everyone's satisfaction when Christian stripped off his boots and uniform and offered them to the woman who had led the assault.

After he had remounted, wearing nothing but his skivvies, to the delight of the natives, I asked him, "Why did you not fight back or at least try to defend yourself?"

He thought about this for a moment . . . "I suppose because I felt I deserved it," he finally answered. "And also because I have never had to fight against a woman . . . or a man for that matter. I'm a pacifist after all, taught to turn the other cheek. I do not know how to fight back."

As we continued our ride through the village, Susie and Meggie suddenly leapt from their horses and ran to greet a magnificent, statuesque black woman, dressed in native attire, the rims of her ears pierced in four or five places, and decorated with small metal rings. Euphemia Washington is her name, we have learned, an escaped slave and one of the Kellys' own party of white women. They say that Phemie fought the soldiers in the Mackenzie attack and was reported to have been killed. Thus upon finding her here alive, the twins were overwhelmed with joy. Their reunion was a moving thing to behold.

We have other wonderful news: Martha's infant son is here in the village, in the care of his father, the Cheyenne warrior Tangle Hair. No one seems to know yet exactly how or why this came about. She has been reunited with her child, and although it cannot be said that this has entirely set her mind right again, she did recognize him on first sight, which seems, at least, to have brought her out of her trance state.

15 May 1876

We greenhorns have been installed in two temporary tipis on the edge of the village, but not yet incorporated into it . . . evidently until the matter of matrimony has been resolved. Once they had settled us here, Meggie and Susie announced that they would be moving back into the village and making themselves scarce for a time.

"When our group of brides arrived," said Susie, "we didn't speak the language, either, we didn't know shite about the customs of savage life, we had to figure things out on our own. Now it's time for you lassies to do so, as well. Ain't that right, Meggie?"

"Right as rain, sister," said Meggie. "Our babysittin' days are over, girls. We're lettin' the Cheyenne take over now. This is their place, their world, and they'll teach you all you need to know about it . . . if you're willin' to learn, that is. And the fastest way that's goin' to happen is if we're not around to hold your hands anymore. We'll check in on you from time to time, but right now we got business of our own to attend to. We're just goin' to leave you with a' coupla pieces of advice. First: if you haven't already done so given what you've been through so far, forget everything you ever knew about the way things work in the white world. Nothing you may be hangin' on to from your old lives applies here, and the sooner you understand that, the easier things'll go for you. This is a different world, with different people who have different beliefs and different ways a' doin' things. And by the time they get done with you, you're goin' to be different, too. All you need do is look at me and Susie to know the truth a' that."

"Aye, and the second thing is," said Susie. "Just remember that for quite some time you will be looked upon as interlopers here, especially by the women. If you hope to be accepted, you need to cozy up to them first. It's true that the men don't let the lasses sit in council, but that's only because they have their bleedin' male pride to protect, and they like to pretend they run the show. But they don't really. You'll find that out. It's the women who have the final say here. The fact is, the husbands go to their wives on all family and tribal matters, and the lasses are free to disagree with 'em, argue with 'em, persuade 'em, cajole 'em, and when that fails, they put their foot down. They got the power. Don't forget that. Make friends among 'em."

"Well, I must say," remarked our suffragist, Lady Hall, "we may consider them savages in other regards, but in this respect, they are certainly more civilized than we."

"Molly McGill," said Meggie then, "if me and Susie may just have a word with ya in private . . ."

We stepped away from the others.

"We just wanted to mention," said Susie, "that even though you ain't any longer the official leader of your group, and they are in the quite capable hands of Lady Hall, you are still the unofficial leader . . . if you understand our meaning. It ain't goin' to be easy here for any of you."

"Will it be harder than what we've already been through?" I asked.

"It will be different. The others count on

you to be strong, which we know you are, and you will continue to be. But you're also headstrong, and you don't take real well to authority, Molly, if we may say so. So we just want to suggest that you don't try to break the rules here, or encourage the others to do so. You'll soon find out that the Cheyenne got their own way a' doin' things. It'll go a whole lot easier for all a' you to just go along with the way things are, and don't try to change 'em."

"Alright, I'll do my best."

And with that the twins took their leave of us.

17 May 1876

We have been put immediately to work by the Cheyenne women. Having grown up on a farm myself, I do not object to physical labor in the open air, and much prefer it to the kind of work I did when we moved to the city . . . which employment, as the Kelly girls suggests, is unavailable where we find ourselves now.

These last two days our primary occupation has been to collect and bring in firewood. This involves climbing into the timber in the hills above the valley, gathering sticks and branches, bundling them with rawhide straps, and transporting them on our backs down to the village. It is not an easy task, and I am fortunate to be rather tall and quite strong. However, it is especially difficult labor for the smaller, slighter members of our group — Hannah Alford and Lulu LaRue, for instance, who are unable to bear the same size loads as I and Lady Hall, the latter who, though not especially tall, is quite muscular. Astrid Norstegard, too, having lived a life of physical activity on the sea and the Great Lakes, hauling nets and baskets full of fish, is a hearty girl, while Maria Galvez, with her Indian blood, and solid little frame gained during her hardscrabble childhood in the Sierra Madre, is surprisingly strong for one of her small stature. Carolyn Metcalf, on the other hand, whose life as a preacher's wife was, by her own admission, quite sedentary, is perhaps the physically weakest member of our group.

For this reason, we decided to form the bundles in varying sizes that could be borne comfortably by each of us. Curiously, the Cheyenne women themselves make little such accommodation, except for some of the older women who appear to be reaching the end of their wood-hauling days and bear lighter loads. Everyone else carries roughly the same weight. Thus when they saw our different-sized bundles, the women were quite disapproving, scolding the girls who carried less; we did not have to understand their language to know that they considered them slackers.

We tried to explain the reason in our still-rudimentary sign language, but finally, I am glad to say, it was Lady Hall who resolved the issue. She simply smiled and told the Cheyenne women in her forth-right and slightly imperious manner: "You see, ladies, this is how we choose to do it." Though they, of course, equally did not understand what she had said, due to her natural authority of character they seemed to get the point. And with only a bit more reproachful grumbling they left us to our own devices.

When all were loaded and we began to make our way single file down the trail, out of the woods and back to the village, Lady Hall said, "Lulu, I think what we all need is a little song while we work, to lighten the load. Might you have something appropriate for the occasion?"

"But of course, *madame,*" she answered. "Lulu has a song for all occasions." She began to sing a charming little French children's song called "Let's Go Walking in the Woods," a simple, sing-along ditty with a refrain — a story about children reassuring themselves against the danger of the wolf in the woods, just as we perhaps needed a little reassurance. Because of their aforementioned understanding of French-Canadian patois, the Cheyenne women quickly picked up the refrain. Even those of our group who spoke no French began to catch on, and soon all were joining in. It was a lovely moment that seemed to bring us together, and even made the burdens on our backs feel a bit less weighty.

18 May 1876

Lady Hall and I went today to see Martha in her lodge, and we were heartened by the sight of her happily doting upon her baby. However, she did not recognize us and remains terribly confused; she appears to remember very little of what has happened to her . . . perhaps this is a blessing, the mind's way of dealing with the terrible violence and abuse she has experienced. To her great credit, Grass Woman, a girl who appears to be no older than sixteen years, has relinquished the role of mother to the boy, and serves, rather, a secondary role as a sort of aunt or nanny.

It is clear, as the Kellys warned me, that the Cheyenne take very seriously their tribal rules and customs, the place and responsibilities of men and women in their society. Being here in the village even this short time, I more fully understand why the twins are so disquieted by my breaches of etiquette. Having brought us into their village to live among their people, they expect us to behave correctly, and I cannot fault them for that.

In addition to our duties hauling wood, the Cheyenne women have now put us to work carrying water from the creek every morning, not only for our own use but also for theirs. We have each been assigned a lodge at which we are to appear at dawn to pick up an empty pouch made from the stomach of a buffalo, which is left for us in front of the tipi. This we each carry down to the river and fill with fresh water, what the Cheyenne call "living" water as opposed to the "dead" water from the night before, the remainder of which the Cheyenne women pour on the ground outside each morning. Once filled, we carry the pouch back to the respective lodge and deposit it in front of the opening. It is cold, wet, heavy work, and there has been much speculation among us about whether or not we are being made slaves, or if they are simply giving us preparatory lessons in the wifely duties, which, conveniently, happen to benefit them, as well.

There is so much to learn about this new world, into which we try to immerse ourselves, making every effort not to judge too harshly some of the customs that seem incomprehensible to us. After all, what else is there to do? Thus we have adopted as our group motto: adapt or perish.

19 May 1876
We have been informed that a feast and a dance is to be held in our honor, this in order to formally welcome us to the village, and so that the young men can have a look at us as prospective wives. "Let us think of it as a kind of savage debutante ball," said Lady Hall when we heard the news.

Some of the Cheyenne girls, who will also be participating in the event, are teaching us the correct steps for the first dance of the evening — a very strict, formalized style which involves a great deal of prancing synchronization of movement. There appear to be variations of this dance, with different steps, depending upon the occasion. I must say that during our first lessons, we find it repetitive and not terribly lively, and we are all hoping that the actual event will be more animated . . . or as Lulu puts it, "bouncier."

"If we want something bouncier," she

said, "I will learn you all how to do the cancan. I think they never seen a real cancan before."

"I would say that is a fair assumption, dear," said Lady Hall.

"But it not so easy to put on a cancan without the right music," said Lulu. "We need horns, trombones, a tuba. And the correct dresses, with petticoats, stockings, and high heels."

"All of which, my dear Lulu, might be rather difficult to come by here in the wilderness."

Never at a loss to edify us on a subject about which she is knowledgeable, Lady Hall continued: "For those of you who may be unfamiliar with the Parisian quadrille, or cancan as it is commonly known, allow me to enlighten you. It is, in fact, a rather risqué — considered by many, even indecent — music hall dance performed primarily by courtesans . . . no offense intended, Lulu . . .

"Indeed, my dearest companion Helen Flight and I had occasion to witness one such performance at the Alhambra Palace Music Hall on Leicester Square in the fall of 1870. A traveling troupe of women dancers from France crossed the channel to perform a ballet called, rather grandly I should say, *Les Nations — The Nations;* I

312

believe they had the intention of making an international tour, which they began in Great Britain as a trial run to see how it would be received."

"*Oui, oui!*" said Lulu excitedly. "But I know those girls! The star of the show, Finette, was my teacher and my best friend. It was she who learn me to dance!"

"Yes . . . well some of the women impersonated men," Lady Hall went on, ignoring Lulu, "and dressed as such, while the others wore long dresses, with, as Lulu suggests, several layers of frilly petticoats, stockings, and heels. During the dance, which involved a series of lewd antics and lascivious bodily movements, those attired as women pulled up their dresses and kicked their legs as high as their heads, exposing their petticoats and drawers, in addition to just a flash of naked thigh above their high stockings. It was . . . well, it was scandalous."

"How did it happen, Lady Hall," I asked, "that you and Helen found yourselves in the audience of such a performance?"

"Ah, well you see, dear, we attended in an official . . . I should say semiofficial capacity," she answered, "at the behest of our dear friend Lord Chamberlain, who was responsible for maintaining public order and decency in the city's theatres and those of its environs. His lordship and his fellow magistrates had been receiving complaints about the sensual nature of this ballet, and he wished Helen and me to provide him with an eyewitness account. Of course, for obvious reasons, he could not attend himself, for it would hardly do for a member of the House of Lords to be seen by the public at such a spectacle. Thus Helen and I were, if you will, serving as his eyes and ears."

"And how did you report back to your lord?" I asked.

Here Lady Hall hesitated for a moment before issuing a small, sly smile. "If you must know, Helen and I found the performance quite . . . exciting . . . exhilarating I should even say . . . all those lovely girls kicking up their heels so exuberantly, exposing their undergarments and the alabaster white flesh of their thighs . . . yes, we told Lord Chamberlain the truth . . . we absolutely adored it! And judging by the enthusiastic reaction of the audience, everyone else appeared to enjoy it as well. As a consequence of our report, his lordship had the police shut the show down the following night, and he sent the troupe immediately back to France. He later told us privately that if Helen and I were so enthusiastic about the performance, it could only have a dangerous effect on public morals."

"But we French are not so bourgeois as the British, or the Americans," said Lulu. "We are not so worried about public morals. We are not so *hypocrites.* Ah, *oui,* close the show down because all who see it have fun!" Here Lulu, being the actress that she fancies herself, assumed a deep voice of bureaucratic authority, wagging her finger sternly. '*Ah,* non, *we must not allow the public to have too much fun . . . fun is very dangerous . . .* très dangereux.' But you see," she continued in her normal voice, "everybody who watches it loves the cancan, for it is a dance of joy and *liberation.* If no one else wish to learn, I will dance alone for the entertainment of our Cheyenne hosts."

Several of us could not resist a laugh at this lively girl's spirit, always so bright and cheerful. We had come to depend upon her good humor to lift our own morale when it sagged.

"I would suggest, dear," said Lady Hall, "that we first consult Meggie and Susie on this matter. It would not do to offend our hosts at the welcome dance."

"If I may say so, Lady Hall," said I, "this is just the kind of thing the twins wish for us to sort out on our own. They made themselves quite clear about that. Personally, I believe that if we avoid displaying the 'alabaster white flesh of our thighs,' as you so sensuously put it, a lively dance would not be considered offensive. Perhaps it might even be a good way to introduce ourselves to our hosts. Of course, no one is obligated to participate."

"I will dance with you, Lulu," announced timid little Hannah, who was the last girl in our group whom I could have imagined making such an offer . . . well, except perhaps for Lady Hall. "I love to dance, and I should like to learn the cancan."

"As would I," I said.

"My people love to dance," said Maria Gálvez. "I will join . . . even though my thighs are brown, not white."

Excellent! said Lulu. "Ah, *oui,* now we have a real chorus line . . ." She looks at us as if counting heads. "But we still have . . . how you say . . . we still have three flowers on the wall."

"Three wallflowers, I think you wish to say, dear," said Lady Hall. "Well, I shall not sit this dance out. I am, after all, the only other person among you, besides Lulu of course, who has actually witnessed a cancan performance. I have to admit that after having seen the spectacle, Helen and I tried a few kicks of our own at home in front of the mirror . . . however, the two of us were so hopelessly clumsy and got laughing so hard that we fell down on top of each other."

"Yes, you see how much fun it is!" said Lulu. "Now we only have Astrid and Carolyn who are still flowers on the wall."

"My country, too, has a long tradition of folk dancing," said Astrid. "Our major instrument of music is the fiddle, and the form of our dance is quite stylized. We, however, are well-covered, even our heads and our arms. I am afraid that the cancan might be a bit too . . . too *French* for me."

"Ah, *oui*," said Lulu, "I imagine you *Norvégiens* even make love dressed in winter attire . . . with mittens on your frosty hands."

I should here mention that although most of us appreciate Lulu's good-natured optimism, I do not include Astrid among our French gamine's admirers. The two are complete opposites in both temperament and character — one gay, chatty, and always positive, the other dark, quiet, with a tendency to brood. I am quite fond of them both, but from the beginning of our journey, they have not been close, and sometimes even at odds. Astrid finds Lulu to be frivolous and vapid . . . and . . . how shall I say this politely . . . of questionable morals due to her former employment. While Lulu finds Astrid to be gloomy, dull, and with a disposition "like low clouds in winter," as she puts it. I've wondered if the fact that Lulu comes from the sunny Mediterranean, while Astrid hails from the frozen north country, does not partly define their differing characters.

"And you, Carolyn," said Lulu, "will you not join our chorus line?"

Carolyn, always thoughtful and with a wry sense of humor, seemed to consider the question for some time. "You know, if one of my fellow lunatics in the insane asylum had come to me six months ago," she said with an ironic smile, "to warn me that I was to be abducted by western savages, taken to live in an Indian village in Wyoming Territory, and there asked to perform the cancan, I would have known that woman had been justly committed. Yet here we all are . . .

"In answer to your question, Lulu, I must tell you that in our church, dancing was strictly forbidden — it was considered to be the devil's recreation, leading to debauchery, fornication, and adultery. Therefore, I have never had occasion to learn how. However, I did once express my mild interest in the art form to my husband, the minister, wondering idly what it would be like to dance a lively Virginia reel. He responded that if I did not put such impure thoughts out of my mind, I risked going to hell, where I would be condemned to dance for eternity in the flames with the rest of the sinners."

"Mon Dieu!" said Lulu. "But I would much rather dance in hell than go to your church! And if you are to be sent there just for thinking about dancing, I can learn you a few steps much more interesting to take down with you."

"Very well," said Carolyn, "you've convinced me, Lulu. I shall give it a try."

20 May 1876
Last evening several Cheyenne women, among them Chief Little Wolf's first wife, Quiet One, his second wife, Feather on Head, and his daughter, Pretty Walker, came to our lodge and presented us with a peculiar gift — seven individual coiled pieces of thin braided rope, which when unwound revealed two long branches attached to the first length. We were pleased to find that both Feather on Head and Pretty Walker speak a good bit of English, taught them evidently by May Dodd. When it became clear to them that we had no idea what we

319

were to do with these items, Pretty Walker demurely parted her deer hide skirt and revealed its purpose. The first length of rope encircled her waist as a kind of belt, knotted in front. The two attached branches passed down between her thighs on either side of her private parts, which themselves were covered by a kind of loin cloth. Each branch was then wrapped around her upper legs nearly to her knees.

"Brilliant!" said Lady Hall. "A primitive chastity belt. How charming."

The Cheyenne women then went about taking what appeared to be general measurements of each of us, which process consisted of looking us over critically, spinning us around and touching us lightly here and there, with a little chattering between them, which, of course, we did not understand. Nor did we understand the exact purpose of this examination, although our actress Lulu suggested that we were being measured for costumes.

"You know, before I took up with Helen," said Lady Hall idly, as one of the women took her measure, "— a liaison that scandalized all of British society, I might add — I was married for two years to Sir John Hall of Dorchester. In the matter of chastity, I'm afraid that my horse has long since left the barn."

"What horse?" asked Lulu, as another woman spun her around.

"My virginity, dear. It is only an expression."

"If m'lady doesn't object," said Hannah, "I would like to wear one of those strings. You see . . . my horse is still in the barn, and I should like to keep her there."

"Of course you would, Hannah," said Lady Hall. "And if you wish to be bound up like a trussed chicken, far be it from me to stand in your way."

"My horse was stolen from the barn when I was thirteen," said Lulu. "I have never seen it since."

"That's the way it is with virginity, dear. Once it leaves the barn, it never returns."

When the Cheyenne women had finished with us, they took their leave.

We know now the purpose of their measurements, for they returned this evening, bearing the most beautiful deerskin dresses for us to wear to the dance, exquisitely embroidered with trade beads and beaver quills. The workmanship is magnificent, especially considering the short amount of time in which it has been accomplished. In addition, the dresses are wonderfully comfortable, draping over our bodies like second skins. Just trying them on, and admiring each other, made us feel a bit more as if we belong. We scarcely know how to thank them.

This evening Quiet One and Pretty Walker also brought May Dodd's daughter, Little Bird, with them to our lodge. Also accompanying them was my friend, the Arapaho girl Pretty Nose, whom I had not seen since our arrival in the village. Little Bird, or Wren as the Kellys tell us May called her daughter, is a beautiful baby. We are all struck by the fact that she is fair of skin, with light brown hair, and blue eyes, whereas Little Wolf himself is quite dark. She clearly takes after her mother. I asked if I could hold the child, and when Pretty Walker placed her in my arms, I promptly, and without any warning whatsoever, burst into tears. The weight and warmth of her little body wrapped in a blanket brought back such vividly painful memories of my own daughter's infancy.

Because the Cheyenne women seem so generally stoic, as, indeed, does the Arapaho girl, Pretty Nose, I was surprised when, upon my outburst, she also began to cry, turning away from us, and covering her eyes.

I gently handed Wren back to Pretty

Walker, approached Pretty Nose, and took her in my arms, her body shaking as she sobbed. When finally her trembling began to subside, I took her broad brown face in my hands, her warm tears running between my fingers. She kept her gaze diverted from mine, her expression one of inconsolable heartbreak. She did not know that I had heard her story, for we had not spoken of such matters when we were riding together, both preferring to keep our respective sorrows to ourselves. Finally, she looked me directly in the eyes. In that long moment, she, too, knew everything about me, and we were bound forever in the confederacy of grieving mothers. I put my arms around her again, and she hers around me . . . we held each other and we wept.

21 May 1876
The night of the dance is fast approaching and we are all quite nervous about it. Increasing our trepidation, this evening we were visited by a character named Dog Woman, who is evidently in charge of organizing all important tribal social events, and whom Pretty Walker brought to our lodge. I say "character" for the Cheyenne refer to her as *he'emnane'e,* which translates to half-man half-woman. We frequently see

Dog Woman about the village, for he/she is much in demand as a matchmaker, with special powers in all matters romantic. Sometimes dressed as a woman, and sometimes as a man, he/she is said to possess the characteristics of both sexes, which evidently earned him/her the status of holy person.

In this particular instance, Dog Woman arrived dressed as a woman. Between Pretty Walker's English and our more limited sign language, we came to understand that the purpose of her visit was to get a sense of which available young men might be the most suitable partners for each of us at the dance, with the goal being that these pairings will quickly lead to matrimony. It was one thing while we were traveling to idly speculate about our future as the brides of Cheyenne warriors, quite another now that the reality of the moment approached in the person of this distinctly peculiar matchmaker.

Dog Woman, whom I must say cannot be counted among the comeliest of the Cheyenne, was dressed in a white woman's gingham dress that must have been purchased at the trading post. She looked us each up and down, touched us lightly here and there, for what purpose we did not know, grunting and muttering all the while in varying tones running the spectrum from approbation to disapproval, alternately nodding and shaking her head crankily. However, when she reached Lady Hall, the Englishwoman held up the palm of her right hand in the universal sign for "stop."

"Do not lay hands on me, madam," she said, in her most commanding tone of voice. "I dislike being manhandled . . . or woman-handled . . . by strangers."

Dog Woman stared at m'lady for a moment, then smiled and nodded her head with a certain self-satisfaction, as if she had come to some important conclusion. Then she moved on to her cursory examination of the next one of us.

We have begun rehearsals for the cancan performance, our largely preposterous efforts thus far providing a bit of comedy to leaven our anxiety, while at the same time increasing it. As we laugh at ourselves and at each other, we do so fully aware that we risk becoming a laughing-stock for all at the dance. Even the irrepressibly optimistic Lulu, our sole "professional," is beginning to express grave misgivings regarding the negligible . . . dare I say, nonexistent talents of her thoroughly amateur troupe. *"Mes chères filles,"* she said, shaking her head sadly during our first rehearsal, "my darling girls, but that is no cancan you dance; that is old ladies shuffling along in the park with their canes. Can you not make your kicks more higher, more energetic than that? You must point your toes to the heavens. My teacher Finette always say, 'Imagine that you kick the stars from the sky.' "

"You know, Lulu," I suggested, "kicking the stars may be setting rather too high a goal for us at this point. Everyone is exhausted from working all day, stooping and bending and carrying. What about if we just imagine kicking one of the mean dogs who prowl the village. Would that not be more realistic?"

It is true that there are a number of dogs in the camp, and some of them quite large shaggy animals. We understand that they are kept primarily as beasts of burden when the tribe travels, carrying small parfleches, and sometimes young children, also as watchdogs and as a source of food, the Cheyenne being particularly partial to tender young puppies, either boiled or roasted over the coals. For the most part, the dogs are friendly enough, but perhaps because we are still perceived by them as outsiders with a different scent than that of the natives to whom they are accustomed, some growl threateningly at us when we pass the lodges in front of which they sleep. They sometimes even make little feints to snap at our heels, which is when a good kick comes in handy.

Perhaps the most fun at our rehearsals is had by Astrid, who, because she is not participating, has the luxury of watching our foolishness and critiquing it. I should mention that the Kelly twins have not yet reappeared. Nor have we had any further news or sight of them, or of Martha for that matter. We have also not yet had the pleasure of meeting the negro woman, Euphemia, or Nexana'hane'e, Kills Twice Woman, as the Cheyenne call her due to her exploits on the battlefield. We catch a glimpse of her about camp now and then . . . truly she is a majestic being.

In the matter of music for the performance, trombones and tubas being clearly out of our reach, we have, thanks to the assistance of Pretty Walker, managed to secure the services of two tribal flute players, a pair of renowned drummers, a fellow who is gifted in the use of rattles, another a master of whistles, and yet another who blows an instrument made of a buffalo horn. It is a strange kind of orchestration, to be sure, but as with everything here, we make do with that which we have.

The flute is proving to be our most versatile instrument. It is widely used by the Cheyenne, for the pure pleasure of its tone as well as for romantic conquests. Indeed, there is a renowned flute maker in the camp said to have the ability to imbue his instruments with the power to make any woman fall in love with the respective flutist. Nearly every evening, we hear the music of a lovelorn suitor wafting gently over the village, sometimes romantic, sometimes even with a touch of tragedy in its tones. It is, after all, springtime, the season of love.

Lulu has assembled the musicians and is trying to teach them the 2/4 time signature, at the same time as she is trying to teach us the correct steps. Besides the high kicks she asks of us, the dance itself is a fairly simple concept, for similar steps are employed in many international folk dances. Most of us are picking it up rather quickly . . . with the exception of Lady Hall, who, as she readily admits, has two left feet. At the same time, she does not seem to recognize her own lack of natural rhythm, nor does it prevent her from having a wonderful time at it. "Ever since my Helen and I witnessed the scandalous performance," she said, "I must admit that I dreamed of the sense of abandon dancing it myself might give me . . . although I never imagined that I should have the opportunity, least of all in a setting such as this."

The music is rather more complicated than the dance steps themselves, for the natives employ a decidedly different beat and rhythm than do we, a pulsing, hypnotic sound overlaid by what to our ear seems at first a wildly discordant chorus, a descending stair-step pattern, repetitive but oddly melodic. It is the music of nature and the wilds, of the landscape itself — the rolling plains, the rushing rivers and burbling creeks, the wind sighing through the grass, shrieking across the winter prairie, the wolves howling, the buffalo hooves pounding the earth. It is the sound of the seasons passing generation after generation, the ancient history of the land and of the people palpable in the beat. The delicate job of choreography for poor Lulu is to somehow meld these very different styles while still allowing the particularities of each to come forth.

Then, of course, there is the not inconsiderable problem of costumes for our dance troupe. Those that Lady Hall described from the performance she and Helen had witnessed in London are clearly not to be replicated here. In addition, out of respect and gratitude to the Cheyenne women, we are obligated to wear the beautiful deer hide dresses and beaded moccasins they made for us with such exquisitely painstaking workmanship. Indeed, we very much wish to wear them, both because they are lovely and as a further sign of our desire to assimilate into their world.

The fire burns low, exhausted, time to sleep . . .

23 May 1876
The Irish twins have resurfaced at a most timely moment, coming to our rescue with what we think will be an acceptable compromise costume. They arrived at our lodges this afternoon, just after we had returned from our labors, which today, in addition to our daily water hauling duties, consisted of digging tubers with the other women in the meadows surrounding the village. This is accomplished with a wooden spadelike instrument, and is not such easy work. However, it was a beautiful day, clear with a deep blue sky, and we were thankful to be out of the timber, and not having to bear our burdens. As we dug our tubers, we sang in the spring sun, and our fellow Cheyenne workers joined us, teaching us some of their own tunes. The singing does help the time

to pass faster, and to make the work go a bit easier.

"Where have you go, girls?" asked Lulu of the Kellys upon their arrival. "What is in the bag you carry?"

"We heard you girls were puttin' on a dance performance," Meggie answered. "It's the talk a' the village. So we've been pluckin' prairie chickens for ya."

"*Mais pourquoi?* . . . why? For what?"

"For your costumes, lass, what else?" said Susie. "We saw the handsome dresses the Cheyenne made for you while they were workin' on 'em. But they ain't exactly cancan outfits from the way you've described them. So Meggie and me figure you could all make little tutus with these feathers and throw 'em right over the dresses just for the performance. Quick change a' costume, you theater folks might say."

"But that is a splendid idea!" said Lulu.

"Course it is," said Meggie. "And what's more, the People love feathers. Maybe it'll even make your dance look a wee bit less peculiar to 'em."

"*Mais non,*" said Lulu, "it is not peculiar. It is very nice and the girls are getting better . . . they can now kick as high as a tall dog's nose."

"Meggie an' me are goin' to dance with

you," said Susie.

"But you have missed the first two rehearsals."

"Don't you worry about us, Lulu. We are a pair of dancin' fools. Show us how it's done right now. We'll catch on."

And so Lulu held an impromptu rehearsal, and it's true that it did not take long for Meggie and Susie to reach our minimal level of skill. They are a welcome addition to our troupe — athletic little things, their natural energy and elfin grace encouraging us all to greater heights. I think we even dared to hope that perhaps our performance might not be such a disaster, after all.

For the tutus, we have all of us cut lengths of fabric from our old "white women" dresses, fashioning a kind of wrap-around skirt to which we have been busy for two nights sewing feathers. When it is time for our cancan, which Dog Woman has officially added to the dance program, we will simply tie the feathered skirts around our waists on top of the hide dresses. These we will grasp in hand and flip up during the dance, mimicking the action of the real cancan dresses, though in far more modest fashion. The leggings and moccasins beneath our dresses are considerably less titillating than stockings and heels, and very little in the way of flesh will be exposed during the performance. We have, however, drawn the line at wearing the chastity strings.

"You'll get rope burn dancin' in those damn things," Susie advised us. "We didn't wear 'em, either. For one thing, Meggie and me didn't have any chastity to protect. And for another, the Cheyenne boys are real gentlemanly toward the girls."

"That's right," said Meggie, "Cheyenne women are famous among all the plains tribes for their chastity . . . which is a funny thing because the tribe has long been great friends and allies of the Arapaho, whose lassies are notorious for bein' loose with their fannies. They say that when a Cheyenne lad starts to polish his knob under the buffalo robes, his father sometimes sends him off to visit the Arapaho for a bit, for he's almost assured of finding a lass or two there who will take care of his needs. Whereas, on the rare occasion that one of the Cheyenne lasses lets her castle be breached before marriage, it will never be forgotten by the tribe. She will be disgraced for life. No man will ever marry her . . . except maybe an old widower who needs someone to do the housework. And see, that makes most of the lads real respectful toward the lasses, makes 'em behave themselves until they're married . . . aye, sometimes the boys won't even go at it on their wedding night. They'll wait four, five days, sometimes even a fortnight 'fore they finally get around to chargin' their weapons. Up to then they just like to lie under the buffalo robes and chat it up with their bride by way of breakin' the ice."

"I find that quite charming," I said. "I've never asked you sisters this, but are you planning to remarry now?"

"No, we already told the old cock twat Dog Woman not to be wastin' her time makin' matches for us," said Meggie. "We're way done with romance. We got more important business to attend to."

"What kind of business?"

"Killin' soldiers. We've joined the women's warrior society Pretty Nose and Phemie set up. We're in training. That's what we been up to these past days."

"And you really intend to go to war?"

"War is comin' to us, Molly, we don't need to go to it. And when it does, me and Susie are goin' to be ready this time. Right, sister?"

"Right as rain, Meggie. Two fiercer warriors than the howlin' Kelly twins the soldiers have never before witnessed. When they see us ridin' down upon them those boyos will shite their pants."

The Kellys' talk of war has made me realize that I have barely mentioned our good Chaplain Goodman since his misadventure upon our arrival . . . so busy have I been with our own affairs. My neglect is also partly due to the fact that we have seen very little of him, for he is installed in a lodge in the village itself, whereas we, due to a matter of protocol, were forced to locate on the edge of it.

We catch glimpses of Christian on the way to and from our labors, and sometimes we manage to exchange a few words. He seems already to have taken exceptionally well to this way of life. The same women who beat him with sticks have sewn him several handsome native outfits, and due to Hawk's recounting to the village of the chaplain's desertion from the Army and his long vision quest alone in his cave, he has been accepted by the Cheyenne as a holy man. The natives are great admirers of such behavior. In addition, Christian catches fish in the river each day and distributes them to poor and elderly people in the village, and anyone else who wishes to have them.

There is a distinct economic hierarchy

here we are discovering, for a family's wealth is based upon the man's abilities as both hunter and warrior. Prowess in the hunt provides the obvious sustenance required to feed the family, as well as the accumulation of hides for trade, for covering tipis, making clothing, bedding, and the other accoutrements of comfort; while a successful warrior is one who is both fearless in battle and adept at stealing horses during raids upon other tribes, and in capturing wild horses. The more horses one owns, the more lodge poles one can transport, therefore the larger and more comfortable are one's tipis. Inevitably, there are men in the tribe less gifted, less brave, or simply less lucky in life, and their families lead a relatively poorer existence. In this manner, it is not so different than our own society and economy, just considerably wilder.

The wealthier Cheyenne also take care of their less fortunate tribal members; they take in or at least support the families of warriors felled in battle, and they provide for the elderly and the infirm. In this way, the selfless actions of Christian Goodman are greatly respected. He is a simple, earnest boy . . . I don't know why I call him a boy, as he is nearly my same age, but his ingenuous good nature has such a childlike quality to it, which, finally, I think, is what allows him to adapt so apparently effortlessly to this new life. Of course, he also has the luxury of not having to worry about being married off by Dog Woman to the suitor of her choice, as do we girls. Should he decide to take a bride, he is free to choose his own. Nor, of course, is he required to dance the cancan with us . . .

It occurs to me that I have hardly mentioned Hawk in these last pages, either, for the simple reason that I have not laid eyes on him since we arrived . . . and here I thought we were unofficially engaged . . . Still, I harbor a small hope that I will see him at the dance . . . Good Lord, does that not sound like the diary entry of a lovelorn schoolgirl?

■ ■ ■ ■

Ledger Book VII
The Strong-heart
Women's Warrior
Society

■ ■ ■ ■

Violence begets but more violence, and from it we learn that there are no limits, no boundaries to the savagery, the butchery of which human beings are capable. Nor can there be any understanding of it, or coming to terms with it. I hope it is true that the meek shall inherit the earth, but in the meantime, sadly, this is the world we have inherited.

(from the journals of Margaret Kelly)

14 May 1876

Me and Susie have left the greenhorns to their own devices. We figure we've babysat them long enough, have done our job by bringing 'em this far. After all, that's what we said we would do, and we weren't all that thrilled about the idea in the first place. Now it's time for them to start sortin' things out themselves, makin' their own way in the village. Aye, and we must say, it's a relief not being any longer responsible for 'em.

So we're turnin' our attention to our own business . . . the important business of war, of vengeance, preparin' to kill soldiers, which moment me and Susie have been living for since they took our wee babies from us. Because they proved themselves in battle during the Mackenzie attack, our Phemie and Pretty Nose were both named war chiefs by the tribal council, and have been given permission by the elders to form a women's warrior society. It is said that there have only been a handful of women chiefs in the long history of the tribe, and only occasionally in times of need when the number of men warriors has been reduced, or when a special woman, or two, comes forward to fill the role . . . Aye, and this is such a time, and Pretty Nose and Phemie are such women.

The men themselves have seven such warrior societies, each with their own specialty and way of bein': the Kit Fox Men, the Elk Soldiers, the Dog Soldiers, the Red Shields, the Bowstrings, the Chief Soldiers, and the Crazy Dogs — this last mostly young warriors, known for their recklessness and the need to prove themselves in battle . . . it is with them our lads rode on that terrible day they took the Shoshone baby hands . . . and brought the vengeance of gods down upon us.

Given the right to name their own society, Pretty Nose and Phemie call us Imo' yuk he' tan à'e — it's a mouthful in Cheyenne, to be sure, but in English it means Strong-heart Women. Me and Susie went to our first meeting today, held in a special ceremonial lodge Phemie put up near her and her husband Black Man's tipi. Only we members of the Strong-heart Women, or those

342

personally invited, are allowed to attend these meetings. And everything said or done there is to be kept secret. It is explained that if we even speak of it to others outside the society, we risk bringin' bad fortune upon us when we go into battle.

When the meeting is over, we ask Phemie in private whether she really believes this or not, for it seems to me and Susie a wee superstitious, though we're gettin' more and more that way ourselves. "It does not matter whether I believe it or not," she answers, "or whether you girls do. All that matters is that the Cheyenne believe it, and in so doing it becomes our reality. In order to attract the best women and to keep them, we must respect their traditions, their beliefs and taboos . . . their superstitions, if you like. If we start talking around the camp about what happens here, even to your friends, word will get out that there has been a breach in our secrecy, and once that happens the Cheyenne women in our society will begin to lose faith in our power, they will begin to think we are going to fail in battle. And then we surely will fail."

Still, me and Susie figure it's OK for us to write down what happens in our meetings, for these pages are private and if ever they are read by anyone else, which is not likely, that means we're dead, and the story itself will be as cold as our corpses.

All the men in their warrior societies have bird or animal spirits upon whom they count to protect them in battle, to make them strong and victorious, and, in some cases, even bulletproof. Figures of these they paint on their war shields, or on their horses, or on their own bodies, our dear Helen famous among the warriors for decorating them with her artwork. Most warriors carry amulets associated with their chosen bird or animal, and attached to their war costumes or their hair — a wing or bird skin, a tail, a tuft of fur, a bone — and some, like Hawk, learn to speak the language of their creature. Phemie has adopted as her animal spirit protector the sandhill crane, for the female of the species is considered the bravest of birds, and if wounded and unable to fly, will fiercely stand her ground to defend her young, will even attack a man. Phemie has learned to make the strange warbling cry of the crane, and we can well imagine how eerie that must sound to the enemy as she rides into battle, for it is damned chillin' even to our ears. She has encouraged each of us to choose a bird or animal as our protector, and me and Susie are discussin' the matter. We wish Helen were here to help us make our choice, for she knew more about the animal world than anyone. We're thinkin' a' askin' Lady Hall if she has any such advice, because she knows her stuff, too.

17 May 1876
The last few days, Phemie has been instructing us in the art of making war. Being city girls ourselves, and having always relied on our husbands and the men of the tribe to provide us with game since we been here, me and Susie never even learned how to shoot a bow and arrow, or a gun for that matter, although in Chicago we carried knives in our handbags, especially during times when we were plying a certain trade that doesn't need to be mentioned by name . . . for now and again we had some real rough customers seekin' our services.

But we're both competent on horseback by now. I'd even say we ride as well as do the Cheyenne women themselves, and most of them don't know how to handle weapons, either, that not being part of a girl's upbringing in the tribe. After a couple days of target practice on the ground with bow and arrow, revolver, and rifle, Phemie and Pretty Nose are now tryin' to teach us how to shoot these weapons from a runnin' horse, which is no easy trick, we can tell you.

Even trickier than that is somethin' they can do, and some of the best but not even all the men warriors can manage. That is, while their horse is at a dead run, they slide from its back onto its side, holdin' on to its mane with one hand and keepin' one foot hooked over its hip. Hangin' on to the side of the horse like this, with their other hand they can shoot a revolver or even a repeatin' rifle under the horse's neck, yet the enemy has no visible target of them to aim at, their own bodies bein' protected by the bulk of the horse.

It's a neat trick . . . course, Phemie has those beautiful long arms and legs to wrap around and hang on with, and Pretty Nose, though not a tall girl, is strong as can be, a fine horsewoman and excellent athlete. Me and Susie are sprites compared to those two — we don't have the reach of Phemie, or the strength of Pretty Nose. Still, we're agile girls, and because we don't weigh a lot, with a little practice we've come at least to be able to slip onto the side of our horses and hang on like that at a run. But we don't dare yet try to shoot from that position. Aye, you fall off a runnin' horse from that position, and you got a big problem, not the least of which, assumin' you survive the fall, is that now you're on foot, totally exposed to the enemy.

Even the other Cheyenne women in our society have not risked tryin' that trick just yet, though all are real competent on horseback. Of these so far there are but four, though Phemie is still tryin' to recruit others. One is the tough old bird Kills in the Morning Woman, who Molly coldcocked on our arrival here. We heard she earned that name some years ago after her son was killed in a fight against a small band of Pawnee warriors. The morning after, she went out all alone before dawn and tracked the Pawnee back to their war camp. She snuck in and killed the lot of them in their sleep, returning to the village with their scalps and horses, and the scalp of her son so that she could return it to him on the burial scaffold and he wouldn't have to go to Seano without his hair. Aye, this is a lass you do not want to get on the wrong side of, which is why we were surprised she took Molly's punch with such good nature. And they've actually gotten to be real friendly together,

Another girl who has signed up is a lass named Buffalo Calf Road Woman, who is the sister of the warrior chief Comes in Sight. The third is Vé' otsé'e, Warpath

Woman, who lost her whole damn family in the Mackenzie massacre — her husband, two children, mother, father, and grand-mother. All that loss has made her go a little crazy . . . as you might say have me and Susie, and ever since she has been tellin' the tribe to go on the warpath rather than waitin' for the warpath to come to us. "All we do is run and hide from the soldiers," she says in our meeting, "and wait for them to attack our villages when they find us. Why do we not find them and attack them first? Why do we not go on the warpath like we used to in the old days?" All we can say about this one is that we wouldn't want to be one of the soldiers who runs into her, either . . . or into any of us for that matter. Hell hath no fury like the vengeance of mothers.

18 May 1876

Another morning of war drills, ridin' and shootin', and learnin' how to work in teams of two, so everyone has a partner to look out for each other. Phemie says this is how her African people hunted and went to war. It's an easy lesson for me and Susie to learn, because we been lookin' out for each other that way since we were in the womb.

Phemie and Pretty Nose are also instructin' us on how to make war cries that chill the hearts of our enemies, as well as how to dress and paint ourselves in order to make those soldier boys shite their pretty blue pants when they see us comin'. Of course, the Cheyenne women already know somethin' about the war outfits, because they been helpin' to dress their men from the start, and no one looks scarier goin' off to fight than a Cheyenne warrior dressed and painted for battle, wearin' a headdress with a tail a' eagle feathers hangin' nearly to the ground.

Still, it's funny how shy the Cheyenne lasses are about fixin' themselves up this way . . . it ain't what they consider to be a real ladylike look, nor is a war cry a sound they've ever learned to make. It goes against everything they been taught all their lives — which is to cook, sew, embroider, erect tipis, butcher animals, flesh hides, dry meat, dig roots, haul wood and water, keep a tidy tipi, and raise the children, among all the other daily work of livin' in the wilds, all the while dressed real modest and demure, not like the men who are all peacocked up when they go off to battle. Yet me and Susie, descended ourselves from a warlike tribal people, have had no trouble at all summonin' up a battle cry that'll shrivel the bollocks of the soldiers, and no lasses in the tribe look scarier than the Kelly twins when we get kitted out in our battle outfits, faces painted and red hair wild about our heads . . . we look like a pair a' red devils.

"That is exactly what we want, ladies," says Phemie. "We want our band of women warriors, small though it be, to strike fear into the souls of the enemy when first they hear and lay eyes upon us. We want to appear before them as a vision of hell on earth such as they have never before seen in their lives, we want them to wonder who and what these creatures are riding down on them. One thing for certain is that these soldiers have never before faced a woman in battle. Of course, some have killed defenseless, unarmed women and children when they storm our villages, but they have never been attacked by a band of women. It is a great advantage for us to sow this sense of confusion in their minds, for all it takes is that one split second of hesitation, that moment of doubt on their part, for us to kill rather than be killed. I witnessed this myself in the Mackenzie fight when the soldiers saw me coming at them with my lance and shield. Of course, being a negro, as well, doesn't hurt, because most white boys are already scared of us."

After we finish the morning drills, Phemie asks to have a word with me and Susie in private. The three of us lead our horses down to the river together, and sit on the bank. The water is high and muddy with runoff now, and we see Christian Goodman fishin' nearby with a pole he made out of a willow branch, driftin' worms through the deep pools and pullin' up one fat trout after the other, which he throws up higher on the bank. He sees us, too, waves, and calls out: "Take some of these trout with you! Take all you want! They are biting today!"

"You know that boy is a Mennonite, don't you?" I say to Phemie. "His people don't believe in killing other human beings."

"Yes, I know," says Phemie. "I have met him. We have spoken. He seems a fine young fellow, and his committment against violence of any kind is a wonderful ideal. I very much admire his devotion to his faith. However, the ideal only works when all men adopt it, as in his community. I do not believe in killing other human beings, either. Except for the fact that they are trying to kill us. Sadly, in our world not to fight back or defend onself results in being imprisoned, enslaved, or exterminated by those who don't observe the same rules.

"I have not yet met any of the new girls

you brought here," Phemie continues. "But I wanted to ask if you think any among them are suited to be warriors in our society. What I saw of that Molly girl, and what you've told me about her encounter with Jules Seminole, leads me to believe that she would be a good candidate."

"Aye, we'd say she's your best bet, Phemie," says Susie, "she's a tough girl, and brave to be sure, but she doesn't like being told what to do. She has what you might call a problem with authority . . . maybe it's because of the time she spent in prison."

"She was in prison?"

"Aye, she murdered a man. We don't know who or why. She also lost a child, a daughter . . . don't know how that happened, either."

"One of the others," says I, "is an Englishwoman named Lady Ann Hall. Does that name ring a bell for you, Phemie?"

She considered this for a moment . . . "Yes, yes, that was the name of Helen's lover, wasn't it? She who wrote the letterpress for her bird portfolios."

"Aye, one and the same," says Susie. "She came out here lookin' for Helen. Signed up for the brides program hopin' to find her . . . and find her she did . . . at least found her bones on the scaffold."

"She is a tough lass herself," says I, "one you could depend on in a tough spot. She'd be worth signing up, but we don't know that she'd be willin', either."

"Anyone else?"

"The Mexican Indian girl, Maria Galvez, and the Norwegian, Astrid Norstegard, are neither of 'em sissies," says Susie. "They are competent lasses. Maria is a real good rider, and Astrid has picked it up quick. After that the French girl, Lulu LaRue, as she calls herself, and the Liverpudlian lass, Hannah Alford, are both sweet as can be, but definitely not warrior material. Nor is the preacher's wife, Carolyn Metcalf. She's a fine woman, and never whines, but she ain't strong enough, and hasn't the temperament to make war."

"So we would say that you might have four possibles outta the seven of 'em," says I. "Though you'll probably be doing well if you get one or two to sign up. You understand, Phemie, that these women, for all they have already endured, have not yet seen what we have seen. Their hearts are not hardened against the soldiers like ours."

We watch Christian fish for a while longer, until he's caught all the trout he needs, which he will distribute to the old and poor. He's gotten right popular with the Cheyenne. He comes over now and sits down next to us. He's already put on some weight in our time here, has filled out considerable since his days when first we came upon him and he looked like a damn ragged scarecrow. It is clear that this life agrees with him.

"I'm pleased to see you ladies out and about on this fine spring day!" says he, sweeping his arm from left to right, as if to take in the entire landscape — the lush river bottom, the broad green meadow stretching away to the timbered hills beyond, the sun shining above. "How can one not thank God for his bounty on such a day as this? For providing us with this beauty, with this fecundity of the earth, with fish to eat for our supper, a warm place to sleep at night, and dear friends with whom to share it all. What more does one need in life? . . . besides, of course, family."

"Nothing more than that, Christian, it is true," says I. "If only God would leave us in peace to enjoy it, to *make* families and to live on here without the sure knowledge that the soldiers are coming to exterminate us . . . again."

"Well, Meggie," says he, "you do know how to put a damper on one's high spirits on a splendid day."

"Aye, that's our specialty, chaplain," says

Susie. "We live in the real world where God sends soldiers to slaughter us and our infants . . . Even on a fine day like this, such things can happen, and we never lose sight a' that."

"And in preparation, Christian," says I, "we been training for war today."

"Oh dear," says the chaplain, the good cheer in his face now darkening another shade, like a cloud passin' before the sun. "Yes, as you well know, I have seen the soldiers in action myself. But it is not God who sends them, that you must understand, it is men themselves."

"Aye, but then what good is he if he can't stop 'em?" says Susie. "What a dirty trick for God to make the earth such a beautiful place, and the men who live upon it so hateful."

"Not all men," says Christian, gently. "And you, Euphemia, it is said around the village that you are a warrior woman, yet you seem to possess a spirit of great calm. What think you on this matter of men and God? Of war and peace?"

"I wish all men were like you and your people, Chaplain Goodman," says Phemie, "truly I do . . . . whites and Indians alike. The world would surely be a better place. I must say that my people are not innocents, either. My tribe, the Asanti, are the greatest warriors in Africa. Indeed, our name itself means 'because of wars.' You see, we are warriors, we exist, because of wars. For not to be is to perish. In this same way, the Cheyenne pride themselves on being the best fighters on the plains. From an early age, a boy is taught that his primary responsibility in life is to go to war. Because his father is often away, occupied in the business of making war, or hunting, stealing or searching the plains for horses, it is his grandfather or another wise old man in the village who instructs the boy in the manly duties of fighting. Before he goes into battle for the first time, the grandfather tells him: 'When you charge the enemy, do not be afraid, do as the other men do. When you fight, try to kill and count coup, it will make a man of you, and the people will look upon you as a man. Do not fear death. It is not a disgrace to be killed in a fight.' "

Christian shakes his head sadly. "This is precisely the opposite manner in which I was raised," he says. "You see, because of our beliefs my father was never away at war, and so he himself was there to teach me the manly virtues. These are to follow the example of Jesus Christ — to love everyone, to live a life of nonviolence, nonresistance, and pacifism. We are taught that killing another human being is a sin, under any circumstances."

"Aye, that's a right pretty notion, Chaplain," says Susie, "but in this country among these people that kind of upbringing would get your family, and you, dead before you were outta your diapers."

"Just because we live in a violent world does not make violence right."

"It is not a question of right or wrong, Chaplain," says Phemie. "It is a question of survival — life or death."

"But you see, for my people," says Christian, "it is only a question, and a rather fundamental moral one at that, of right and wrong. Is it right, for instance . . . is it a manly duty for warriors on a raid against an enemy, to cut the hands off infants, as did some of your young Cheyenne men — your own husbands, Meggie and Susie, didn't you say? — when they attacked the Shoshone village on the afternoon before the Mackenzie attack?"

"Aye, 'tis true, Christian," says I, "we been tortured by that event every day since, wonderin' if perhaps it was God's own retribution that set the soldiers upon us with such cold fury the next morning."

"God does not act in retribution," he

answers. "That is the way of mankind, for what does violence beget but more violence, more murder, despair, and heartbreak?"

And so the four of us sit in silence for a while on the riverbank, lost in our own thoughts. Finally, Christian stands and collects some of his trout in a burlap bag, leaving another one for us to fill, and more than enough fish to distribute to our own family and friends. We thank him, and he waves as he walks away, bearing his sack over his shoulder. "God bless you," he says in a quiet voice.

"That is a fine young man," says Phemie.

We continue to sit there on the sunny bank, just the three of us now, listenin' to the flowin' creek. It is a fine day, with the spring birds pairin' up, singin' and flirtin' in the trees, and we don't want to give up just yet this moment of quiet and peace. Maybe after our talk with the chaplain, who is so innocent and faithful to his faith, me and Susie feel a wee ashamed of our terrible thirst for vengeance. It is true that our stone hearts are a heavy burden to bear, but it seems to us that until we have our revenge we will never be able to set them aside. There ain't hardly a moment in the day . . . or in the night for that matter . . . aye, it is the nights that are the worst . . . not a moment when we do not feel the weight of our frozen babies hanging from our breasts, or see their wee blue faces in our dreams.

"And what about those baby hands, Phemie?" says Susie. "Our husbands had newborns of their own at home, and yet they slaughtered and mutilated Shoshone babies. We decided that night when we found out, that we could no longer live with 'em, we never wished to ever look upon 'em again . . . baby killers . . . what lower crime is there than that? How could we ever come to accept them again? We were fond of those boys, me and Susie were, but they deserved to die in the attack that morning . . . Yet Christian Goodman is right, ain't he? God didn't send our husbands on that raid against the Shoshone, nor did he send the soldiers against us. Those were the acts of men, yet God doesn't even have the power to stop 'em."

"Of course he is right," she answers. "He and his faith hold the moral high ground, of that there is no question. Violence begets but more violence, and from it we learn that there are no limits, no boundaries to the savagery, the butchery of which human beings are capable. Nor can there be any understanding of it, or coming to terms with it. I hope it is true that the meek shall inherit the earth, but in the meantime, sadly, this is the world we have inherited. Perhaps the only moral distinction we can make, and hardly a difficult one at that, is that in order to survive, we must fight against and kill soldiers, or be killed by them . . . but we do not kill babies."

"Aye, and the soldiers don't generally bring their infants to the battlefield, do they now?" says I. "That is where the tribes are so vulnerable. But I cannot imagine our women warriors, all of whom but you, Phemie, are mothers . . . or at least were mothers . . . I cannot imagine them killin' other women's babies. That's the business of men."

"We shall talk about such matters at our next meeting," says Phemie. "And just so you girls know . . . I, too, am going to be a mother."

Me and Susie are taken back by this news, for Phemie always said that she did not want to have children, and she even wore the chastity string to ensure against it. "Is that a wish, Phemie, or a fact?"

"Both."

"You must believe in a future then to bring a baby into this world."

"One day I neglected to don my chastity string . . . perhaps I did so on purpose for I have not worn it since. Black Man, who remained a patient and loyal husband through my long unavailability, took full advantage of the opportunity, and I confess that I have not objected. Now I have no other choice but to believe in a future."

"And you are going to carry that baby to war in your belly?"

"I have no other choice in that matter, either, do I?"

It is just then that we hear a commotion in the hills across the river, the war cries of our scouts, a sound we know all too well. Me and Susie feel the shivers and gooseflesh runnin' over our skin. Is it possible that the Army has discovered us? We all stand to gather our horses and return to the village, when suddenly we get a glimpse of a lone horseman cresting one of the far hillsides, headin' our way, his mount at a dead run, disappearing from our view into the swale on the other side, behind him five Cheyenne warriors ridin' hard in pursuit. A moment later the horseman crests the next hill, disappears again, and a third and fourth, our warriors closing fast behind him. Now he appears on the high bluff just above the riverbed, downstream from us. Here on the crest, he is forced to rein up suddenly for below him the hillside has been carved out by the river, forming a steep-cut bank of loose soil and rock, too treacherous to ride down, and surely impossible at a gallop. We get a bit of a look at him now. He is clearly not a soldier for he is dressed in a fringed buckskin outfit, and a broad misshapen cowboy hat cinched up to his chin with a rawhide tie-down, his face thus obscured. We see now that he rides not a horse at all, but a big gray mule. He looks behind him, clearly sees the warriors closing in, their war cries louder now, though they are not yet visible to our view. And damned if he doesn't urge his mount over the edge of the embankment. The mule sets its front hooves in the loose soil but begins to slide sideways, it looks like a sure wreck comin', like the poor beast is goin' to roll over with his rider. But somehow he manages to straighten himself and he sits back on his haunches, the rider too leanin' back in the saddle against the downhill pull. Together they slide down the embankment to the river below.

The warriors have appeared now at the top of the bluff, where they mill about on their ponies, clearly not plannin' to follow. The rider begins crossin' the high swollen river, his mule havin' to swim the middle part of it, until his hooves find bottom again and he splashes out on our side. Now he wheels his mount around, looks up at his pursuers, takes off his hat, gray braids spilling over his shoulders, waves it in the air at 'em, and calls out in Cheyenne. Me and Susie figure a rough translation is: *You didn't catch me, you sons of bitches! You didn't count coup on old Dirty Gertie, did ya now?* And then she whoops it up, laughin' an' flappin' her hat.

At this the head scout on the bluff, a fella named Medicine Wolf, raises his lance, shakes it at her, and returns her laugh in good-sport acknowledgment that she beat 'em fair and square.

Gertie turns her mule back around and sees us standin' on the bank upriver. She rides over to us, her fringed pants drippin' wet. "Well, I will be goddamned," says she with a smile, "fancy runnin' into you gals out here."

"You outdid yourself, Gertie," says Susie. "That was some entrance, even for you. But why were those scouts chasin' you?"

"Because I breached their perimeter, snuck right past 'em. It's a game we play. They knew it was ole Dirty Gertie all along, but by the time they figured out I had got through, I had enough of a lead on 'em. They wanted to catch me and count coup on me to save face for lettin' me sneak past. But my old mule here . . . for all his other fine qualities . . . cannot outrun an Indian pony, and it's lucky for us we came up on that cut bank when we did . . ." She pats her mule on the neck . . . "Ole Badger here knows how to slide downhill on his ass."

Gertie looks at Phemie, smiles, and nods. "Yeah, I heard from the Arapaho that you come back from the dead, Euphemia. That makes two of us."

"Hello, Gertie," says Phemie. "And I heard the same about you from them. I'm glad we meet again here, rather than on the hanging road to Seano that you and I were so close to taking."

"I'm mighty glad, too, darlin'," says Gertie. "Then again, we're all headed that way one of these days, an' some of us sooner than others."

"How did you find us, Gertie?" Susie asks.

"You gals always ask me that same question, and I always give you the same answer: I used to live among these folks, remember? I know all their favorite campsites. I figured Little Wolf would look for a protected valley, a little out of the way from his regular haunts, a place to hole up for a while and replenish supplies. They had nothin' much more when they escaped from the Red

Cloud Agency than the clothes on their backs, and pitiful little of those to boot. There ain't no richer country than this here. An' you know I've always had a good nose for an Indian village, I'm like a damned coyote that way, can smell it on the wind from miles away."

"You bring news for us, don't ya, Gertie?" says I.

" 'Deed I do, ladies, 'deed I do . . . but let's not get ahead of ourselves, let's not spoil our reunion just yet with talk a' business. I see you been fishin'," says she, pointing at the pile of fat trout Christian left on the bank. "I sure could stand to eat a couple of those beauties for supper. You gonna invite me to stay over, ain't ya?"

"Aye, a' course we are," says Susie. "You can stay with us as long as you like, Gertie, you know that. You come at a good time, for the Cheyenne are holdin' a dance in a few days to welcome the greenhorns and to pair 'em up with husbands. You should stay around at least long enough for that."

"You gals know there ain't nothing ole Dirty Gertie likes better than a damn Injun dance," says she. "It's been a real long time since I been invited to one. Hell, if I get the notion, I may even cut a rug myself. When I was your age, I could dance with 'em all night long. By the way, how those new gals doin', anyhow?"

"They're doin' . . ." says I . . . "still gettin' settled in, but we'd say they're doin' as well as can be expected. It was a long ride for 'em here . . . for all of us . . . some things happened along the way . . . unexpected things . . . you know how that is, Gertie."

"Yeah, things have a habit a' happenin' that way in this country, don't they?" says she . . . "unexpected like. I figured you gals'd have plenty of news for me, too."

"Aye, Gertie, you have no idea the news we got. We'll tell ya all about it over a trout dinner tonight."

19 May 1876
So last night me and Susie get Gertie all fixed up in our lodge, with a real comfortable backrest and sleeping place, and we share a fine dinner of trout grilled over the fire. We got an old widow woman livin' with us, Mó'éhá'e, Elk Woman. She's from the Southern Cheyenne band and lost her family at the Sand Creek massacre in Colorado in '64. Afterward she came to live with Northern Cheyenne relations, who are also gone now. She's all alone in the world, so we've taken her in. She looks after us around the tipi, and for our part in the

bargain, we see that she's got food, shelter, and a warm place to sleep. Our own needs this way are met by relations of our dead husbands, who hunt for us, bring us hides, and supply us with lodge poles. It is the Cheyenne way to look after their own, and though we don't have much, we got enough.

Because Gertie was living with the Southern Cheyenne at the same time and lost her own family in the massacre, she and Elk Woman know each other. They have a little reunion of their own, reminiscin' about old friends and family way back when. It is sweet and sad at the same time for me and Susie to listen to 'em . . . there is so much loss, so much heartbreak in this big country.

We tell Gertie about Martha, and about Molly's rescue of her from Jules Seminole, her return here to find her baby, and how she's still not right in the head. When we finish the story, Gertie sits real quiet for a time, thinkin' things over, her face set hard as granite.

"The son of a bitch," she whispers finally, shakin' her head. "When I got back to Camp Robinson after my visit with ya in Crazy Horse's village, I heard that right before they put Martha on the train to Chicago, the Army took her baby away from her and returned him to Tangle Hair. I

figured they didn't want her goin' home bearin' hard evidence of the brides program."

"That's what Meggie and me been thinkin', too," says Susie.

"I heard they sent an escort of two soldiers with her on the train," says Gertie, "and that they had to carry her on board, kickin' and screamin' for her baby. But how the hell did Seminole get his hands on her?"

"We don't know the answer to that, Gertie," says I. "She doesn't seem to remember any of it . . . or if she does, she ain't talkin' . . . before Molly got away with her, Seminole introduced Martha to her as his wife."

Son of a bitch," says Gertie again. "Jules Seminole's wife . . . real pretty fate to imagine, ain't it? No wonder she don't want to remember. All I can figure is that somehow she escaped her soldier escort and got off the train. She must have been tryin' to get back to her baby when Seminole came upon her. One thing I do know is that the Army has been loanin' him and his scouts out to guide private parties of cattlemen, land speculators, mine owners, and journalists. They want to prove to the white world that they got the region more or less secured from Indian depredation, that it's safe now for settlers. The government don't want to scare away the moneymen, or the homesteaders, with more stories about white folks gettin' scalped, which is about all the newspapers out here report anymore, even if they have to make it up. Martha musta run into Seminole while he was guidin' one of those bunches."

"Aye, the day Molly came upon him and Martha, Hawk's scouts reported a party of white men camped upriver from us, with some Crow among 'em. We figured that's what Seminole was doin' there."

"You mark my words, girls, I'm gonna get that son of Satan if it's the last thing I do on this earth. As if I didn't already have enough reason, doin' that way to our poor Martha just gives me more."

"She's a lot better than she was, Gertie," says Susie. "But we still don't know if she'll ever really be right again. We're thinkin' maybe it'd be better if she never remembers."

"I seen things like this before," says Gertie. "Hell, I been in this country so damn long now, I figure I seen about everything . . . I'll wager that somewhere deep down, some part of Martha remembers, and that one day, no matter how hard she tries to keep it buried there, that memory is goin' to bubble up to the surface like one a' them damn hot spring geysers. And when it blows, God knows what'll happen to her. I just hope you gals are around."

"Aye, now it's your turn, Gertie," says I. "We know you came here for a reason, so let's hear your news."

"You know, ladies, I been thinkin' on it all evening," she says, "and I decided we got some time for all that. I'd like to tell ya my news in front of the new gals, too. Saves me havin' to repeat myself. Things is happenin' back at the fort, that much I'll say right now. But they ain't gonna happen overnight. So if I tell ya now or I tell ya in a few days, it don't make no difference, see? I need to talk to Little Wolf about it first, too, seein' as how he's the Sweet Medicine Chief, and is the one who's goin' to call the shots. So let's don't get all worried about it just yet."

"Gertie," says Susie, "Meggie and me got worried about it soon as you rode in today. Aye, we know damned well you didn't come all the way out here just for a social visit."

"You gals know me too well. And maybe that's so. But why not we just call it a social visit these first few days. I got some catchin' up to do with other folks here, too. I'll let ya all know everything before the dance. Wouldn't be fair not to, especially if old Dog

Woman is fixin' the greenhorns up with husbands . . . because what I got to tell ya might change some a' their minds about that . . . or maybe it won't. One way or 'nother, it'll be a hoot to watch those gals meetin' their betrotheds, and Injun dancin'."

We tell Gertie that she's goin' to see more from 'em than just Indian dancin', but we don't spoil the surprise for her. It's funny, ain't it, how even though we all know there's another shit monsoon on the way, as Gertie calls it, we still manage to find somethin' to hang on to. Aye, we know more or less why she's come to see us again, we see the black storm clouds gatherin' on the horizon, we feel the cold wind blowin'. But still, me and Susie are lookin' real forward to the dance, too. It brings back memories of how it was with our group when we first came out here. We watch these lasses tryin' to settle in with the tribe, and it's like gazin' in a mirror with us and our old friends reflected back . . .

"Damn, we were so young and innocent then, weren't we, Gertie?" says Susie. "We had no idea what was headin' our way. Just a wee bit over a year now since we arrived, and look how the whole fooking world has turned upside down . . . it seems like ten years, and we feel like we're a hundred years old . . . and we sure ain't innocent any-more."

"Oh, hell, you pair a' Irish scamps," says she, "you gals ain't been innocent since you was five years old."

And we all get a good laugh outta that, because even though we know Gertie is only playin' with us . . . she's right.

22 May 1876
Gertie has been to powwow with Little Wolf, and this morning she's comin' to meet with us and the greenhorns. Me and Susie are nervous about what she has to say, for we been enjoyin' these past few days of not knowin' the full details . . . course we understand damned well that somethin' big is afoot . . . somethin' which is likely to involve more travelin,' more runnin' . . . and just when we're gettin' rested and settled in the new village.

We get there just about the same time Gertie does, and we can tell straightaway, just from lookin' at her face, that for now, anyhow, the social visit is over indeed. After she says hello to the lasses, she doesn't waste any time gettin' down to business.

"Ladies," she begins, "on May twenty-ninth . . . that's one week from today . . . General George Crook will be leaving Fort

Fetterman on the banks of the North Platte River, Wyoming Territory, with fifteen companies of cavalry and five companies of mule-mounted infantry — well over a thousand soldiers altogether, headed northwest toward old Fort Reno on the Powder River. For support he'll be travelin' with a mule train of one hundred thirty-six wagons and a couple hundred pack mules. This I know because Susie and Meggie's old pal here, Jimmy the muleskinner hisself, aka Dirty Gertie, will be meetin' up with 'em at Fort Reno to take charge of one a' them wagons, presently being driven by my assistant muleskinner, a fine boy named Charlie Meeker.

"At about the same time," Gertie continues, "the Dakota column, commanded by General Alfred Terry, will be marchin' out of Fort Abraham Lincoln on the western bluffs of the Missouri River, headed west toward the Yellowstone. Terry leads fifteen companies, nearly six hundred soldiers, including twelve companies of the Seventh Cavalry under the command of Lt. Col. George Armstrong Custer. And, ladies, that ain't all . . . a third force, the Montana column, commanded by Col. John Gibbon, is leaving Fort Ellis, east of Bozeman, movin' west to meet up with the Dakota column on the Yellowstone.

"The War Department is callin' this campaign the Bighorn and Yellowstone Expedition, the largest military force ever deployed on the Great Plains, the plan bein' to throw a net a' soldiers around all the remaining hostile Injuns — Lakota, Cheyenne, and Arapaho — still at large from the Black Hills of the Dakotas, south to the Platte River, and west to the Yellowstone. That, a' course, means these folks here . . . and you gals . . . yup, I'm mighty sorry to have to tell ya this, but you all are hostiles now, too.

"I should also mention somethin' I didn't bother to tell Little Wolf, because it wouldn't mean anything to him, and it don't change a thing. And that is, travelin' with Crook's column are five members of the national press, reporting for nine newspapers across the country — the *New York Tribune, The New York Herald,* the *Chicago Tribune,* the *Chicago Times, The Chicago Inter-Ocean,* the *Omaha Republican,* the *Cheyenne Sun,* the *Rocky Mountain News* of Denver, and the *Alta California* of San Francisco. See, the government wants to make it clear to the whole goddamned nation that not only is this the largest campaign ever against the Indians, it's also gonna be the last. The reporters have been invited along to confirm to the public that we're wipin' the blood-thirsty savages off this land once and for all, and it'll soon be secured for God-fearing American people . . . that is to say, the white homesteaders, miners, and ranchers who are takin' over this country in the name of God and manifest destiny . . ."

This news, that me and Susie had been more or less expecting . . . although maybe it's even worse than we expected . . . . the greenhorns receive real quiet for a long time, while everyone has a chance to think things over.

Finally Astrid breaks the silence: "What is manifest destiny?"

"Basically, it means that American settlers have the divine right," says Gertie, "givin' to 'em a' course by God his ownself, to steal the natives' land, even though it was deeded to 'em fair and square in the treaty of Fort Laramie in 1868. See, soon as gold was discovered two years ago in the Black Hills, the government real quick took the land back, said the treaty was no good anymore."

"And why does the government have a divine right to do that?" Astrid asks.

"Because God says so, because he loves us so much, honey."

"Why?"

"Because we're special."

"Why?"

"Yup, now you've got to the real question, missy," says Gertie, "and I can't tell ya that I have a good answer for it, either."

"I have been called many names," says Lulu, "many of them not so nice. But no one has ever before called me a hostile."

"Interesting, isn't it?" says Molly. "We went from being part of an important government program to help assimilate the Cheyenne, to being captives of the Lakota, to being fugitives without a country . . . and now, suddenly, we've become hostiles in the eyes of the United States Army. All without having done a single thing."

"Crikey, it appears that we are in the stew now, does it not?" says Lady Hall.

"Before I come up here," says Gertie, "I led my mule train along with General Crook's Army from Camp Robinson in Nebraska to Fort Fetterman. That was the first stage of the march. If you could see that mass of cavalry and infantry travelin' in formation across the plains — the support wagons and pack mules behind 'em . . . the whole goddamned shootin' match stretchin' out a mile long and a mile deep, yup, you gals'd get a real . . . good . . . sense of the stew you're in."

"How long before they reach us, Gertie?"

Molly asks.

"A force that big travels real slow, honey. It's lucky to make ten miles a day. They'll stop at old Fort Reno to rest up a spell. And they'll be waitin' there on their Indian soldiers to show up. Yeah, that's somethin' else I ain't told ya yet. Right now General Crook is travelin' with his three chief scouts — Frank Grouard, Louis Richaud, and Baptiste 'Big Bat' Pourrier. But he's got a hundred or so Shoshone warriors who have promised to join the command at Reno, and at least that many Crow. See, Crook likes to 'fight Injuns with Injuns' is the way he puts it, because Injuns know how Injuns think, so he enlists warriors from enemy tribes of the Cheyenne and the Lakota, or even members of their own tribes if they're willing. But I can't tell ya how long they'll stay at Reno . . . at least a week, anyhow, I'd say. An' I saved the best part for last . . . guess who'll be leadin' the Crow warriors and scouts? Yup, none other than our ole pal Jules Seminole. He ain't shown his face around any of the forts since he killed me . . . or at least thought he did. But I heard it from Big Bat that he's comin' here, wouldn't be like that bastard to miss out on the big show."

"But, Gertie, charged as a spy and a traitor," asks Molly, "if it were found out you were giving information to Little Wolf about the movement of the troops, wouldn't you be?"

Gertie nods. "Oh, hell, honey, they wouldn't bother chargin' me or goin' to the trouble of a trial. They'd just hang my scrawny ole neck from the highest tree."

"And yet you've worked for the Army for a long time?"

"Girl's gotta make a living, honey, which ain't an easy thing to do in this country. And what better cover for a spy and a traitor is there than workin' for the enemy? Still, I gotta say this again to you gals, especially to you, Meg and Suse: you know better than any that I seen a lot of death in my time in this country . . . way too much . . . a lotta real ugly death . . . men, women, children, babies . . . slaughtered . . . scalped . . . burned . . . mutilated . . . white and Injun alike, and my own babies among 'em. I'm tryin' to help these folks, see? and I'm tryin' to help you . . . But that don't mean I want to see a lotta soldiers killed, either. Many of these new young recruits from the East are immigrants just off the boat from all kinds a' different countries — Ireland, Scotland, England, Germany, Poland — you name it. They're just kids lookin' for room and board and a payin' job, and this is an easy one to get because the Army needs bodies to pump up the troops, and they'll take any able-bodied man who signs up . . . and some who ain't even real able. Hell, most a' these boys got nothin' against Injuns, they don't know a thing about 'em. They're just doin' what they're told to do."

"Aye, which is to kill the Indians they got nothing against, right, Gertie?" says Susie. "War is war. It's kill or be killed. Always been that way, always will be. They're on that side, we're on this side, and the side that kills the most of the other wins."

"Yeah, and what I'm tryin' to tell ya is that your side ain't gonna win. I know I can't talk you gals outta fightin', but you greenhorns, you could still make a run for it."

"And where would you propose we go?" Lady Hall asks. "And how would we get there?"

"I make the same offer I made to ya back in Crazy Horse's village. I'll escort ya south down to Medicine Bow station and put ya on the next train east. Why, I'd be doin' the Army a favor. Since they got all that press travelin' with 'em, they'd have some real trouble this time explainin' a bunch of dead white women among the Injuns after they kick your butts in another massacre . . . which, believe me, they will. And since the brides program has been abandoned and was a secret to begin with, chances are most a' you could melt right back into polite society . . . ya know, move to different towns, take on different names, become respectable white women again."

At this Molly laughs. "As opposed to white whores livin' with savages?"

"Exactly that, honey. Been there myself."

"Doesn't that sound like a lovely idea," says Carolyn. "And thus you escort us down to the train station, Gertie" — she holds her hands out to her sides — "dressed like squaws, correct? For you see, we have no other clothing than this. Nor, of course, do we have money for train tickets."

"I been savin' money outta my pay," she says. "I got enough for your train tickets, but maybe not quite enough for proper white women clothes for all a' you."

"That's very generous of you, Gertie," says Carolyn. "But imagine our reception at the station and on the train itself. And what would we do, each of us, disembark at random towns along the way, 'to melt right back into polite society' as you put it? You think the authorities wouldn't ask questions? You think news of our respective arrivals would not appear in the local newspapers?" She flips one of her braids off her chest. "You think the ladies of the town would welcome us into their homes for tea and biscuits, and admire our savage hairstyles?"

Gertie shakes her head sadly. "No, honey, I don't expect that'd happen," she says. "It's true that polite society ain't quite ready for you gals, you think I don't know that? It's never been ready for me, neither, because I never been a respectable white woman."

"Nor have we, Gertie," says Susie.

"Me neither," says Lulu.

"A girl can't get much less respectable than a life sentence in Sing Sing," says Molly.

"I beg your pardon," says Lady Hall, "not to try to set myself apart from or above you fine ladies, but I do consider myself to be quite respectable."

"Were that the case, m'lady," says Susie, "you wouldn't be among us, would you now? For neither was Helen respectable in the eyes of polite society. You two are outsiders, just like the rest of us, as was May, and that's how we all got here."

"Look, girls," says Gertie, "I was just tryin' to paint a rosy picture of a possible alternate future for you. 'Cause don't ya see? I'm tryin' to save your lily-white asses. You don't have much of a chance either way, truth be told, but you got a better one runnin' than you do stayin' with these folks and waitin' for the shit monsoon to strike again. An' the only thing I can tell you for sure is that it is bearin' down on you, from all sides, right now."

This gets everybody's attention, and a long quiet falls over the greenhorns, broken finally by Maria. "But I can never be a respectable white woman," says she, with a tone of some regret, "because my ass is brown."

And no matter how scared these lasses are by what Gertie has just told 'em, damned if we don't all manage a good laugh.

■ ■ ■ ■

Ledger Book VIII
Dancing Under
the Moon

■ ■ ■ ■

From those seated around the dance circle there arose assorted exclamations, growing in waves . . . of surprise? astonishment? shock? disapproval? appreciation? Perhaps they were enjoying our performance, or perhaps they wished to scalp us for it. We did not know, and what's more, we didn't give a damn . . .

(from the journals of Molly McGill)

26 May 1876
The dance has come and gone . . . and I hardly know where to begin to describe it . . . or all that came before . . . and after. There is much to tell . . .

The dance and feast were announced first that morning by the village crier, who walked through camp recounting the news that festivities would begin with the setting sun, and telling the people where they should congregate for the event. Next Quiet One, Feather on Head, Pretty Walker, and Pretty Nose came to our lodge, bearing shawls cut from bright-colored trade blankets for us to wear over our dresses, and bringing with them another woman, Alights on the Cloud, who is said to have big medicine in matters of romance. They led us down to the river, where they stripped us of our work clothes, bathed us ceremoniously, washed our hair, wrapped us in buffalo robes, and led us back to our lodge. There they rubbed us with bundles of sage and other wild herbs, slipped our hide dresses over our heads, draped the shawls around our shoulders, and rebraided our hair, into which they weaved small bones and shiny shards of metal.

Once again, Lady Hall did not submit to any of this, as she had made it quite clear that though she planned to participate in our cancan, and even wear a dress and tutu, she would not join us in the courtship dance to be put on display to the young men. Nor did she have any intention of being paired by Dog Woman with one of them. "I tried marriage once," she said, "largely for the sake of propriety. But, for rather obvious reasons of which I think you are all more or less aware, it simply wasn't for me."

"When May and the other white women came to us," said Pretty Walker as they worked upon the rest of us, "the People were very rich." She made the expansive sign language gesture that indicates great wealth. "We had many possessions from trade — white man bells and beads of silver and rings of gold, shiny rocks of glass dug from the earth, bright coins that flashed in the sun and in the flames of the fire. But now we are very poor. We had to leave everything behind when the soldiers attacked our village. We lost everything. Yet the soldiers took nothing, as we do when we make raids upon our enemies. They did not even take our food. They burned it all — our food, our hides, our riches, all burned. Now we are very poor. This is why we have little to give you for the dance, except the dresses we made and the shawls, and these few scraps of metal to shine in your hair. My father, Little Wolf, says it is a good thing for the People to be poor, for now we must learn to live again in the old way. But still, we wish we had pretty necklaces and rings to give to you."

"The dresses you made for us are beautiful," I said. "And the shawls, too, which will keep us warm in the night air. We have no need of those other things."

Now Alights on the Cloud arranged us in a circle, standing facing outward, and began to paint our faces, one by one, with various designs meant, presumably, to encourage romantic thoughts among young men. Despite that, Lady Hall agreed to be thusly made up, for Alights on the Cloud had worked with her friend Helen Flight and learned much from her artistry. "In addition to honoring Helen's talents by bearing the work of her apprentice," said m'lady, "I do not wish to call undue attention to myself by being the only paleface in the dance."

Pretty Walker instructed us to look straight ahead and not at one another. If we did not follow this procedure correctly, she said, we would break the sacred circle, which would make for bad medicine and spoil the entire evening. When Alights on the Cloud had finally finished painting the last of us, Pretty Walker told us to all turn around in unison, so that we faced inward in our circle. We did so . . . and stared at each other in a long moment of stunned silence, broken only by small gasps of astonishment. Although our identities were given away by certain personal characteristics — height, hair color, Lady Hall's breeches, etc. — the greasepaint rendered our faces virtually unrecognizable to one another, a transformation so complete that we had to consciously seek out these other features to identify who was who.

"May I be the first to say," remarked Lady Hall, finally, "that you ladies all look splendidly, fiercely savage. Why, I wager were we to look in a mirror, we would scarcely recognize ourselves, let alone each other. It's brilliant, don't you see? This allows us a liberating sense of anonymity. It is as if we are attending a masked ball, our true selves disguised, unrevealed. We are free to be whomever we wish. Yes, I believe we are going to dance tonight as we have never danced before."

Just before sunset, the Cheyenne women led us to the site of the dance. Drums beat rhythmically as a huge orange sun hung suspended over the western mountains, mirroring the flames from the bonfire. Seated in a broad circle around the fire were rows of tribal members, chatting animatedly while waiting for the festivities to begin, the dancers themselves beginning to assemble on the edge of the circle. Overseeing all this, the social director, Dog Woman, bustled fussily about. She wore the same cotton gingham dress, adorned by multiple bead necklaces around her neck, metal rings on her fingers and in her ears, and on her head an incongruous Abraham Lincoln–style top hat, from which protruded an array of eagle feathers. Dog Woman was assisted by a young woman whose name we later learned was Bridge Girl, but dressed as a boy, and said to be a Sapphist, the two of them scolding unruly children, changing seating arrangements, and adjusting the costumes of the dancers.

The men dancers wore face paint less

elaborate than our own, and magnificently feathered headdresses, their arms and leggings equally decorated with plumage. They looked like nothing so much as prairie roosters, practicing their dance steps and displaying to the hens. The women dancers were dressed more simply, in hide dresses and shawls not unlike ours, their faces unpainted, their moccasins and leggings trimmed modestly in fur. It occurred to me that so much of their culture is learned from nature, and as in the bird world itself, the male frequently has a brighter, more colorful and elaborate plumage than the female.

As the sun began to drop behind the mountains, the dancers took their places. This first was to be the welcome dance, by which we were to be formally introduced to the tribe, and the correct steps of which we had learned in our lessons. More drummers joined in now, their pulsing beat coming from different sides of the circle, echoing off the surrounding hills, joined then by flute players, followed by gourd rattlers, all together creating a strangely rhythmic, while at the same time discordant cacophony . . . a sound that civilized ears might at first hesitate to call precisely music.

When the native dancers were in position — the women in one row, the men in another — Dog Woman gave them the signal. They began to move slowly, lightly, gracefully, their moccasined steps in concert with one another, at the same time in harmony with the music, giving it further definition as if the dancers themselves were silent instruments, joining the orchestration. As they danced, the two lines, men and women, began to merge, though each individual continued to dance alone. They merged then parted again into their separate lines, merged and parted again, a kind of preliminary courtship dance that suggested they were not quite prepared yet to become partners.

Dog Woman now signaled to us, and we took our position in a line behind the Cheyenne women, where we could mimic their steps until we settled into the pattern. We began tentatively but soon were performing a credible version of the dance. The Cheyenne women now turned to face us, and we continued to dance in unison, the beat picking up in tempo.

"Bloody Hell!" said Lady Hall, "but we've got the rhythm now, ladies!" She herself danced with a somewhat exaggerated gait, her step more exuberant than it was graceful, although whatever she lacked in style, she more than compensated for with enthusiasm. "By God, I do believe I was born to dance!" she said, which remark elicited a good deal of giggling among the rest of us.

At another signal from the social director, we and the Cheyenne women danced forward until we faced each other directly, then back again, forward, and back. The men, too, turned around and danced behind the women, forward and back. Now as we danced forward the Cheyenne women parted so that we passed between them, and met the men dancing forward. Then the two lines of women turned around so that we faced each other, and danced forward, passing again so that this time the Cheyenne women met the men dancing forward. It was a dance as simple and hypnotic as the music itself, which all this while had been gradually increasing in tempo, so that the steps came faster. I don't remember exactly how many times we repeated these passes, three, four perhaps, but at some point the Cheyenne women faded out of the dance, and we were left dancing with the men. When we danced forward toward them and came face-to-face, they did not look us directly in the eye, as seems to be the way among these people. Yet we all had the sense that the man each of us met in this manner was the one chosen specifically by Dog

Woman to be our prospective mate . . . I confess a sense of deep disappointment that mine was not Hawk, nor indeed had I yet seen him here this evening. The music continued faster and faster, drums and flutes and rattles, the steps quickening equally, faster and faster, and we lost ourselves in the moment . . . until suddenly, and without warning, the music stopped . . . the dance was over.

We left the dance circle, and it took us a moment to catch our breath. There was now to be a short intermission after which we would perform our cancan, and then the general social dancing would begin, and the food roasting already on the fires would be served. Meggie and Susie now joined us, carrying the sack with our feathered tutus. They were in full face paint themselves, white with bloodred slashes on their cheeks, their eyes also rimmed in red, their curly hair unbraided, like wild red bushes growing from their heads. Although they are identical twins, we are usually able to tell them apart by certain differences so subtle that they can hardly be specified — a way of moving or reacting, a particular facial expression. Yet with their face paint they were virtually indistinguishable from each other, which renders them somehow doubly frightening; truly they looked like twin devils. With them was their friend Phemie, to whom none of us had yet been introduced.

"You lassies did real well," said one of them. "We could tell that the People approved of the way you danced. You were real respectful to the correct steps."

"Aye, and you all look good," said the other. "The paint agrees with you. This is our friend Euphemia Washington, an African princess and great warrior. She came to watch our cancan, and also to dance a step or two herself when the social dancing begins. She's shown the Cheyenne a few African tribal moves of her own. You will see, this girl can dance."

I am very nearly as tall as Euphemia myself . . . perhaps even as tall. I towered over my schoolmates as a child, and was taller than most of the boys. However, Phemie has such a presence . . . a kind of regal bearing . . . that when I stood before her now, I had the strange sensation, and perhaps for the first time in my life, that I was short. We all introduced ourselves briefly.

"You know who else is here, girls, don't you?" said one of the twins. "Sittin' right over there, with her baby in her lap? That's right, sittin' beside Gertie, it's our Martha come to watch. Now are you girls feelin' ready?"

"Mais oui," said our choreographer, Lulu, "but of course we are. The welcome dance was good warm-up, but now the real show begins. Costumes, my girls!"

All of us, including the Kellys, but with the exception of Astrid, who had chosen to sit this dance out, donned our feathered tutus. We had had only one dress rehearsal the day prior, and although Lulu tried, as usual, to put on her most positive face, she was clearly not impressed by our efforts.

Dog Woman signaled to us that it was time to return to the circle for our dance. Many more Cheyenne had arrived by now, and more continued to arrive. Later we guessed there were over three hundred people in the audience, possibly even a greater number, all seated in rough rows around the circle. With the village of tipis spread up and down the valley, none of us had any real sense of the number of residents here, nor had we ever seen so many together in one place. We have all noted since this adventure began that it is virtually impossible to find anything to compare our life here to the world we once knew, a notion that Meggie and Susie have repeatedly reinforced. However, that doesn't prevent us from trying to do so, simply in the largely vain hope of creating some small, familiar point of reference. The dance thus far was clearly no exception, except perhaps you might say that with the people of all ages gathering and seated, to me it bore some faint resemblance . . . yes, very faint, indeed . . . to a summer concert in the park in New York.

With the sun set and night descending, the crest of a full moon now appeared over the hills to the east. The fire behind us burned high, the flames flickering over the eager dark faces of our audience, young, middle-aged, and old, their brown eyes sparkling.

"Good Lord," said Carolyn, "look at them all . . . I had no idea we would be dancing in front of so many. I don't know that I can do it. My legs feel like they weigh a hundred pounds, I can barely lift my feet off the ground."

"But it is normal, a little stage fright," said Lulu. "Sometimes it is even good. Once the dance begins your legs tell you what to do, you will see."

"I think I am going to chunder," said little Hannah in a terrified voice.

"What does that mean?" asked Maria.

"It is a vulgar Liverpudlian term for vomiting," said Lady Hall, "which I have told you, Hannah, never to use in my presence. Nor are you going to do that. I forbid it. Steady on, girl. You are one of our most lithesome dancers, but with vomit all down the front of your lovely dress, you will certainly spoil the effect. Do I make myself clear, dear?"

"Yes, m'lady. I'm sorry."

"Right, lasses, I think that's quite enough talk of legs freezin' up and puke," said one of the twins. And then finally she identified herself: "It's time to put on our show. Meggie and me'll show you all how it's done. Start the music, Lulu."

"But Dog Woman does not yet give me the signal."

"Ah, forget about the old cock twat," said Meggie. Start the bleedin' music, Lulu. This is our show. And remember, girls, it's what everyone came to see. Let's give 'em their money's worth. And lassies — while we're at it, and given everything Gertie has told us we got to look forward to — let's even try to have a wee bit of fun, why don't we?"

Lulu gave the signal to her musicians, who were scattered about the circle. The drummers took up the 2/4 time beat she had taught them, and the flutists and the rattlers followed suit, the buffalo horn man blowing in where appropriate. Just as we began our little routine, with some modest warm-up steps, Astrid came into the circle and joined us beside Lulu. She wore a feathered tutu herself, where she got it we did not know, but she took up the dance in perfect step with the rest of us. "I could not be the only wallflower," she said. "Don't worry, I know all the steps from watching your rehearsals. I practiced in private."

"Wonderful!" said Lulu. *"Formidable!"*

The word "fun" has not been frequently springing to our lips these past days, weeks, months, and the notion itself seemed at first strangely out of context. Although we have shared a good deal of laughter in our time together — much of it ironic rather than joyful — I could not remember the last time I actually had fun . . . not in prison certainly . . . not since my daughter died . . . not since we moved to New York, except the good times she and I shared together . . . despite that man . . . And I think the others must have been thinking similarly. Yet Meggie's use of this common, yet oddly foreign word seemed to free us up somehow, to relax us, to make us realize that after all we had been through, and all the uncertainty of what lies ahead, perhaps we deserved to have a little fun. We felt a wonderful sense of camaraderie with everyone together in our own little performance, and suddenly I think we stopped worrying about how the Cheyenne would receive it — after all, under the circumstances, what difference did it really make? — and we began dancing for ourselves, for the sheer joy of it, which, after all, is the whole point. We danced first in a line, then with each other, switching partners as we had rehearsed, looking at our friends' bizarrely painted faces and preposterous homemade feather tutus, and we laughed, even the often dour-faced Astrid ... we laughed.

The enormous white moon had cleared the eastern horizon, and now illuminated the scene like a giant lantern. With the music increasing in tempo, we came to the final portion of our routine, the grand finale as it were. We danced back into our chorus line again, all nine of us — Meggie, Susie, Lady Hall, Hannah, Astrid, Maria, Carolyn, Lulu, and I — facing outward toward the people. "Remember, *mes filles,*" Lulu called out, "kick the stars from the sky! You can do it!" And so we did, or at least we imagined we did, which is the same thing really; flipping our tutus up, while laughing like madwomen, we kicked those stars right out of the sky.

From those seated around the dance circle

there arose assorted exclamations, growing in waves . . . of surprise? astonishment? shock? disapproval? appreciation? Perhaps they were enjoying our performance, or perhaps they wished to scalp us for it. We did not know, and what's more, we didn't give a damn. We danced with greater and greater abandon, we laughed and we kicked as high as we could. And now the people were laughing with us, or perhaps at us, what difference did it make? For they, too, appeared to be having fun. Some of the children now ran into the dance circle, kicking their legs up, squealing and falling down laughing from their efforts. This was clearly a gross breach of dance etiquette, for Dog Woman, having now completely lost control of the event, frantically tried to shoo them away. But there is power in numbers and the children were not to be denied their chance to do this wild new dance. They simply scattered like a flock of birds at her angry approach, coming back together to dance at another place in the circle. And then my little Mouse came to me dancing, kicking her slender, willowy little legs higher than any of us but Lulu had achieved. Her broad, brown face beaming, her eyes sparkling in the firelight, she took her place beside me and followed our steps perfectly.

We repeated our entire routine twice, dancing far longer than we had intended, until we were so out of breath that we had to stop. Which was just as well, for the social dance, with its unauthorized beginnings, was now well under way, more adults having joined the children in the circle. Mouse, too, with all the spritely energy of a six-year-old, danced off with her little friends. We had clearly forever earned the enmity of Dog Woman for fomenting this dance riot, for she scowled, scolded, and angrily wagged her finger at us.

As we were catching our breath, some of the young men who had danced with us at the welcome dance stood together a short distance away, having removed their head-dresses and with blankets wrapped around them, eyeing us out of the corners of their eyes in that curious manner the Cheyenne have of watching you without looking at you. Here again perhaps was something we could compare to our former worlds, the shyness of young men in matters of romance, a common behavior that transcends cultures and societies, savage and civilized, no matter how different their customs.

Dog Woman had joined the boys in close conference.

"The old twat is advisin' 'em," explained

one of the twins, unidentifiable again, "on how to cast love spells upon you lassies she matched 'em up with in the courtship dance."

"But my boy looked barely past adolescence," said Carolyn. "It is absurd. Are we to be married to children?"

"Aye, see, the Cheyenne have lost a good number of their warriors in these past years of the Indian wars," said the other twin, "and there are more younger men available for marriage than older just now. But some of 'em aren't as young as they look."

"I like the boy I danced with," said Hannah. "He seems my age."

"Mine is nice, too," said Maria.

"Aye, that's because you girls are still babies," said one of the Kellys.

"I am not a baby," Hannah said. "I am seventeen."

"And I, too," said Maria. "But I am old for my years, for when Chucho el Roto took me from my family, I am only twelve. I like to find a nice boy here."

"I have eighteen years," said Lulu, "and I have been with too many old men. I also prefer to marry a young, gentle man with soft brown skin who will be kind with me."

"Well, it's true that Dog Woman has a good eye for matchmakin'," said Susie.

"They say she can think like a man and a woman at the same time . . . which seems a stretch to Meggie and me . . . but we liked the lads she paired us with, too . . . aye, at least until they went off to war and murdered babies . . ."

"Here's what's going to happen now, ladies," said Meggie. "After Dog Woman gets finished givin' those boys instructions, they're goin' to come over to you, one by one, and take you aside. They're goin' to stand in front of you and open their blankets. That is an invitation for you to step inside, if you are so inclined. Then they'll close the blankets around you. You don't need to be afraid about this, they ain't goin' to hurt you, or try to have their way with you, they're just goin' to talk to you, by way of gettin' familiar. Aye, see that's how courtship works around here with the young lads. They'll tell ya about themselves, they'll talk about this and that — the dance, their family, the weather, they'll boast about their prowess as hunters, maybe they'll even tell ya a story — though, a' course, you won't understand any of it. And when they're finished, they'll open the blankets and let you go. See, that's just the first step. These boys are well brought up and real respectful."

"And what if we do not wish to get into the blanket with them?" I asked.

"Somehow me and Susie just knew you were goin' to be contrary about this, Molly," said Meggie. "Right, sister?"

"Right as rain, Meggie," said Susie. "You don't need to get in the blanket if the lad doesn't please you, Molly. You just shake your head no. He'll close it up around him again and walk off. He'll be humiliated about being rejected, and his friends will tease him, but he'll get over it."

"I am twenty-two years old," I said, "and the boy I was paired with looks to be about thirteen."

"Aye, Mol, don't try to kid us, girl," said Meggie, "we know damned well who you're holdin' out for. But don't get your hopes up. Our May got to marry the big chief Little Wolf, but you ain't her, and I'm sorry to tell you that you ain't goin' to get Hawk."

"You know, if I may just take this opportunity to say so, girls, I have grown tired of being unfavorably compared to your perfect little friend May Dodd."

"We never said she was perfect," said Susie. "May had her faults."

"Really? To hear you speak of her I never would have guessed. What kind of faults?"

"Truth be told, and God rest her soul, she

was a bit of a tart, our May was . . . though me and Susie are hardly ones to be throwin' stones in that regard."

"A tart? How so?"

"You seen that baby of hers, haven't ya, Molly?" Susie asked. "You think she looks anything like Little Wolf? May did the nasty with Captain Bourke before we even got to the Cheyenne. Aye, an' he bein' a good Jesuit boy, engaged to another at the time . . . She was a warm number, May, she seduced him recitin' Shakespeare — the Bard, she called him — that was Bourke's soft spot. The little girl you saw here in the village is his daughter."

"And why do you say I'm not going to *get* Hawk?"

"Because he is obligated to marry his dead wife's sister," said Meggie. "That's how it works here. And bringin' you, a white woman, into the household, is never a good idea. May herself found this out livin' in the same tipi as Quiet One and her sister, Feather on Head . . . that is, until they all eventually became friends."

I was crestfallen to learn that Hawk is required to marry his wife's sister, though I tried not to show it.

"Which is why we're telling you that when your thirteen-year-old dance partner screws

405

up his courage enough to come around and open his blanket and invite you in? . . . you might just want to reconsider your answer. Aye, given what's comin', believe us, you'll all need a man to protect ya."

"Perhaps, but I don't need a boy to protect me," I said. "I can take care of myself."

"I should say we've done rather well without men thus far," said Lady Hall, who had remained uncharacteristically silent during this conversation, clearly the notion of being wrapped in any boy's blanket of no interest whatsoever to her. However, now Dog Woman's assistant, Bridge Girl, herself clad in a blanket, approached and stood before Lady Hall, regarding her directly. "Good evening, Lady Ann Hall," the girl said in perfectly enunciated English, with a distinctly British accent. "I knew your friend, Helen. She spoke often of you. She was my special friend, too. She taught me to speak your language. I loved her." Bridge Girl smiled and opened her blanket wide.

Lady Hall looked at the girl for a long moment. *Bloody hell,"* she said, finally, with a smile, "my Helen, the devil! I should have known she would find herself a little friend out here. Yes, thank you, my dear, I don't mind if I do." She stepped inside the blanket, and Bridge Girl closed it around them.

"Didn't Meggie and me tell you the old twat had a canny talent for matchmakin'?" said Susie.

I decided to take my leave of the group then and return to our lodge. I did not wish to face my young partner with an open blanket. I was embarrassed, and more disheartened by what the twins had told me about Hawk's marital responsibilities than I had any right to be. After all, I barely knew the man, and he hadn't even come to the dance tonight. And yet I had fabricated and held on to a preposterous fairy tale about marrying him, as if by doing so I might have another chance . . . at what? I wasn't even sure . . . Peace? Happiness? Escape from my former life? Escape from my guilt over the death of my daughter? I already know perfectly well that there is no escape. Getting released from Sing Sing was the easy part, but I remain forever a prisoner of my memories. What a fool I had been to harbor these small secret dreams . . .

I could not leave without at least briefly saying hello to Martha and Gertie, and I went over to where they sat, with Phemie beside them. "I am so pleased to see you here tonight, Martha," I said. "How lovely you look. And such a handsome little gentleman."

Martha regarded me with an expression of some confusion. "But who are you?" she asked. "How do you know my name? Have we met?"

I looked at Phemie, then, who gave me a gentle smile and shook her head.

"Forgive me," I said, taking her cue. "It's just that I've heard so much about you from Meggie and Susie, I feel as though I know you. My name is Molly. Molly McGill."

"Ah, and you are one of the new girls?" Martha asked.

"Yes, I suppose you could say that. Did you enjoy our dance?"

"My friends and I used to dance," she said, "but except for Phemie, Meggie, Susie, and me, all the others have gone home now."

"Oh? And why haven't you gone home, Martha?"

Martha looked confused again, as if trying to remember. "Yes," she said nodding, "Yes, I was on my way home. But on the way, I lost my baby boy." She gazed lovingly down at her child. "My little Tangle Hair. I had to come back to find him."

"I'm so happy you did," I said. "And how is your little donkey, Dapple?"

"But you know Dapple?" she asked.

"Yes, I do. A fine little fellow."

"Why, he is doing splendidly, thank you

for asking. Now that you mention it, you do look vaguely familiar to me . . . perhaps I have seen you about the village?"

"Altogether possible," I said.

I took my leave then, with Gertie promising that we would have a visit soon in a quieter setting.

As I was leaving the dance, Phemie called me from behind. I stopped, and turned as she approached. "May I have a word with you in private, Molly?" she asked.

"Of course."

We stepped a bit outside the light cast by the fire. "As you can see, Martha still has a very incomplete recollection of events, and people," Phemie said in her softly beautiful, melodious manner of speaking. "But gradually, little by little, her memories are returning, though often imperfectly."

"Maybe that is the best way," I said.

"I know what you did for her, Molly. Susie and Meggie told me everything. And I know Jules Seminole all too well. You are a courageous woman."

"No, I am not . . . really . . . I was just trying to get away from him."

"But you took Martha with you, without even knowing who she was. You didn't have to do that. You could have left her behind."

"I wouldn't leave a dog behind with that

man if I could prevent it."

"One day, I hope we will have our chance to avenge Martha," Phemie said, "and the rest of our friends, for all that Seminole has wrought. It is that which I wish to speak to you about. As you must know, Pretty Nose and I have formed a women's warrior society. We meet privately, as tribal protocol dictates, and only members or prospective members are allowed to attend. In the short time that you have been here, you may already have heard mention of some of the men's warrior societies. Each of these has four young women attached to it, who are referred to as *nutuh'ke' â,* which means 'female soldier.' However, these girls are not actual members of the society, nor do they go to war. Their duties are primarily social — they attend meetings, they take part in the singing and dancing, and they cook for the men. They are usually pretty girls, all from good families, and it is considered an honor for them to be asked to fulfill this role, which they do in much the same way as a nun devotes herself to her vocation.

"I tell you this so that you understand the distinction between our warrior society and those they call female soldiers. You see, we actually train for war, and when it comes, we will fight side by side with the men.

410

Pretty Nose was given permission by the tribal chiefs to form this society because she has proven herself in battle . . . as, I believe, have I. We both fought against the Army when Mackenzie attacked our village . . . we counted coup, and we killed soldiers. I was gravely wounded myself and thought to be dead, but my husband, Black Man, came back for me. He took me to the Arapaho village of a chief named Little Raven. The medicine men there cared for me and brought me back to life. When we heard that Little Wolf had escaped from Camp Robinson, we came here to rejoin his band.

"All this I want you to know, because I wish to ask you to join our warrior society. I can see that you are a strong girl, and I know you are brave, even if you deny it. The Kellys tell me that you are also a quite competent horsewoman. All these are qualities I seek in my warriors. And one other . . . anger."

"Why anger?"

"Because it hardens the desire for vengeance." Phemie was wearing a pair of men's breechclouts, which she now untied and let fall to the ground; naked from the waist down, she turned her back to me, reached behind, and touched a prominent raised scar just above her buttocks, the waxy skin that covered it shining in the moonlight. "Do you know what that is, Molly?" she asked.

"No."

"It is a brand, the initials of my white slave master, burned into my flesh when I was eight years old, the same year he took me into his bed. I show it to you so that you know I understand the power of anger. It is for the reminder of this brand I have carried for most of my life, and will carry for the rest of it, that I am a warrior."

"I am so terribly sorry, Phemie," I said. "Such terror . . . such horror you must have borne . . . But you do not even know me. What makes you think that I am angry?"

"Meggie and Susie have told me you lost a child, though they don't know how. They said you were in prison for murder, though they don't know who you killed or why. They said you are willful and bullheaded, and don't take well to authority. That sounds like an angry woman to me."

I told Phemie that I appreciated her invitation, that no one had ever asked me to join a warrior society before. And I admitted that it sounded like a more interesting occupation than hauling wood and water, and digging tubers. But I also told her that I was not seeking vengeance, and I did not wish to go to war. "We saw soldiers die, Phemie," I said, "along with members of our own party, during the attack on our train — frightened young men who had never been west of the Mississippi. I will do what I have to do to protect myself and my friends, but I don't want to kill soldiers."

"Believe me, Molly," she said, "if you stay among these people long enough, protecting yourself and your friends will require that you kill them, or be killed."

I saw with dismay that I had not left the dance soon enough, for out of the corner of my eye I spotted my partner coming toward me, wrapped in his blanket. He was clearly highly nervous, and as he approached, he kept his eyes diverted, even as he stopped in front of me and opened his blanket. He was two heads shorter than I, and if I exaggerate by stating that he looked to be thirteen years old, I do not when I say that he couldn't have been a day older than sixteen.

"Your future husband stands before you, Molly," said Phemie with a deep, rich chuckle. "Step inside and you begin your life as this fine young man's squaw. If it is any consolation, he is from a very good family."

It was at that moment that another man,

leading three horses, came up behind us. He spoke softly to the youngster, who closed his blanket around himself and with downcast head turned away and hurried off. Dog Woman, having witnessed this scene, now bustled over toward us, squawking like an agitated chicken and waving her arms. The man spoke softly again and held the horses' lead ropes out to her. Immediately calmed by this gesture, she took them in hand and answered in a tone of what sounded like gratitude. Then she turned and spoke something to me, which, of course, I did not understand.

"What is happening here?" I whispered to Phemie.

"Hawk just purchased you from Dog Woman for three horses," she said.

"And am I commanding a good price?" I asked with a smile.

"A very handsome sum," said Phemie, laughing, "which has clearly changed the old charlatan's mind about the most suitable match for you. She just gave you her official benediction to marry Hawk."

Hawk now spoke a greeting of some sort to Phemie in Cheyenne, and she answered him in kind. "Hawk is a fine man," she said to me. "He and I fought together at one point during the Mackenzie attack. Good luck, Molly, think about my offer. All I ask is that you come to one of our meetings."

She turned and left us, and I stood alone then with Hawk in the shadows of the moon, feeling oddly shy and speechless. The dance continued in the circle, the flutes, the rattles, the drums in their hypnotic, pulsing beat, the fire still burning bright, the moon high now in the sky, lighting the prancing dancers like a beacon. All of our girls had returned to the dance. From this little distance, I could tell them apart only from the grace of their steps . . . or lack thereof — Lulu with her professional élan; Maria, sprightly as a nymph of the woods; Carolyn, surprisingly graceful for one who had only just begun dancing; Astrid with a step as fluid as the sea of her homeland, and coupled with, of all people, our good chaplain, whose religion he had told us prohibited this recreation. "With the exception of square dancing," he had explained, "which is permitted, as there is no physical coupling of partners, a contact which risks inappropriately inflaming the passions." Yet here was Christian dancing with wild abandon that had all the appearance of passion inflamed. Then there was Lady Hall, dancing with Bridge Girl . . . two more enthusiastic left feet I have never before witnessed;

and Hannah, so often timid in demeanor, as lively afoot as a Liverpudlian elf.

Having tried to calm my racing heart by watching my friends for this long moment, I turned finally to Hawk, and all I could think to say was: "Thank you."

He led me in silence back to his lodge. An old woman sat inside tending a small fire in the center. She rose as we entered, spoke a word to Hawk, and left through the opening without looking at me. Hawk indicated that I was to sit down. He took a tin trade pan of warm water from beside the fire, and dipping a cloth into it, he began to clean the greasepaint from my face.

"Are you ever going to speak to me again?" I asked. "After all, if we're getting married, it would be nice to have a little conversation between us."

"Yes, after you learn Cheyenne," he answered with a wry smile.

"That's not fair. I am trying to learn it. You should be willing to speak your maternal language. Remember, as the son of a white woman, you, too, are considered white by your tribe's own beliefs."

"I am not white, nor does your tribe accept me as one of their people."

"That is true."

"I wish for you to lie with me at my sleeping place," he said when he had finished cleaning my face. "I wish only to talk to you. This is why I speak your language now."

"That sounds like a splendid idea," I said, and I laughed. "I am too nervous to do anything but talk."

"As am I."

We lay down beside each other at his sleeping place, fully clothed beneath the buffalo robes. "Who was that old woman?" I asked.

"My grandmother," he answered, "the mother of my Lakota father."

"Why did your mother speak English to you when you returned from the Indian school, if she did not wish for you to learn the language?"

"We only spoke English in private," he said, "never when others were around. She wanted me to be Cheyenne. When I came back from Indian school, I had more English than she. Even though she did not wish to return to the white world, she wanted to keep some contact with her past, which she did by speaking her first language with me. That was a private place we shared."

"As you and I must share it," I said. "Until I learn your language we have no other means of communication."

"You know more about my life than you

have told me about yours," Hawk said. "You know what happened to my mother, my wife, and my child. Now tell me your story. Tell me about your daughter."

"That is something I am not yet able to speak of . . . not to you . . . not to anyone."

"Then we have nothing further to say to each other."

"I'm sorry. I cannot."

We lay beside each other in silence for a long time, our clothed bodies touching lightly. When Hawk's breath came deep and even with sleep, I began to tell my story in a whisper:

I grew up on a farm in upstate New York. I was an only child. My father enlisted in the Union Army at the outbreak of the War between the States, and he was killed at the Battle of Appomattox in April of 1865, three days before the surrender of the Confederate Army. My mother and I had kept the farm going as well as we were able to, with the help of a neighboring farmer's son. After my father's death, I also taught school in the one-room schoolhouse after the former mistress, Miss Nichols, died suddenly of heart failure; I had always been a good student and I loved to read, and though I was only fourteen years old, there was no one else in the community to fill her position.

I married the neighbor's son, who was six years older than I. I was already tall and physically mature for my age, and to marry young and start a family was not so uncommon in farm country. I gave birth to a baby girl . . . Clara, I named her.

My mother hoped we would stay on the farm, but my husband detested farming. He was a dreamer, one of those men never content with his lot in life, always blaming others for his troubles — he blamed his parents, my father, my mother, me, he blamed even our baby daughter, Clara, for standing in the way of his dreams. He dreamed of moving to the city to be involved in the burgeoning financial world there, which he eagerly read about in the newspapers. He imagined himself becoming a banker, sitting in an office behind a mahogany desk, wearing custom-made suits and patent leather shoes, not, as he put it, "spending the rest of my life scraping cow dung off my boots."

When our daughter was three years old, we finally decided to move to the city. There was no question that my mother would be able to run the farm alone, and so we sold it, and she purchased a small cottage in town. We went to New York City. It was the worst decision of my life, one I have regretted every single day since.

I hated the city from the beginning, the filth, the close quarters, the hordes of people. I missed the farm terribly, and right away things began to go badly for us, as I had feared they would. My husband . . . I will never speak the man's name again . . . my husband seemed to believe that he would somehow be welcomed into New York's financial world, that doors there would open magically for him, although he was just a country boy himself, and all he knew about it was what he had read in the newspapers.

The only job he was able to find in a bank, finally, was as part of the crew that cleaned it after business hours. He learned very quickly that this was not a position that would lead to custom suits and patent leather shoes. He told me that while they were cleaning, he sometimes liked to sit for a moment behind the bank president's desk, which was the closest he would ever come to realizing his dreams. By then of course I knew all too well that my husband was a weak man, but in our society girls are taught to stay with our men, no matter what; we are not given any other choice.

I managed to find work teaching at a school in the Five Points neighborhood. This was my first exposure to the slums, a terrifying place of shocking poverty, human suffering, debauchery, and crime. It was there that I met the people who ran the Children's Aid Society, and I took a second job working for them. My duties included placing children without homes in one of the many orphan asylums with which the organization worked, or in one of the lodging houses they themselves operated throughout the city. There were so many children living on the streets, especially in Five Points, many of them belonging to immigrant families who found themselves unable to care for all their offspring. Some we sent on orphan trains to live with farm families in the Midwest, and I helped organize one group that was sent upstate to the country where I had grown up. How I longed to go back there with them. And I should have. I should have taken Clara and gone home. For not having done so, I will never forgive myself . . .

My husband had started drinking, and our marriage further deteriorated. He began to miss work, and to spend his time and our money in disreputable taverns among the most lowlife of companions — bums, drunks, drug addicts, and petty criminals. Of course, he blamed me for all his failures. If he had only come here earlier, he said, when he was younger, he could have made a start in the business. If I had not "tricked" him into marrying me, by burdening him with a child, he could have had a grand success. But no, because of me he was stuck for those years on the farm, his best years when he would have had a chance to get ahead, to make something of himself, but now it was too late for him. Virtually every day, I heard some variation of this litany of his woes.

We had already moved three times since we had been in New York, each time to less expensive lodgings. We were not yet living in a tenement building, but we were not far from it. We had rented a tiny, shabby row house on the Lower East Side, just on the edge of Five Points itself. It seemed clear that we were locked in a deadly downward spiral from which there was no escape. Although I had taken on more work to try to make ends meet, teaching school and part-time employment with a charitable foundation are hardly high-paying positions. My days were increasingly long, the hours often irregular, and I was always exhausted. I was entirely supporting the family now, my husband barely working at all, except for rare odd jobs, the proceeds of which he immediately drank or gambled away. When he wasn't in the taverns trying to cadge free drinks or passed out in an alley somewhere, he stayed home drinking whatever cheap alcohol he managed to acquire on the street. Sometimes he went out and did not come home for several days. I never asked him where he had been, I did not wish to know, and I began to pray that one day he would not return.

He became increasingly violent when he drank, breaking dishes, chairs, and tables in his drunken rages. It was only a matter of time before he began to strike me, accusing me again of ruining his life, the same old cowardly recitation of self-pity and blame. I was taller than he, and strong enough that I could usually defend myself against his assaults, and by then he was usually so drunk he would fall down and pass out before he could hurt me too severely.

Clara was six years old now, and despite all our family troubles, a beautiful, cheerful, trusting little girl. When she wasn't in school, I often had to leave her with neighbors when I was working, for I could no longer trust her father to look after her. I had to pay them for watching her, which was yet another drain on our already desperate finances.

One evening while we were eating dinner, Clara mentioned that her friend Cristina, who lived next door and whose family were immigrants from Romania, had received a bicycle from her parents for her birthday. Clara said she wished she could have a bicycle, too. I will never forget how her father looked at her in that moment, with an expression of such loathing, as if this simple wish of a little girl to have a bicycle was meant as a personal reproach to him for his failures. Then he leaned over and slapped her across the face. He had never hit Clara before, and she was so shocked, so hurt that it took a moment for the tears to well up in her eyes. Finally, she broke down and began bawling. I took her to her room and tried to console her. "Daddy didn't mean to hurt you," I said. "He's just having a hard time at work, that's all. Of course you can have a bicycle, darling. We will go look for one soon, I promise."

I left her in her room, and went back to the kitchen table. "If you need to hit somebody," I said to him, "you hit me. But if ever you lay a hand on our daughter again, I will leave you, I will take her with me, and you will never see either of us again."

That is where the story should end. That night, after he passes out, I should pack our bags, and before he wakes in the morning, Clara and I will have left to go back upstate to my mother's house. But it does not end there, and no matter how many times I relive it in my mind, I cannot change the ending of this story, there is no going back . . .

Early the next morning, a Saturday, two women colleagues from the Children's Aid

Society came to our house. They needed my help in situating another group of orphans who had been found living in an abandoned, rat-infested building in Five Points. Both my husband and Clara were still asleep, and I left them there together and went with the women. I left my daughter alone in the house with her drunken, insane father, in order to look after the children of strangers . . .

I had not expected to be gone the entire day, but I was and I didn't get home until nearly dark. I found my husband passed out on the kitchen floor, two empty bottles of cheap gin beside him. I called out for Clara. She did not answer. The dusky evening light and oppressive silence of the house filled me with dread. I felt the terror rising in my breast. I ran into her room. She was lying facedown on her bed, naked, the sheets around her soaked in blood, her tiny body bruised, her face battered, swollen, nearly unrecognizable. Her father had beaten her to death. I hugged her to my breast, weeping in a state of utter hysteria, thinking that this was all a terrible mistake, this could not have happened, this is only a nightmare from which I will awaken, and when I release her and look at her again my daughter will be alive, and so happy that I am home. Please, please, let it be so . . . let it be so . . . but it was not.

I went into the kitchen then, oddly calm and deliberate now, and I tied my husband's hands and legs firmly with twine; still he did not wake up. I took a large kitchen knife from the drawer, knelt beside him, and pressed the blade against his throat. His eyes popped open, and I let him have a good look at me. Then I cut his throat, and watched the light fade from his terrified eyes.

I walked the several blocks to the nearest police station, still carrying the knife, my dress covered in the blood of my daughter, and now that of my husband. I told them what I had done. They handcuffed me and had me lead them back to the house. I was arrested and accused of murdering both my daughter and my husband. The city assigned a lawyer to my case; I pleaded guilty to the latter crime, and innocent to the former. The trial was covered by all the newspapers, with lurid headlines. Some women colleagues from the aid society testified on my behalf, but I refused to take the stand, refused to say a word in my own defense. My mother came down from upstate for the trial. Of course, she knew I had not killed my daughter, and she begged me to testify. The jury convicted me for the murder of my husband, but were split on the charge of the murder of my daughter. The judge took pity upon me, and instead of condemning me to death, sentenced me to life imprisonment in Sing Sing. I wept when he delivered the sentence, not because I was relieved, but because I had prayed to be hanged and put out of my misery. Now I knew that I would have every day, all day for the rest of my life to mourn my daughter, to torture myself for my own culpability in her death.

In a grotesque irony, my husband's and daughter's bodies are buried side by side in paupers' graves somewhere in the city, the precise location of which I was never told. It was not expected that I would ever be released from Sing Sing to have occasion to visit their graves. I cannot bear to think of my little girl resting for eternity alongside the man who killed her, and when I learned about this brides program, the first thought I had was that if I was accepted in it, and if I survived, perhaps one day I could go back there, I could find Clara's grave, have her disinterred and take her back to bury in the country. It was only this slender hope that gave me any reason at all to live. I did not protect my daughter from her father when she needed me. For that I can never forgive myself, nor do I deserve forgiveness. But one day, perhaps, I will take my little girl home, away from that monster once and for all, as I should have done so long ago.

My daughter's murder, the strain of the trial, and my conviction and imprisonment were all too much for my mother. Five months later, I received a letter at Sing Sing from an old farm neighbor, with an obituary enclosed from our small-town newspaper. It said that she had died of a broken heart.

All this I whispered to Hawk beneath the buffalo robes of his sleeping place. I knew he was awake now, though I had no idea how much he had heard or how much he had understood. What could he possibly know about life in the city, about slums, homeless children, aid societies, the American trial system, Sing Sing . . . about drunken fathers who beat their daughters to death? Such a thing is simply unheard of in their world. Indeed, as we have learned since we've been among them, Cheyenne parents never punish their children physically, never whip or spank them, rather they teach them correct behavior by advice and counsel, and by example. So I could only imagine what Hawk must have been thinking as I recounted this terrible story, which he had no possible means of understanding. Still, I believed that I owed it to him, and as painful as it was for me to tell, I felt some small sense of relief for having finally unburdened myself of a heavy silence I had carried all this time.

We lay together without speaking. Finally, Hawk sat up, removed his deer hide shirt, breechclout, and leggings. He raised me gently to a sitting position and lifted my dress up over my head. Then we lay down together and he took me in his arms. I smelled again the faintly wild scent of his skin. He held me, warm against him, enveloped in the buffalo robes and in the sanctuary of his smooth, muscled body. I buried my face in the crook of his neck, and I began to weep. I wept for the release of my story, for the pain and terror of my little girl at the end of her life, the memory of which will live inside me for the rest of mine. And I wept for the silent tenderness this man showed me. Whatever he had understood, or not, he knew there were no further words to be spoken between us, nothing left to do in this night but to hold me in his arms.

■ ■ ■ ■

LEDGER BOOK IX
UNDER THE
BUFFALO ROBES

■ ■ ■ ■

When one's child dies young, their death
becomes the defining moment, not only of
their short life, but also of our own. Everything before then, everything they were,
everything we were, everything they and
we would have become together is canceled, erased like chalk from a blackboard . . . because they are no longer, as
we are no longer.

(from the journals of Margaret Kelly)

25 May 1876

Me and Susie have a fine time dancin'. We get to laughin' our cacks off with the greenhorns during the cancan . . . that's the most damn fun we've had in a long time . . . and the people are all havin' fun with us, too. We keep dancin' afterward, until finally we take a breather and sit down with Martha, Gertie, and Phemie. Most a' the lasses are takin' their turns in the dance circle, too, sometimes alone, sometimes with each other, and sometimes with the partners Dog Woman has set 'em up with. Lulu, Hannah, and Maria have all spent time in the shadows a little away from the circle, wrapped in the blankets with their boys, though we ain't had any reports about how these powwows are goin' just yet, for they are all back in the dance now.

Lady Hall is steppin' up a storm with Bridge Girl, havin' the time of her life it appears. And we'll be goddamned if the chaplain hasn't taken to the circle with Astrid. We don't believe that Dog Woman has approved this pairing yet, but the two of 'em make a grand couple, and they move right pretty together.

"That wee Hannah lass," says Susie, watching the performance, "is tiny as a mouse's diddy, but she can dance, can't she?"

"Aye, sister," says I. " 'Deed, she can. And a' course, ain't Lulu bleedin' deadly on the floor? And you can see that Maria's got savage blood in her step, too, can't ya? Why, she could damn near pass for Cheyenne."

"Aye, funny ain't it, how they asked for white women in the trade," says Susie, "and our government sent 'em Phemie in our group, and a Mexican Indian, as dark-skinned as them, in this one?"

"That's somethin' I've always admired about these folks," says Gertie. "They don't judge people by the color of their skin. Remember, Phemie, how the first name they gave you when you come here was Black White Woman? But that was just a way to call you, to identify you, they didn't judge you by it or think any less a' you."

"Yes, since we arrived here," Phemie answers with a deep chuckle, "I have always been treated as an equal . . . and that is not an experience we negro folk often have."

"Martha," says Gertie, "if you should get a hankerin' to take a turn in the dance circle yourself, you got four babysitters right here, dyin' to look after your little boy."

"Oh, no, thank you, I couldn't," Martha answers. "I can never leave little Tangle Hair again, except when I go outdoors to do my toilet, and then Mo'ke a'e watches him for me."

It's funny the holes Martha has in her memory, the things she remembers and those she doesn't. She seems to believe now that May and the others have somehow gone home rather than having been killed, as if she's forgotten the attack altogether, even though she surely remembered it when we were back in the place where it happened. It's like every time she goes into one of her trances, everything that happened before gets erased in her mind. Thankfully, this has not happened since she was reunited with her baby. Gertie tells us Martha didn't even remember Molly when she came by to say hello, even though Molly is the one who rescued her, and has even been to visit her once with Lady Hall at Tangle Hair's lodge here. Yet Martha does remember Phemie and Gertie, me and Susie and all her dead friends.

"By the way," says Susie, "where is Molly? We haven't seen her since she was sitting here with you lasses."

Gertie and Phemie laugh together. "We think she's under the buffalo robes with Hawk," says Gertie.

"Go on!" says me and Susie together. "Get out!"

The two of 'em look at each other, smilin' like Cheshire cats. "It's true, girls," says Phemie.

"But Hawk didn't even come to the dance?" says I.

"Like hell he didn't," says Gertie, "he just didn't dance, is all. Brung three of his handsomest horses with him as a gift to Dog Woman. It's damned amazin' how fast she decided that Molly and Hawk were made for each other. It appears they went straight back to Hawk's lodge. Why, I 'spect they're at it right now."

"An' just after me and Susie got finished tellin' her she wasn't goin' to get Hawk. Shows what little we know, right, sister?"

"Aye, Meggie," says Susie, " 'Tis the God's truth . . . we Kelly girls never have been real canny in matters of the heart."

"Nor real lucky," says I. "Well, good for Molly. She set her cap for Hawk right from the start, and it appears she got him, after all."

So me and Susie take another turn in the dance circle. We think it does us good . . . aye, the music and the motion kinda our way a' forgettin' our own memories for a brief moment . . . well, maybe that's not exactly what I mean to say . . . for ours are memories that don't ever get forgotten. Let's say instead that we lay those frozen corpses down gently at the edge of the circle as we enter, for there must be lightness in the act of dance and they weigh us down so that so we couldn't possibly step light. Aye, and it is such a relief to do so that me and Susie can hardly stop all night . . . we prance and kick and leap and laugh, dancin' wild with the lasses, with the Cheyenne lads, with the chaplain, too, havin' the time of his life, whirlin' dervishes we all are, lost in the fire, becoming flames ourselves under the full moon.

26 May 1876
We continue our war drills with Phemie, and we're gettin' to be passable shots with the bow and arrow . . . we can release three arrows in a row from our horses' backs at a dead run, drawin' them from the quivers on our back, all in two shakes of a lamb's tail.

The Springfield carbine rifles are a wee bit heavy for us, so we been given Colt .45s and Army-issue holsters to wear on our hips, and we've learned how to draw the guns, slip onto the sides of our horses, hangin' on to the mane with one hand, one leg hooked over the horse's haunch, and shootin' under their necks, just the way Phemie does . . . well, almost as good as she does.

Me and Susie are ridin' wild paint prairie ponies that have been trained for war by a lad named Votonéve'hamého, which in our tongue means somethin' like Winged Horses Man, a young bucko famous among the People for his gift at breaking and training broncos . . . to the point that he is said to even be able to teach a horse to fly. Aye, course we don't know about that part . . . but we do know his services are much in demand and that we're real lucky to have these mounts, the only reason bein' because he so respects Phemie and wants all her warrior women to be astride the best possible horseflesh. Ours are lively, quick-steppin' little ponies, a perfect fit for a pair a' lively, quick-steppin' little lassies like me and Susie. Due to their training they ain't a bit gun-shy, nor do they spook when we make sudden movements — steady creatures, even when we get clumsy as still happens from time to time. We've named 'em Noméohtse, Going with the Wind, and Áme'háohtséhno'ha, Flying Horse . . . you know, just in case there really is something to that flyin' business and we might need to take to the air, we figure we'd better give 'em names that would allow for that special talent.

27 May 1876
Me and Susie ain't seen the greenhorns since the night a' the dance, an' so today we decide to go for a visit. We want to see what progress they're makin' gettin' settled in with their Cheyenne families. After what Gertie told us, we expect we'll all be on the move again soon . . . to where, as usual, we do not know. But with our new responsibilities to the Strong-heart Society, we ain't goin' to be in any position to be lookin' out after 'em when the shite monsoon strikes. Also, we gotta admit, we want to catch up a little on their romantic lives . . . for reasons . . . what's the grand word I'm lookin' for, Susie . . . aye, for *vicarious* reasons. Those days may be long gone for us, but we still like to hear the stories . . . they remind us of our own group, our more innocent days, an' sometimes we need somethin' a

little hopeful to think about . . . like love and romance.

They tell us they're still being courted by their lads, who come around every evening, wrapped in their blankets, opening them wide and taking them in for a little conversation.

"He chats me up for a while," says Hannah, "and then I tell him about meself, about me brothers and sisters, me mum and me dad . . . Course we can't understand a word the other is saying, but somehow we're comin' to know each other anyhow."

"Mais oui," says Lulu, "and my little prince, too, is the perfect gentleman. I have never known a boy so sweet, so gentle, so different from any of the men I have ever been with before."

"My man," says Carolyn, "and I use the term loosely . . . showed me on his fingers how many years he has. "He hardly looks it, but he assures me that he is eighteen. I have never had a younger beau before, but I must say, it is rather exciting. I danced like a wild woman the other night . . . I completely lost control of myself . . . It was quite liberating. I must confess to you girls . . . now that I'm getting used to the idea, I wish for that boy to take me . . ." She laughs, blushes, and puts her hand over her mouth. "Good Lord, do you know that I have never before spoken . . . or even dared to have such a thought?"

"That we can well imagine, Carolyn," says Susie, "from what you've told us about your husband. Not exactly a wildcat between the sheets, we expect."

" 'Wildcat' would not be a term that leaps to mind when describing the pastor," says she. "However, my young man has been the picture of propriety. I fear that perhaps I am too old for him . . . perhaps I do not excite his passions."

"Don't you worry about that, missy," says I. "For once the courtship period ends, and you lassies move into the lads' lodges, and they get over their natural shyness, you'll find that these boyos are bleedin' savages under the buffalo robes . . . and we mean that in the best possible way. Still, you may need to take matters into your own hands to get him started . . . if you understand our meaning."

"Oh, dear, yes, I . . . I believe I do," says Carolyn, blushing again.

"Our boys needed a little encouragement, too, ain't that right, sister?"

"Right as rain, Meggie," says Susie. "But once we gave 'em a taste of our charms, there was no holdin' 'em back . . . three, four, five times a night they were at us."

"Oh, dear," says Carolyn again, with a small, nervous laugh.

"And you, Molly," says I, "why, we heard that you and Hawk kind of skipped the courtship period altogether and went right into the state of unholy matrimony. Ain't that so?"

"My personal relationship with Hawk is my private business," says she, "and none of yours."

"Talk around camp is that you've already moved into his lodge," says Susie.

"Yes, that much is common knowledge," says Molly. "It is what goes on inside the lodge that is not your business."

"That's alright," says I, "because me and Susie got real good imaginations. You do understand that in the eyes of these folks, now that you've moved in, that means you two are married?"

"Understood, thank you."

"All we can tell the rest of you lasses is this," says Susie. "Don't be wastin' any more time before goin' under the robes with your boys. After what Gertie told us, we'll be on the move again soon. While we're still here, you all need to make honest men of 'em, get settled in their tipis. They may seem young to you, but these lads have been trained for war since the day they were born. They will all prove to be competent warriors, and the greatest responsibility they have is to protect their families from harm. You'll be safer with them than you will alone or together."

"Me, too, am already married," says Maria. "My boy and me . . . he says his name is Hó'hónáhk'e . . . went under the robes the night of the dance. He was very sweet with me. He did not hold a loaded gun to my head the way Chucho el Roto liked to do when he had me. He used to say that when the day arrived I no longer pleased him, he would pull the trigger. That excited him."

"Jaysus Christ, lassie . . ." says I. "If that is all you know of the act, then we'd say you've made yourself a fine match with young Hó'hónáhk'e, which, by the way, means Rock . . . It's good that you didn't waste any time. We did the same with our lads . . . for different reasons maybe . . . We figured the sooner we lived up to our end of the bargain and had our savage babies, the sooner we'd be able to get our lovely little arses back to Chicago. See, we were plannin' to leave the little buggers with the Cheyenne. Susie and me never had much in the way of maternal instincts . . . maybe because we never had a mother to show us how. And then, of course, soon as they popped out . . . oh hell, even before really, we fell in love with 'em, and life took on a whole other meaning to us. We figure that a woman lives three different lives in this way . . . or at least that's how it's been for us . . . there's one life before you become a mother, a second after you do, and a third when you lose a child."

" 'Tis the God's truth, Meggie . . . and you and me are in the third life. We ain't ever going back to Chicago now, for we have the final business of mothers to attend to right here. Aye, someday people'll be readin' in the history books about the fightin' Kelly twins, scourge of the Great Plains."

28 May 1876

Now me and Susie are real surprised when Molly comes to see us in our lodge today. It is the first time she has done so, and we don't even know how she found us. She scratches at the opening real polite and when our old widow woman, Mó'éh'e, opens the flap and invites her in, she steps to the left and sits down by the entrance, just like the Cheyenne expect visitors to do, which impresses us no end.

"You be learning the ways of the People,

Molly," says Susie.

"I've been trying to take your advice and observe their rules of etiquette," she says. "Although these are sometimes difficult to determine."

Elk Woman fills our trade pan with water and boils up some coffee Gertie left with us. We make a little awkward chitchat with Molly, wonderin' why she came, and realizing that except for a few short conversations between us while riding on the trail, all this time since we first met the greenhorns back in Crazy Horse's village, the three of us have never really been alone together in a social kind of way. It ain't completely comfortable, either.

As if reading our minds, Molly says: "I imagine you girls are wondering why I came to see you."

"Aye, lass, that we be wonderin'," says Susie.

"It just occurred to me that we've never really talked, just the three of us. That is to say, there have always been others around, we've never had a single private conversation."

"There ain't a whole lot of privacy in an Indian village," says I, "as you may have noticed by now. So why *have* ya come to see us, then, Molly?"

She laughs. "Well . . . to have a private conversation."

"And what about, lass?"

"Gertie described a rather dark future for us all, didn't she? And since then I got to thinking . . . I've been thinking that we don't really know each other, beyond some vague details of our respective lives. We've been at odds a good deal, you girls and I, and I know you haven't always approved of my behavior . . . I'm not even sure you like me. And that's alright, too, I don't blame you for it, truly I don't. But I do like you both, and I admire you . . . and I think in many ways we are a lot alike . . . or at least we have much in common . . . we share a similar wound. What you said yesterday, Meggie, about the three stages of your lives . . . before you're a mother, after you're a mother, and after you lose a child . . . that made an impression on me, for I know exactly what you mean. That's how it's been for me. It appears that more bad things are going to happen to us soon, things that are completely out of our control. Maybe even we're all going to die, or at least some of us are. You girls seem to have resigned yourselves to that fate, and for a long time, I thought I had, too. But I don't want to die anymore, not yet. And if I do . . . if any of us do . . . I don't want it to happen without us leaving something behind with each other . . . some memory of kindness between us, some vestige of friendship . . . Do you understand what I'm trying to say?"

"Not quite yet," says Susie, "but go on, lass."

Molly laughs again. "Yes, I'm not sure I know what I'm trying to say, either. Maybe it's simply that I'd like for us to be friends. For instance, I'd like to know something about your babies, other than that they are dead, and how they died. I don't even know their names."

"As you have never spoken the name of your daughter."

"Clara. My daughter's name was Clara."

"That's a grand name, Molly," says I. "Yet you know more about our girls, than me and Susie know about yours. Because you have never even told us how Clara died."

"I haven't told anyone about that . . . until Hawk just recently. Along the lines of what you said yesterday, when a child dies . . . and I hardly need tell you girls this . . . when one's child dies young, their death becomes the defining moment, not only of their short life, but also of our own. Everything before then, everything they were, everything we were, everything they and we would have become together is canceled, erased like chalk from a blackboard . . . because they are no longer, as we are no longer."

"Aye, that is so, Molly," says Susie. "It's just like you said: 'my daughter's name *was* Clara' . . . for she *is* no longer, as you are no longer her mother. Our girls were just wee babies, you see, only a few weeks old when they died . . . three weeks and two days, to be exact. They had no past to speak of . . . maybe they had memories of the warmth of our wombs at the end, we hope so. The only memories we have of them are of carryin' them in our bellies, of their birth, of them as tiny, cheerful infants, and, of course, of their cold death, one by one. Mine were named Bird and Egg, Vé'ése and Vòvotse, those are Cheyenne baby names, and if they had lived they would have been given other names as they were growing up. But like you say, Molly, that is never going to happen . . . all of that is gone, all of that has been erased. All that remains of them now is the constant knot of pain in our guts, where once they were."

"Mine were named Curly and Baldy," says I, "Péhpe'e and Oo'estséáhe, because one had hair already and one didn't . . . it's how I could tell 'em apart. Those babies will never learn to walk or talk, to run or play . . ."

"My daughter was beaten to death by her father," says Molly in a real small voice, and we see in the dim light of the tipi that tears are running down her cheeks. "She was six years old . . . she . . . she wanted a bicycle . . . that's all . . . he killed her because she wanted a bicycle."

"Jaysus Christ," says Susie, shaking her head. "Aye, we understand now, lassie. And you killed the bastard, that's why ya went to prison, ain't it?"

Molly just nods because she can't talk now for her weeping. And me and Susie are cryin', too . . . for our dead children, and hers, and for our former selves who died with them, who, like Molly says, are no longer.

Molly stays the night with us in our tipi, and we send old Mo'éh á'e to Hawk's lodge to tell him where she is so he won't worry. We fix up a sleeping place for her and we talk late into the night. She tells us how she feels about Hawk, that she's in love with the lad, the first time she's ever really been in love in her life, she says. She tells us that after they have had a bit of a "honeymoon," Hawk intends to speak to Bear and Good Feathers about taking the orphan girl, Mouse, in to live with 'em. She tells us how guilty it makes her to have these feelings — both for Hawk and for the child — because her life is going on without her daughter, after all . . . and she feels like she's abandonin' her. Me and Susie try to reassure her by saying just what she was tryin' to tell us — that the person she was as Clara's mother died with her little girl, but maybe now she has a chance at a fourth stage of life, as the wife of a man who loves her and as another child's mother. And, a' course, Molly, being Molly, turns that right around on us and says if we really believed that, then why don't we try to make another chance for ourselves.

To this Susie answers: "Ya see, Molly, you already got your vengeance by killin' the man who killed your daughter. Meggie and me can't rest until we get ours."

"I'm sorry to tell you this, girls," says she, "but there is no rest with vengeance. It doesn't make you feel any better, it doesn't relieve the pain. There is only the slight satisfaction of retribution that at least the man responsible is also dead."

"We'll take that," says I. "That's better than nothin', ain't it?"

"But you won't even be killing the men who were directly responsible for your daughters' deaths."

450

"Aye, that satisfaction we won't have, it's true, but at least we'll be strikin' a blow against the Army that sent the men who were responsible. And who knows, maybe we'll get lucky and find ourselves engaged in battle against some of the soldiers who attacked us that morning. A girl can dream, Molly."

"You ladies are incorrigible," says she.

"That we are, lass, that we are."

"And by the way," says Susie, "we do like you, even if we don't always show it. You know, the thing is, Meggie and me got an image as a pair of tough street lassies to protect. And even if it ain't entirely true, we been guardin' that image our whole lives as a way to defend ourselves, keep folks at arm's length. The fact that you came on as tough as us, maybe even tougher . . . aye, it's true that kinda rubbed us the wrong way sometimes."

Molly laughs at this. "What you see as my toughness, girls, is largely an act, too . . . just as you say, to defend myself. My real self is more like what you have witnessed tonight — a weak, weepy, grieving mother, filled with remorse and guilt."

"But you're filled with love, too, Mol," says Susie. "That much is plain to see."

It's a good thing that Molly came to visit,

because by the time she leaves us this morning, we feel like we're all the very best of friends.

■ ■ ■

LEDGER BOOK X
OF LOVE AND WAR

■ ■ ■ ■

We have little left to hide from one another, and no pretenses. How unladylike, how unthinkable it would previously have been to admit aloud to the taking of physical pleasure, how shocked women of polite society would be were they to overhear us. Yet to us it is a perfectly natural conversation among friends, without shame or embarrassment. Life in the wilds offers certain freedoms not readily available to the so-called civilized.

(from the journals of Molly McGill)

27 May 1876
On the morning after what it is now understood was my wedding night . . . although not exactly as every girl might have imagined it to be . . . I woke up in Hawk's lodge, still in his arms. I had that hollow feeling in my stomach upon remembering all that I had spoken to him, as if the unburdening of it emptied me, drained my heart, my blood, my very soul from my body. Perhaps I had held on to this story for so long, not wishing or able to share it with anyone else, as a way of holding on to my daughter. Because once I let go, I knew she would be gone from me for good, and I would never be able to change the ending for her . . . a vain hope, of course, but one I have held close.

I was not sure if Hawk was awake now or still sleeping, for his breath came even, but he began to move against me, our bodies warm together under the buffalo robes. I felt him strengthening against my belly, and the first tentative twinge of my own desire, a feeling barely remembered. I pressed my breasts against his chest, my lips to his neck, inhaling his man scent, and I felt our hearts beating together in unison as if we had known each other for a very long time. There was new life sprouting here between us, like the unlikely spring grass in the ruins of the massacred village, offering at once a sense of comfort and renewal, as well as the pain and heartbreak the Cheyenne say lives on forever in the earth . . . and in us.

Hawk whispered something to me in his own language, in a voice so soft and gentle. He touched me in the same way, and I opened myself to him. And then we were covered and absorbed by each other in that private world that there are no words to describe.

29 May 1876

Gertie left us this morning. I came from Hawk's lodge to say good-bye to her at the communal tipis I had shared with the others. Only Lady Hall, Maria, and I have already moved into the lodges of our respective mates, the others still being courted by their boys . . . it is hard to think of them as men, and even more so, as warriors. Yet for the sake of protection, the twins are encouraging all of our girls to get settled in our *husbands'* lodges . . . such a strange notion that still seems . . .

Gertie had just finished saddling her big gray mule and was strapping on her Army saddlebags. All there was to say on the matter had been said, and a nervous silence fell over us as we watched her work. Finally, she put her foot into the stirrup and swung into the saddle.

"Well, here we are, then," she said, nodding down at us. "Don't know when I'll see you gals again . . . depends on what Little Wolf decides to do. But no matter what is to come, I want to tell ya all something before I leave. I want to tell ya how much I admire you . . . all a' you. I admire the hell outta you. I know it ain't been easy what you been through already, but you done yourselves proud. An' I never heard a bit of whinin' from you, either. You're damn fine women, every damned one a' you, and it has been my honor to know you."

Now Gertie looked around at the village lying so peaceful in the valley, smoke curling from the tops of tipis, children playing in front of their lodges, women, two or three together, fleshing hides, tanning, butchering, cooking, quilting, chatting easily among themselves, giggling softly from time to time. And then she looked up and took in the landscape beyond — the birds singing in the trees of the river bottom, the morning sunlight sparkling off the flowing water, the greening foothills, behind those the snowcapped peaks of the Bighorns, and on the other side of the river, the hills and bluffs running off to the plains. "It ain't such a bad life with these folks, is it?" she said. "Takes some gettin' used to, no doubt a' that . . . as you've all well learned. But once you're accustomed to their ways, and get in the habit of livin' wild, it ain't a bad life at-tall . . . that is, if others'd just leave ya alone. I loved it myself, loved all of it, I miss the hell out of it. But like I told ya, it ain't a life that can last, and it's comin' to an end here real soon. I hate to see you caught up in all this, but I can't do much more for you now. Whatever happens, you gals take good care a' yourselves, take good care a' each other. Stay as strong as you've been this long . . . stay even stronger . . . you'll need be."

"But Gertie, when the Army comes," I asked, "you'll be with them, won't you? Might we not see you then?"

"No, honey, course we don't travel with the troops when they go into battle. We stay back in a base camp some distance away. Some a' the teamsters may go along on mules as civilian fighters. But not me, I'll be with the supply wagons . . . Anyhow, that'll be way too late to be stoppin' in for a visit."

Gertie reined her mule around. "Adios, gals," she said, touching the brim of her grimy, misshapen, sweat-stained hat. I thought I detected tears welling up in the corners of her eyes. But maybe it was only because I was looking through the veil of those clouding my own. "And say good-bye to those damned Irish rascals for me, too," she added. "May we all meet again under happier circumstances . . . and I don't mean on the hangin' road to Seano, neither. You all stay away from that place. I have it on good authority that it ain't all it's cracked up to be."

Now Gertie took her hat off and lightly slapped her mule's hindquarters with it. "Git on down the trail, old Badger," she said, and as the beast broke into a trot, I could then see plainly the streaks of tears on her cheeks, sparkling like the flowing river in the sun. I know Gertie was thinking that she would never see us alive again, because that's what we were all thinking.

2 June 1876

Ours is to be a short honeymoon, indeed, for yesterday morning, the camp crier came through the village, announcing that we were to begin taking down our lodges and packing up for travel. Hawk left to attend a powwow and smoke with Little Wolf and the chiefs of the other bands, including that of a contingent of well over a hundred Lakota warriors and their families, who rode in yesterday afternoon and set up a camp near ours.

Hawk's grandmother arrived at our lodge shortly thereafter to show me how to dismantle the tipi, and to help me at it, as this is something we have little experience with. Her name is Náhkohenaa'é'e, which Hawk translates as Bear Doctor Woman. Cheyenne names seem to spring from either physical attributes, accomplishments, talents, events in which the individual has participated, and very frequently from the animal and bird kingdom, or from some combination of more than one of the above. When I questioned Hawk further about his grandmother's name, he told me this story:

When she was a young woman her name was Méstaa'ehéhe . . . Owl Girl, because she was said to be able to see in the dark. One morning she was walking from her family's camp to another nearby village to visit a sick relative, when she was overtaken by a sudden thunderstorm with lightning and pounding hail. She took refuge in a cave that was often used by the People for such purpose.

When her eyes adjusted to the dim light inside, Owl Girl saw that she was not alone; there was a mother grizzly bear with a cub curled up against the back wall of the cave. Grizzlies are considered to possess supernatural powers and are greatly feared by the Cheyenne; there is a taboo against killing them. In the early days, before they were largely hunted out by the fur trappers, the big bears weren't confined to the mountains but often roamed the open plains and were a great risk to travelers. They could run a short distance as fast as a horse and would chase down people on foot and devour them.

Now the cub began whimpering and poking at its mother, and Owl Girl could see that there was something wrong with her, for she did not move. Perhaps, for this reason, the girl was not afraid of the mother grizzly, and she crawled back to have a closer look. The mother bear only watched her and did not appear to have the strength to attack or even to move. Now Owl Girl saw that she had a deep wound on her chest around which flies buzzed and inside which maggots crawled. She nearly vomited from the smell.

The sudden cloudburst was over quickly and Owl Girl left the cave and went down to the river, where she filled her water bladder, and filled another pouch she carried with mud. Then from the bank she gathered various grasses and wild herbs the Cheyenne know to have healing power, and she returned to the cave. First she poured water on the mother bear's wound and picked out all the maggots. Then she made a poultice of the mud, grass, and herbs and gently applied it to the wound. All the while she talked to the mother bear, who flinched in pain at her touch but did not struggle; she just kept her small yellow eyes, like shiny marbles, focused on the girl.

Later Owl Girl told the People that the mother grizzly thanked her, told her that a fur hunter had shot her with a musket rifle, the ball from which must have passed all the way through her shoulder. No one doubted that the bear had spoken to the girl, due to the grizzly's well-known powers.

When she had finished dressing the wound, Owl Girl told the mother bear that she was going to return to her family's camp and bring food for her and her cub. This she did, carrying the haunch of an elk one of her brothers had killed. She did not allow any of her family to accompany her back to the cave, nor did they wish to, for they recognized that the girl had come to some kind of understanding with the bear, which their presence might upset. Also, of course, they were terrified of grizzlies.

For three days, Owl Girl fed the mother bear and the cub, and each day she changed the poultice. On the fourth day when she returned, they were gone. Over the next two years as the cub grew, the girl would see them periodically by the river, or near the cave when she walked to visit her relatives in the nearby village. Owl Girl knew that they were following her, and she had the sense that the mother bear was watching over her. After two years, grizzly cubs leave their mothers, but the girl continued to see the bear now and again, and the last time she saw her, she had two new cubs with her. And that is how Owl Girl got her new name, Bear Doctor Woman.

Náhkohenaa'é'e has been kind to me these few days . . . at least she presents a kindly demeanor. Although the old woman does not speak very much, I have found that she knows some rudimentary English, perhaps learned over the years from listening to Hawk and his mother. This was the first time the two of us had actually been alone together, and as we worked she spoke to me in a mixture of English, Cheyenne, and sign talk, so that between the three languages, and by watching her work, I was able to sort out what I was supposed to do.

This involved first packing all the contents of the lodge into leather parfleches, a kind of primitive suitcase. These are then strapped to a travois, a sort of primitive wagon without wheels, made from two poles between which are stretched a piece of canvas or leather, one end of the poles then attached to a harness which in turn is attached either to a horse, a large dog, a woman, or a child, depending on the size of the load.

Next we began unstitching the leather thongs that connected the stretched buffalo hides covering the lodge poles themselves, then folding and bundling the hides, which we also packed in parfleches. I was grateful for the old woman's gentle instruction and her patience with my own relative awkwardness at this work. Clearly, it is a function she has performed many thousands of times in her life, a primary duty of the women, and she worked quickly and efficiently, as did all the others who were dismantling and packing up their lodges around us. Some hummed or sang softly as they worked, and I learned that there are specific songs connected to this particular labor, which create a certain odd harmony, a kind of steady, pulsating musical hum hovering in the air above the village.

When we had finished packing the lodge, Bear Doctor Woman, in a mixture of English and sign talk, said: "Happy me Little Hawk" — he has told me that his grandmother still calls him affectionately by his childhood name — "has new wife."

"Thank you. And happy me you happy," I responded in kind.

She nodded and smiled at me. "I see Little Hawk mother you," she said, touching my hair, which I translated to mean that I reminded her of Hawk's mother, due to our common fair hair. And perhaps this is one reason she has been so kind to me . . . and one reason Hawk has fallen in love with me . . . yes . . . there, I have said it. I believe that he does love me.

I put my hand over my heart, nodded, and again said: "Happy." I remembered the one piece of romantic advice my own mother gave me, which tragically I did not take, and that was to marry a man who loved his

465

mother, which clearly Hawk had.

By midmorning, the entire village of over three hundred lodges had been completely dismantled, and the travois, pack horses, dogs, women, and children fully loaded for travel. Mounted on Spring, I hoped as we began to move out that I would find some of my friends to join as we rode, although given the sheer number of people, and the fact that our tipis had been so spread out, this seemed rather unlikely. For precisely this eventuality, we had appointed our Lulu and any of the other girls who might be riding with, or near her, to begin singing a French song called "Frère Jacques," one she had not yet taught our Cheyenne women. In this way, if we were within earshot, we might at least have a general idea of their location in the mass of travelers, which must number well over a thousand, and all departing at slightly different intervals. It had struck us that having spent so much time together these past months, and become so interdependent, with this sudden separation, we missed each other. Indeed, it was the simple comfort of friendship, the knowledge that we were in this together, that had sustained us throughout the entire ordeal.

We were traveling north along the foothills of the Bighorns, roughly following the

Tongue River below. Of course, other than our general direction, we white women had no idea where we were headed; as always we simply follow. At some point later that morning, we turned slightly east, dropping down out of the foothills and entering the plains, moving due north again. It was easier traveling over the flatter terrain, especially for the pulling of the travois, and as we spread out, we had a clearer view of the immensity of this expedition — men, women, children, young, middle-aged, and old, some walking, some pulling travois, some on horseback. The members of the various warrior societies traveled loosely together, mounted on their fleet, fast-stepping ponies, wearing their war headdresses and carrying their painted shields and lances. The Lakota warriors who had joined us rode with their people, a little apart from us, also wearing headdresses and other accoutrements of their profession. Bands of scouts from both tribes fanned out in all directions, and in the midst of the main body of travelers were two vast herds of horses, which represent the true livelihood of these people, driven by men, women, and boys, some mounted, some afoot and with the help of dogs. Here in the plains the effect of this massive migration was a breathtaking spectacle of fluidity, colorful waves of man and animal following the contours of the land, alternately rising on the hills and disappearing into the swales, a natural living single organism moving across the plains.

Finally, from a distance, I heard the faintest sounds of Lulu singing, then as if being relayed, came the same tune from different locations in the expedition, some distant, some closer, as others of our group heard and joined in. I, too, began to sing and as always the act brought me a sense of joy, hope, and strength. I peeled Spring off from those beside whom I rode and headed toward what sounded like the nearest other singing, and so did my friends, and in this way we began gradually to converge. And delighted we were to see one another, until we all rode together again in reunion, singing our hearts out, the Cheyenne who were traveling around us smiling, laughing and nodding at the antics of the white women whom they still find as strange and exotic as we do them.

As we rode together, we caught up with everyone else's news, and our respective marital situations. Lulu has been claimed by a young man named, charmingly, No'ee'e, Squirrel. "I never know a boy who treat me so gentle, so sweet," she said, "who be so polite with me. He treat me like a precious thing he is afraid to break. He believe my horse not yet leave the barn, because no good Cheyenne girl lets it out before marriage. So I pretend that is so . . . why not?"

"Me bloke, too, is a sweetie," said Hannah, "Hotóáso is his name, Little Buffalo. I was so nervous . . . but blimey if he wasn't also, because he had never been with a girl before. It took three nights for him to get up the courage . . . and then when I just barely brushed his willy with my hand, he got so excited he shot his spunk all over me."

"Bloody hell, Hannah!" said Lady Hall. "Must you really discuss such vulgar matters? Just the sort of filthy business that disgusts me about relations with men . . . rendered all the more revolting in your wretched Liverpudlian vernacular."

"I'm sorry, m'lady, but as you know, I have brothers. It is from them I learn such things."

"Astrid, tell me," I said. "I saw you dancing with the chaplain. Did Dog Woman not arrange a union for you with a Cheyenne boy? Where are you living?"

"I am living chastely in Chaplain Goodman's lodge," she answered. "We have fallen in love, but because of his religion, we must wait until we can be married in a proper ceremony by a minister ordained in his faith. Dog Woman could not interfere with our arrangement, because Christian is considered to be a holy man, with certain rights of his own."

At this Lulu laughed. Although they seem closer since the dance, she clearly still enjoys teasing Astrid. "*Mais ma petite amie norvégienne,* my little Norwegian friend, you have long wait to find a minister out here to make a marriage for you. We live with the Cheyenne now, you must make a Cheyenne marriage like the rest of us . . . all you need do is touch by accident his . . . how you say, Hannah?"

"His willy."

"We maintain separate sleeping places to avoid such temptation," said Astrid.

"Ah, but do you not see that is exactly your problem? You who have already been married, whose horse is long gone out of the barn. Some night after he falls asleep, you must slip under his buffalo robes with him. He is a good Christian boy . . . they are very . . . how you say, *frustré* . . . very frustrated? . . . I know this from the gentlemen's club where I worked. Some of my clients bring their sons to me to learn them the pleasures of the body. The boys say their mothers tell them they will go blind if they play with their willies. Can you imagine? *Oui,* it is certain, Christian will not be able to resist when you touch him there. But one more advice, *ma petite amie:* take off your mittens first!"

At this we all had a good laugh . . . except poor Astrid. "I do not wear mittens, Lulu," she said. "I don't know why you always say such things about me."

"You know I just say for fun."

"I must agree with Lulu, Astrid," said Carolyn. "After my long and astonishingly tedious marriage to the pastor, I find the simplicity of the Cheyenne arrangement to be quite liberating. Indeed, I have had more marital relations with my young fellow, Vó'hó'k'áse — Light, we would call him, isn't that charming? — in three days than I had in ten years with my first husband, with whom the act, free of even the pretense of pleasure, was undertaken strictly for the purpose of propagation. As Lulu suggests, do not wait for the blessing of God to sanctify your marriage, my dear, for out here in the wilderness, that may never arrive."

Simply due to the fact that we are able to discuss these formerly taboo matters with

such good-humored frankness and direct-
ness, it was hard not to recognize how much
we have all changed in these past months.
Surely this big country has opened us up to
a new way of being, while at the same time
binding us ever more tightly together. We
have little left to hide from one another,
and no pretenses. How unladylike, how
unthinkable it would previously have been
to admit aloud to the taking of physical
pleasure, how shocked women of polite
society would be were they to overhear us.
Yet to us it is a perfectly natural conversation among friends, one without shame or
embarrassment. Life in the wilds allows
certain freedoms not available to the so-
called civilized world.

As the day wore on, riding together, chatting away, surrounded by the other tribal
members, borne across the plains in this giant wave of man and animal, it eventually
occurred to us that we had completely lost
our bearings. Although we had thought it a
splendid idea to locate each other by song,
we had made no similar arrangements to
find our way back to our own families. We
had also begun to understand that as infor-
mal as our procession appeared at first, it
possesses a certain inherent form and function, clearly passed down through the many

generations of this nomadic existence. Everything and everyone have their designated place and order. Clearly we had not yet learned the key to this form.

"I dare say," offered Lady Hall as we considered our predicament, "it would not do us a bit of good to ask directions of our fellow travelers, would it now? For there is no fixed point in a fluid movement such as this. Indeed, I think it quite possible that we might never find our way back."

We finally decided that our only option was to stay together and wait for the movement to finally halt when it came time to pitch camp for the night. And when that happened, one by one, as we hoped they would, our mates managed to locate us — exactly how, of course, we have absolutely no idea. These people own an inexplicably precise sense of such matters . . . like homing pigeons . . . or in my case, in the way a hawk flying high in the sky locates a mouse on the ground. When Hawk himself appeared to fetch me, he wore that wry smile on his face with which he frequently greets me. I have come to appreciate his sense of humor. I find it oddly refreshing that he does not take me entirely seriously, for this creates a good-natured lightness between us that helps to prevent me from taking myself too seriously.

Of course, our traveling night bivouacs are considerably rougher and simpler than our full village encampments. Bear Doctor Woman has also been helping me to set up our temporary lodge each evening, and to commence food cooking, and by dusk Hawk rides in from whatever position in the procession his warrior society has taken up that day.

Two days ago, after Hawk had located me with the other girls and led me "home," I found, to my great embarrassment, that Náhkohenaa'é'e had already set up our camp alone and started our dinner cooking. Yet she smiled gently upon our arrival and did not seem to hold it against me. Even before I could thank her she slipped discreetly away, as she did last night and again this evening. The old woman is clearly being respectful of our newlywed status; in each other's presence we are still frequently shy, awkward, tongue-tied, love-struck, while full of an inchoate passion that can hardly wait to be released under the buffalo robes where we are able to divest ourselves of our timidity. It is difficult for me to write of this . . . . just to think about it brings a hot

474

flush of blood to my chest and face.

I rode today with Mouse seated in front of me, as we often do. She is such a slip of a thing that Spring does not mind at all bearing us both upon her back. Indeed, the child seems to bring forth the equine's own maternal instincts, for she nickers softly when Mouse appears, and nuzzles her affectionately with her nose, which makes her giggle delightedly.

As we ride, we give each other language lessons, pointing at various objects, parts of our bodies, the sky, the horse, each of us identifying them in our respective tongues. Sometimes we just chatter away to each other, hoping the other might understand a word or two of what we each say. And sometimes we sing one of Lulu's little ditties in French. She is a bright, alert little girl, with a certain impish manner about her, and I can see already that with a child's natural facility to absorb language, she will learn English considerably faster than I will Cheyenne . . . although I feel that I am making modest progress.

As we were riding thus today, Phemie joined us atop a tall, white prairie stallion, which she explained was a new addition to her and her husband's string of horses. It is a snorting, prancing, long-legged, wild-eyed, high-spirited beast, upon whose back Phemie looks more regal than ever.

"How did you find me in this mass of travelers, Phemie?" I asked.

"I know where to look," she answered simply. "You have not come to my women's warrior society meeting yet, Molly."

"I have not, Phemie. As I told you, I have no interest in being a warrior."

"Do you have interest in protecting your life and that of your friends?"

"Of course."

"Of protecting our Cheyenne people, particularly the mothers and their children? Of protecting this child?"

"Yes, of course, I would do everything I could toward that end."

"Then to fight with us is everything you can do, Molly. Our scouts have located a massive force of Army troops moving in our direction, clearly the Crook expedition that Gertie told us of. Relays have sent word that Crazy Horse and Sitting Bull, as well as other Lakota bands, are on the way to join us. They recognize the strength in numbers, and the necessity of fighting together. Like us, the warriors travel with their families, who can no longer be left behind in unprotected villages. The Army has well learned that this is our greatest vulnerability, the easiest way to defeat us . . . rather than fighting our warriors, the generals prefer to attack our women, children, and elders, and to destroy our villages. I need you in our society, Molly. Don't you see? We require all the soldiers we can enlist . . . men and women."

"But I know nothing about waging war, Phemie."

"You know how to shoot a rifle, and you are a fine horsewoman. That will have to suffice. Come to our meeting this afternoon after we make camp. I will send Pretty Nose to lead you there. Little Wolf is gathering the heads of all the warrior societies for a council, including the chiefs from the Lakota and Arapaho bands who are already here with us. Pretty Nose and I will be attending. It is, perhaps, the first time in the history of the tribe that women have been invited to participate in council. We will know more after the powwow. All I can tell you for certain now is that we are going to war, and sooner rather than later."

"Did you know that Hawk and I are planning to adopt this little girl, Phemie?" I said, putting my arm around Mouse. "She lives presently with the old couple Bear and

Good Feathers. She's an orphan."

"Yes, I knew her family. They were fine people."

"And if I go to war, she risks losing me, as well."

"Her parents died in the village that morning, defenseless, like so many others, Molly, because we were not prepared. But now we are no longer waiting passively for the Army to attack us. We are traveling to unite with the other bands of Arapaho and Lakota, and the chiefs are leading us to a strategic position from which we will attack them."

"You know, Phemie, to wage war against our own government is not precisely what I and the other girls signed up for."

"That is what our group believed. However, we learned the hard way . . . and too late . . . that, in fact, it was exactly what we had signed up for. Our government plans to exterminate us. And so this child is all the more reason for you to fight."

Phemie reined her white stallion, who wheeled in a tight circle, snorted, whinnied, threw his head, and kicked both back feet out behind him, whether from sheer wild exuberance, or rebellion against being tamed and restrained, it was hard to say. Perhaps a combination of the two.

"Is that horse even broke, Phemie?" I asked.

"More or less," she answered with a smile. "I'm working on it, but he's the kind of horse that never gets fully broke. He's got too much heart. He needs to run." She touched her heels to his flanks, gave him his head, and off they dashed.

With her queenly bearing and sonorous voice, Phemie commands such natural authority that it is hard to say no to her. I decided it could not hurt to at least attend her meeting. In so doing, I was under no obligation to join. It is true that despite all we have heard from Meggie and Susie about the horror of their own experience, and from Phemie, and all that Gertie has told us, our own group has nevertheless held tight to the illusion that somehow an attack upon our band could be avoided, that the specter of war was only that — a phantom, a bogeyman — one that would never actually come to pass . . . not to us, surely . . . perhaps it is simply the blind faith of human nature to believe thusly. Only a handful of days ago we danced with joy and abandon, we married, we moved into our husband's lodge . . . or in Ann Hall's case into the lodge of her new paramour . . . we made love . . . well, except for Astrid and

Christian, that is . . . Can it be possible in the face of all this new life, strange though it be, that we are really going to war? Facing death? It seems already a long time ago that I wanted to die . . . I know it is crazy under these desperate circumstances to even entertain the thought, but I want now to have Hawk's baby. And perhaps this is all I have left to give to you, finally, my darling Clara . . . life to another.

True to her word, this evening after we had pitched our camp, Phemie sent Pretty Nose to lead me to the meeting of the Strong-heart Women's Warrior Society, as they call themselves. The girl, too, came mounted, for with the arrival of the various Lakota and Arapaho bands, the encampment has spread out even farther across the plains.

One finds riding through a large Indian village that there are distinct "neighborhoods" — each laid out in circles or a connecting series of circles, the tipi openings all facing east to greet the morning sun. In this way extended family groups often camp together. The richer tribal members with more horses take up positions in proximity to one another — partly as a practical measure in order to share secured horse corrals guarded by their young sons. In the same way, the members of each of the warrior societies also tend to cluster in common circles, as do similarly the poorer members of the tribe. Finally, the outcasts, who have been banished for various tribal offenses, are required to camp some distance away from the others in their own circles, or often even one family alone. And, of course, the Lakota and Arapaho bands take up separate campsites, which in their appearance and atmosphere, their colors and attire are as distinct as the various ethnic neighborhoods of New York City.

I had seen Pretty Nose briefly at the dance, but we had no opportunity to speak that night. Now as we rode through the camp, I asked her if she had remarried yet, for generally the wife of a fallen warrior is taken in as a second or third wife by one of her husband's brothers or cousins, or failing that, by a best friend.

"I do not yet wish to remarry," she said. "One day I will accept another husband. It is the duty of all women to bear children because the People need warriors. Without warriors we cannot defend ourselves, and therefore the tribe cannot survive. And we must bear daughters to look after our warriors."

"But if you are supposed to be a mother,"

I said, "how can you also be a warrior? Do you not have to be one or the other?"

"In our tribe, when our men are killed in a fight with another tribe, the women in the camp go around weeping and begging the young men to go to war and kill some of the enemy who killed their relations. It is only in this way that their keening can be stopped, for the killing of the enemy brings comfort, it wipes away our tears. Instead of asking young men to go to war for me, I myself go to kill the enemy, to wipe away my own tears."

I must remember to tell Christian Goodman about this when next I see him, for although not intending to, Pretty Nose had quite succinctly described the absurdity of war, the pointless circle of vengeance, like a dog chasing its tail. If all Cheyenne men are warriors, taught from early youth that no pleasure on earth equals the joy of battle, that death in war is the noblest, most glorious end for which a man can hope, then all women are breeders, put on earth to keep the tribe well supplied with future warriors, who will grow up to kill their enemies, and be killed by them, generation after generation after generation. It is, in her short, simple telling, the entire history of the human race.

"And tell me," I asked, "has killing your enemies wiped away your tears?"

Pretty Nose did not answer, or even look at me. She just gazed off into the distance with that expression on her face I had noticed the very first time we met. In it, I recognized again all the heartbreak, the anger, and the anguish I myself bear.

When we reached the lodge in which the meeting was being held, in addition to Phemie, Meggie, Susie, and several Cheyenne women of my acquaintance, I was surprised to see that both Maria and Lady Hall were also in attendance.

"I did not know, Ann, that you had enlisted to fight the soldiers."

"Like you, Molly, this is my first meeting," she answered. "Bridge Girl has convinced me of my responsibility to avenge the murder of our dearest companion, Helen Elizabeth Flight."

"And you, Maria," I said. "You are married now. What has made you decide to become a warrior?"

"My mother was a full-blooded Indian of the Rarámuri tribe," she said. "We are a peaceful people. When the Spanish came into our country, they took us from our homes and made slaves of us. The Jesuit missionaries had us build their churches, cut down our sacred trees of the Sierra Madre, and dig gold from the earth . . . all this in the name of their God. Phemie has told us of her mother's people, who lived on the other side of the world. She tells this same story — captured by the slave traders, taken from their homeland, beaten, raped, murdered, enslaved, and made to do the work of the whites. And here among the Cheyenne, it is again the same — the whites kill all the buffalo so that the People have nothing left to eat or to cover their lodges with, or to warm them in the winter; they steal their land so that they can dig gold and put their cows here to eat the grass, they cut down the trees in the sacred land of the Black Hills to build their houses. They put the People on reservations, which they are forbidden to leave, where there is no game to hunt and no food to eat, for the white Indian agents there steal and sell it to other white people. Those who refuse to go to the reservation, or who try to escape, they kill. That is why I go to war, Molly."

I have to admit that Maria's was as clear and simple a justification for taking up arms against the Army as any I had yet heard.

During the meeting, Phemie explained a bit about the tactics of her and Pretty Nose's military society, the fact that all were divided into teams of two. As Ann and I would be the newest members, and had not as yet participated in any training exercises, I was to be paired with Pretty Nose, and Ann with Phemie herself . . . It seems that my attendance at the meeting was to be considered my consent to join. At the same time, I felt a certain strange detachment from the proceedings, as if I were in the midst of a dream, watching myself and the others from a distance, with the comforting knowledge that I would eventually wake up.

Phemie told us that at the powwow this afternoon, Little Wolf and the other chiefs agreed that based on information received from the scouts regarding the location of the Army, and the direction in which it was traveling, we would now turn due west toward the Rosebud and Little Bighorn country, where the considerable forces of Crazy Horse and Sitting Bull will join us. Even traveling with our families, we can still easily outpace the ponderous Army caravan with its cavalry soldiers and their horses weighed down by heavy gear, its support wagons and mule strings stretching out behind, and the raw young infantry recruits Gertie spoke of, many of whom have clearly never ridden before, or so say the scouts who spied upon them and were greatly amused as the soldiers were trying to learn to mount their mules. It is inconceivable to a native of the plains that a man might not know how to ride, and it gave the scouts confidence that we could not possibly lose to such an inept enemy.

"We shall continue our training as we move," Phemie concluded, "or in the case of Molly and Ann, you will begin it. You must also both be aware of the fact that nothing said here at our meetings can ever leave this lodge. The rule is total secrecy."

I managed to negotiate the return trip to Hawk and my lodge alone. I am beginning to get a sense of the lay of the encampment, which maintains its general form when we pitch new camps en route. Hawk was there when I arrived and he knew, of course, where I had been, and for what reason.

Hawk, too, had attended Little Wolf's powwow. "I fought beside Phemie," he said. "She is a fine, brave warrior. But it was her first fight, and she almost died. War is the work of men, not women. I do not wish for you to die."

"Nor I you," I said. "But Phemie and Pretty Nose believe that the tribes need all the warriors they can get, whether men or women."

"But you are going to have a baby now . . .

my baby."

I laughed. "Well, that certainly remains to be seen, doesn't it?"

"No, it has been seen," he said, quite seriously. "Woman Who Moves against the Wind came to me today to tell me that you are with child."

I laughed. "But that's ridiculous. Who is she? How could she possibly say such a thing?"

"She is a medicine woman. She had a vision. In her vision, you and our son were killed in battle."

Despite my utter disbelief of such nonsense, I felt a terrible chill of gooseflesh run over my skin. "But we do not have a son, Hawk," I said. "Nor is it possible for anyone, including me, to know if I am with child given the very short time we have been together."

Hawk placed his open palm lightly on my stomach. "Yes, you have a child there. And you, too, I believe, know this. I do not wish to lose another wife and another child."

"Nor do I wish to lose a husband. Why must either of us go to war? Why can't we just run away?"

"And where would we go?"

"Someplace where we can't be found . . . north, to Canada."

"And leave our families, our tribe, our friends?"

"No, of course not . . . we take them with us. We all go."

"That is not a decision for you, or I, to make," he said. "I go to war because it is my duty to defend the People, and the earth upon which the Great Spirit put us to live. It is the duty of all men. But it is not your duty. Your duty is to bring our child into the world, and to care for him, to see that he survives and grows up. Woman Who Moves against the Wind says that if you do not go to war you will not be killed, nor will our son."

"I was ready to die until I met you. I wished to die. Yes, I wish now to have your baby, to live in peace, and yet we do not have that choice."

"We do not."

There was a great storm that night. The summer solstice was only a few weeks away, and the days were lengthening. We watched the evening clouds building on the distant horizon, like ragged black mountains rising from the earth. Then a cold prairie wind announced their coming, pushing the huge bruised masses rolling and roiling across the plains, lit inside by violent strikes of purple lightning, the grumbles of thunder like an Army of angry gods approaching.

And then, because we are newlyweds who wish to do something that points toward life rather than death, Hawk and I slip under the buffalo robes. I imagine this is what lovers have done throughout history, faced with the prospect of annihilation, for what else is there to do? We do not speak further of this conundrum that has no solution, but poses only the question of who fights and who doesn't. And in the end everyone fights, we fight for survival, for the survival of the people, of the children, an instinct common to all animals, all species.

The storm overtakes us, envelops us, hard rain drumming the hides of the tipi, the night sky as black as the bowels of a mine, the enraged wind screaming, the thunderous voices of the gods exploding like cannons with long, staccato blazes of lightning. Naked under the robes, the tempest driving us ever deeper into our private world, we caress each other, and as the flashes light our tipi, we look in each other's eyes, we watch our bodies move together, brown against pale. I run my hands over his smooth skin, the hard muscles in his arms and shoulders, his legs and belly, I press my face against his neck and smell the faint animal fragrance of his wildness like the soft supple

489

odor of an antelope hide, I taste him on my lips like a field of wild herbs and roots dug from the earth, we press our mouths together, a cool mineral flavor like licking a smooth river rock polished for millennia by clear flowing water, our bodies pressed tight, here we take refuge from the great storm, entering, surrounding, and protecting each other, becoming for that blissful moment one being without a conscious thought between us, only these feelings, these scents, these sounds, these tastes, these pure sensations of passion . . . of love . . .

■ ■ ■ ■

LEDGER BOOK XI
THE BATTLE OF THE
ROSEBUD/WHERE
THE GIRL SAVED
HER BROTHER

■ ■ ■ ■

Love makes fools of people . . . gives 'em hope when there is none, makes 'em believe in a future where one doesn't exist.

(from the journals of Margaret Kelly)

15 June 1876

Between travel and trainin' for war, me and Susie been far too busy to make journal entries. Our band is workin' our way west from the Powder River into the valley of the Rosebud — rich country, with grass thick for the horses, and large buffalo herds to meet our needs. Here we're camped near Crazy Horse and his Oglala Lakota band, and Sitting Bull with his Hunkpapa Lakota people. Other Lakota bands are said to still be joining us, the Minneconjou and the Santee. A few days ago Sitting Bull held a Sun Dance . . . he himself danced two days and two nights, slashing himself about the arms and chest a hundred times as a sacrifice to the Great Spirit, who in return sent him a vision in which he saw the white soldiers falling into his village headfirst like grasshoppers. This was taken by all as a sign that we would win the fight against the

493

Army, and it greatly encouraged the People, gave them hope of victory.

Tonight we are camped in the valley of Ash Creek west of Rosebud Creek. The scouts report that Crook's force of over one thousand soldiers are on the march and already in the area. Travelin' with the Army, they say, are nearly three hundred Shoshone and Crow warriors and a hundred or so armed civilians who have joined the soldiers.

It is now certain that we are soon to engage the enemy, and the Strong-heart Women are ready for battle. Have we butterflies in our stomachs? Aye . . . at least some of us surely do. Only Phemie seems undaunted, true as always to her queenly nature, which offers the rest of us a wee bit of courage. She's managed to convince Lady Hall, Maria, and Molly to join our warrior society, and all three of 'em seem to have the same jitters as we.

It's funny, because Molly is the most reluctant of us all about goin' to war. And not because she's a coward, because we know that ain't the case. It's because she's crazy in love . . . plain and simple. She told us she asked Hawk if they couldn't run away together, north up to Canada where maybe they could live in peace. She says she wants to have a baby by him. Imagine that . . .

bringin' another infant into the world now? . . . after everything we told her happened to us and ours . . . not to mention her own. This world is no place for babies, she oughta know that. Aye, love makes fools of people . . . gives 'em hope when there is none, makes 'em believe in a future where one doesn't exist.

Molly says she doesn't want to kill soldiers, that she's not going to fight, because Hawk doesn't want her to. She's only goin' along to look after her friend and partner Pretty Nose, because she feels obligated to do so. We told her that in our opinion that makes for a real poor warrior, and we told Phemie, too. What good is a warrior who is not goin' to fight, and who wants a partner like that? We wonder if maybe the chaplain ain't been workin' on Molly with his turn-the-other-cheek crock a' shite.

Phemie just chuckled in that deep way of hers that sounds like it comes up from way down in her belly, and said: "Don't you girls worry about Molly. Pretty Nose told me that she still wants her as her partner. In the heat of battle, she will do everything she can to protect Pretty Nose, and the rest of us, and that includes killing soldiers if she has to. You'll see, she will rise to the occasion. I would not have asked her to join our society if I did not believe that."

All me and Susie can say is that Molly is real lucky to be partnered up with Pretty Nose. That lass wears an unreadable puss, if ever there was one, which we have never quite been able to figure out . . . we can't tell if she's mad or sad, or both, nor 'ave we ever seen her smile . . . but she can ride and shoot, fire an arrow, throw a lance, a tomahawk, or a knife like no one else . . . maybe even better than Phemie, or at least as good . . . and she does it with a kind of quietness . . . an intensity that's scary to witness . . . We figure that's why the elders made her a war chief, because she's got both the talent and the stone coldness of a mother's vengeance like a force of nature. Aye, she'll take good care of Molly, though no matter what Phemie says, we still ain't so sure it works the other way.

16 June 1876
Pretty Nose and Phemie have been to war council this morning between Little Wolf, Crazy Horse, Sitting Bull, the Minneconjou warrior named Hump, the Santee leader, Inkpaduta, and the heads of each of the warrior societies from all the different bands, two dozen or so. They say it's a council never before seen in the history of

the tribes, for never have so many come together to fight the soldiers.

Afterward, Phemie tells us to begin gettin' our tack, weapons, horses, and war outfits ready, because the scouts say Crook's troops are on the move again and that tomorrow the battle begins. Aye, *tomorrow* . . . speakin' of the jitters, even though we knew this news was comin', it sets a whole flurry a' butterflies loose in our guts. To be sure it's one thing trainin' and thinkin' about the glories of battle, the heroic acts we will commit, the enemies we will smite, the sweet vengeance we will take . . . and it is quite another when the moment is actually upon us . . . it is only then that we begin to question if we are really up to the task.

As if readin' our minds, Phemie says: "Wake well before dawn, ladies. Dress for battle, get your horses from the corral, and come to our communal tipi. There we will paint each other's faces. As the paint transforms us into warrior women, and the fierceness of our respective visages reveal themselves to one another, our nerves will settle, and we will feel a great calm descend upon us, like a flutter of butterflies settling quietly on a field of wildflowers. With this calm will come an invincible courage, and that is the spirit we shall take into battle."

It's funny, 'cause just Phemie's words alone calm our jitters. This is the time me and Susie been waitin' for, the time that's kept us alive these past months since our girls and our friends were taken from us. We ain't sissies, we ain't goin' to let our nerves get the best of us, we're the Kelly sisters, white Cheyenne, Strong-heart warrior women, scourge of the Great Plains, we're here to kill soldiers, scalp and cut off their bollocks.

So we've taken as our animal protector the kingfisher bird, because it's a cocky little creature, the way it dives so bold into the water to catch fish with its long beak. We've even cut our hair to resemble the ragged crest of feathers that sticks up on its big head, and we've learned to make the bird's piercing rattling cry that is sure to strike terror into the hearts of our enemies. Helen Flight's friend and protégé, Bridge Girl, who is now tipied up with Lady Hall, has painted images of the kingfisher on our horses' chests, and lightning bolts on their legs. She may not be anywhere near the artist Helen was, but she learned a few things, and she does good work.

Aye, we are ready for battle, me and Susie. This is our time.

Like Phemie told us to be, we're up before dawn that morning, we dress and walk down to the roped-off horse corral by the river, where the boys take turns sleepin' by a small fire and walkin' the perimeter to guard against enemy horse thieves. We find our mounts, bridle and saddle 'em, and lead 'em to the meeting lodge just as dawn is breaking. The others are similarly arriving and three other boys are gathered there to look after the horses.

The old crone, Tóhtoo'a'e, Prairie Woman, who lives in Phemie and Black Man's lodge has a fire burning inside, with a pot of stewed buffalo meat and roots simmerin', a tin coffeepot steamin' beside it. It all smells grand, and though we didn't think we had much appetite when we first arrived, we do now. Everyone sits down in a circle around the fire, and Tóhtoo'a'e pours us each a half tin cupful of coffee. After she has taken the stew off the fire and it has cooled a bit we pass the pot around and each take some out with our fingers. Everyone is real quiet, lost in our own thoughts for the day, and no one wishes to break the silence.

Finally Phemie says: "We stay together today as much as possible. You've all ridden this country enough now to know the general lay of the land — the draws, hills, and valleys. That is a great advantage to us, and one the soldiers do not have. Remember, we take our direction from Pretty Nose, she is our leader, she makes the decisions, and we follow. As we have worked on in our drills, we strike fast and hard, and we fall back. The soldiers are more numerous than we but they are ponderous and move slowly. Our ponies are quicker, more agile, and we move like the wind.

"We will encounter infantry troops as well as cavalry. As long as the infantry men are mounted on their mules they will be easy targets for us to strike. However, when engaged they will dismount and form skirmish lines and then they will be dangerous, for there will be at least some skilled marksmen among them, and they have longer-range rifles than we. Do nothing foolhardy such as trying to ride in on them. And always keep an eye out for riflemen hidden on the tops of the hills. Remember, our strategy is to surprise, strike fast and deadly, then fall back and regroup before we strike again.

"If in the confusion of the fight . . . and believe me, it will be confusing at times . . . if you get separated from our group or lost, try to join up with any of our other warrior societies, or those of the Lakota or Arapaho. You do not want to be caught out there alone. This is your first battle; be strong, be brave, but take no unnecessary risks. Except . . . remember our cardinal rule: we do not leave one of our own wounded on the battlefield. We are the Strong-heart Women. We take care of each other."

After Phemie finishes talking to us in English, Pretty Nose addresses her women in Cheyenne, saying roughly the same things.

Now we set about painting our faces, me and Susie workin' on each other. We've already worked out our designs, we're both goin' with red greasepaint background and yellow lightning bolts on our cheeks. We figure that'll scare the shite out of the bluecoats when they see twin visions of hell bearin' down on 'em, faces painted, our wild red hair shaped like the crest of the kingfisher.

Molly and Lady Hall are not usin' the face paint. "I do not wish to hide behind a mask," says Molly. "If I must do this, I shall do it as myself, and not disguised."

It is daylight now when we step back outside. We gather our horses, check our gear and weapons. We're all sportin' shirts of flannel, cotton, or buckskin; men's buckskin breechclouts and leggings; moccasins of deer, elk, or buffalo hide; we got coats of bright-colored blanket with loose sleeves and a hood, made special for us by the women of the tribe. Me and Susie carry Army Colt .45 single-action revolvers holstered at our waist on the right side, these taken off the train that was carryin' the greenhorns, and lucky we are to have 'em, too. Hangin' from the left side of our gun belts we got trade scalping knives in beaded sheaths, and small tomahawks for close-in fighting. On our backs, we each got a quiver of arrows, and light bows tethered to our saddles, these in case we run out of bullets.

The other girls are similarly outfitted with some variations depending on their preference and ability with certain weapons. For instance, Molly has her Colt .45 and a Winchester 1873 rifle. Even though she says she ain't goin' to fight, she says in case she has to, she wants at least to be prepared, which we take as a good sign. Phemie carries a lance and a rifle in a scabbard at her side, and a holstered Colt; Pretty Nose and Buffalo Calf Road Woman got pistols, rifles, and coup sticks, because that is a big part of the Cheyenne war tradition, the means by which they amass honors on the battlefield. Me and Susie ain't at all interested in countin' coup or gatherin' honors, we just want to kill.

As we're mountin' and preparin' to move out, damned if Christian Goodman doesn't ride into our camp. He's dressed in buckskin and moccasins, and he wears his hair in braids with a single feather stickin' out of the back of his beaded headband. His skin is bronzed now from our many days in the saddle, and he looks like any other brave. We don't need to say that he ain't carryin' a weapon.

Phemie asks him what he's doin' here, and he says he's comin' with us. Phemie says that ain't possible, because he's not a member of our society, and we only allow women.

"Believe me, I do not wish to be a member of your society," says he. "I am simply accompanying you as a spiritual advisor." Aye, just what we need among us as we go into battle . . . another noncombatant.

"We are going into battle, Christian," says Phemie. "There will be soldiers shooting at us."

"Yes, of course, I am well aware of that. Precisely why you need spiritual support."

"You will only get in the way, and you might be killed. I do not wish to be responsible for you."

"I fully understand the risk. I will not get in your way, nor are you or anyone else responsible for me. Indeed, it is I who feels responsible for your souls in this ungodly venture. And, after all, Phemie, you can hardly prevent me from following along, can you?"

Phemie just shakes her head, reins her big white stallion, and we ride out to join the other bands who are coming together on the hillsides.

The Sioux scouts are reporting to Crazy Horse, who sits his horse on a rise, and the Cheyenne scouts to Little Wolf, mounted on the crest of another hill. The two chiefs still ain't bosom buddies, but at least they've agreed to fight together. And in their war headdresses, the feathered tails of which fall nearly to the ground, they make an impressive sight. After each has a brief parlay with the scouts, as if by some invisible signal, the warrior bands begin to ride out in different directions. Course, all we know to do is what we been told, and that is to follow Pretty Nose.

We ride down valley for a half hour or so, catching sight of other bands cresting hills or comin' down side draws that empty into our valley, some of 'em joining us. We begin to hear scattered gunshots in the hills above, then the sound of coyotes howling, except it ain't coyotes, it's a signal from the scouts, because Pretty Nose turns her horse in that direction and kicks him into a gallop up the hill. We follow, as do at least three other bands.

Reaching the top, we see Indians ridin' hard down below in the swale but they ain't Cheyenne, Lakota, or Arapaho. We been told there would be Crow and Shoshone warriors in the fight against us, and we see now that the Army has outfitted 'em all with red sashes worn across their chests so that the soldiers don't mistake 'em for us. Many of these are also wearing Army cavalry hats with the tops cut out, and feathers stickin' out of 'em, and some have blue cavalry coats. We see now why they're runnin' because comin' down the far hill toward 'em, spread out, whoopin' up a storm and shootin', is a mass of our own warriors, three times the size of theirs. Now and then the Crow and Shoshone, whichever they be, we can't tell, turn in the saddle and shoot at their pursuers. Pretty Nose must assume that the fleeing Indians are heading back toward the main body of the Army, because instead of joining the chase she keeps us to the top of the hill and we follow along parallel to 'em, the same direction they are taking. Yet more warriors have joined up with us now.

It is not long before we spot the first infantry troops headin' our way. We know they're infantry because like the scouts said, they're ridin' mules. They see us, too, and just like Phemie said, they dismount, form a skirmish line on the ground, and begin shootin' at us. We start to spread out, and here is where, as she also warned us they would, things start right quick to get confusing. The soldiers have the longer-range Springfield rifles, of which we were only given two, one Pretty Nose carries, the other Phemie, they being the best shots among us. As we spread out, horses at a dead run, with the sound of gunfire, Indian yells, and bullets flyin', it is impossible to keep track of anyone besides our own partner and even that ain't easy. In addition, behind and among and surroundin' us on all sides now are a mass of at least two to three hundred other warriors . . . Lakota, Cheyenne, Arapaho, and more comin', so that our group begins to get broken up and separated from each other. Some of the bands splinter off to approach the soldiers from different angles, others going after the enemy Indians. Me and Susie get swept up in a wave of horsemen galloping down a side draw, and by now we've completely lost track of the others. We're hopin' that at least some of our women got carried away with us.

We have a little cover in the coulee, but we're still gettin' fired on. Those in the band with whom we now find ourselves ain't re-turnin' fire yet, because the riflemen are still out of our range. At least two separate battles, maybe more, are being fought now, crossing and overlapping, as all the groups have splintered, chasing and being chased, charging and countercharging. All we can hear now is more gunfire, bugles blowing, horses whinnying, and the battle cries of all sides, white and Indian. It's like some crazy dream that doesn't make any sense.

As we reach the head of the draw, ridin' hard, we come out on a kind of bench where we are fully exposed again. The first skir-mish line of riflemen that was shootin' at us see now that we've outflanked 'em. They begin to remount and fall back, but a second line holds their ground and keeps firing. Two warriors' horses near us get shot out from under 'em with great pained bel-lows as they go down, and we see one La-kota ridin' right alongside shot out of his saddle. Me and Susie just keep ridin' toward the soldiers hard as we can. I don't know what we're thinkin' . . . it's just exactly what

Phemie told us not to do. Aye, the fact is we're not thinkin' at all, we're just ridin', and later when we talk about it, we realize that we were both in a kind of trance, only one thought between us, and that was to catch one of those soldiers and kill him. Bullets are flyin' all around us now, but we don't care, we don't worry about gettin' hit, and we ain't scared, either, we just keep ridin' . . .

Now we've practically reached their second skirmish line, and those soldiers, too, begin to fall back, but they don't remount their mules. They're backin' up on foot, firin', some of 'em droppin' their rifles and running in panic. One of the retreating riflemen in front of us stops to reload his rifle. But when he sees me and Susie bearin' down on him, he drops it and draws a revolver. For some reason . . . I don't know why . . . neither me nor Susie even think to take our Colts from their holsters, instead I pull my tomahawk from my waist and we both together make the high, shrill rattlin' cry of the kingfisher, risin' from our chest, and comin' outta our mouths like the bird itself lives in there. We're close enough to him now that the soldier must see we're a pair a' girls, screamin' like crazed banshees, our horses still at a dead run toward him.

He points his revolver at me and fires, I hear the bullet whistle right past my ear, I can feel the hot sting of wind off it. We rein up at the last second, our little prairie ponies skiddin' to a halt, and we both leap from their backs and onto the soldier, topplin' him over backward. He cries out as he falls and drops his gun. When we land Susie rolls off to the side and draws her knife from the scabbard and I'm on top straddlin' him. I raise my tomahawk high and look down into his eyes, wide in terror. *"Please don't kill me,"* he says, *"I didn't mean ya no harm."* But the tomahawk is already comin' down, as if swingin' itself, cleaving his skull right between the eyes, sprayin' me with blood. Susie has her knife out, rips his hat off his head, lifts his coppertop hair in one hand and slices off a good-sized chunk of scalp with the other. I unbuckle the lad's belt, yank down his trousers and skivvies, and Susie cuts his nut sack off, raises it in the air with the scalp, the whole mess drippin' warm blood through her fingers, the two of us howlin' like a pair a' she-wolves on a fresh kill . . . in the red mist of battle there is no time to think about what we've done, that will come later. The other warriors are now chasin' down the rest of the infantry-men, who run in disarray, overwhelmed by our sheer numbers, one by one they are caught, killed, scalped.

Though it's hard to say for sure as we've lost any sense of time, the battle goes on for a good six hours, up and down the valley of the Rosebud and its tributaries — like this first, a series of disconnected skirmishes between our different bands, Army forces, and enemy Indians, all movin' through the hills, draws, and creek bottoms, makin' charges and countercharges, retreats and counterretreats, attackin' and fallin' back. It ain't anything like we expected it to be, and doesn't seem to have any form or sense to it . . . but then maybe that's just the way war is . . . Me and Susie join up with a number of different bands in the course of the fightin', we're independent warriors now, separated all this time from our society, killin' three more soldiers between us and takin' their trophies like we did the first.

Comin' down a side valley of the Rosebud we run across Buffalo Calf Road Woman, the first member of our group we've seen since we got split up. She's ridin' now with the warrior band of her brother, Chief Comes in Sight. We don't have time to ask if she knows where the rest of the Strongheart Women are, and even if we could, we probably wouldn't be able to find 'em

510

because after all the movement and confusion, we ain't even sure exactly where we are.

As we come back into the main valley of the Rosebud, we encounter another detachment of cavalry and Comes in Sight leads us in a charge against them. He's shootin' a Winchester repeatin' rifle, and he swings onto the side of his horse, hangin' on with one arm around the neck, and one leg hooked over the horse's hip, firin' the rifle with one hand from underneath the horse's neck, just like Phemie showed us how.

But it seems that some a' the soldiers have figured out how to deal with this strategy, for one of 'em shoots Comes in Sight's horse, who goes down hard, the chief himself rolling free, but clearly hurt in the fall, and he's lost his rifle. He manages to get to his feet as several soldiers ride toward him, firin' their revolvers, bullets hittin' the dirt all around him. He does not run, but stands his ground, pulls a knife from its sheath, and begins to sing his death song. Just before the soldiers reach him, his sister, Buffalo Calf Road Woman, swoops in on her horse, holding her arm out to her brother. Comes in Sight grabs hold, swings on behind her, and together they make their escape. It is a beautiful thing to see and a right proud moment for us to witness, and me and Susie give our best Indian yell in appreciation. And that is why this battle will always be known to the Cheyenne as Where the Girl Saved Her Brother.

Not long after this, the Army troops begin to withdraw from the battlefield, the shootin' becomin' more and more sporadic until it dies out altogether. We figure we've whipped 'em and they've had enough. We hear cries of triumph from different bands in the hills around us, who must be thinkin' the same.

We begin makin' our way in what we believe to be the general direction of our village, following the flow of the other bands, everyone exhausted and filthy from the long fight. As we're ridin' the crest of a hill, we see down in the valley below, our Strong-heart Women travelin' with other bands, headed the same direction as we. Me and Susie give one of our kingfisher whistles and the lasses look up and see us. We wave at each other, and we ride down to join 'em, so happy to be reunited.

Christian Goodman watches us ride up and as we get close the look on his face changes from one of relief to see us alive to one of horror. *"God help you,"* he says in a real low voice. I guess we kinda forgot how we look, with scalps hangin' from our belts, our faces, hands, arms, and clothes splattered with the blood of those we killed, four pair a' bollocks danglin' in a bloody sack off the pommel of Susie's saddle. *"God help you,"* says he again.

"Well, it'd be a wee bit late for that, Chaplain," says Susie. "As you can plainly see, Meggie and me have gone savage, and God has surely forsaken us."

"God help you," he says a third time. "I should have been there to stop you."

"You could not 'ave stopped us, Christian," says I. "Of that we can assure you. We were possessed by the devil."

"That I can clearly see."

"And did ya have any luck stoppin' these lasses?" asks Susie. "Surely you all fought, and killed, did you not?"

"We did," says Phemie.

"But we don't see any scalps on your belt, Phemie," says I.

"I do not take scalps," says she. "Nor, as you girls know, is it a practice I encourage. Warpath Woman took them, as did Kills in the Morning. I'm sure you will hear of it tonight in the victory dance . . . if, indeed, a victory it was."

We can't help but notice that Phemie seems awful subdued, distracted, and as we look around at the others, we realize there are a couple missing. "Where are Molly and Pretty Nose?" Susie asks. "They get separated from you, too?"

Phemie shakes her head and looks like she's about to break down. We ain't ever seen her like this, she seems . . . she seems weak. "They're gone," she finally manages to say.

"Gone?" says Susie. "What the *fook* does that mean, Phemie? You mean *dead*?"

"Dead or taken prisoner," says she. "We're not sure which."

"But what in bejaysus happened?"

"In that very first fight when we lost sight of you girls," she says, "we ended up joining a large band of Lakota, chasing the Crow down valley. At least, we thought we were chasing them . . . But they led us into a ravine where there were many more of them hidden in the hills above. It was a trap. Pretty Nose and Molly were riding at the head of our charge and when the cross fire ambush began, Pretty Nose's horse went down. It rolled over on her and pinned her to the ground. Molly dismounted to help her. They were quickly converged upon by Crow warriors who came out of the river bottom. That is the last we saw of them. Those of us with guns were firing at the attackers, while trying to ride up the slopes of the ravine. It was a bloodbath, at least two dozen Lakota warriors went down. It was a miracle all of us weren't killed."

"You mean to say you left Pretty Nose and Molly there?" says Susie. "What about the cardinal rule you said was so important, Phemie? How did it go? . . . *'We do not leave one of our own wounded on the battlefield. We are the Strong-heart Women. We take care of each other.'* Ain't that what you said?"

"Yes . . . that is what I said," says she. "And it was I, as second in command after Pretty Nose, who ordered the others to retreat. It would have been suicide to stay in that ravine, and I was not prepared to sacrifice our entire society."

"Or yourself, that is to say," says Susie.

"Sister, that is enough!" says I. "You can't be talkin' like that to Phemie. You know as well as I if there'd been anything else to do, she'd 'ave done it."

"It's alright, Meggie," says Phemie. "Susie is right. Molly and Pretty Nose were trapped one way or another, and I made the decision to cut our losses. I take full responsibility. I'm not proud of it, and perhaps I should have sacrificed myself with them. As it is, I am resigning my position in the

Strong-heart Women's Society, because . . . yes . . . I broke the cardinal rule. And if the tribal council wishes to banish me for it, I will accept that punishment, too."

"Utter . . . bloody . . . nonsense!" Lady Hall speaks up. "Phemie did everything possible. She defended the rest of us heroically, standing her ground in the ravine, riding back and forth shooting at the ambushers in the hills and providing cover while the rest of us fled to safety. Had it not been for her actions, all of us would have been killed. And had you girls been there to witness it, you would understand that."

Suddenly Susie breaks down and starts to bawl, as if the full horror of the day has descended upon us with this news. "I'm awful sorry, Phemie," says she, "I had no business talkin' to ya like that. I know you ain't a coward. I am so sorry. Please forgive me. I . . . I just can't believe we've lost Pretty Nose and Molly."

"Nor can we, Susie," says Phemie. "Our first battle . . . It is a dark day for us all. And it was I who convinced Molly to join our society against her wishes."

"Jaysus Christ," says I, "if they were taken alive, we know what'll happen to 'em. Remember, Gertie told us Jules Seminole would be leadin' the Crow war party? If that filthy bastard gets hold of 'em, they'd be better off dead."

When we arrive back at the village that afternoon, with the other bands also comin' in, there is a strange mix of celebration and mourning — trilling by the women at the return of their victorious warriors, and keening for those brought in dead or wounded, lying across the backs of horses or dragged on travois.

It is considered that we have won the battle, for it is the Army that retreated, and later that night, though me and Susie don't feel like it at all, we are obliged to attend the victory dance. The scouts report that General Crook, having suffered heavy losses, has withdrawn all his troops from the area, and is on his way back to his supply camp to lick his wounds. Course, none of us can stop thinkin' about Molly and Pretty Nose, wonderin' whether they be dead or alive, and if still alive what terrible fate has surely befallen them.

We are required by tribal etiquette to dance and display our trophies of war . . . it'd be rude not to, for to the Cheyenne these provide physical proof of the victory, and offer them solace for our own losses . . . or so they believe. It is said by the others in the dance who were among our group when we engaged the infantry, that me and Susie, Ma'ovésá'e' heståhkehá'e . . . Red-haired Twin Women they call us . . . led the first charge, and our courage inspired the other warriors to follow us into battle . . . but we know that ain't true, for we weren't bein' brave . . . it was just our stony hearts of vengeance that drove us to do what we done. Aye, it's true we are savages ourselves, incapable even of feelin' remorse for our actions . . . or so we believed.

We leave the dance just as soon as we can and return to our lodge. We are knackered and all we wish to do is to crawl under the buffalo robes and sleep like the dead. But even that luxury we are denied, for in the middle of the night Susie shakes me awake.

"You're havin' nightmares, Meggie," says she, "you're cryin' out in your sleep. I thought at first you were awake. You said, *'Holy Jaysus, what 'ave we done, sister?'* "

"Aye, Susie, I was dreamin' . . . I was havin' a nightmare . . . it was terrible . . . I was dreamin' that we were murderers you and me, we were cuttin' the hands off babies . . . they were screamin', lookin' us in the eye and screamin' . . . we killed babies, Susie . . ."

"No, Meggie, no we did not, we would never do such a thing. We killed soldiers today, not babies, remember?"

"They were just boys, Susie. That first soldier we killed was just a scared kid."

"He was shootin' at us, Meggie, he was tryin' to kill us."

"We ain't spoken of this yet, but we may as well now. That boy was a Paddy, and you know it as well as I do. Did ya not hear his brogue, Susie, when he begged me not to kill him? He was an Irishman."

"Aye," says she in a tiny voice, "I heard it, Meggie, but I didn't want to say."

"Jaysus Christ, sister, we cut off his damned bollocks, didn't we?"

"That we did, four pair of 'em we got. It's what we've always said we were goin' to do . . . remember? An' today we finally got our chance. We got our revenge."

"Did it make ya feel better, Susie? Did it bring our girls back, or make ya feel better about their dyin'?"

Susie doesn't answer that question for a long time. She gets back under the bed of buffalo robes and blankets, puts her arm around me and cuddles up, like we've done to comfort each other since we were wee girls . . . and just when I think she's fallen asleep again, she whispers at last: "No, sister . . . no . . . it did not."

And now Molly and Pretty Nose are

gone . . . two more dear friends lost in these wars. Is there no end to it?

■ ■ ■ ■

Ledger Book XII
Hell

■ ■ ■ ■

I spotted him when they were still a little distance away, leading his party down the hillside into the encampment . . . a man, if one can call him such, whom it would be impossible to mistake for another. Greasy black hair falling in curls to his shoulders, black Army Stetson worn sideways with the top cut out and eagle feathers protruding from it, black knee-high cavalry boots, the seam split halfway down, navy blue cavalry jacket and pale blue breeches with yellow stripes, all filthy, stained, surely never washed . . . I could almost smell his stench from here, could feel the bile rising in my throat, the cold fear washing over me. I knew that this time there would be no escape . . .

(from the journals of Molly McGill)

17 June 1876

Hell . . . and more to come . . . I will tell from the beginning . . . as long as I have strength to write, and am permitted. Our women's warrior society's first battle went terribly wrong . . . and right from the start. We were riding with a mixed band of Lakota and Cheyenne, in pursuit of a mixed band of Crow and Shoshone who were fleeing down valley from our superior force . . . or so we thought . . . they led us up a side canyon, riding hard, turning to fire at us. I rode beside my partner, Pretty Nose, who returned fire, although I did not.

The canyon narrowed into a kind of ravine with steep bluffs on either side, and as our soldiers rode in, the trap was sprung. The gunfire began all at once from both sides of the bluff, and from the creek bed at the base of the ravine . . . an ambush, a bloodbath, chaos, horses screaming and falling to the bullets, our warriors shot out of their saddles, Pretty Nose's horse was hit, went down on its knees, and rolled sideways. She scrambled to be clear of it but her right leg was caught beneath his withers as he fell. I dismounted to try to help her, taking hold of the horse's bridle and pulling up with all my strength. Struggling to rise, he raised his head just enough to take some of the weight off her leg and Pretty Nose managed to drag herself free. The horse fell back, wild-eyed, flared nostrils running blood, but before we could both mount Spring, five warriors with rifles came running toward us out of the creek bottom. There was no point in trying to draw my Colt, and Pretty Nose had lost her Winchester in the fall. "Ooetaneo'o," she said to me, which I knew meant Crow. They surrounded us, clearly surprised to see that we were women. They poked both of us with coup sticks. One of them snatched the reins from my hand, and the Colt from my holster, dragged us into the creek bottom, and threw us to the ground behind the embankment. The shooting continued . . . there was no escape for our soldiers . . . nowhere to run . . . except to turn and ride back out of the ravine, or try to ride up the hill to the bluffs above, ground held by our attackers . . . Our captors took up their positions behind the bank and resumed firing. I crawled up and looked out to see if I might identify any of our women . . . more of our warriors shot and tumbling from their mounts . . . others afoot, running, shot down, horses falling, screaming, flailing . . . the floor of the ravine littered with bodies of man and animal, some writhing in agony . . . cries, gunfire, mayhem . . . I caught a glimpse of Phemie riding hard on her white stallion, returning fire alternately toward the bluff and then toward the riverbank. I saw Christian Goodman also riding in the thick of things, hollering at the top of his lungs, though I could not make out what he was saying, a prayer no doubt . . . Before I could look further, one of our captors pulled me roughly back down beneath the undercut bank.

Gradually the shooting subsided, and the Crow and Shoshone who had been stationed on the bluffs rode back down into the ravine, as those in the creek bottom came out, all yipping, shaking their rifles in the air in triumph. Then began the grisly business of taking scalps, mutilating the dead, collecting weapons and horses that were still alive and uninjured. Presumably our captors felt that we represented sufficient spoils of war for they did not participate in these post-battle activities. Instead we were ordered in sign talk to mount Spring, and surrounded by the five Crow, now also mounted, we began to make our way out of the ravine. I could think of nothing but our compatriots, and could not imagine that any of them had survived the onslaught. Now as we rode through the killing field, I dreaded coming upon their bodies, or seeing them desecrated by these acts of barbarism. Yet I could not prevent myself from carefully scanning each body we passed, mildly heartened not to see anyone I recognized. Perhaps by some miracle our women had escaped after all.

Near and distant gunfire, bugles, Indian yells, and the cries of soldiers issued from the hills, valleys, and draws in what seemed like all directions, giving us some sense of the broad scope of this battle. When we reached the top of the bluffs, we kept mostly to the high ground, moving generally southeast. We had periodic sightings of skirmishes raging below. After traveling nearly an hour and traversing three valleys, we arrived at what appeared to be the main encampments of the Crow and Shoshone, the bivouacs of each tribe separated by a sizable herd of horses, guarded by armed boys. There were also a dozen or so women in the respective camps, who as we rode in began to trill in victory when they saw that their warriors brought captives. All came out to inspect us, some grabbing at us roughly, uttering what were clearly insults in their mocking guttural tongues. "Keep your head high and your eyes straight ahead, Molly," Pretty Nose advised me. "Do not look at them, do not show fear."

When we reached the rope horse corral, the women who had followed dragged us off Spring's back. One of the boys led her into the corral, uncinched her girth strap, slipped off the saddle and her bridle, and released her. I wondered if I would ever see my horse again, though that was the least of my worries.

Our captors seemed now to be arguing over which of them owned us. One of the women tugged at my hair and muttered something. Another grabbed Pretty Nose roughly by the arm and began to drag her, limping, away. It was clear that we were to be separated. Pretty Nose tore her arm free and made sign talk to the woman, obviously saying that she did not wish to be manhandled. Then she looked back over her shoulder at me, not pleadingly or afraid, but proud, defiant, with a small smile, as if to set an example and to give me courage . . .

which she did.

Similarly, two women, one on either side of me, chattering angrily, grabbed hold of my arms and began to pull me away. They were surprisingly strong though far smaller than I, and I, too, shook free of them, raising a fist to make my intention understood. I walked between them then to a rough lodge set among a number of others . . . not exactly tipis but crude shelters made of curved willow branches with canvas coverings. They shoved me to a seated position, bound my hands together with a rawhide thong, and tied a rope around my ankle, the other end of which they attached to a wooden stake driven into the ground with a rock . . . I was tethered there like the family dog.

I do not know exactly how much time passed . . . five, six hours, perhaps longer. Our captors had returned to the battlefield, and for most of that time I could still hear the distant gunfire. Periodically, wounded warriors came in, or those needing fresh horses. At some point one of the women gave me a tin cup of water, which I was able to drink between my bound hands, then a small strip of dried buffalo meat. By mid-afternoon the shooting had become increasingly sporadic, and then finally ceased altogether but for an isolated shot now and again. The various bands of Crow and Shoshone warriors, some of them sporting fresh scalps on their belts, began to return to the encampment with victory ululations met by joyous trilling from the women . . . and occasional keening as the bodies of their dead were brought in.

He was riding with one of these bands, as I dreaded he would be . . . I spotted him when they were still a little distance away, leading his party down the hillside into the encampment . . . a man, if one can call him such, whom it would be impossible to mistake for another. Greasy black hair falling in curls to his shoulders, Army Stetson worn sideways with the top cut out and eagle feathers protruding from it, black knee-high cavalry boots, the seam split halfway down, navy blue cavalry jacket and pale blue breeches with yellow stripes, all filthy, stained, surely never washed . . . I could almost smell his stench from here, could feel the bile rising in my throat, the cold fear washing over me. I knew that this time there would be no escape . . .

Please, come for me, Hawk, wherever you are, I beg you . . . find me, save me . . . please . . . I know you'll come . . . please, hurry.

After he rode into the encampment, it took Jules Seminole very little time to locate me . . . "Ah, *ma belle,* my beauty! When they told Jules that a blond white woman had been taken captive, I knew . . . I knew that you had come back to me to beg my forgiveness, I knew you could not stay away for another moment, that your love was too strong to keep us apart any longer." Now he fell to his knees beside me, swept his hat off. "Yes, my darling, Jules forgives you, I forgive you for everything . . . you see, I know why you stole my bride, for you could not bear to share Jules with her, you had to have me to yourself, so you took her away. It is perfectly normal. *Oui, mon amour,* but now, at last, your dream has come true, it will just be you and Jules from now on, a lifetime of love together . . ." He smiled his revolting rotten-toothed grin, cruel, mocking. "Yes, a lifetime of taking pleasure in each other, pleasure and pain such as you have never before known, my darling, that Jules can promise you. Ah, *oui, ma petite,* beginning this very day, surely the luckiest day of your life, you will drink the sweet nectar of Jules's love juice . . . every day for the rest of your life . . . and you will taste the divinity candy of his darkest, his most forbidden recesses . . ."

I vomited. I had only the bit of water I had drunk earlier and a small bite of the buffalo jerky in my stomach, but it came up without warning, in a wave of disgust and terror. "You'll have to kill me," I managed to say. "I'll bite it off. I'll rip your throat out with my teeth."

He slapped me so hard that he knocked me from my seated position to the ground. I lay on my side with my face in the dirt, breathing hard, trying not to cry, making no effort to sit up again.

"*Mais non,* that you will not do." Seminole spoke no longer in the wheedling, unctuous tones with which he had been addressing me. Now his voice seemed to come from another person — hard, vicious. "*Au contraire,* you will do exactly what I tell you to do, exactly as I wish for you to do it. For you see, in addition to Jules's many other talents, I have pliers and excellent dentistry skills. I rather like to be in the mouths of toothless women . . . a sensation like no other. However, such a procedure as pulling your teeth will collapse your face and ruin your looks, which would be a terrible shame for a woman so lovely as you. As to killing you, *oui, bien sûr,* that, too, can be easily arranged. But not yet. For that would be a punishment far too easy for you. Do you realize that Jules's precious jewels were swollen for a week after our last meeting? You stole his horse, his wife, his gun, you did grave damage to his manhood, not to mention insulting his dignity. You have a great debt to pay Jules before you will be allowed to die. And by then, you will be begging for death."

Seminole grabbed a handful of my hair and pulled me back to a seated position on the ground. He had thick arms and a swarthy simian build, and I was struck again by his strength, as I remembered from our first encounter.

"I'm begging for it now," I said.

"Far too soon, *ma petite putain*," he said, "my little whore, first you have your debt to pay."

"You know the warrior Hawk, do you not?" I asked.

Now his tone changed again, becoming oddly whiny and defensive. "Of course, Jules's mother is Cheyenne," he said. "She is the sister of the Sweet Medicine Chief Little Wolf. Jules grew up with Hawk." A shadow crossed Seminole's face. "My uncle Little Wolf banished Jules from the tribe. That is why Jules rides now with the Crow. When we were boys everyone liked Hawk. He was a fast runner and won all the races, he was always the best at games, the best rider of horses, the best shooter of the bow, and of the rifle and pistol. And even then, it was said that he was a shape-shifter and could become a hawk, that he could fly like a hawk. Everyone admired him. Jules was not well liked, for his father was a Frenchman from Canada, a trapper, who was not well liked by the People, for he brought alcohol among them. Jules wanted to be friends with Hawk, but Hawk did not like Jules. Jules was not gifted at games, or running, or at all the other things that Hawk could do so well . . . Jules had no special talents, no one admired him. Hawk ignored Jules, he mocked him. Jules does not like to be made fun of. Now tell me why do you ask Jules about this man Hawk?"

"Because I want you to know that he is my husband," I said, "and I am going to have his son. If you violate me, if you force me to do any of the vile things of which you speak, if you harm me in any way, you know what Hawk will do to you, don't you? You know what he is capable of. He will hunt you down, and you will suffer terribly before he kills you. I am certain that he is already on his way here. He rescued me the last time, and he will rescue me again."

Seminole laughed, as if suddenly terribly

relieved. "Ah, *mon amour,* you see you have come back to Jules at just the right moment. I had no idea you were married to Hawk. I am so sorry to give you this sad news, but as his wife, you deserve to know the truth: Hawk was killed today in battle, one of the Army long-gun soldiers shot him from his horse. Jules witnessed this himself. So you see, now you are free to remarry, to realize your dream of spending the rest of your life with Jules. Together we shall raise Hawk's son as our own. Don't you see, my beauty? This will bring us even closer together."

"You're lying, I do not believe you."

"*Mais ma belle,* why do you think he hasn't come already to save you?" Seminole asked. He looked up in the air. "Look, not a single hawk in sight this afternoon. See, only the vultures circling, waiting to feast on the remains of the dead. Your Hawk, my darling, has been shot from the sky, falling to earth just as he fell from his horse. I only hope his people have recovered his body before the scavengers reach it. It would be such a shame if he had go to Seano with no eyes, and his entrails pecked out."

That was all it took to cause me to fall completely apart. I began sobbing violently. Although I did not want to admit it, either to Seminole or to myself, I believed what he said. Hawk would have found me by now, he would have come for me if he could . . . I know he would have . . .

"Well now, *mon amour*," said Seminole, "no sense in crying over it. Jules is going to remove the rope from your ankle, but I will leave your hands tied, for I do not think that you are as yet entirely trustworthy . . . although, believe me, you will soon be as docile as my former wife, Vóese'e, Happy Woman, as Jules so lovingly named her.

"We are going to retrieve your little pony from the corral, while everyone here is packing up the camp. You and Jules will ride side by side, like a real couple, to the supply base of *mon cher* Général Georges Crook, where my warriors will receive their pay for scouting and battle services rendered, and where Jules will receive his next orders. There we will spend the night . . . and you must now begin to imagine all the intimate acts you will perform upon Jules as a loving wife on her wedding night. Ah, *oui* . . . we shall be alone together at last, my darling . . . And tomorrow we will return to our village to the west, where we will commence our true life together. You will be the most obedient of wives to Jules. For if you are not . . . and I do hope you understand this . . . the life of your unborn child will be in the gravest danger."

I pulled myself together then. It was one thing to wish death for myself, quite another to sacrifice the child that grows inside me. That thought was all I had left from which to draw strength. I remembered Pretty Nose's proud, defiant courage and I tried to summon some of it for myself.

One of the horse boys cut Spring out of the corral and returned my tack. The camp packed up and we rode out. I tried without success to spot Pretty Nose in the procession as we left. But after we had been riding for a half hour or so, I heard her soft, sad voice beginning to sing one of the songs Lulu had taught us, "Vive la Rose," "Long Live the Rose," about a girl abandoned by her lover. Pretty Nose was letting me know where in the procession she was, and that she was alright. I turned in the saddle and finally got a glimpse of her; we smiled at each other, and I took up her song, so that she would know, I, too, was alright . . . even if neither of us really was.

"Ah, *mon amour*!" said Seminole when our song came to an end. "I had no idea you sang so beautifully, and in French! *Quel plaisir!* You will sing songs of love to Jules every day! How that excites him! But, please, you need not worry about Jules ever leaving you, *ma chérie,* or you ever leaving him, for that will never happen, we are inseparable. Such a perfect, loving couple we shall make, united forever, morning and night in our unquenchable passion!"

As we rode, Seminole kept up a running discourse of filth and madness, alternately and without warning, becoming at times strangely civil, even banal, speaking both English and French, or a mixture of the two, turning in the saddle to address me as if we were intimates taking a pleasure ride. Other times he didn't appear to be speaking to me at all, but involved in some bizarre interior dialogue, in different voices, alternately whiny, argumentative, absurdly tender, all punctuated by crazed laughter. He obviously found his own company highly entertaining; I began to have an ever clearer and more chilling sense of how truly insane he was. I knew beyond a doubt that he had the power and the depravity to break me, as he had broken Martha in both mind and spirit, and that the only defense I had was to find in him some point of weakness, some opening . . . In the meantime, all I could do was to make the smallest, most tightly closed package of myself in order to try to preserve my own sanity. *Keep your head high and your eyes straight ahead . . . do not look at them, do not show fear,* Pretty Walker had said to me.

"Tell Jules, my darling, why you carry the ledger book upon your back," he asked. "Are you an *artiste*? Do you have other secret talents Jules has not yet discovered?"

"I keep a journal," I said.

"You are a writer?" he asked.

"No, I just keep a journal."

"And have you written about Jules?"

"Yes, as a matter of fact, I have, in one of the earlier ledgers."

"Ah, you write about Jules? How wonderful, I am so happy, so proud!" he said. "You must love him very much." A shadow crossed his face. "But Jules does not know how to read. If only I had known that one day someone would write a book about me, I would have insisted upon learning."

"It is not a book, and it is not about you. It is a journal, and you just appear in a few entries."

"You must read them to Jules!"

"I do not have them with me . . . obviously," I said. "All my old journals are in a parfleche that Hawk's grandmother now keeps for me . . . However, if you let me go, I could certainly ride back to fetch them, and bring them to read to you."

At this Seminole laughed like a madman.

538

"Ah, *mon amour,* Jules is so happy to see that you have a sense of humor. That was one thing missing in my marriage to Vóese'e . . . the girl you know as Martha . . . I must say, the poor thing was not very much fun, she did not know how to laugh, or to make me laugh. But I can see that you and Jules will laugh much together."

"That I would very much doubt."

"Tell me, my precious, is Jules as dashing a hero in your book as he is in real life?"

"I told you, it's not a book, it's not about you. And, no, you are neither dashing nor a hero in the few entries in which you are mentioned."

"But in your book, you must surely speak of Jules's irresistible animal attraction, *non*?"

"I may have used the term 'animal' to describe him . . . although that would seem rather generous."

At this insult, Seminole's cheerful mood just as quickly evaporated. He glared at me and I expected that he was going to hit me again. "Ah, *oui,* that does not make Jules laugh, that hurts Jules's feelings. Jules never forgets insults. Be assured, Jules will pay you back for that."

Seminole's strange combination of evil and infantilism, his changeable moods and voices, kept me constantly on guard. He had a compulsion to wound and terrify, while at the same time a bizarre need to be accepted, admired, even loved by his victims.

"You're right, I am writing a book about Jules," I said in an attempt to placate him, "an entire book about him. He has many different sides to him, Jules does. Yes, he possesses a certain undeniable animal attraction. However, I also point out that he could use a bath every now and then."

At this Seminole laughed again. "Ah, that is much, much better, my love! Jules knew it, a whole book about him! If only I could read. You will read it to Jules, won't you, *ma princesse*? Do you know what Jules will promise, my darling . . . because he is so deeply in love with you? I promise I will take a bath once every month . . . I swear, once every month without fail . . ." And he laughed, and laughed.

The afternoon winds had come up, blowing ominously to suit my own sense of doom. But at least it helped to make conversation more difficult, and to drown out Seminole's words as we rode.

We traveled south and west for perhaps three hours, until the sun was just setting and we reached the edge of the Army base camp in the valley of Goose Creek. We kept to the hills on the perimeter without entering the encampment itself, but close enough to have a sense of the vastness of it — huge corrals of mules and horses, endless rows of supply wagons, canvas soldiers' tents, cooking, dining, and medical tents all set up in military formation. Cavalry and infantry companies were still arriving from the battlefield, bringing with them the dead and wounded, attended to by doctors and orderlies. Fires burned near several mess tents as cooks prepared supper. After all this time in the wilds, it was strange to witness this relatively orderly outpost of civilization, and I cannot say that I did not experience a certain twinge of nostalgia . . . even longing. Then again, it occurred to me that but for one bite of dried beef, which I promptly vomited, I had not eaten since this morning, and perhaps it was simply the familiar smell of white-man food cooking that inspired these thoughts.

Seminole halted us in the hills a good distance away from the Army encampment below, and his band pitched its evening bivouac. He was going off to collect pay from the quartermaster for his warriors and scouts, and clearly did not wish for me to be seen by any of the Army personnel. He turned me over to the same two sullen women who had taken charge of me before.

They reminded me of prison guards I had known, handling me roughly and contemptuously as they tethered me again to my stake, clearly enjoying their power over the powerless. Before Seminole left, I asked him if he could at least free my hands so that I could continue working on my "book" about him while he was away. He was so pleased by this notion that he agreed, untying my hands and speaking sternly to the women, presumably telling them not to let me out of their sight. I took the journal from my back and assumed the squatting position, learned eventually by all prisoners in solitary confinement, so that one's butt does not rest on the cold stone floor of the cell.

My keepers sit cross-legged by a small fire in front of the makeshift stick shelter they have constructed, cooking meat impaled on sticks that they hold over the flames. From the smell, I identify it as either elk or deer, for buffalo has a particular odor of its own. They do not offer me any, nor, despite my hunger, do I ask.

Undated entry

After Seminole had been gone for well over an hour, three soldiers rode into the far end of our camp. My first impulse was to cry out to them for help, but then suddenly in a tumult of confusion I realized that to be rescued by the soldiers would only result in captivity of another kind. Presumably, because I'm a white woman and clearly a captive, they would take me in, but then they would surely want to know who I was and where I had come from. What plausible lie could I possibly tell? And when they found out the truth, which they undoubtedly would, what would they do with me, send me back to prison? It had never occurred to me until this moment that there might be a worse fate than being Jules Seminole's "wife" . . . for at least here, I had a chance of escape, while there is no escape from Sing Sing.

The soldiers rode slowly through the camp, stopping as they went to speak with the Crow. They appeared to be asking questions, as if searching for someone in particular, for those they consulted pointed in our general direction. When finally they reached the hut beside which I was tied, the highest-ranking of them, a captain it appeared from his uniform, addressed my women keepers in native tongue. They answered, gesturing toward the Army camp. I realized that they must be looking for Seminole. The soldiers regarded me with obvious curiosity. I kept my eyes downcast, in my squatting position, trying to be as inconspicuous as possible. My attire gave no suggestion that I was not myself a native, my face covered with dirt after the long day, my skin darkened in our time under the plains sun, my braided hair equally filthy, though still noticeably fair. The captain now looked at me, then asked the women another question . . . I assumed demanding why was I thus tied. They answered. He dismounted, handed his reins to one of the soldiers, walked over, and squatted in front of me. He spoke to me in what I recognized to be the Cheyenne language, and I realized that the women must have told him I was a captive from that tribe.

"I'm sorry, I don't really speak the language yet," I answered.

"You are Caucasian, madam?" he asked in astonishment.

"Yes."

"A captive?"

I picked my tether rope off the ground and held it up to him. "It would appear so, sir, yes."

"I am Captain John G. Bourke. May I ask who you are, and how you came to be here?"

"That is a long story."

"Where were you captured?"

"I was riding with the Cheyenne during the battle on the Rosebud."

"Riding with the Cheyenne? In what capacity?"

"As a warrior."

"I am afraid that I do not understand, madam. Please explain yourself."

In that moment, Seminole himself galloped up to the hut, as if he knew the soldiers were there and was clearly agitated about it. The captain stood and turned toward him. Seminole leapt from his horse, coming to attention and offering a kind of absurdly exaggerated salute. It occurred to me that were he not also insane and depraved, he would simply be a buffoon. Little wonder that Hawk mocked him when they were boys.

"Ah, *mon cher capitaine,*" he said, "*mais quel plaisir de vous voir,* what a pleasure to see you, my dear Captain Bourke." He swept his arm out in an expansive gesture as if to indicate the grand premises. "Welcome to my humble abode. Jules has been looking all over for you in the supply camp, and finally I was told that you had gone to find me. To what does Jules owe the honor of this visit?"

"What is the meaning of this, Seminole? Who is this woman?"

"She is an enemy warrior, *mon capitaine,* fighting with the Cheyenne, and taken prisoner by my men during the battle."

"But she is a white woman," said the captain.

"Ah, *oui,* that is correct, *mon capitaine.*"

"Fighting with the renegade savages against the United States Army?" said Bourke, clearly confused. He turned and addressed me again: "You do understand, madam, that for a citizen of the United States to ride into battle as a soldier of an enemy army is an act of treason?"

"I'm not really a citizen of the United States, Captain."

"Tell me your name, please."

"Mé'koomat a'xevà . . . which, as you appear to be fluent in several native tongues, you may know translates into English as something like Woman Who Kicks Man in Testicles."

At this, Bourke actually blushed, and I remembered that the Kellys had told me he was a devout Catholic, and rather straight-laced . . . although clearly less so in his relations with May Dodd. "Are you mocking me, madam?" he asked.

"No, of course not, that really is my name."

"Your Christian name, please?"

"I don't have one, sir. I was reborn into the Cheyenne tribe. And I am married to a

Cheyenne man, a warrior named Hawk . . . perhaps you know him? As Wyoming and Montana are only territories and not states, you could say that I am, by marriage, a citizen of the Cheyenne nation."

"There is no such thing as the Cheyenne nation, madam," said Bourke. "This is the United States of America, and we claim sovereignty over these territories. You are a traitor, and will be charged as such."

"Mais non, non, mon cher capitaine," Seminole protested, "My dear Captain Bourke, Jules must respectfully remind you that the agreement our esteemed Général Crook made with his Indian scouts is that renegades wounded or taken prisoner by our warriors during battle, including women and children, belong to us, not to the Army."

"Yes, Seminole, renegade prisoners of enemy tribes," said Bourke.

"*Exactement, mon capitaine.* You heard the lady speak herself. She is Cheyenne, a member of an enemy tribe."

"She is a white woman, and this is a bizarre situation, to say the least. But we will get to the bottom of it. You will release this woman into my custody right now, Sergeant Seminole. Untie her. I assume she has a horse. Fetch it. In addition, you are to report to General Crook as soon as possible. He is ordering all his head scouts to come in. He wishes to get a rough sense of the full scope and size of the Cheyenne and Lakota force we met today. The battle did not go as the general had expected it would. We do not suggest that the Army was beaten; however, the savages fought with a good deal more ferocity and tenacity than anticipated, as well as a certain tactical prowess we have rarely seen from them. We suffered considerable losses."

Perhaps it was due to my own sheer exhaustion, fear, rage, and sense of utter hopelessness, but I could not prevent myself from speaking up then. "You said it yourself, Captain, there is no such thing as the Cheyenne nation. However, they believe there is, as the Lakota believe there is a Lakota nation. Having been here long before us, they also believe that they have certain inalienable rights to continue living on the land their ancestors have walked for a thousand generations . . . land I might add that your government, which now claims sovereignty, gave to them recently by treaty. They fought today with tenacity and ferocity as you put it, for the simple reason that they are making a last stand in defense of their country . . . not yours, not mine, not the United States of America, *their* country.

They have had enough treaties broken and land stolen from them, enough Army attacks upon their villages in the dead of winter, the slaughtering of defenseless women, children, and elders. Indeed, my understanding, Captain Bourke, is that you yourself participated in such a massacre upon the village of the Cheyenne chief Little Wolf this past winter in which your . . . shall we say your dear friend May Dodd and others of her party were killed. Is that not correct, sir?"

Bourke went pale at my outburst and looked at me with an expression of shock and incredulity. *"Good Lord,"* he said in a low, tremulous voice, nearly a whisper, "but . . . but this is madness. How dare you address me in this manner, madam? Who are you? Where have you come from? How did you get here?"

21 June 1876

This entry and much of the last two, I write from a tent in the supply base camp of General George Crook's troops of the Bighorn and Yellowstone Expedition. I wear leg shackles to effectively preclude any escape attempt, and I am guarded on all sides by armed soldiers, which equally discourages the brief nostalgia I felt for the comforting embrace of civilization. Nevertheless, I am fed, I have bathed and been given clean attire — a man's cotton shirt and trousers, which because of my height, fit me adequately, with a belt to cinch them up about my waist, although it does seem strange to wear white-man clothing again. My ledger book was temporarily confiscated from me and transcribed, in case it might hold information of interest to the War Department. Captain Bourke returned it to me himself, and seemed particularly solicitous on this point, largely, I believe, because May Dodd had kept a journal, which was presumably burned by Mackenzie's Army, along with everything else in the village. As a literate fellow, particularly admiring of Shakespeare, according to the Kelly sisters, I suspect that Bourke adheres to the principle of preserving the written word, even something as humble as one of my ledger books.

Before they led me away from Seminole's camp, I begged the captain to intervene on Pretty Nose's behalf. But this he would not do. She was the Crow's captive, he said, to do with as they pleased. As we rode out, I began to sing another of Lulu's songs, "Au Claire de la Lune," "By the Light of the Moon," in the hopes that she would see me leaving with the soldiers. I was briefly heartened to hear her take up the song with me, until the doleful tone of her voice told me of her own suffering. I worry as much for her fate as I do my own.

This is my fourth day here now as the Army attempts to sort out what disposition is to be made of me . . . I have answered no questions about my identity, given neither my name nor any details of where I came from, for why should I help them facilitate my return to Sing Sing?

The captain came to see me this morning, as he has each day. He brought me several new pencils, which I appreciate. He seems a decent and rather tortured fellow himself. However, I can't help but wonder if his new kindness to me is not simply a means of trying to gain my confidence.

Today he told me the Army was willing to recognize that I had been coerced into fighting with the Cheyenne, and that if I cooperated, at least told them my name and where I came from, they would not bring treason charges against me. All would be forgiven and they wished only to return me as quickly and quietly as possible to my previous "civilian" life, whatever and wherever that may be.

He then told me that the War Department

was well aware of the fact that a group of white women, volunteers in the Brides for Indians program, had been mistakenly sent west this past February, though the program itself had been terminated. Of course, they knew of the attack on our train by what they assumed was a band of Lakota warriors.

"In addition to all the young Army recruits," Bourke said, "a number of these women volunteers were also killed in the attack, and their remains eventually identified. Others had wisely defected along the way, and these, too, have been identified. However, it appears from records obtained by the War Department that seven of the total number of women remain unaccounted for. It has been assumed that this was simply a clerical error — sloppy record keeping on the part of a defunct and frankly illegal government program — although there has been speculation that possibly these missing women had been taken captive by the renegades. In any case, madam, the records are presently on their way here, and should arrive within the next day or two. I am asking you now if you were among this group? Is that how you came to be with the Cheyenne? And are there others still with them? It is critical that you tell me so that we might take measures to protect them."

"As you took measures to protect May Dodd and her friends, Captain?"

Bourke looked away with an expression of genuine anguish on his face. He did not answer me.

"If I am a prisoner of war," I said, rattling my shackles, "as I clearly appear to be, I continue to exercise my right to tell you nothing. And if I am not a prisoner, then you must release me."

Bourke stood to leave me. "That, madam, I am afraid I cannot do."

Despite my shackles and my ever-dimming future, one aspect of my incarceration I must admit I rather appreciate — in addition, of course, to the luxuries of a bath and palatable food — is the opportunity to be alone. Solitude is not readily available in the general course of tribal life, and certainly not to our group since the very beginning of this adventure. I listen now to the afternoon prairie wind rising outside; one can hear it coming from a good distance away, and as it arrives, it wraps over and around the tent, rippling the canvas walls. I feel a strange sense of calm and solace in being thus enveloped, in finally having this time to myself — no longer running, free of the endless travel, free of the constant work making and breaking camp, of the dust and dirt, free of the specter of impending war with its constant anxieties, and actual war with its chaos and brutality — time to reflect, rather than simply to react.

I have a chance, finally, to think about Hawk. When we parted on the morning of the battle, he asked me again not to go. He told me he was obligated to ride with his own warrior society, the Dog Soldiers, that Little Wolf was in charge of making the plan of battle for all the warrior societies, and that he must follow his chief. He said he would not be able to look after me, and he placed a single hawk feather in my hair. "This is all the protection I can give you," he said. "Stay here in the camp with my son, keep him safe, bring your little Mouse here and look after her. I beg of you." But in my typically pigheaded fashion, which Meggie and Susie have always said was going to get me in trouble . . . and so it has . . . I felt that I could not disappoint my women, could not let my partner Pretty Nose go into battle alone . . . and thus despite Hawk's entreaties, and even though I did not wish to go to war, I went anyway . . . and this is where that decision has brought me . . . .

what a fool I am.

Is it true what Seminole said? Was Hawk shot? Is he dead? Do I really believe he has the ability to know where I am, that he will come for me? That he can turn himself into a raptor? To fly? Or was it simply a trick of ventriloquism on his part? . . . for the only thing I know for certain is that he can mimic the cry of a hawk in a voice indistinguishable from that of the bird itself . . . and he can make it sound as if it is coming from the air. But fly . . . ? Have I gone mad? It is a notion counter to all reason, to all we know about the physical world around us. Of course, people cannot turn themselves into birds, they cannot fly. They do not converse with bears as Hawk said his grandmother had . . . as if it were the most normal thing in the world. Had I suggested any such thing to my students when I was teaching school, I would surely have been branded a witch — tarred and feathered, turned out, shunned . . . or worse, burned at the stake.

Yet reason and the physical world, the nature of reality itself, is simply different among the natives . . . less rigid, broader, more fluid. It reminds me of the Kellys' advice to forget everything we ever knew or learned in our past lives, for none of it applies here. The natives have a way of putting it themselves: "the real world behind this one," they call it, suggesting that what we see and understand of the surface world is but a façade, which they are capable of navigating beyond. And so it is that in living among them, such things as shape-shifters, talking bears, men turning into birds and flying, all seem somehow plausible.

Being thrust back into the rational realm of civilization has prompted these thoughts on my part, these questions, these grave doubts. It is like the first few moments upon waking from a vivid dream, while one is still in that limbo state between one world and another, not certain where the line lies between the two, or even which is which. Gradually at first, and then all at once, the actuality of the physical world overwhelms that of the dream. Perhaps this is what is happening to me now. Life with Hawk and the Cheyenne is the dream, as was my captivity by Seminole a nightmare, all beginning to fade in the face of this, the real world, to which I have been so abruptly returned.

And something else . . . . I feel my daughter's death more acutely here again . . . for it is here that it happened. Not that I ever forgot her in my short, fledgling life with

Hawk, but somehow there the pain was mitigated by being immersed in a strange, alien place in which Clara had never lived, in which we had never lived together. I long to sink back into that dream, to have Hawk's baby, all of us women together in our lodges, with our husbands and children, living a simple life in nature — but without war, without violence.

22 June 1876

Captain Bourke returned again this morning, bearing a thick folder of papers. He asked for permission to sit, and he took the chair across from mine at the small traveling campaign table that furnishes my tent. He opened the folder and withdrew several sheets of paper from the top, his dark brow furrowed, wearing not at all a triumphant expression, but one of genuine regret.

"From the physical description," he said, "height, weight, eye and hair color, this would appear to be your dossier, madam, or may I address you now as Mrs. Paterson, Mrs. Molly Paterson?"

"No, that you may not do, Captain. I go under my maiden name, Miss Molly McGill, and you may call me that, but not the other."

"However, you were listed under the name

Paterson in the brides program, is that not correct?"

"Yes. But I am telling you, it is no longer my name."

"And your residence was Sing Sing Prison in New York?"

I nodded.

Bourke looked again at the papers in his hand. "I now understand, Miss McGill," said Bourke, sadly, "why you were reluctant to reveal your true identity. A convicted murderer serving a life sentence . . ."

"As you can see, Captain, the brides program was not terribly selective."

This prompted a slight ironic smile from the captain. "May I assume that you were wrongly convicted, Miss McGill?"

"Not at all. Guilty as charged."

"And you feel no remorse?"

"None. Would it make you feel better if I did, Captain? You're going to send me back, aren't you?"

"It was not my decision to make," he said, "but, yes, you are to be returned to New York as soon as possible. You will be transported by Army escort to the Union Pacific station in Medicine Bow. There you will be met by officers of the U.S. Marshals Service who will accompany you on the journey to New York."

I lifted a foot, rattling again my chain. "Wearing these, I assume?"

"That will be determined by the marshals."

"And when do I leave?"

"Within forty-eight hours. There is still paperwork to be completed. I'm sorry, Miss McGill. Truly, I am. You have clearly led a difficult life, and been hardened by it."

"Living in New York with a drunken wastrel husband who murdered our daughter does that to a girl, Captain . . . not to mention two years in prison, much of that in solitary confinement . . . or for that matter this life I have led thus far on the plains. I expect your friend, May Dodd, was equally hardened by her experiences, was she not?"

A shadow crossed Bourke's face, and he looked away but did not answer, the pain in his expression mixed with a certain confusion. It became clear to me how incomprehensible May's life as a woman, and mine, were to the captain . . . he seemed to be searching for a way to forgive us our trespasses.

"I met your daughter while among the Cheyenne, Captain."

"That is quite enough, Miss McGill," Bourke snapped. "My personal life is none of your concern."

"I am concerned about all children. Especially those living with what remains of the free tribes, given U.S. Army policy toward the disposition of these people."

"You know nothing about Army policy, madam."

"You would be surprised, Captain, how much I have learned. I only mention your daughter because I thought you might like to know that she is a lovely, happy, beautiful child. But she, too, is at risk."

And with that Bourke, furrowing his dark brow in the same expression, once again took rapid leave of me.

23 June 1876

Although, of course, I could not mention to Captain Bourke that I knew Gertie, I had hoped she would learn I was here and come to see me. And so this morning she has. We embraced when she arrived at my tent, and I broke down, so relieved was I to see a friendly face, a luxury I will soon be denied.

"Easy now, honey," she said, holding me tight. "It's alright, you goin' to be OK."

"No, it isn't alright, Gertie, and I am never going to be OK."

"I know, I know . . . and there ain't nothin' more I can do for you either, honey. You know that, too, don't you?"

"There is nothing anyone can do for me."

"Cap'n Bourke sent me," she said. "He thinks you're a tough cookie . . . a 'hard woman,' he said. I guess he ain't seen you fall apart like this."

"Nor will he ever," I said, my tears subsiding. "Why did he send you?"

"Knowin' I was close to May, he thinks maybe you'll open up to me, give me some information about the others. He don't want the same thing happenin' to them as happened to her and her friends, not to mention his child. He's a good man, the cap'n . . . really he is . . . but like everyone else he's caught up in the system . . . he's a soldier, after all, and like all soldiers he takes his orders from his superiors. Course, he don't know I already know all about the others. He don't know about Meggie and Susie, neither, except for some wild tales circulatin' among the enlisted men about a pair a' painted, red-haired banshees seen ridin' with the renegades at the Rosebud — killin', scalpin', and cuttin' the nuts off soldiers, they say they were. I gotta tell ya, those damn Irish scamps got these young recruits spooked real bad."

"It's just what the girls said they were going to do, Gertie."

"Look, I know you ain't goin' to tell the

cap'n a damn thing about the others, and a' course neither am I. Him askin' me to come here just offered a good excuse to see you. He's also signed me on to take ya down to Medicine Bow station, 'cause he trusts me. He's sendin' a dozen soldiers to escort you, ten on horseback and two with you an' me in the wagon, with strict orders not to let you out of their sight for a minute. Hell, honey, you won't even get to take a pee in private."

"I can't go back to prison, Gertie . . . I just can't. I've known freedom now . . . maybe for the first time in my life. I've fallen in love with a good man, and that's also a first time. I'm going to have Hawk's baby, or so says the medicine woman. You know what happens, don't you, to women who give birth in Sing Sing? They take their babies away as soon as they're born, put them in the care of a wet nurse, and send them to an adoption agency. I can't go back there, Gertie. I'd rather die. Do you understand what I'm saying? I'm not asking you to try to help me escape, because I know you can't do that, and I know there is no escape. But I do have a favor to ask of you."

Gertie looked at me questioningly for a long time. Finally, as if she had sorted out in her mind some version of what I was going to ask her, she nodded, and said: "I'm not gonna want to do your favor, am I, Molly?"

"No."

"Then don't even bother askin' me, honey . . . because that I cannot do."

"Let me at least ask you this then, Gertie. If Captain Bourke doesn't confiscate my ledger book before we leave here tomorrow, they will when we get to Medicine Bow. The government and the Army is not going to let any written evidence of their chicanery survive. I'd like to make one last entry. Will you come back in an hour, and take it yourself?"

"What do you want me to do with it, honey?"

"I don't know, Gertie . . . put it to some good use if ever you can. I'll leave that up to you. All my other books are in the care of Hawk's grandmother. Who knows what will happen to them, either? They'll most likely be consumed in flames by the end of these Indian wars, as were May's."

"Sure, honey, I'll take it, and I'll keep it safe. You're right, they won't let you leave with it. When the time is right, I'll see that it gets into the hands of someone who, like you say, can maybe put it to good use, who can tell your story of what happened out

563

here. I'll be back for it in an hour."

"And Gertie, one last thing, I want you to promise me that after I give this to you, you won't read it until you return from taking me to Medicine Bow."

Gertie looked hard at me again, then finally nodded reluctantly and said: "Awright, honey, I promise."

My darling Clara,
I don't know what, if anything, lies beyond this life . . . having gone before me you surely know more about it than I. What I do know, my little girl, is that the dead do not read the journals and letters those of us still living address to them. And so I write to myself, but with you in my heart, as I have throughout this ordeal. I seek your forgiveness, which you cannot give, and knowing that as well, only I can forgive myself, which I cannot do, either. The grand tragedy of life is that we can never go back to fix our terrible mistakes. Everyone should be allowed to do so, just once. Instead, all we can do is to relive them, over and over and over again, to torture ourselves endlessly with questions to which there are no answers. *Why did I leave you there with him? What was I thinking? Why didn't*

I take you to the neighbors? I'll tell you why . . . because you were sleeping so peacefully, and I didn't want to disturb you. Yes, instead of disturbing your sleep, I left you there to be beaten to death.

I enjoyed a brief moment of peace, a respite of solace and escape here with Hawk. I was loved and held close. I saw a future lying ahead with him and your unborn brother. I thought that perhaps in this way, I might be able to earn your forgiveness and my own. But that hope, too, has now died. I write not in a spirit of self-pity, but one of resignation, of acceptance. I am ready. I am coming for you, at last, my dear, darling Clara.

Your loving mother.

And that is all I have left to say in these pages. My adventure comes to an end, and I rest my pen once and for all.

■ ■ ■ ■

LEDGER BOOK XIII
THE RETURN
OF MARTHA

■ ■ ■ ■

War is funny that way . . . aye, it's kinda
like the first time ya let a boy inside your
knickers . . . it's usually a big disappointment, a letdown, maybe it even leaves you
feelin' a little sick to your stomach. But
then another part a' you wants to try it
again, and when ya do, knowin' more or
less what to expect, it's that much easier,
and even easier the time after that, until
pretty soon, damned if you don't get to
likin' it. And that's how it is with makin'

war . . . not so different really than makin'
love.

(from the journals of Margaret Kelly)

21 June 1876

With all the travelin' these past months, I'm gettin' pretty competent at writin' in my ledger book off the back of a horse. Aye, we're on the move again — west and north, our ranks swellin' with the addition of the "reservation" Indians who have joined us, more joinin' up all the time. These are mainly Lakota, with some Cheyenne and Arapaho, who had already surrendered and were livin' at the agencies. As word spread of Sitting Bull's Sun Dance vision in which the white soldiers were fallin' into his camp headfirst like grasshoppers, followed by our victory on the Rosebud, the boyos been sneakin' off the res by the hundreds to hook up with us, even though it ain't permitted. Life there is bleedin' boring, nothin' for 'em to do all day long. They want to hunt and fight again, because that's what a lad lives for in this country, it's everything he's ever

569

been brought up to do. Take that away, and they got nothin' left.

No tellin' how many we are now, no way to count . . . a couple thousand maybe, all the bands comin' together, movin' in roughly the same direction, separated a little and leavin' at different times, but all with the same destination in mind — the Little Bighorn country. We should reach there this evening. We hear the buffalo herds are thick up that way, the summer grass already tall for the horses. Aye, when it comes right down to it, that's all these folks really need to survive, buffalo and grass. That ain't really askin' so much, is it?

Now that we've left the Rosebud, we're all feelin' that we've also left Molly and Pretty Nose behind once and for all. Somehow we been holdin' on to small hopes that maybe they're still alive, maybe they'll manage to get away and make their way back to us. But now it looks like they are truly lost forever, and we'll never know exactly what became of 'em. That's how it is in this big country, stretchin' out in all directions, so indifferent to the puny lives of human beings . . . sometimes it just swallows people up, and leaves not a trace of 'em behind.

Other bad news is we've learned that Hawk took a bullet, lost a lot of blood, and nearly died. They say it was his nana, Náhkohenaa'é'e, Bear Doctor Woman, who saved his life, that she made a special poultice to stop the bleeding and sat up in his lodge, singing to him for three days and nights without sleeping herself. They say he's better now but still too weak to travel, so they left him behind on the Rosebud with the old woman, two of his male cousins and a nephew to hunt and look after him. We been holding on to one other slim hope, and that is if Molly and Pretty Nose were still alive, Hawk would find 'em and bring 'em back to us. But that hope, too, is gone now, for they say it'll be a good long time before he's up and about . . . even longer before he soars again . . . if you believe in such things . . . Either way, we figure the longer those lasses are missing, the less chance we have of ever seein' 'em again, nor would we know where to begin looking. It breaks our hearts so bad we can hardly bear to look at each other without bustin' out in tears.

And so we have arrived this evening, as planned, and I write this now from our lodge in a side valley of the Little Bighorn, the biggest damned Indian village we ever seen, and still growin' as other bands and

571

more reservation Indians continue to arrive. We first saw it from the high ground as we were ridin' in, and it took our breath away, maybe three miles long and a half mile wide, how many thousands of Indians it's impossible to guess . . . includin' our number, we figure six, seven, eight thousand? The old widow, Elk Woman, who looks after me and Susie, says it's the biggest encampment she's seen in her seventy-six summers, spread out so far in the valley that once you're down in it you can't see from one end to the next, maybe the biggest assembly of tribes there's ever been.

Though it ain't far away from the Rosebud, it's different kind a' country here — broader valleys and big, rollin', mostly tree-less grasslands, but for the cottonwoods and willows in the river bottoms, up high a shimmerin' spread a' hills and arid buttes running away to the horizon that never ends. It's enough to make a lass dizzy . . .

22 June 1876
Aye, now we'll tell of the finest thing that happened this morning . . . me and Susie are up early, it ain't quite dawn yet, and despite its size the camp is real quiet, everyone still asleep in their lodges, the only sounds the first timid songs of the morning

birds, the soft nickering of the horses in the corrals, and an occasional halfhearted bark of a dog. The sound carries so in the still, clear air of daybreak that we can hear the hoofbeats of a single runnin' horse in the hills above the valley . . .

We part the tent flap and can just make out the silhouette of a lone horseman against the pearly gray skyline . . . a lone horsewoman, I oughta say, ridin' bareback, gallopin' across the horizon, long braids flyin' behind her like banners. She turns her mount and comes down the hillside toward the village still at a dead run, and that's when we see it's Pretty Nose herself comin' toward us.

Because we have decided that in an encampment as large as this one, we need to stick close together or risk losin' each other, the rest of our warrior society is camped around us with their families. That includes Lady Hall and Bridge Girl; Maria and her husband, Rock; as well as our noncombatant lasses — Lulu and her boy, Squirrel; Carolyn and Light; Christian and Astrid. These last two me and Susie are convinced have given up waitin' for a Mennonite preacher to magically appear on the plains and marry 'em in the eyes of God, and gone native like the others, which is to say livin' as husband

and wife. Now, one by one, our women begin to come out of their lodges and take up the trilling, wakin' up the whole damned village, others comin' out to see what the commotion is all about, and joining in . . . and then others . . . the sound spreading like a wave across the valley floor, for it is a universal signal among the tribes that one of our own, in this case whether it be Cheyenne, Lakota, or Arapaho, has come home safe to us. Aye, it is something to hear this trilling rising on the air with the promise of dawn, taken up by a thousand women and girls in the village, maybe two thousand even . . . it sends gooseflesh like an army of ants crawlin' across our skin.

Pretty Nose rides in and dismounts, her horse lathered and breathin' hard. Me and Susie, bein' the affectionate souls we are, can't help but take her in our arms and give her a big hug, the others gatherin' around. She doesn't waste any time tellin' us what we all want to know — what happened to 'em, how did she get away . . . and most of all, what happened to Molly? She tells us her horse got shot and went down, her leg trapped beneath, which is the part we knew from Phemie. Molly dismounted to help her. That's when the Crow captured them, and after the battle was over, they were taken back to the Crow bivouac and separated. She says the warrior who claimed her dragged her into his stick hut . . . and though she doesn't say as much, we can tell from the way she lowers her head and looks away that he did to her what all men will do when they take a lass captive . . . *goddamn the filthy bastards* . . . She says he tied her up so she couldn't escape, came back later, untied her and made her take down the hut. She says the whole camp packed up and traveled south, and that she and her captor were ridin' in the rear, while Molly was ridin' up front . . . aye, just as we had all feared, with none other than Jules Seminole leadin' the party. She says that because they were so far apart she and Molly only got a glimpse or two of each other as they rode.

She says they traveled down to the big Army supply camp on Goose Creek, where Crook had retreated to lick his wounds after we kicked his arse on the battlefield. They pitched their own camp for the night a bit away from the Army. Her captor forced her back inside his hut . . . to do to her again we know, without her sayin', what he'd done before . . . the *bastard* . . . Later that evening, after the sun set, three soldiers rode into the Crow camp, and sometime after that Pretty Nose heard Molly singin' one of Lulu's songs. When she managed to look out through the opening of the hut, she saw that Molly was being led away by the soldiers.

It was nearly dark now, and her Crow captor had fallen asleep. He wore a knife on his belt, which he'd taken off and tossed aside. She reached out real slow, real careful, slid the belt toward her, slipped the knife from its sheath . . . and slit the wanker's throat. Good for her . . . the fooking *bastard*.

She says she waited a couple more hours with the dead man bleedin' out beside her, until she figured all the others, except the boys guardin' the horses, had gone to sleep. Then she crawled out of the hut on her belly and all the way like that to near where the horses were corralled. She waited there a good long time, watchin', and gettin' a sense of what the horse boys' routine was. They took shifts sleeping, and every now and again, whichever one of 'em was on duty would walk around the perimeter of the corral to make sure all was well. She timed it so that when the boy did this, and she knew he was on the back side, she stood and moved real quiet toward the corral. There was a pile of halters with lead ropes near where the other boys were sleeping. She picked one up and ducked under the corral rope. Pretty Nose has always had good relations with horses, she has a calm, sure way about her that puts 'em at ease, and they didn't spook or make a sound when she came among them.

She picked out the biggest, strongest-lookin' mount she could find and slipped the halter over his head. Using the knife she'd taken from the Crow she killed, she cut the corral rope, swung onto the horse's back, pressed her heels to his flanks, gave her best Indian yell, and busted out at a gallop. She says she knew that with the rope down and the disturbance she caused, the other horses would spook and bolt, which would distract the horse boys and slow down any pursuers. And so it did. Still, she knew some would chase her, and she rode as hard as she could push that horse without killin' him. There was enough moon and a sky full of bright stars to light her way. She says she got back to our old camp on the Rosebud about daybreak yesterday morning, and there she found Hawk, bad wounded, with his grandmother, cousins, and nephew lookin' after him. She holed up all day until darkness fell. They fed her and she got some much-needed sleep before she rode out again after dark to follow our trail.

And so here she is . . . and now, in addition to gettin' Pretty Nose back, we know that Molly is still alive. Aye, that gives us a little somethin' to hope for again. We don't know what the Army will do with her . . . but at least we can be thankful she's no longer with Jules Seminole.

We feed Pretty Nose, and Mo'éh á'e makes up a sleeping place for her in our tipi. She is about the toughest lassie we know . . . but she is one knackered girl. We know that she will never speak further of what happened to her during her captivity. It is not the way of these people. We know that from our own experience, when it happened to me and Susie with May and the others. And Pretty Nose knows that we know without her havin' to speak of it. You put it away someplace tight inside yourself, and do your best to keep it there. That's how things work in this country . . . life goes on, no matter what happens, you make your way, best you can, through the trials and hardship, the pain and suffering . . . and maybe, if you're real lucky, with a wee bit of happiness mixed in . . . until one day it doesn't go on anymore.

23 June 1876
This afternoon, the chaplain gathers us all together to announce his intention of goin'

down to Crook's camp himself, to try to recover Molly back from the Army.

"That's all very well, Christian," says Lady Hall, "but how do you intend to do that? You are a deserter, they will arrest you, and quite likely execute you. And we will have lost yet another of our merry band. That will simply not do, sir. I will not permit it."

"Molly risked her life to help me," says he, "and she saved mine in the process. I don't know how I intend to do it, but I owe it to her to try. I owe it to the good Lord."

"And I, too, am going with him," says Astrid. "Molly is our friend, she has been good to me, to all of us."

"Why, I'll be comin', too, then," says Hannah. "Molly 'asn't done anything wrong, why wouldn't the Army just give her back to us? At least we know where she is now, and if we don't go for her, it may be too late, we may never know again."

"I daresay, Hannah dear, I must agree with you," says Lady Hall. "If we do not act posthaste, Molly could be spirited away forever . . . back to serve her prison sentence, God forbid. Therefore, allow me to make a proposal: do you ladies remember what Miss Gertie told us? That the Army, the government, would send us back where we came from? Now that may cause no particular hardship to those of us who came here from some relatively benign place, of our own free will with no strings attached . . . I speak, specifically, of myself, Hannah, and Astrid. However, others who came out of less fortunate circumstances . . . Carolyn, for instance, Molly, Lulu, and Maria, you have much more to lose by being sent back. Why don't those of us who are at less risk make the journey to General Crook's camp and plead Molly's case? That, of course, does not include you, Christian, for the aforementioned reasons. But what can they do to the three of us? We signed up for the program, and the program ended without our knowledge. They cannot send us back to prison as they can Molly; or to an insane asylum as they can Carolyn; or deport her back to face a homicidal Mexican gangster, as they can Maria; or a pimp in Saint Louis, as they can Lulu. Nor can they court-martial us . . . nor, it seems to me, can they arrest us, or otherwise prevent us from going upon our way. We are civilians, after all, and we have done nothing whatsoever illegal."

"Aye, m'lady . . ." Susie points out, "unless one counts fightin' against the United States Army at the Rosebud."

"Ah, well, yes, that is clearly the part we

do not mention, isn't it, dear? No one will recognize us. It goes without saying that you and Meggie will not be joining us on our little excursion, for you two are far more easily identified . . . in addition to the fact that you have had more . . . shall we say . . . more intimate contact with the soldiers than have we."

Now the chaplain makes the case that it was his idea to go to Molly's aid in the first place, and he says he won't allow Astrid to go without him. Furthermore, he points out that for obvious reasons, none of the Cheyenne scouts will be willing to guide their party back to Crook's camp, nor will they be capable of finding the way there alone. "The fact is, you need me," says Christian.

At this, Lady Hall, stubborn and bossy as she can sometimes be, has to admit that the chaplain makes a good point. And she allows finally that he should come along. "Provided, that is," says she, "that you stay out of sight when we get there, and do not try to enter the Army supply camp yourself."

"Agreed."

Just as all these arrangements are being made, who should arrive in our family encampment but Martha, and without her baby we are all surprised to see. With all that's been happening we've hardly seen the lass these past weeks, for she spends all her time with her own family, and never lets her son out of her sight. But as she trots in on her little donkey, Dapple, she seems a different person than last we saw her . . . aye, she seems like her old self . . . maybe even better than her old self . . .

She slips off the beast and comes toward us with a firm step.

"Has something happened to little Tangle Hair, Martha?" asks Susie, concerned.

"I heard Molly was taken," says she, ignoring the question. "I heard she was taken by *that man.*" This last she says in a kind of rattlesnake-like hiss.

"Indeed she was," says I. "But she's escaped him now."

"Nobody escapes Jules Seminole," she says. "Don't you understand that? He never lets you go. Even if you get away, he comes back for you, he haunts your dreams, he takes you again and again and again. *That man* must be killed, and a stake driven through his black heart. That is what I intend to do, once and for all."

"But what are ya talkin' about, Martha?" asks Susie. "How ya plannin' on doin' that, lass?"

"Where is Molly? I am going to her. She needs me. I'm the only one who knows what it's like. I'm the only one who can stop him. She saved me once, she gave me back my life, my son. And I shall give her back hers. She's going to have a child, you know? A boy. Woman Who Moves against the Wind told me. But she is in grave danger, and so is her son. I must find her, I must go to her, I must save her."

"You're talkin' crazy now, Martha," says I. "Ya can't do any of those things. And what would ya do, anyhow, leave little Tangle Hair again?"

"He will be fine in the care of Grass Woman. He will wait for me to return. He is a good boy."

"But Martha, dear," says Lady Hall, "we are leaving tomorrow to travel to General Crook's supply camp and try to gain Molly's release. That is where she is now. She is no longer with Seminole."

"Excellent," says she. "Then I shall come with you. Seminole will be lurking not far away. Of that I can assure you . . . I know *that man.*"

"Dear, if the soldiers should see you there," says Lady Hall, "and happen to recognize you, they will send you back to Chicago. You will lose your son again."

"I will go in my disguise as Red Painted Woman. No one will recognize me. You girls didn't even recognize me at first. They'll think I'm just another squaw . . . which, indeed, I am."

At this, Susie barks an astonished laugh. "But how do ya even know that's what everyone called ya, Martha?"

Martha looks at her with a withering gaze and says: "*Honestly,* Susie . . . do you really think I'm *that stupid*?" And this makes all of us laugh, which even gets a laugh out of Martha. Somehow she has come back to us, and stronger than ever, and we got no idea how, or why. Now all agree that if she wishes to go with the contingent to Crook's camp, so be it. We have to say that m'lady is the perfect emissary to plead Molly's case, and we trust her to take care of Martha, too . . . although given how Martha is behavin', it seems like she may be able to take care of herself.

As Lady Hall points out, there is no question of me and Susie goin', or Phemie for that matter, who would be even more recognizable to the Army than us, for Gertie told us that her reputation as a warrior goes all the way back to the Mackenzie massacre. She says the soldiers who were there still speak in hushed, frightened voices of the tall negro Cheyenne they call the Black Panther, who fought so fierce and bare-chested against them. Speakin' of Phemie, she's the only one not camped with us, and we don't know where in the hell she is. None of us have seen her since the Rosebud battle. She didn't come to the victory dance that night, nor did she ride with us on the way here. And in an encampment this big, it'd be almost impossible to find her.

Pretty Nose tells us that on the way here last night she came upon the tracks and then the night bivouac of yet another Army regiment who must also be following our trail. We figure it's some part of the Montana and Dakota forces Gertie told us about. But whoever it is, with all the soldiers in this country now, one thing for sure is that there will be more blood spilled, and the Strong-heart Women's Warrior Society will ride again . . . aye, especially now that we got Pretty Nose back. Me and Susie intend to be in on the action, again, and we bet Phemie'll come out of hidin' for the occasion, too.

War is funny that way . . . aye, it's kinda like the first time ya let a boy inside your knickers . . . it's usually a big disappointment, a letdown, maybe it even leaves you feelin' a little sick to your stomach. But then another part a' you wants to try it again, and when ya do, knowin' more or less what to expect, it's that much easier, and even easier the time after that, until pretty soon, damned if you don't get to likin' it. And that's how it is with makin' war . . . not so different really than makin' love. It's true that me and Susie weren't real pleased with ourselves after the Rosebud, but with the passage of a mere couple a' days, baskin' in the respect of the Cheyenne for our bloody deeds on the battlefield, the shame has begun to fall away. As it does, we are left again with the bottomless pit of our vengeance, the need to fill it up with more blood, more dead soldiers. Aye, we are warriors, savages, damned in the eyes of man and God, that much is sure. We follow a new God now . . . and maybe that, after all, is what drives men . . . and women to war . . . like a drug you can't get enough of . . .

■ ■ ■ ■

LEDGER BOOK XIII
(CONTINUED BY
LADY ANN HALL)

■ ■ ■ ■

Flying

23 June 1876

On this, the eve of my departure on our mission to free Molly, snug in my tipi with my little friend Bridge Girl, I, Lady Ann Hall of Sunderland, finally pick up the pen, having successfully prevailed upon Meggie and Susie to allow me to take with me this, their very last ledger book, nearly half the pages of which are still blank.

I must confess that given all the ledgers those girls have filled in the course of this strange adventure, I have felt rather slighted. After all, as the author of the letterpress to my dear friend Helen Elizabeth Flight's seminal ornithological portfolio, *The Birds of Great Britain,* I am the sole published author among us, and yet, if I may speak frankly, our self-appointed, unofficial *auteurs* have been quite stingy in sharing their precious paper with me. And while not meaning to cast aspersions upon their respective literary talents, I find it difficult to believe that two largely uneducated twin sisters, who effectively lived as street people . . . fond as I am of them, would it be awfully catty of me to say "streetwalkers"? . . . in Chicago's Irish town . . . (By the way, as a small reminder to myself, I must mention right here that I fully intend to tear these pages out of the ledger for my own keeping before I return it to the Kellys); while our other author is a young woman who grew up on a farm in upstate New York, teaching country children in the same one-room schoolhouse in which she herself was educated . . . well, all of that to say I simply find it difficult to believe that their combined skills would be up to the task of doing justice to our tale. And yet . . . upon reading these few pages here contained in Meggie's hand, I must admit that those two Irish scamps, as we all refer to them, have a certain lively, if, perforce, unsophisticated writing style, but one true to their nature and redolent of their true voice. To Molly's literary efforts, of course, I cannot speak.

In any case, with no ledger books left to them, and not exactly being welcome any longer at the trading posts to replenish their supply, it seems unlikely that the Kellys will be able to continue their journals, even if they wished to. For their part, they seemed quite willing to bring them to a close, and presented me with these last clean pages, in order that they might focus full-time upon their ghastly business as warriors.

"Aye, Lady Hall, go on then, you're welcome to it," said Meggie to my request, "me and Susie 'ave said what we 'ave to say. And with the Army headed this way again, and judgin' from the size of our own forces, this next battle promises to be the grandest yet, one for the history books, and me and Susie ain't goin' to miss it."

" 'Tis the gods' truth, we'll be plenty busy, m'lady," added Susie, "makin' a place for ourselves in those books. But you be sure to bring this back. An' if we don't make it, you give it to our old tipi lass to put with the others. Elk Woman is her name, Mo'éh á'e."

And so it is that I take up the pen to tell whatever remains to be told, or, I daresay, until I simply run out of paper, whichever comes first.

24 June 1876

From our first evening bivouac,
somewhere in the foothills of the
Bighorns:

True to his word, the chaplain has proved to be an efficacious guide. With the expectation that the Indian scouts of the approaching Army troops would certainly pick up and follow the trail that the Cheyenne, Arapaho, Sioux, and we among them took from the Rosebud to the Little Bighorn, Christian wisely decided upon an alternate route, skirting a wide berth farther west and then south, a somewhat longer, elliptical passage but one where we would be far less likely to encounter enemies, with which this region is clearly rife.

In the matter of arms, Christian and I each carry Winchester rifles, and I a Colt .45, in my case, both for the protection of our little group and in order to feed us, he, of course, solely for the latter purpose given his religious convictions. For the hunt, we confine ourselves to small game, largely rabbits and prairie grouse, which are easily obtained and less time-consuming to butcher and prepare. We need to travel as lightly and quickly as possible, for, of course, we have no way of knowing how long Crook's Army will stay where they are, or how long they will keep Molly with them. Saddle-hardened as we all are by now, and having traveled this first day from dawn to dusk, we expect to arrive at our destination

by midday tomorrow. Too knackered now to
write further . . .

25 June 1876
And thus we have arrived as expected, and
have found a secluded campsite along a side
creek of the Tongue River, roughly a mile
and a half from the Army base camp. Christian immediately set about catching trout
for our lunch. It has already been determined that he, Astrid, and Martha will stay
back here, while Hannah and I go in alone.
We can have no real idea of how we might
be received. I am dressed in my tattered,
much-mended waistcoat and knee breeches,
Hannah in demure native attire — a deerskin shift with moccasins and leggings. Even
if we do not exactly look the part on first
view, we hope that between our accents and
relatively fair hair, we can quickly present
ourselves to the soldiers as respectable white
women. Of course, we carry no weapon with
us, so that we cannot in any manner be
considered threatening . . . simply an ec-
centric British noblewoman and her maidservant, out for a Sunday ride in the wilderness. I feel for some peculiar reason like
Don Quixote, with his loyal retainer Sancho
Panza, off to tilt at windmills.

27 June 1876

Well, then, I daresay, it did not go as we might have hoped . . . We rode into the Army encampment on their main wagon route, and were promptly stopped by guards, who regarded us with puzzled expressions and asked us to identify ourselves.

"I am Lady Ann Hall of Sunderland," I said in my most patrician tone, "and this is my maidservant, Hannah Alford of Liverpool."

"And what business brings you . . . *ladies* . . . here?" asked one of the guards in an insolent tone.

"I have come to request an audience with General George Crook."

"An audience?"

"A meeting, good sir. I should like to *meet* with General Crook."

"Would ya now, ma'am, and on what business might that be?"

"That might be *business* between me and the general, sir."

"Go fetch Captain Bourke," he said to the other, regarding me with an equally insolent expression. "Tell him there's a *lady* here askin' to see the general."

The second soldier did as the first told him, and a scant ten minutes later, returned with the captain in tow. I must say I was jolly well interested in meeting the man in person, having heard a good deal about him from Meggie and Susie, particularly on the subject of his romantic adventures with our distinguished predecessor, May Dodd.

He introduced himself. I must admit he is a handsome, manly fellow, with an air of natural gallantry about him, and I could see how he might have turned an impressionable young woman's head. He told the two guards to look after our horses, and led us inside the camp to a tent that seemed to have been set up as a kind of administrative office. There he seated us in front of a campaign desk, and took a seat himself on the other side.

"I understand, madam, that you have requested an audience with General Crook."

"That is correct, Captain."

"You must understand that the general is a very busy man. It is quite irregular for civilians, not to mention women, to be calling upon him at a supply base camp in a theater of war. May I ask you, madam, what would be the purpose of this meeting?"

"It has come to our attention, sir, that one of our colleagues, a woman by the name of Molly McGill, may be in your care."

The captain furrowed his dark brow in an

expression of concern, and, I detected, genuine sadness. "I see . . . a colleague . . . yes, of course, I see . . ." He pulled some papers from a basket on top of the desk, and rifled through them. "This Brides for Indians program," he said in a low voice, as if speaking to himself, "has been my bête noire for almost two years now. *Utter madness . . .*" Pulling several sheets of paper from the bundle, he looked at me, and at the paper in his hand, then at Hannah, and back at the paper. "Lady Ann Hall and Hannah Alford, both of Great Britain, I presume?"

"Exactly so, Captain," said I. "A pleasure to be formally introduced, sir."

He smiled wryly and nodded. "The pleasure is all mine, Lady Hall . . . Miss Alford."

He looked at the next sheet, studied it for a moment, and regarded us again. "I see that you both have the rather unusual distinction of volunteering to the program without having been in previous situations of any particular distress or urgency."

"Which is to say, Captain Bourke, that we were not patients in a lunatic asylum, incarcerated in prison, or fleeing some other equally desperate history? Yes, that much is quite true. I volunteered of my own free will and for a very specific reason — to discover what fate had befallen my dear friend, the artist Helen Elizabeth Flight. Perhaps you knew her, sir?"

Bourke nodded, clearly pained at these memories. "I did, Lady Hall. Helen was a fine woman. On the few occasions when I saw her, I very much enjoyed discussing the flora and fauna of the region. She was quite knowledgeable, and a great talent."

"Indeed."

"And have you discovered Miss Flight's fate?" he asked.

"I have, sir, yes. The Army killed her."

Again Bourke winced, as if almost in physical pain. "She had taken up arms against us, Lady Hall," he said. "May I assume that you and Miss Alford were not participating as combatants with the Cheyenne, as was, by her own admission, your colleague, Miss McGill?"

"You may so assume, Captain. Our place was strictly with the defenseless women and children." This I stated with a certain tone of irony.

"And of what service can General Crook be to you, madam?"

"He can release Miss McGill, to us, of course, sir. She may have been riding with the Cheyenne when taken captive by your criminal scout, Jules Seminole, but Molly was not acting as a warrior. May we see her, sir?"

At the mention of Seminole, Bourke raised an eyebrow. "Miss McGill is no longer here, madam. She left yesterday with a military escort headed to Medicine Bow station. There she will be turned over to agents of the U.S. Marshals Service who will conduct her back to her former residence in New York."

Hannah and I exchanged a worried glance. "I see."

"I am most curious to know what dealings you have had with Sergeant Seminole, Lady Hall."

"None, personally, sir," I answered quickly, realizing that I had said far too much. "We just know of him by way of his bad reputation among the Cheyenne." I took a deep breath and stood. "Well then, I see that we've come on a fool's errand, Captain. I believe we've taken up enough of your time. We shall be on our way."

"Where will you go, madam?"

"We will return to the Cheyenne, sir."

"As you must well know by now, Lady Hall," he said, "that is hardly a safe place to be these days. I could place you both under protective custody."

"That will not be necessary, Captain," I answered, uncertain from his tone whether he meant this an offer or a threat.

"Tell me, please, are there others of you with the Cheyenne?"

"Others of us, Captain?"

"You know quite well what I mean, madam. Other members of the brides program. Are there presently other white women living with the tribe?"

"The various bands under different chiefs move around a great deal these days, Captain," I equivocated, "as you must certainly know — coming and going, chased hither and yon by the Army. I really could not say if there are any other white women among them."

"Please, sit down, Lady Hall," he said, indicating my chair. "If you will excuse me for a moment, I shall see if General Crook is available for a conference. I believe he will be very interested in meeting you."

As soon as Captain Bourke left the tent, I whispered to Hannah, "We must leave here right now, dear."

"Methinks the very same, m'lady."

Hoping to avoid raising further suspicion, we walked briskly, but as nonchalantly as possible, back to where the guards had tied our horses to a hitching rail. We thanked them politely, mounted, and turned the horses back down the wagon road, heeling them into a trot, and then a light lope. It is then that we heard Captain Bourke shout at the guards. "Stop those women!"

In unison, we kicked our horses into a full run and turned off the road into the hills, galloping all the way back to our camp along the creek, where we told the others to quickly gather their affairs. They asked no questions, and were saddled, mounted, and ready to head out in short order. Only when we were moving again did the chaplain ask: "Where are we going?"

"Medicine Bow station."

"And why is that?"

"That is where they're taking Molly. As I most feared, they're sending her back to Sing Sing. Do you know how to get to the station in Medicine Bow, Christian?"

"It is there where I first arrived after I was conscripted into the Army," he answered. "It is nearly due south, but I would guess over two hundred miles from here."

"She is being escorted by soldiers. They left yesterday morning. Can we overtake them?"

"If Molly is being transported by wagon, which I would expect, we should be able to travel considerably faster than they. But

600

even if we do find them, what then? Do you have a plan, Lady Hall?"

"None whatsoever, sir. I have only the sense that the farther away from us she gets, and the closer to that train, the less chance we have of ever bringing her back."

The chaplain had no trouble locating the main route south, for ever since the completion of the transcontinental railroad in 1869 there has been sufficient traffic to well mark its passage on the face of the landscape, largely due to the movement of the Army troops back and forth. He estimated that we could reach Medicine Bow in seven days or less, and if we were lucky and kept up a steady pace, we could cut the trail of Molly's party within two days.

And thus on we rode, as fast as we could push our horses and Martha's briskly trotting little donkey, blindly following the chaplain, with no plan, on a virtually impossible mission, our spirits subdued. With the Bighorn mountains to the west, and the plains to the east, the only limits to the horizon were of sight, and we felt again our sheer smallness and helplessness in the face of this immense land. We felt no stronger, no more important or permanent than the grains of grit that stung our faces in the wind. And no one felt like singing.

■ ■ ■ ■

Tonight we are camped along a tiny trickle of a creek, just far enough off the main road to be hidden from view to anyone passing by. The country is more arid here, the Bighorn mountains receding farther to the west. We encountered not a single other traveler on the road today, which was a relief, for another of my worries was that we might cross paths with one of the band of brigands who are said to rove this countryside, preying on the weak and defenseless. With only one man among us, and one, at that, who won't raise a hand against others, we are awfully vulnerable.

Undated entry
Time has passed and due to desperate circumstances, duress, and exhaustion, I have lost track of the date. Much has happened . . . I shall try to tell of it . . . try to make sense of something that makes none.

In the morning of our second day after departure from the Army supply camp, we came upon a family of pitifully poor Indians traveling north — a husband and wife, an old woman, who we presumed to be a grandmother, and two small boys — of what tribe we were uncertain, but we guessed they had come from the Indian agency. By the look of them, they appeared to be near starving. We had heard stories from other reservation defectors who had joined us on the Little Bighorn, that the white agents who were in charge of distributing government-issued rations to the surrendered Indians routinely stole the shipments and sold them at a profit to settlers. The old woman rode a bony, swaybacked horse with a swollen belly, while the parents and the boys walked. When they came abreast of us, the entire family enviously eyed a brace of jackrabbits Christian had shot at dawn near our overnight camp, which now hung from the pommel of his saddle, and was meant for our midday meal.

The chaplain and Martha were the most gifted of us with the sign language, and they both spoke to the family in hand gestures, the chaplain pointing down the road. I understood that he was asking if they had passed any other travelers. They answered, yes, and made the signs for wagon wheels, horses and soldiers, and other signs I was unable to read myself.

"God bless you," Christian said to them, making the gesture of thanks and handing down the rabbits to the grateful mother, a satisfactory transaction to all parties. And to us he said: "They are not far ahead now. "Only a several-hour ride, if I understood correctly."

"But how do we know it is Molly's party?" I asked.

"They say there was a white woman in the wagon with the driver, and two soldiers," said Martha, "and ten more soldiers on horseback."

"Oh, crikey, an escort of a dozen soldiers, is it? I daresay, that will present a challenge."

"Have you been working on your plan, Lady Hall?" asked the chaplain.

"Night and day, sir."

"And what have you come up with?"

"Absolutely nothing."

"We shall trust in God."

"Easily said, Christian. Let us hope that he has a plan."

"God always has a plan."

Those proved to be prophetic words on the part of the chaplain, for the scene we came upon several hours later was nothing any of us might have imagined, or planned for. We spotted them from some distance away, and knew that it was, indeed, Molly and her escort with whom we had caught up. The road here ran along a high, arid, red rock bluff, the cliffs carved over the eons by the Powder River, which wound its way through the broad green valley a hundred or so feet below. On the crest of the bluff, unbroken by so much as a single blade of grass, the wind blew hard as a hammer and chisel, sculpting the rocks and stinging our faces.

Their procession appeared to have come to a halt here, and the soldiers had dismounted. As we approached closer, we saw why . . . Molly stood on a promontory at the very edge of the cliff; the soldiers were gathered in a cluster roughly a hundred feet behind her. Between them and Molly stood another figure whom we were unable to identify from a distance, but whom I assumed was the driver of the wagon. We were still sixty or seventy yards away from them, and with all sound stolen by the wind, and so intent were they, our arrival had not yet even been noticed.

There seemed no reason for us to approach cautiously now, and we kicked our mounts into a gallop. We had nearly reached them before they heard us. The soldiers turned and readied their weapons, and Christian waved his arm in the air, calling out: "Don't shoot! We are friends! We come in peace! Don't shoot!" The wagon master, too, had turned, and as we came closer we recognized that it was none other than our friend Gertie. The only person who did not turn to look at us was Molly. She remained motionless on the edge of the cliff, gazing intently into the abyss below, the fierce wind swirling her blond hair around her face, threatening to push her over the edge.

We reined up beside the soldiers. One of them stepped forward, his rifle leveled at us. "I am First Sergeant Matthew Broughan, the commander of this detachment. State your business, please."

"We are friends of the prisoner," I said, dismounting, and making it up as I went along. "We come from General Crook's camp on Goose Creek. Captain Bourke told us to present ourselves directly to you, Sergeant Broughan. Please, sir, what is happening here?"

"The prisoner is threatening to jump. We have agreed to stay back while our mule-skinner tries to talk her out of it. For what reason did Captain Bourke send you, madam?"

"So that we might join you for protection on the trip to Medicine Bow. We, too, wish to take the train."

He looked me up and down, and then at the rest of our group, who remained

"Don't do anything foolish, missy," she warned.

I approached Molly.

"That's close enough," she said. "Stop right there. What do you want, Ann?"

"Well, you could start by getting down from there, Molly."

She laughed. "I, too, am afraid of heights," she said. "That's why I haven't jumped yet. You know, it is the strangest thing, but I have had this dream nearly all my life, ever since my parents took me to Niagara Falls when I was a little girl. I've dreamed of being here on this very edge, about to jump. It is as if this place has been waiting for me all this time."

"And have you ever jumped in your dream?"

"Yes, always, I always jump eventually. And I always soar like a bird. It's a wonderful feeling. But first I stand here for a while, looking down, terrified. I jump, finally, in order to stop being afraid, for I know that when I do, I will fly . . . free."

"Listen to me, Molly. This is not a dream, and this time, you are not going to fly. Let me turn and walk back toward Gertie, and just as I reach her, I'll take the reins of my horse and begin to mount, and when I do you run to me, quick as you can, and leap on behind. We'll make a dash for it, you and I."

"Thank you for offering to risk your life for me, Ann, but with the two of us on your little horse, you know we could never outrun the soldiers. They will catch us and put my leg shackles on again, and I will be sent back to Sing Sing. And you will all be arrested for trying to help me escape. Don't you see? This is the last, the best, the only chance I have to be free." Molly turned again to face the edge, raising her arms out to her sides like wings.

"Don't do this, Molly, please," I begged, beginning to weep now, *"please don't jump."*

"Turn and walk away, Ann. I'm sorry . . . good-bye, my friend."

It is then that I heard the high, shrill shriek of a hawk overhead, and looked up to see it above, wings set and soaring on the wind, weaving and dancing in the air like a child's kite.

Molly, too, looked up. "I knew you would come for me, Hawk," she cried. "I knew it, I've been waiting for you." Arms still spread wide, she leaned forward to fall from the cliff.

"No, please, Molly, don't!" I screamed, collapsing to my knees and putting my hands to my face, unable to watch, sobbing in ter-

ror now.

I do not believe in native superstitions that tell of people becoming other animals, or making themselves bulletproof by painting figures on their body, or of men flying like birds . . . But in the very next instant when I lowered my hands and looked up again, two riders had appeared on the ridge, riding north toward Molly at a full gallop . . . it was Pretty Nose on her dappled paint and Phemie, on the cliffside, astride her big white prairie pony. As they approached Molly, Phemie crouched low in the saddle, leaning down to her right, and holding out her arm, crooked like a scythe. With the horse barely breaking stride, Molly grabbed hold and as if she was but a wisp of a girl, light and agile as a spirit being, she swung onto the horse's back behind Phemie. I stood and in the split second it took them to thunder by, Molly looked directly at me and smiled . . . a smile both triumphant and amused. "I told you, Ann," she cried, her words streaming behind her as they passed, "in my dream, I always fly!"

Now carried on the wind, I heard Hannah scream, and scattered exclamations of shock and horror, and I turned to look back at Gertie and the others. They wept and cried out, the chaplain uttering ululations of grief to the heavens . . . Gertie raising her clenched fists in the air. *"Goddamn you, Molly,"* she roared, *"goddamn you, why didya have to do it? Why didya jump, goddamn you!"* Only Martha did not weep, but seemed to be gazing calmly off toward the ridge with a slight smile on her face.

The soldiers, too, milled about, shaken; some had turned their backs, scuffing the ground with the toe of their boots, muttering and swearing. *"Son of a bitch, she did it!"* one of them hollered. *"The crazy bitch jumped!"*

Had I gone bloody mad? Did I imagine it all? But when I turned again, I saw the two horses, one paint and one white, galloping north along the bluff, bearing our three Strong-heart Women — an Indian girl, a black girl, and a white girl — all retreating into the distance.